A Pattern of Lies

A Pattern of Lies

Charles Todd

HARPER LUXE

An Imprint of HarperCollins*Publishers*

A PATTERN OF LIES. Copyright © 2015 by Charles Todd. All rights reserved. Printed in the United States of America. No part of this book may be used or reproduced in any manner whatsoever without written permission except in the case of brief quotations embodied in critical articles and reviews. For information address HarperCollins Publishers, 195 Broadway, New York, NY 10007.

HarperCollins books may be purchased for educational, business, or sales promotional use. For information, please e-mail the Special Markets Department at SPsales@harpercollins.com.

FIRST HARPERLUXE EDITION

HarperLuxe™ is a trademark of HarperCollins Publishers

Library of Congress Cataloging-in-Publication Data is available upon request.

ISBN 978-0-06-239310-4

15 ID/RRD 10 9 8 7 6 5 4 3 2 1

*For Kathryn Kennison, for Dick, for Drew—and
for everyone at Magna Cum Murder. We love you all!*

*And for Maggie of the lovely eyes, who was
very dear to me, and for Clarissa, our English cat,
who welcomed us every time we came through the
door, and who slept on my bed when I wasn't there,
next to the computer.*

A Pattern of Lies

Chapter One

Canterbury, Kent, Autumn 1918

I didn't know much about the little town of Cranbourne, on The Swale in northeastern Kent, only that its abbey had been destroyed by a very angry Henry VIII when the abbot of the day refused to take the King's side in certain matters. What stone was left had been transported to France to shore up the English-owned harbor in Calais. A young Lieutenant by the name of Merrill, standing by me at the railing of the *Sea Maid,* had told me about that as we came through the roads and edged toward where we were to dock. That was in 1915. Shortly after that, we were caught up in the rush of disembarking and finding our respective transports, and I doubt I gave it another thought.

2 · CHARLES TODD

My next encounter with Cranbourne was while I was assigned to a base hospital in France. A critically ill patient was brought in for further surgery, and he sometimes talked about the village during his long and painful recovery.

All in the past, that.

And then yesterday I accompanied a convoy of badly wounded men to hospital in a village just outside Canterbury, in Kent. The hospital specialized in internal wounds, and it was a shorter journey to go directly there than to travel all the way to London first, and then arrange transport all the way back.

They'd made the crossing from France safely, every one of my patients, even though Matron had been worried about the gravest cases. All the same, I was relieved to find a line of ambulances waiting for us in Dover, and again when the train pulled into Canterbury's railway station. Soon after that we had every man in a cot with a minimum of fuss. Most of them were too exhausted to speak, but they knew they were in England, and their smiles were enough. Home. Alive. And on the way to recovery. I hoped it was true. Then I saw Lieutenant Harriman, the most seriously wounded, weakly giving me a thumbs-up, and I thought, *Yes, they'll be all right now!*

By three in the morning, we'd coaxed them to swallow a little thin broth before wearily seeking our own beds, leaving the night staff in charge at last.

Late the next morning, I said good-bye to the men and to the nurses who had come over with me. They were needed in France, but I had earned a few days of leave.

One of the doctors kindly ran me back into Canterbury to await my train to London.

I was happily counting the minutes before I could call my parents in Somerset and tell them when to expect me in Victoria Station when I discovered that my train was delayed. Three *hours*, the stationmaster informed me, although from his gloomy expression, I didn't hold out much hope of reaching London until midnight at the earliest. *Well, so much for that,* I thought, resigned to further delays. My telephone call would have to wait until I knew more.

Rather than sit in the busy, noisy railway station, I decided to walk for a bit. It was a fine day, and I'd always enjoyed Canterbury. Leaving my kit bag in the growing pile of luggage pushed to one side for the London train, I looked at my watch to check the time, then set out.

A handsome town with its bustling markets and its famous cathedral, the one always associated with the tomb of the Black Prince and the martyrdom of Thomas à Becket, Canterbury had much to offer. I could pass a pleasant hour or two exploring, and then call in again at the station for the latest news. If the train was still delayed, I could count on a quiet lunch somewhere nearby, and even browse in the shops, although many of them had very little to offer these days.

Before very long, I came across a hidden gem of a garden open to strollers. Half an hour spent enjoying the autumn flowers blooming along a narrow stream was heavenly. There was so little left of beauty in the parts of France I saw every day, only the hardy poppies and a few wildflowers that straggled in any patch of rough ground. I badly needed something else to think about besides torn bodies and bloody bandages, consoling amputees and long vigils at the sides of dying men. Sitting on one of the benches, I closed my eyes and listened to the bees in the blossoms at my feet. For once I couldn't hear the guns in France, and I let the Front fade away.

Over my head in one of the lovely old trees growing along the stream, a jackdaw began to call, confused by this sudden burst of warm weather here in the autumn. I smiled as I listened to him.

Feeling myself again, I set out for the High Street shops. Along the way I passed the Army recruiting office where men could enlist. In the early days of the war, August and September 1914, in particular, these had been nearly overwhelmed with volunteers, men who were determined to get into the fight before the Kaiser changed his mind and sued for peace. It didn't quite happen that way, and it wasn't long before the Government had had to turn to conscription to fill the ranks.

The office looked rather forlorn, and through the open door, where a shaft of warm sunlight lit up the posters and the enlistment forms and the polished shoes of the officer seated behind the desk, I could almost catch a feeling of resignation. As if, with the war ending, this little room, once a small shop, had lost its usefulness and was just waiting for someone in London to remember it existed and close it down. A sign, perhaps, that the war *would* end, that no more men would be asked to die for King and Country.

Strolling with no particular goal in mind, I soon found myself making my way toward the cathedral precincts. This was a lovely place to spend a quiet hour, and when I came to the massive Christ Church Gate set into the high wall, I stepped through it and walked down to where I had the best view of the west front.

For a moment I simply stood there, looking up at the three ornate towers. It occurred to me how fortunate the French had been not to lose any of their great cathedrals. Damaged, some of them, but they would survive. Far too many of their lovely old village churches had fallen to artillery barrages. The sun was warm on my face, the view splendid, and in spite of the others here in the broad precincts, passing me on the walk, I was reluctant to step inside just yet.

Someone called my name.

"Bess? Sister Crawford? Is that you?"

I turned toward the speaker, and he exclaimed, "Good Lord, it is!"

I didn't recognize him at first.

He had filled out, his dark hair thick now and well cut. It had been shaved to attend to his head wound, although it was the wound in his side that we thought would surely kill him. But it didn't, although he'd been quite thin and gaunt by the time he'd been stable enough to transport to England.

"Captain Ashton," I exclaimed, and held out my hand in greeting as he came to meet me. But he grasped the hand and leaned forward to kiss me on the cheek. "How *well* you look."

"Thanks to you and the good doctors. And it's Major now," he added, touching his insignia. "How are you? And what are you doing in Canterbury?"

I explained about the wounded, and he nodded. "It's a good hospital. I spent some weeks there myself, if you remember. Do you have time for a cup of tea?"

"Yes, in fact, I do," I said. "They've no idea when my train will come in, and I've been passing the morning seeing the sights. Two minutes more and I'd have been inside the cathedral, admiring the stained glass windows."

"My luck that you hadn't gone inside. Otherwise, I'd have missed you." He fell in step beside me, offering his arm. There was the slightest sign of a limp in his gait, but he walked steadily along the path, and I was glad to see it.

Captain Ashton—as he was then—had been very popular with the nursing staff. He was an attractive man, of course, but his sense of humor in the face of his severe wounds had won our admiration. Refusing the morphine as often as he could manage it, he did everything he was told with a smile, however shaky that smile might be, and made light of his suffering. It was true, there were many in that surgical ward in far worse shape than he was, but we'd worried endlessly that we might finally lose him to infection and loss of blood.

"I don't have to ask how you are, Bess," he was saying. "You look well. Tired, yes, God knows, don't we all? But still the prettiest Sister in the ward."

I looked up at him. "And you haven't lost your skill at flattery. I thought you were to be married as soon as you'd recovered?"

As I watched, a shadow crossed his face. "Yes, well. She died. In the first wave of the Spanish flu. I didn't get home in time. They were burying her when I arrived."

"I am so very sorry, Major." I meant it. I'd read him letters from his betrothed when he was too ill to read them himself, and written to her as well, to answer for him. Eloise was her name, though he called her Ellie, and I'd come to know her, in a way. I couldn't think of a finer match for this man. I had so wanted him to survive and come back to her. A small victory for two people amidst the chaos of war.

"I wouldn't have had her suffer another hour. But I could have wished she'd lived until I was there to hold her hand." He looked up at the tall cathedral gates to hide his pain. "But there it is." Clearing his throat, he said, as he had so many times in the ward, "This too shall pass us by."

We walked on in silence, and just beyond the gates he found a tearoom and ordered for both of us.

For a time we chatted companionably. About mutual friends, about those we'd lost, about the prospects, finally, of peace. I asked about his parents, and he asked after my mother and the Colonel Sahib.

"What brings you to Canterbury? Are you on leave, or on your way back to France?"

His fingers toyed with the milk jug for a moment, and then he said, "I've had trouble with my hearing. It's coming back now, but when the tunnel went up nearly beneath our feet, I wouldn't have heard an artillery barrage. I was luckier than some of the lads. The shock wave killed them. At any rate, I was sent home and told to give it time. I don't think the doctors in France held out much hope, but I've got another week before I meet with the medical board, and I have every reason to think they'll clear me now. Of course, if they whisper all their questions, I might still be in trouble," he ended with a smile.

Laughing, I said, "That's wonderful news. Still, I'm sure your mother was glad to have you safe with her for a little while."

"Look, why not come home with me for an hour or two? My mother will be very happy to see you."

"Do you live here in Canterbury now?" I asked.

"No. But not all that far from here. Not by motorcar. Cranbourne. It's a small village up on The Swale."

"Cranbourne," I repeated, all at once remembering. "Of course. And it had an abbey in the distant past."

"A ruined abbey," he said, nodding. "Did I tell you about it? I must have done." Without waiting for an answer, he went on. "I ran in this morning to speak to the police. But Inspector Brothers isn't in. I was told to come back later."

"The police?" I asked, surprised.

He looked out the tearoom window, not meeting my eyes. "There's been a spot of trouble. The police seem to be dragging their feet doing anything about it. Nothing to worry you about. But it would cheer my mother to no end to see you again."

When the Major—then Captain Ashton—had been so severely wounded, somehow Mrs. Ashton had got permission to come over to France and nurse her son. A small woman with snow-white hair, the same lovely blue eyes as the Major, and a spine of steel, she refused utterly to believe that he would die, and without getting in the way of the nursing staff, she sat beside him and read to him and fed him broth without a single tear shed. Only one evening, I'd discovered her in a room where we stored supplies, her face buried in a towel so that no one would hear her. It was the only time. I never knew where she went to cry after that. Or if there had only been that one moment of weakness.

"How lovely," I said, and meant it. "But first I should be sure about my train. There might be news."

"We'll call in at the railway station first."

"Then I'd like to go, very much."

"Good." He settled our bill and guided me down the street to where he'd left his motorcar.

News of my train was not very reassuring.

"There's a troop train coming through shortly, and it will be filled with wounded going back," the harassed stationmaster told us. "I'd find a room, if I were you, Sister. It could be morning before I've got anything for you."

"Never mind," the Major said. "But let's collect your kit, shall we?"

I looked at the baggage—now piled high by the side of the station, even overflowing onto the platform. I could just see mine squeezed between a large steamer trunk and the wall.

"A very good idea," I agreed, and Major Ashton helped me extract it. I could just picture what my clean uniforms must look like now, crumpled into a wrinkled twist. But there would be an iron I could borrow in Mrs. Ashton's kitchen.

As we walked back to his motorcar, he said, "There's more than enough room at the Hall. The hotels are crowded, and you'll be better off with us."

I protested that I didn't intend to presume on his mother's hospitality, but he said firmly, "Nonsense. You can't wander around this town all day, only to discover there will be no train after all. Tomorrow the lines should be straightened out."

I hoped he was right. I still had my heart set on reaching London.

And so we threaded our way out of Canterbury and took the main road toward Rochester, the old Watling Street of the Romans.

The countryside was so beautiful. Roadside wildflowers had gone to seed, but the hedgerows were still thick and green, and sometimes trees along the way provided a canopy of cool shadows overhead.

Major Ashton said, his eyes on the road, "Do you think you could manage to call me Mark? God knows we've known each other for several years. It wouldn't be improper, would it? And 'Sister Crawford' reminds me too much of my wounds."

We were not encouraged to call patients by their first names. It fostered a familiarity that was unprofessional. But the Major was no longer my patient, and so I said, "Thank you. Mark, then."

"Much better." He turned his head and grinned at me. Those blue eyes were twinkling. "I still look over my shoulder when someone calls 'Major' to see who it is they're speaking to."

He was young to have achieved his majority. Thirty? But the war had seen the deaths of so many officers that it was more a mark of survival than time served, as it had been before the war.

We were enjoying the drive in silence when the Major said, "Bess, don't say anything about the explosion."

"When the tunnel went up?" I asked, turning to him in surprise. "Doesn't your family know that's how you lost your hearing?"

It was his turn to be surprised. "Sorry. No. The explosion and fire in Cranbourne. Hadn't you heard about it? Two years ago, it was. I wasn't here, but it must have been as bad as anything in France. Over a hundred men were killed."

"I didn't know—what happened?" I couldn't imagine anything in a village that could cause such terrible damage.

"It was the gunpowder mill. No one knows what happened. It just—blew up."

I remembered then that his family owned a mill where gunpowder had been made for over a century, and in early 1915, the Government stepped in and took it over, increasing size and production to meet the needs of a nation at war.

"There was a fire as well," he was saying. "God knows whether it was the cause of the main explosion or if it started afterward in the dust. I can't believe anyone survived the blast. Still, no one could get to them in time, and that has haunted my father to this day. It was a Sunday, Bess. There were no women in the mill because it was Sunday. Or the loss of life would have been unthinkable."

"How awful!"

He took a deep breath. "Everyone's first thought was sabotage. Well, the mill is close by The Swale, it could have happened that way. A small boat putting in at night? Easier to believe that than think the unthinkable, that it was caused by carelessness. At any rate, the Government sent half a hundred men down here, scrambling over the ruins almost before they had cooled. They searched the marshes for any sign of a boat sent in by a submarine or even a small ship out in the Thames roads; they searched houses and barns and woods and even the abbey ruins in the event the Germans had sent a party in force and it was still hiding somewhere. For six months we had German fever. The captain who was our liaison with the Army was insistent that it must be sabotage, and so neighbor looked at neighbor, wondering who might be a secret German sympathizer. My father was very worried, I can tell you, with suspicion rampant, and even his own movements looked into. Unbelievably ugly. And then the Government found no evidence to support that theory and simply went away."

The amount of gunpowder produced here must have been of immense value to the war effort. The Germans would have been delighted to see the mill put out of business. There had already been a gunpowder crisis that had shaken even the Government. And of course a mill *had* to be located near water, because water was needed in the manufacture as well as to transport the gunpowder to the scattered factories where shell and cartridge casings would be filled with it. No one wanted to see wagons of gunpowder on the rutted and wretched roads.

"And then?"

"It was assumed that something must have gone wrong, that a spark must have set off the chain reaction. It's a dangerous business to start with, milling the ingredients and producing something that can be used in shells and ammunition. The powder has to go off, of course, when fired. But God help us, not before. Everyone knew it meant hazardous working conditions. It's why the pay was so good. But some felt the Government had been pushing too hard to increase production, ignoring proper safety precautions. My father was often at odds with Captain Collier over that. Still, the demand was there. All of us knew it. The Army alone, never mind the Navy, could have used twice the powder we produced."

He said nothing for a moment. And watching his hands clench on the wheel, I knew there was worse to come.

"Recently, don't ask me why, there have been different whispers. New rumors. Gossip. Finger pointing.

It began with more questions about the fire. How that had started—when—and why it had been so intense. Whether it had been deliberately set."

"Deliberately—but that's tantamount to *murder.*"

"Precisely. It makes no sense at all. Still, it was well known that my father had never been happy with the Government's terms when they took over, and it was whispered that he was afraid, given the improvements they'd made, that they would refuse to turn the mill over to him again when the war ended."

"Your father?" I repeated. I had never met him, but I did know Mark, and I knew Mrs. Ashton. I couldn't imagine either of them putting money before the lives of the people who had worked for them before the war, even though those same people might be employed by the War Office or the Army for the duration. It was impossible to imagine.

"Mark, perhaps you should take me back to Canterbury. I can't believe your parents will want visitors in the midst of such worries." He'd meant well, but now I could see it was not the best of ideas. "They have enough on their minds."

"On the contrary. You aren't *someone,* a casual acquaintance. You saved my life. You'll be good for their spirits. Look. I didn't intend to tell you any of this, Bess, but I thought, if you'd read about the explosion, you might say something, a sympathetic comment acknowledging what my father must have been through. At any rate, it's my mother I'm most worried about. She tries to keep our spirits up, but I know she's afraid for my father if this wild suspicion gets out of hand. I can't believe it's likely to go too far, but then it's my father we're talking about, and she's vulnerable."

"What does your father have to say about the accusations?"

"Very little. He tends to think that anyone who knows him will recognize them as the foolishness they are." Mark glanced across at me. "My father has always been a proud man. He tries to live up to his duties and obligations and expects other people to measure him by how well he succeeds. Some find that—I think the word would probably be *distant*, or *impersonal*. But he's been responsible for the livelihood of a good many families, and he takes that seriously. I don't think any of those trying to bring him down understands how much the destruction of the mill has affected him. They couldn't believe what they do, if they knew."

We'd been angling north and a little west, and I could hear seagulls in the distance. Out there somewhere to my right would be the Thames Estuary, broad and emptying into the Channel.

"But surely he can tell them where he was, when it happened."

"That's just it. He was seen earlier talking to someone just outside the mill. And then when the explosions began, first the large one and then the smaller ones that followed, he was on his way home. He ran back down to the River Cran. It was low tide, so he waded across, and started toward the mill just as the dust was settling. He stopped and just stood there, looking at the wreckage, shaking his head. Others had run toward the blast as well, and they saw him. For some reason, he just turned and started back the way he'd come. He told me later he was going after men and whatever tools he could find, to try to look for survivors. Before he'd even reached that side of the Cran, the first flames were spotted."

I thought to myself, *Oh dear.* For those looking for answers to explain the deaths of their loved ones, there was always enough circumstantial evidence to support whispers and rumors and finger-pointing. Sudden shocking death was unbelievable, unbearable, and people needed someone, human or divine, to blame for their loss.

I said, trying for a lighter note, "Surely those who know your father well will prevail. The fact that he rushed to the scene shows he cared, that he would have helped if he could. If anything at all could have been done for those poor men."

"God, I hope so. I don't want to go back to France leaving my family in such straits. The trouble is, even our friends have begun to fall away. They've made excuses of course, but it's clear they must be having doubts of their own. Or are reluctant to find themselves included in the rumors and gossip. Whatever the reason, they've simply avoided us. My mother's circle of friends has been particularly distant. She pretends it doesn't matter, but I know it must hurt."

We had come down a long hill through the outskirts of the village, mainly Victorian cottages and bungalows, straggling down toward its heart. Soon we were among the shops and a collection of older buildings, a number of which appeared to date to the days when the abbey flourished. Almshouses, lodgings for guests, abbey offices? A few had been converted to other uses, but it appeared that people still lived in many of them. One was particularly charming, with window boxes of geraniums and stone urns beside the ancient wooden door. And then we were in a small but busy square. I couldn't help but notice the glances as we drove through. Followed by a quick turn of the back as people recognized the motorcar. Even I could see that they were deliberately shunning us. A refusal to acknowledge so much as setting eyes on an Ashton— not even curious to see who else was in the vehicle. I felt an uncomfortable chill. In some fashion their snubs seemed worse than hostile stares would have been.

For Mark's sake I tried to keep my eyes on the attractive older houses scattered about the square, giving it its charm. But I was well aware of what he must be feeling.

We followed the street out of the square, and soon I could just pick out the roofs of buildings along the river. Three of the roofs looked fairly new.

"Why did you wish to speak to the Canterbury police?" I asked, reminded by a glimpse of the police station down a side street.

"There have been some—problems. Property damage mostly. The local constable isn't keen on dealing with it. I decided to have a word with Inspector Brothers." He cast a quick smile my way. "I promise you, no one will come crashing through the windows as we sit down to lunch."

I was of two opinions about that. But I could also better understand why he felt a visit from me might take his mother's mind off what was happening. If only for a few hours.

We turned off into another narrower street where I could see the long high wall that must once have enclosed the abbey. As old as it was, the wall was surprisingly intact, with trees on both sides of it and shaded walks following it. A nursemaid with a child in a pram was strolling along there, a brown-and-white dog trotting by her side.

The Major only followed the wall for a short distance, turning away, then turning again, and soon we were running down toward the River Cran. I could now see the sheds by the water, the sort that seem to line quays everywhere, catering to the needs of ships and boats. Some of them were long enough for sail mending or making rope from raw hemp. Beyond, on the far side of the river, the land rose slightly higher than this side, rough ground at a guess.

I expected the Major to continue to the river, but he stopped just above the sheds, where the road began to slope sharply toward the water. And I could see that what I'd thought was rough ground must actually be the ruins of the powder mill.

I noticed that Mark didn't turn off the motor. We weren't getting down, then.

At first I wasn't really certain what I *was* seeing. There was so little left to tell me what had once been here.

On the far side of the little river, tall grass had taken over. Scattered through it were stones that were nearly invisible here at the end of summer's growth. A jumble of them, without definition. About fifty yards farther on was what appeared to be an open wood that had been caught in a very bad storm. A dozen or so trees had struggled to leaf out, but most were torn and shredded and some were even beginning to show signs of rot, limbs dangling, bark peeling. I realized that the mill had been set in the wood, to keep the buildings cool and to lessen the blast force if something went wrong. Only this time the wood too had suffered badly.

Among the trees lay even more rubble from the powder works, and I began, slowly, to pick out the jagged remnants of roofless walls, stumps of foundations, clusters of unidentifiable stones that could have been anything. There were even what appeared to be corners that no longer had sides. It was as if a fretful child had begun to build a village, tired of it, and kicked it over. There must have been a crater as well, just as there would be in France when a shell exploded. But I couldn't be sure whether I could identify that from here, the land was so uneven, hummocky, and strewn with debris.

Considering a busy mill had once thrived there, it was still a raw and ugly wound on the landscape.

Even in the last century, gunpowder wasn't made in a single structure but in stages. I knew only what

I'd heard discussed by the officers in my father's command, debating the various kinds of gunpowder and their properties. I knew that it didn't "blow up" in the traditional sense of the word but expanded as it ignited. And I knew there was a rigid formula that produced the best powder, before being milled into small particles of equal size. Each stage was carried out in its own buildings, to lessen the danger of explosion. And so a powder mill was a collection of structures clustered among trees. Whatever had happened in this place had destroyed the lot. A single explosion powerful enough to create a chain reaction until there was nothing left.

Potassium nitrate—saltpeter—made a better gunpowder than sodium nitrate. And alder trees made the best charcoal for the formula. That was something else I'd heard. But for some time now gunpowder works all across Britain had begun to produce cordite instead of traditional black power, and that was a much more complicated recipe. With far more chances for something to go badly wrong. All I really knew was that the length and thickness of the "cord" in the manufacturing process determined how it would be used in munitions.

In 1915, a severe shortage of acetone, necessary to the process, had nearly shut down works all over the country. The loss of the Ashton Mill on the heels of that must have been devastating.

Though hardly an expert, I'd seen enough of the shelling in France to understand that here too something quite disastrous had happened, and that when it did, a great many people had died.

Pointing, Mark described the scene for me. "The walls were thicker on this side of the buildings, so that any blast would point away from the town just behind us. And the buildings were spaced for safety. Yet there's hardly a wall standing now. We'll never know how many survived the first blast. Or if any did." He paused, to let me resurrect the mill site in my mind. "When they took over the mill, the Government put in railway lines to bring in workers from The Swale villages. This was necessary to replace men who had enlisted. A good many of the new workers were women, along with some older workers from the brewery when it closed for lack of men. Three hundred souls to start with, and more as the demands of the war increased tenfold. Thank God it was a Sunday. The Fire Brigade came racing toward the blast, but there was no way to contain it or what followed. Several firemen were injured trying."

Turning slightly, he pointed north of where we were sitting. "That's The Swale." I could just see a line of blue water far to the right, at the foot of what appeared to be marshland. "It runs between the Medway to the west and the Thames Estuary to the east, and of course the Cran empties into it. Across The Swale from us is the Isle of Sheppey. Quite marshy where it faces us, just as it is on this side. The abbots sent wool and barrels of mutton and hops and other goods down the Cran to ships waiting to cross to France. Much of the gunpowder went out the same way, to the munitions factories where the cartridges and various types of shells were filled. Artillery, Naval guns, mortars—whatever the War Office ordered. There used to be a small fishing fleet in Cranbourne as well, a survivor of the days of merchant ships."

I looked to my left. There was no sign of any railway station, nor the tracks coming into it. Both must have disappeared in the blast, save for a twisted length of iron that must have come from the train shed. I could pick that out now.

"We've never had any trouble. Not in over a *hundred years*. Not a single explosion."

I could hear the distress in his voice. The Ashtons had been proud of that record.

I remembered what he'd said earlier, that it was dangerous work, but paid well. And again that it was feared that the Government had been pushing too hard for larger and larger outputs of powder. After all, there was a war on . . .

The Cran was hardly more than a stream now, a narrow channel that must have been wider at one time. It would probably have been dammed long ago to feed the mill. A tidal river, presently at low tide, for the small craft anchored there were literally high and dry, tilted to one side, most of them waiting for the incoming flood to give them buoyancy once more.

I couldn't see what lay beyond the trees.

From something I'd heard the Colonel Sahib—my father—say, there were munitions factories somewhere out there on Sheppey, where women loaded shells and casings with the gunpowder brought from here. He would have known about them. And about the Ashton Powder Mill, surely. Of course there had never been any reason to speak of them to me. These were military matters.

I looked again at the ruins. Very much, I thought, like the abbey we'd passed, torn down by a very angry King. Only no one had wanted this rubble for Calais harbor. It lay where it had fallen two years earlier.

"Thank God, the tide was out that morning," Mark was saying. "A Sunday, no one about, no boaters or picnickers, no families strolling along the water. Only the men working inside. Or the toll could have been staggering. As it was, the blast took out windows for miles, lifted roofs right off the sheds on our side of the Cran, blowing in their doors. For that matter, we lost windows at Abbey Hall, and also part of the roof. Masts of ships in the Cran and The Swale were broken like sticks. And the earth shook like something demented. That was felt as far north as Norwich. Even Canterbury was badly shaken. There were any number of injuries all over this part of Kent, mostly from falling tiles and masonry or broken glass. Many people thought the Germans were shelling Canterbury."

I tried to imagine that morning, and failed. Frightened villagers rushing out of their houses to find out what had happened—and then, finally, *knowing*. And rushing on in horror to where we were sitting now. Their worst fears realized. A hundred men . . .

"The dust cloud was enormous. Stones rained down on everything. My mother heard them falling all around our house. I've always thought it was that dust cloud that set off the fire. Or at the very least fed it. But there's no way to prove that."

He sighed. "The main question after the explosion was, should the powder mill be rebuilt? The Government looked at the ruins, calculating the cost of removing all that rubble before they could begin.

Asking themselves where to find the manpower to begin the task. But there was even a division of feeling about that. For some it was sacred ground, where their loved ones lay buried. For others it was well-paid work, and if the mill wasn't rebuilt, many would be unemployed. In the end, it was decided to expand a mill elsewhere. Although Captain Collier did everything in his power to convince the Army to rebuild, my father was blamed for their decision as well, accused of not fighting harder for reconstruction for the simple reason that the new powder works rising on the site would belong to the Government, not to him. And the mill has always been our greatest source of income. Not the sheep or the fields—the gunpowder. What's more, we couldn't begin to consider rebuilding ourselves. The cost would be prohibitive because of what had to be carried away even before we could start."

I had seen enough, and I was about to tell him so when an egg smashed into the windscreen directly in front of where I was sitting. Before I could stop myself, I threw up my hands to protect my face as it shattered. Another smashed on the bonnet, leaving a smear of yellow yolk.

Mark was swearing under his breath, already out of the motorcar, giving chase. It had happened so fast, I'd caught only a glimpse of whoever it was who'd thrown

the eggs. A boy? A man? I could remember trousers—
a cap pulled low. Mark, clearly, had seen him too, but I
couldn't tell if he'd recognized the person.

I was also out of the car, shouting his name. He was
too angry, and if he caught the miscreant, he was likely
to do something he'd regret later.

Mark stopped just as he reached the shed corner.
He'd forgot about me in that moment of blazing anger.
And I realized, as I caught up with him and could look
down the long line of sheds, that whoever it was had
vanished—most likely into an open doorway—before
Mark could follow him.

"Did you recognize him?" I asked.

"Worst luck, no." He stood there for a moment, then
he turned back toward the motorcar. "It's hopeless.
There are a hundred places he could hide."

"Has this happened before?" I asked, still shocked
by the suddenness of the attack. "You mentioned property damage—this was very personal."

Shaking his head, he answered, "Nothing so direct,
believe me." He helped me to climb into the motorcar
again, and shut my door. "A wall or two pulled down.
Sheep herded out into the marshes. A refusal by one of
the shops in the village to fill my mother's order. The
hop fields—they were once the abbey's—uprooted.
The oast houses damaged. When we put up a watch,

whoever it is seems to know where, and strikes at us in another part of the estate."

"And you said the local man refused to help. I expect he probably knew who might have done such things and didn't want to act."

Mark was quickly reversing, back to a point where he could turn the motorcar and return to the street that followed the abbey wall. "He called it high spirits. Restless lads, their fathers in France, their mothers out of work since the explosion. Constable Hood did come out, I'll give him that, looked around, shook his head, and said from the lack of evidence it was impossible to tell who might be responsible. It was true, of course, there was little to go by. But it was hardly helpful. And yes, my father also believed Hood had some idea who was behind what was happening, that was the worst part. And so the attacks went on. I think the constable must have known they would." His face was grim as he turned to me. "I'm sorry, Bess. I shouldn't have brought you down here to the river, but I thought—it seemed to be the best way to explain what happened."

"And this is why you wished to see the inspector in Canterbury."

"Nor was it the first time."

"But the explosion was what? Two years ago? It's understandable that people would have been upset at the time. But now?"

"For over a year after any chance of sabotage had been discounted, it was seen as a great tragedy. We were all affected by what happened. My parents attended every one of the memorial services. Then about four months ago—June, I think it was, although I can't tell you precisely when, I was in France—there was talk. At first a whisper, and before very long a rumor. And then open speculation." He shook his head. "Sometimes I have wished it *was* as simple as sabotage. We'd be united in blaming the Germans."

"Yes," I responded slowly. "It's the whispers that are hardest to stop. And the rest follows."

He turned to me. "Shall I take you back to Canterbury?"

"Of course not. I'm made of sterner stuff than that." I said it with a smile, and he returned it. But I could read the embarrassment in his eyes.

"Good girl!" After a moment, he added, "They must have thought you were Clara. Otherwise they wouldn't have dared—" He broke off, still quite angry.

"Who is Clara?"

"My cousin. She's come to stay with us for a bit."

I wondered if the "bit" was since the troubles had started or before.

It was even possible that with Mark only temporarily in England, Mr. Ashton had arranged for Cousin Clara to be there in the event that something happened to him. It was a foolish notion, I chided myself. Throwing eggs and tearing down walls in a field were not likely to escalate to murder. All the same, I couldn't quite shake off the feeling that things were beginning to change, and not for the better. And perhaps Philip Ashton had feared that from the start, setting his defenses quietly in place.

Chapter Two

We were driving down the lane that followed the abbey wall, branches of the trees marching beside us spreading like a canopy overhead. I could feel the tension lessening in both of us.

"Did Mother tell you? The Hall was once the old abbey guesthouse. It's been in the family for generations."

I could see it at the far end of the lane now, the same dark stone of the wall passing beside me, tall and quite old, with lovely windows framed in paler stone, some of them filled with diamond-paned glass. As we reached the door, the drive broadened into a circle. Over the door was a seal in an oval of richly colored stained glass.

"The abbot's coat of arms," Mark was saying, "although I have no idea which abbot. At a guess, it was the one who built the house."

The door flew open as if someone had been watching for us and a young woman—Clara?—with fair hair and an oval face came flying down the short flight of steps. As soon as she saw me, she stopped short, saying, "*Oh . . .*" as if a visitor was the last thing she expected.

Mark was out of the motorcar at once. "What is it?" he asked, as if fearful of bad news. "What's happened?"

"The morning post. More nasty unsigned letters threatening us. I tried to keep them from your mother, but I think she could read my face. She just held out her hand and I had no choice but to pass them over to her. Were you able to speak to Inspector—" She saw the slime of the egg on the bonnet. "Oh, dear. Where did this happen? Did you see who did it?" But her gaze turned to me, as if I'd been the cause of the egg throwing.

He hastily made the introductions as he opened my door to hand me out, then added, "Inspector Brothers wasn't in. Or so it was said. They wouldn't tell me when he'd be back. And so I came home. I brought Bess to cheer up Mother."

Clara said over her shoulder to me as she led the way inside, "Aunt Helen will be so pleased to see you." But there was little welcome in her tone of voice. "You're the Sister who took such good care of Mark? Yes, I thought so. I've heard Aunt Helen speak of you often."

We were in a large hall where what appeared to be a Georgian flight of stairs led to the upper floors. Passages led off to the right and left, embracing it. The exterior might be recognizable by the abbot who built the house, but sometime in the past, someone had taken it upon himself or herself to make the interior more fashionable. And dark woods had given way to brighter wallpapers. Here in the entrance it was a very handsome pale green printed with Chinese scenes, some of them picked out in gold leaf: the tips of the pagodas, the patterns on clothing, and the harnesses of horses catching the light.

"Where's Father?" Mark asked, setting my kit bag by the stairs as Clara and he turned to their right.

"In his study. Brooding, I think. I went in to ask him when he'd like his lunch, and he wasn't in the best of moods. At a guess, he'd decided he should have gone into Canterbury himself."

"That wouldn't have done at all. Take Bess in to see Mother. I'll go and speak to him."

He left me with Clara and went back the way we'd come, disappearing toward the far side of the stairs.

Clara opened the door into a sitting room decorated with blue-flowered wallpaper and a blue patterned carpet, giving it the air of a summer garden. I couldn't see Mrs. Ashton at first. Her chair was turned toward the windows as if to shut out the rest of the room. But when Clara said brightly, almost as one might to a child, offering a treat, "Aunt Helen? Mark has brought Sister Crawford to see you," she was out of her chair at once, staring at me.

"Is it you? Bess, dear, how wonderful to see you again." She came to me, embracing me, adding, "Where on earth did Mark find you?"

"I was in Canterbury this morning waiting for my train to London. I'm afraid it's been delayed. I went for a walk to pass the time, and Mark and I ran into each other by the cathedral."

"Yes, he's always liked Canterbury. But I thought he was going to"—she broke off, then quickly went on—"to run an errand for his father."

"Inspector Brothers wasn't in, and the desk sergeant wasn't very forthcoming about when he would return."

"Ah, you know about our situation. Just as well." She managed a smile. "There won't be any awkwardness now. Do come and sit down, Bess, and tell me how you are? Clara, could you ask Mrs. Byers to set another place for lunch, please?"

Clara said, "Of course," but left the room reluctantly, as if she'd prefer to share our chat.

Mrs. Ashton and I rearranged her pretty blue chair so that I could sit by her, and she asked my news. I tried to remember anything I'd heard recently about the Sisters and the doctors who'd worked on Mark's wounds, adding, "And I saw Matron not three weeks ago. They thought she'd caught the Spanish flu, but it was only a rather nasty cold."

"The Spanish flu has taken its toll here," she said. "Did Mark tell you about dear Ellie? Yes? Well, I must admit that it was an ordeal for all of us. And five of our neighbors didn't survive. Mark's old Nanny succumbed to it, as well as one of the housemaids. I'm glad Matron is all right. She's a remarkable woman. She was another one who refused to give up on Mark." She glanced toward the door as we heard voices in the passage. "I've been happy to have Mark at home, even so briefly," she added quickly, lowering her voice, "although I know how eager he is to go back. Selfish of me, but he's my only child. I take each gift of time to heart."

The sitting room door opened and I looked up to see Mark and his father standing there. The resemblance between father and son was strong. At Mr. Ashton's heels was a liver-and-white spaniel. It stared at me with interest but was too well behaved to bark or come forward to sniff at my shoes.

The older man looked tired, and there were dark circles under his eyes, as if he hadn't slept well in some time. I thought too that he must be under a good deal of stress, for his coat was larger in the shoulders than it ought to have been, indicating he'd lost weight recently. Still, he smiled in genuine welcome and took my hand as Mark introduced us.

"I'm glad you've come," he said in a deep, warm voice. "If only to thank you for saving my son's life. But I must also apologize to you for the shocking behavior you witnessed there by the river. I wonder sometimes if the war hasn't brought out the worst in some people, just as it has the best in others."

"It was unexpected," I agreed, "but no harm done. I was grateful to Mark for showing me what a calamity had occurred here. I hadn't known." Mark had warned me not to speak of the explosion, but after Mr. Ashton had brought it up, I could hardly deny all knowledge of it.

"The Government thought it best not to publicize it." He went over and kissed his wife's cheek. I realized that he'd been out this morning as well, and she had been waiting anxiously for his return. It explained the chair turned toward the window, from which she could hear anyone coming up the drive.

"I've asked Bess to stay for lunch," she said to her husband.

"And I was about to suggest that she stay the night. From what Mark has said about these delays at the

railway station, she won't see London before tomorrow morning late. Safer and more comfortable here, I
should think."

I protested, not wishing to intrude, but Mr. Ashton
frowned. "Nonsense. The hotels are crowded, and
the railway people are likely to put off telling you that
it's hopeless until it's too late to find a suitable room.
There's nothing pressing in London, is there?"

Smiling, I thanked him and agreed. I had a little
leave, I looked forward to seeing my parents, but a
day more or less wouldn't matter. And truth be told,
I wasn't particularly eager to find myself in a hotel the
Nursing Service wouldn't approve of. It was very strict
about such matters.

"Good, that's settled, then," he said, briskly rubbing
his hands. He gestured to the spaniel and it went obe-
diently to the hearth rug and settled for a nap. "Now
to business. I saw to the mending of another stretch of
stone wall—"

"Again?" Mrs. Ashton asked sharply. "You said
nothing about it this morning."

"I didn't know then. Baxter came to fetch me as
I was walking out. We attended to it ourselves. I've
decided the less said, the better. No sense in encouraging others to try their hand at troublemaking."

Clara came then to tell us that lunch had been
served. "A little early, but I thought you'd prefer it to

tea. And Mrs. Lacey wants to look in on her sister this afternoon, if that's all right."

"Mrs. Lacey is our cook," Mrs. Ashton explained to me. "Her sister has been recovering from a chill and doesn't have her full strength back. Yes, do tell her to go on, my dear, and take a little of that soup her sister liked. It will keep up her strength."

She led the way to the dining room, along this same passage, and Mark followed with his father while Clara went to speak to Mrs. Lacey. The spaniel came with us and disappeared under the table.

It was a cold luncheon, and after eating whatever the hospital canteen could provide, I found it delicious. But Mrs. Ashton apologized for the shortages. "If we hadn't had the foresight to increase the number of hens we keep, we'd be no better than most. And much to our surprise, one of the housemaids is a marvel with them. As a girl, she looked after her mother's flock."

My mother had also looked to increase the chickens we kept in Somerset. Beef and pork allotments were stringently rationed, while chickens were a little less so if grown for a household.

It was a pleasant meal, and no one mentioned the problems facing the Ashtons and Abbey Hall. I was glad I had come here.

The Ashtons and Clara regaled me with descriptions of what it was like trying to communicate with poor Mark while he was as deaf as a post. Hasty searches for pen and paper when encountering him unexpectedly, falling back on shouting loudly in the hope of being understood, and then charades. They made it sound entertaining, but I knew it must have been very difficult for everyone. And Mark took it all with good grace, and laughed with us. But I could tell that his experience with silence had been worrying, because he'd never been able to believe his hearing would come back. I'd dealt with similar cases in France; I could read the signs.

We finished our meal and took our tea in Mrs. Ashton's sitting room. Even Clara seemed to be less ill at ease, realizing, I think, that I was only a temporary threat. I had to smile. Much as I cared for Mark, I wasn't in the market for a husband, certainly not with the war still going on. Then I found myself wondering how long she'd had this attachment to Mark. Since Eloise's death or before? Because attachment there was.

Then at two o'clock, without warning, everything changed.

After the tea tray had been removed, Mark and his father went off to speak to someone about estate matters, and I could see that Mrs. Ashton was tiring. All that vivacious chatter at lunch had been a mask. It worried me, because I'd seen how strong she was in France when Mark's life lay in the balance. But she was under a great deal of stress, and I wondered if she was sleeping at all.

She offered to show me to my room, and on our way, Mrs. Ashton suggested that I might find the abbey grounds a pleasant place to stroll, if I cared for a little exercise after our lunch. "It's safe enough," she told me, "and Clara sometimes walks there." As I thanked her, I realized that this was the perfect excuse for me to allow Mrs. Ashton to rest, rather than entertain her unexpected guest. She gave me directions, urging me to treat this as my own home and enjoy myself, even offering to accompany me.

"You mustn't worry about me," I said, smiling. "If I can find my way across the north of France, I'll have no trouble. I only need to follow the abbey wall to a gate." And if further proof was necessary that I'd done the right thing, I noticed that she made no objection.

"Of course you can!" she'd answered brightly. "An hour? That should be just right to see everything."

I went down the drive with every intention of visiting the abbey ruins. Instead, when I reached the corner of the wall, I found myself walking back toward the river.

No one could mistake me for Clara now; my uniform would be the first thing anyone noticed. And so I felt relatively safe. Shocked as I'd been by the suddenness of the eggs flying at the motorcar, I had come to realize that they weren't intended for me, and indeed, neither egg had been meant to hit the passengers. It was just a show of meanness, and if I'd been the Ashtons, I'd have taken that to heart.

My own reason for going back was to get a better picture of the scene, because it had occurred to me at some point during lunch that once I reached London, I might ask my father, the Colonel Sahib, what he knew about the explosion and whether something could be done to ease the situation here before it actually became dangerous. If the police were taking such a hands-off attitude, perhaps the Army might have a quiet word in someone's ear about it. In India, my father had made something of a reputation for himself by defusing issues that way. The local people had come to respect him and understand that they could approach him. The remote hill tribes were a mutual enemy, and that had helped smooth the way too—no one wanted to find *them* on the doorstep, taking advantage of our troubles.

As it was, I found the quay deserted. The tide was only just turning, hardly stirring the beached boats. A pair of seagulls, spotting me, came flying out of nowhere to inspect me in case I was bringing their luncheon. They were raucous, and intent on making sure I knew they were about, but I ignored them.

This close I could get a better view of the ruins. I could see where Mr. Ashton must have forded the river before realizing that there was nothing to be done for those caught in the blast. I paused, looking to my right toward The Swale, and the low-lying Isle of Sheppey beyond. Marshy indeed, there, and also on the far side of the Cran below the mill. There the land sloped, running down to The Swale, while on this side of the Cran, rising ground kept the land dry, fit for sheep and hops and whatever else the abbey and now the Ashtons chose to grow.

I was shading my eyes with my hand for a better look at the island, cut off from the Kent mainland by The Swale, when someone spoke from just behind me, making me jump.

"The Isle of Sheep. It's what *Sheppey* means."

I turned. Several of the shed doors had stood open as I walked along the river, but the interiors had appeared to be empty. Now, in the one nearest me, a man was lighting a cigarette. Then he leaned back against the frame.

He must, I thought, have heard the gulls and stepped out to see what they were on about.

Tall, but not as tall as Mark, fair, hazel eyes, his expression lively with curiosity.

"Sorry. I didn't mean to startle you. I was working behind the boat."

I could see a rather large sailboat hull sitting on a cradle in the dimness of the interior behind him. His hands were covered in dust, as if he'd been sanding, and I could see flecks of it on his face. I couldn't help but wonder if he'd been the egg thrower. Or knew who it was.

Without waiting for an answer, he went on. "You're a nursing Sister. Did you bring someone to Cranbourne? Anyone I might know?"

"Actually, I'm a guest at Abbey Hall," I said.

He frowned. "Indeed."

"I was one of Major Ashton's nurses. I met his mother when she came over to find him."

"Ah. And so you've walked down to see the scene of the tragedy."

Turning back to the river, I said, "It's not the best of times to be a visitor. Earlier someone threw eggs at the motorcar when Major Ashton brought me here."

"Not a very friendly welcome," he agreed. "If you're wondering if I threw them, the answer is no." But from the tone of his voice I gathered he'd have preferred something a little more lethal.

"As a matter of interest, were you here when the mill exploded?"

"I was." He looked with distaste at the cigarette he was holding, then pitched it in the river beyond us.

"Not working in here, surely?" I asked, gesturing toward the open shed.

"God, no. The doors were blown in, and the place was a disaster. Paint and varnish and all the rest scattered every which way." He inclined his head in the direction of the hull. "I hadn't begun this one—or it would probably have been matchwood."

"You're a boat builder?"

"I was, until the war put an end to it. No one is buying pleasure craft these days."

"I expect not."

"There was a flying club out on Sheppey. I was a member, as it happened. When war came, I wanted to fly. Early in 1916 I crashed coming in with a machine that was barely holding itself together. That put paid to my war. I should have gone down at sea." He pointed to his foot. "A softer landing, if a wet one."

I could see that his right boot was high, protecting a stiff ankle.

"Not much use when you can't fly any longer. Even the Army wouldn't take me. Hardly surprising, if you can't climb the ladder when the whistle blows," he went on. "Or race across No Man's Land. There's a splinter of something nasty lodged near my heart as well. No one would operate. And there you have it."

I thought perhaps he'd explained his presence out of a sense of guilt for not being in France. There were uniforms for the wounded who couldn't be returned to duty. He was wearing worn corduroy trousers and a cotton shirt to work in. "It's very dangerous to try," I said. "But you can still build your boats. There's something to be said for that." Then I realized how neatly he'd changed the subject so that he hadn't had to talk about the explosion.

"This is a perfect place for such a mill," I went on. "I don't see why they decided not to rebuild on this same site." Two could play at this game of misdirection.

"It would cost more and take longer to clear the land before putting up another building. They've moved on. Besides, it's a grave now, isn't it?" He pointed to the line of warehouses. "It was rumored they might turn these into a new factory. But the town protested, and I think it finally dawned on London that where there had been one catastrophe, there could very well be another, and this time, the town—or a large part of it, at any rate—might go up with the buildings. They were damn—very lucky, the last time."

"But why was it suspicious, this blast?"

He answered grudgingly, "Ashton Powder had had a very good record. The mill had been here since the Napoleonic Wars, if not before, and there had never been any trouble. That's rare, dealing with gunpowder."

"Then what went wrong two years ago?" I persisted.

"People got careless. Or nervous. One mistake is all it takes to level such a place. And there was the pressure to produce more and more powder. The munitions factories were running flat out. Collier did his best to keep them busy. God, if you were in France, you've heard the guns, you know how many they lob over in a single hour. All those shells have got to come from somewhere. And the powder to fill them."

I knew, all too well. The ground shook, the very air seemed to vibrate as the big guns pounded a sector. Men lost their hearing, as Mark had done, or had such severe headaches they couldn't function. Some developed such a shock to the nervous system that they couldn't stand.

All those shells have got to come from somewhere . . .

I turned back to the ruins. "You don't think about that, do you? Where the shells come from. It just seems there's an endless supply." Changing the subject, I said, "Does *everyone* in Cranbourne believe that Mr. Ashton started that fire?"

"There are two camps. The survivors of those lost in the explosion needed someone to blame. A casual spark seems a very dubious source for such tragedy. After all, as I said, it had never happened before. And Ashton was there. As it began."

"And the other camp?"

"They've lost their livelihood, haven't they? And they too want to blame someone."

"Are you among those last?"

He shrugged. "I'd like to hold someone responsible too. I knew many of the men who were killed. It's comforting, you know, to find someone to blame. It says that God isn't cruel, it's Man who caused such pain and loss. You can rage at a man. It's harder to rage at God."

He hadn't really answered my question, but I let it go. I was starting to walk on, when he said, "Let me close these doors. I'll walk back with you."

I could see his limp as he shut the long, heavy doors. He didn't bother to lock them. Coming to join me where I stood watching the tide run in fast, he said, "They wouldn't put a hospital here, you know. Even though the Ashtons and others with large houses offered. Too close to the mill."

"That's interesting," I said. We walked a little way, and I asked, "How *did* the fire start? The explosion was bad enough."

"Nobody knows. But it put paid to any attempt to find out how the explosion occurred. Or to look for survivors who might have known the truth."

Which must have pointed an even stronger finger at Philip Ashton.

The man was looking closely at me. "You're very curious about all this."

"Wouldn't you be?" I gestured toward the blackened ruins. "Even two years after the explosion, it's frightful. So many lives lost?" I shook my head. "If there is any place where ghosts walk, it's there, across the river."

I'd meant it metaphorically, not literally. But I saw the shock in his eyes before he turned away.

"Do you believe in ghosts?" he asked after a moment as we left the river behind and turned toward the abbey.

"I don't know," I replied. "I've never seen one."

He didn't quite know how to take that answer.

We parted company at Abbey Lane, and he nodded to me before turning to go. "Enjoy your stay," he said. With bare politeness.

"Thank you," I said. And as I walked back to Abbey Hall, I wondered what he'd seen in those ruins that had made him take me so literally when I spoke of ghosts.

When I walked into the hall, Clara was just coming down the stairs. "There you are! Aunt Helen is lying down. Is there anything I can do for you? Do you remember the way to your room?"

"Yes, I do, thank you, Clara." Turn right at the top of the stairs. Third door on my right. "I'm sorry to put everyone to such trouble."

"It's no trouble at all. Would you like to see Aunt Helen's garden? It's a part of the old abbey, and quite lovely. I shouldn't wonder if it had been an herb garden. Monks knew a great deal about healing. Somehow it has managed to survive for centuries. That's rather remarkable."

"I remember your aunt talking about it to Mark while he was feverish," I said lightly. "I'll enjoy seeing it."

We walked in silence to a door at the side of the house that opened into the garden. And we stepped out into a little bit of paradise.

There were still herbs, many of which I recognized, in beds that were separated by perennials. And in the stone wall itself here and there were pockets of tiny wildflowers that spilled down in miniature falls of color. As if holding on to summer as long as possible in this protected space. At the bottom of the garden was a slightly raised terrace where graceful iron chairs, painted white, sat beneath an arbor that was thick with wisteria vines, still green. That, I thought, must be Helen Ashton's personal contribution to this wonderful space.

"This is really lovely." But as we stepped out into it, I began to notice that no one had deadheaded the blooming plants or trimmed the wisteria recently, a measure of how little time Mrs. Ashton had spent here of late. A measure too of her worry?

Stopping to admire a display of flowers I didn't recognize, I became aware of Clara's frown.

"You nursed Mark when he was so ill? Aunt Helen came home singing your praises. She said you saved his life with your care and your training."

She was jealous. I'd realized that but hadn't expected her to be so blunt about it.

I smiled. "That's very kind of her," I said quietly. "The truth is we had the best doctors imaginable and an experienced nursing staff. And Mark wasn't the only miracle they've worked."

"Yes, well, Aunt Helen seldom mentions them."

I said, turning to look straight at her, "I've nursed hundreds of men since I finished my training. Mark was special because his mother had come to help us in any way she could, and we didn't want to let her down.

We didn't want to have to tell her one morning that her son hadn't lived through the night."

She stared at me as if I'd bitten her.

"I see" was all she could manage before she turned away. Then, without looking at me, she added, "I'm so sorry. It's just that she's so very happy to have you here. And Mark is as well."

"I expect my arrival helped to take their minds off what's been happening. What's the old expression? A change of trouble is as good as a holiday? Sometimes it's true."

To my surprise, she flushed, saying again, "I'm so sorry. I—Mark and I—I've been in love with him since I was fourteen."

"Then you've nothing to fear from me."

"Thank you," she said ruefully. But we both knew that Eloise was her rival still. And that was as it should be. Mark would have to mourn before he could turn elsewhere.

We walked on, down to the terrace, where I admired the small pools that had been put in on either side.

"The monks would have kept fish in the pools," she said. "Stocked for use as needed on holy days. Alas, there are none in here now. There was a story I read once, when I was a child. About a monk who had made friends with the carp in the fishpond, only to discover that a curse had been put on it, and when the curse was lifted, a prince stepped out of the water. In gratitude, the prince built a great abbey where only a poor wooden one had stood. I remember coming here as a little girl, looking for the fish, determined to find the prince."

We laughed together as we turned back toward the house. But her prince had found another princess. Eloise had got there first.

Over the wall, toward the front of the house, came the sounds of carriages coming up the drive. Their pace didn't sound like that of casual visitors. Too brisk, the wheels rattling loudly. I could hear one of the drivers reining in the horses.

Clara's face was white. "Oh, God, who can that be?"

Side by side we hurried up the garden to the door into the house. I could hear someone coming down the stairs. Mrs. Ashton. She called to her housekeeper, and there was fear in her voice.

We reached the hall just as a fist pounded on the door.

Clara started forward. Mrs. Ashton barred her way. "Let Mrs. Byers open the door. Come with me to the study."

Mark was already standing there on its threshold, listening, his gaze going to his mother's face as the three of us hurried toward him. Behind him, Mr. Ashton had risen from his desk.

I watched as the housekeeper came up from the kitchen, walking steadily toward the sound of the knocking, but before Mark could shut the study door behind us I saw that Mrs. Byers's hands were clenched in the fabric of her dress.

Mr. Ashton was at the window now. He said to his wife, "It's nothing to worry about, my dear. I expect it's the police. They've found our young vandals."

"They'll want us to be magnanimous and not press charges," Mark answered him, but there was bitterness in his voice.

As if by agreement, we took chairs, trying to look as if this was no more than a social call. Mark replaced his father by the windows, his back to the room, while his father resumed his seat behind the desk. As voices reached us from the hall, I heard a low growl and realized that the spaniel was under the desk at its master's feet. Mr. Ashton spoke to it, and it was quiet again.

After what seemed an eternity, we heard Mrs. Byers's tentative tap on the door, and then it swung open.

All of us, except for Mark, could see the man standing there, and the uniformed policemen behind him.

He was of medium height, perhaps forty-five, dark haired. There was a grim expression on his face.

Not one of us believed now that this call was about young vandals.

My heart flew into my throat, and I reached out for Mrs. Ashton's hand. She clasped my fingers fiercely until they hurt.

Philip Ashton rose. "Inspector Brothers," he said calmly.

"Good afternoon, Mr. Ashton. I've come from Canterbury with a warrant for your arrest for the murder of these men." He held out several sheets of paper, and I could see that they were filled with names. "I shall be happy to read them to you, sir, if you insist."

"I know the names of these dead," Mr. Ashton said. "They are engraved on my soul. What evidence is there that I have caused their deaths?"

"You were at the mill earlier in the day, Sunday the second of April 1916, before the first blast, behaving suspiciously, and there again just after the explosions brought the buildings down, standing at the very spot where the flames rose as you were hurrying away. This has been attested to by a dozen people who have come forward and given their depositions. They were rushing toward the river, and they report that your expression as you turned their way was gleeful."

"Gleeful? I see. And what possible motive could I have had for destroying my mill, much less wanting these men dead?"

"A court will hear that in due course, sir. I am here to take you into custody on the charges brought."

"Yes, certainly." He glanced toward his wife, standing still as if turned to stone, her blue eyes stark in her pale face. "Will you give me a few minutes to say good-bye to my family, and to give my son instructions about my affairs?" I could see Inspector Brothers hesitate. "I give you my word, Inspector. I will come through that door in ten minutes' time and accompany you to Canterbury without fuss."

Reluctantly—I think he was all too aware of the constables at his back, prepared for any resistance—the Inspector agreed. Stepping back into the passage, he shut the door, and all of us could hear his voice issuing abrupt orders for his men to wait outside.

I would have left, to give them privacy, but Mrs. Ashton was still gripping my hand as if it were a lifeline to hope.

Philip Ashton came across the room to her and put his arm around her shoulders, pulling her close. "Nothing to worry about, my dear, it will all be resolved shortly. I want you to be brave and not do anything rash."

I couldn't imagine Mrs. Ashton doing anything rash, but I thought the words were meant for Mark as well.

He nodded to me, then turned to his niece. Clara was striving to hold back tears as she said good-bye.

"It might be best for you to go home," he urged her. "Will you think about it?"

And then he was conferring in a low voice with his son, close by the window.

Without looking at us, three women still standing there like marble statues, unable to speak, he crossed the room. Mrs. Ashton put out her hand then as if to stop him, but let it drop. He opened the door, stepped through it, then shut it firmly behind him, and we could just hear voices as Inspector Brothers took him in charge. As well as the soft *clink* of handcuffs.

The spaniel went to the door, scratching on it and whining.

Chapter Three

As their footsteps faded in the distance, Mrs. Ashton said distractedly, "He has nothing with him. His razor, comb—a change of clothes, shoes—a blanket, if where they put him is too cold." But she didn't move.

Mark cleared his throat. "Later, Mother. He'll be all right until later. I must speak to Mr. Groves as soon as possible. That means running into Canterbury." Through the open study windows we could hear the front door closing and then the carriages beginning to move down the drive. It was so loud in that room, as if the sound had come rushing back to invade and fill the silence.

For a moment no one said a word.

"Mark, perhaps it would be best—" I began, thinking that it would be an imposition for me to stay under the circumstances.

Mrs. Ashton put out her hand. "Bess. No. You mustn't leave." Then to her son, she said, "I'll see to his valise now. You must take it with you. It will make him more comfortable."

Clara stepped forward. "I'll help," she offered, but Mrs. Ashton shook her head.

"Thank you, dear, but I'd rather attend to it myself. You might speak to Mrs. Lacey about some sandwiches, and a Thermos of tea. I don't know what they serve in such places." And she walked from the room like someone in a dream, only half her mind on the present.

Clara hurried after her, turning in the direction of the kitchen. The spaniel slipped out between them, and I could hear it scratching at the house door, asking to be let out.

Mark stared at me, but I don't think he saw me. Then he shook his head and said, quite simply, "Hell."

I waited, not wishing to intrude. I couldn't imagine the police coming to take away the Colonel Sahib right in front of me. A shiver went through me at the thought. After a few seconds Mark's gaze sharpened, and I knew he was back in the study once more.

He said, as if apologizing, "There was nothing I could do. You do see that?"

"The last thing he would have wished is for you to make a scene. It would have been all the harder on your mother."

"I felt like knocking Brothers down." His voice was suddenly quite savage, the aftermath of shock.

"It would only have made matters worse for your father. And very likely they'd have taken you as well, and where would your mother be then?"

"Yes. Still." He took a deep breath. "I don't know if they'll let me see him. But Mother will insist that I try."

Collecting my wits, I said, "They'll search the valise. A formality, a precaution. And look at the food. You mustn't argue. Let them do what they must. Then they'll let your father have his things." I wasn't sure if this was true or not, if they'd take away the razor and anything that he might use to harm himself. But I knew that it mattered to Mrs. Ashton, and if only a few things reached her husband, she'd be able to breathe more easily.

"You're quite right. Yes. I'll remember." And then his anger came surging back. "My father. Taken away in handcuffs. Of all the stupid, ridiculous, *absurd* things to do." He slammed his fist down on the back of the chair nearest him, not noticing the pain. "Why would he kill men he knew, men who'd worked for him, men who'd worked at the brewery until it closed? He knew them all by name. It was a point of pride to be able to call a man by his name when speaking to him. He paid a decent wage. He saw to it that they had decent housing. There are cottages on the far side of the abbey for those who needed a place to live. What in God's name could he gain, blowing up the mill?"

"If there's little or no evidence, if it's only rumor and speculation, the police will sort it out soon enough." But Brothers had mentioned depositions. That was far more serious.

Mark frowned. "I can't imagine who these 'witnesses' are. According to the Army there was only *one* witness. I'd nearly forgot about that. He claimed he was fishing out in The Swale. Surely he can swear that when my father walked away that morning, the buildings were still standing, the men inside still alive. And that my father had nothing to do with the fire any more than he'd had to do with the explosions."

"Who is he?" I wondered if it were the boat builder. And if it were, if he would testify on behalf of Philip Ashton.

"A man by the name of Rollins. He calls himself a fisherman, but he spent as much time as possible far away from the sound of his sister's voice, and fishing may have been an excuse. Their father left them the cottage in equal shares, I hear, and it's very likely he enlisted to escape her. The trouble is, he was recovering from a wound at the time of the explosion. He must have gone back to the Front soon after the Army interviewed him about any signs of German incursions in the marshes. I don't believe he's been on any of the casualty lists. He must be still alive." He was clutching desperately at straws.

"Will they bring him home, do you think, to testify? Surely they must, if he can refute the testimony of these other witnesses."

"God alone knows," he said, a touch of despair his voice. I knew this looked bleak; I could understand his gloom as his anger subsided. "Well, we'll accomplish nothing if I don't go and find Groves." He crossed the room and said, "Bess, I'm so sorry. First the eggs and now this. But the worst is over, surely—they've got what they wanted, the whisperers and the rumor-mongers. Groves has been the family solicitor for years, he'll know what to do next. How to turn this around."

It was whistling in the dark, but at least as soon as the solicitor came into the picture, the police would have to behave.

I wondered if that would satisfy anyone who had driven the police to take action today. But I said bracingly, "And you will, Mark, between you. I'm sure of it. And don't fret about me. I had nothing more pressing on my calendar than a few days of rest in London. I'll see your mother through this shock, and then she'll be herself again. I've never seen a more determined woman than Mrs. Ashton when she was in France. And she pulled you through. She'll not let anything happen to your father."

His face brightened a little. "I'll be on my way. Mrs. Lacey and Mother should have the valise and those sandwiches by now." He touched my shoulder in a comradely fashion. "Truth be told, I'm glad you're here. Eggs and Inspector Brothers notwithstanding."

And he was gone. I waited there in the study until the hall was quiet once more, and then I went in search of Mrs. Ashton.

Instead I found Clara in the sitting room, a handkerchief in her hand and her eyes red.

"I don't want to go home," she said wretchedly. "I want to stay here and help in any way I can. I want to stand by Mark, and Aunt Helen."

It was none of my business—Philip Ashton had expressly asked her to consider leaving. For the sake of her own good name. There was no reason for her to be involved and it would be best for her to go. "I think you should stay," I said gently. "At least in the beginning. They'll have so much on their minds. They'll need someone to see to things, to make certain they eat and go to bed, and that Mrs. Lacey knows what to order, and the staff goes on as before."

"Then why did Uncle Philip urge me to leave?"

I answered reluctantly. "Perhaps he feels there's worse to come. There will be more accusations, I should think. People will talk freely about him now, of course; they'll say things that are unforgivable because they feel they can. That he's guilty. This business might even come to trial, Clara, and that will be very hard for Mrs. Ashton to go through. Whatever is to happen in the next few days or weeks, your uncle wanted to spare you. To keep you from being dragged into this wretched business. And at some point, you might have to do just that. Leave. Where is it that you live?"

"In Berkshire," she said. "My mother was Aunt Helen's sister."

"There won't be the talk in Berkshire that there will be here. You will need a lot of courage to hear what's being said about your uncle, and not be hurt or angry. And you'll have to help your aunt to handle it as well. Now go put cool water on your face before Mrs. Ashton sees how upset you've been. It will hurt her to see you cry."

In France I'd often been responsible for training the younger nursing Sisters and more than a few volunteers. Many of them had been shocked and frightened by their first experience of battlefield wounds, so different from the cases they'd worked with in hospitals in London. It made me feel ancient, but I'd had to learn to cope, just as they would have to do—or be sent home. And Clara had had a shock too. Not torn bodies and the constant, nerve-wracking sound of guns day and night, but it was no less devastating to watch her uncle taken away by the police on a charge of murder.

She looked a little mutinous, as if she resented my suggestion that she put her own feelings aside for the sake of her aunt. But if she wanted to stay here in Cranbourne, she would have to be strong.

Then she gave me a quavering smile and went out of the room.

Thank goodness, I thought to myself. *When I leave, she'll be all right.*

I wanted to stay out of the way for a bit to give everyone a chance to deal with this shocking turn of events. Putting on a good face for the sake of a guest is very hard when pacing the floor or throwing something would make one feel better.

And so I slipped into the drawing room, expecting to find it empty at this time of day.

Instead I found Mrs. Byers, the housekeeper, standing by the front windows, her hands clasped tightly together. She must have watched Mr. Ashton leave.

She turned quickly when she heard me enter, expecting Mrs. Ashton. Her face was streaked with tears and she was hastily trying to hide them when she saw who it was.

"Don't mind me," I said, putting up a hand to stop her from hurrying out of the room. "I've come here for the same reason you must have done. To give Mrs. Ashton a little time alone."

Mrs. Byers took out her handkerchief and blew her nose. "I don't know who is behind what's happening, but it's *wrong*. I've been housekeeper here for twenty years and Mr. Ashton is no murderer. Do you think I'd have stayed, even for a minute, even for Mrs. Ashton, if I thought he'd had anything to do with the disaster at yon mill? All those men, blown to little bits or burned to death—I ask you, what sort of person could do such a thing? It was an accident, pure and simple. God knows it couldn't be anything else." She realized all at once that she was speaking to a guest in the house. Drawing herself together, she put her handkerchief away and was about to beg my pardon.

I said quickly, "Who could hate the Ashtons enough to cause them so much trouble?"

"God forgive me, and haven't I stayed awake at night wondering who was behind all the mischief?" she asked bitterly. "And I can't think of anyone vile enough."

"It could be more than one person."

"Whoever it is, they've spread their lies through the village. The butcher's order is wrong, or the meat already turned. We send the horse to be shod, and it's done backward. The post goes astray. A ha'penny's worth of nails is strewn in the drive one morning. Mr. Ashton's little boat is splashed with a dark red paint. Like blood, it was, and running everywhere. Another time the lines were cut and the mast hacked at."

I couldn't hide my surprise. "Did Mark know all of this?" He'd been home for several weeks, he must have known. But he hadn't mentioned these other problems.

Mrs. Byers shook her head. "We were warned not to upset him. After all, he had enough trouble of his own. I felt that sorry for him, and everyone shouting in the hope he could hear a little. Mrs. Ashton didn't want him to worry about his father. As it was, he learned soon enough that something was going on."

"Surely the staff has been questioned? By Mr. Ashton, if not by the police. Someone must have over- heard talk. Some might know a name to begin with. A few must have family living there in the town."

"Not that many of them. What's more, they all appear to be as much in the dark as I am."

Or pretended to be . . . It would be hard on the servants here, having to choose between their own families and the family they worked for.

"We did have to let one of the maids go at the end of March this year," Mrs. Byers told me with some reluc- tance. "She had lost both her brother and the man she was to marry in that explosion, and I think it slowly turned her mind. When we all believed it must have been sabotage, she hated Germans. She was volunteering for every committee in sight, knitting stockings and caps for our soldiers, then rolling bandages on her day off, even talking about going to work at the munitions plant over on Sheppey, to make the shells to kill more Germans. When it was decided there was no sabotage, she seemed to settle down a bit. I was all for letting her go; I thought she was apt to unsettle the others with her flights of fancy about Germans everywhere. Mrs. Ashton felt sorry for her. Besides, her mother had worked here before her death, and Mrs. Ashton was willing to give the girl the benefit of the doubt, for her mother's sake."

"Has she ever come out and said anything against the Ashtons? Mr. Ashton in particular?"

"Not until that last day, when I paid her what was owing to her and gave her a little extra to tide her over while she found other work. That was Mrs. Ashton's doing too. Then she said outright that Mr. Ashton had put me up to letting her go, that he couldn't bear looking at her because she was a daily reminder of two of the dead on his conscience."

"But why did you let her go, if Mrs. Ashton was against it?"

"She wasn't doing her work properly. I'd find a grate that hadn't been cleaned, a fire that hadn't been laid. A bed made worse than a junior maid could do the task, and the like. We were shorthanded already because of the war, and now one or the other of the staff had to go along behind her. I tried to talk to her, but she sat there without speaking, and I don't think she heard a word. I've wondered what it was troubling her. But she would never say. I didn't have any choice but to tell her enough is enough."

"Do you think she could have been behind the whispers? She knew the family better than most of the other survivors. She would know best how to hurt the Ashtons."

Mrs. Byers frowned. "Oh, I can't think Betty would do such a thing."

But I wasn't as easily convinced. *Someone* was behind the trouble here. If the maid hadn't taken an active part, someone might have used her knowledge of the family for their own ends.

"How long after Betty had left employment here did the harassment start?"

"Much later. A matter of several months." Her tone of voice told me she thought this eliminated Betty from any list of suspects.

Perhaps it seemed a long time to Mrs. Byers but certainly not to someone who was already turning his or her attention to Philip Ashton as the person responsible for what happened.

Four months ago, the rumors began.

June, Mark had said. When we were so grateful the Americans were joining in the fighting. When the Marines held out at Belleau Wood against all odds. When it seemed that the war might actually end in victory. Only it wasn't quite as certain now.

How did it begin? A suggestion here, a comment there? Gaining no momentum at first, but slowly casting a shadow of suspicion over the Ashtons as more people passed on what they'd heard and finally began to believe it themselves.

I remembered something Mark had said. "And the Ashtons' friends—neighbors. Do they believe these accusations too? Is there no one who would step forward and offer his help or defend Mr. Ashton?"

"Not to speak ill of anyone," Mrs. Byers said, turning her head to look out the window, "but I was that surprised when acquaintances stopped calling and invitations stopped coming. I don't know that their friends believe all they hear, mind you. But where there's smoke, there must be fire, if you take my meaning."

I did. It was very English to avoid unpleasantness, to adopt a wait-and-see approach to anything that smacked of being disagreeable. And certainly Philip Ashton was not a warm man, the sort of person who drew others close. He had been very kind to me, knowing how his wife felt about me, but I had glimpsed a formality that must often have kept people at a distance. Mark had said much the same thing. Which meant in times of trouble, there were few who would risk censure by standing up for him. His arrest wouldn't help matters. It would be seen as proof that friends and neighbors had been right to stay away, however much they might pity Mrs. Ashton.

Mrs. Byers cleared her throat. "It's wrong of me to be gossiping about the family," she said. "If you'll excuse me, Sister, I have my duties to attend to."

I let her go. There was no reason to keep her, and as she brought her anger and distress under control, she was less and less likely to confide in me, a stranger and a guest.

But I couldn't help but think that whoever was behind this persecution would have seen the fruition of his or her plan as the police led Philip Ashton away to gaol on multiple charges of murder. People in the square wouldn't look away from the police carriage taking him to Canterbury. They wouldn't want to miss that sight.

From now on, the Ashtons would have enough to worry about to satisfy anyone.

I had stepped out into the passage, intending to go upstairs for half an hour, when Mrs. Ashton came out of the sitting room, saying, "Ah. There you are, Bess." With an uneasy sigh, she went on. "I sent everything I could think of with Mark. Philip will want to be presentable, whatever happens, and at least he'll have a decent meal tonight. I don't know how the police will view our bringing in food on a regular basis, but that's all right. It's important for him to make the best of things, even the sort of food they insist on providing."

I thought as I followed her and sat down next to her favorite chair that she was trying to convince herself that her husband would be taken care of. People like the Ashtons had never set foot in a cell. Gaol was as foreign to them as the harem of a Turkish pasha.

I smiled. "I'm sure he'll manage well. He's the sort of man who can."

Her blue eyes flashed warmly at the praise. "Yes, you're absolutely right, my dear. He *will* manage. I must remember that. And it will be our duty to support him in any way we can think of."

Her concern was evident, but so was her absolute certainty that right must prevail, that her husband would come home again as soon as this unfortunate mistake had been sorted out.

There was a scratching at the door, and Mrs. Ashton rose quickly to let the spaniel in. It went directly to the hearth rug and curled up with a forlorn sigh.

"Poor Nan," Mrs. Ashton said gently, coming back to her chair. "You don't understand, do you? Well, neither do I."

It occurred to me then how very little I knew about Philip Ashton. The gracious host who'd welcomed me might be quite different in other circumstances. I had only the views of others to judge by, and his family, his staff, would wish me to believe the best of him. Yet, to be honest with myself, I couldn't even be sure he was innocent. But for Mark's sake and Mrs. Ashton's sake, I prayed that he was. He'd certainly dealt with his arrest with a coolness that spoke of a strong self-control. He'd resisted any temptation to argue or struggle or run. And that was a measure of his strength of mind.

But cool nerves and self-control could work both ways, as I'd already seen.

I remembered that one of my friends in Somerset— sadly dead at the first battle of Mons—had told me about his time at University. How the town and the gown were always at odds, living together in an uneasy alliance. It was certainly true between Cranbourne and Abbey Hall, and not because of any of the public drunkenness, bawdiness, and outrageous pranks that annoyed the citizenry of Oxford. The question was, what had turned the usually cooperative relationship between the village and the Hall so sour? Was it the recent deaths of so many men, or had it been stewing under the surface for a much longer time, waiting for the right circumstances to burst through?

But when I tried to approach this idea obliquely, Mrs. Ashton shook her head and told me, "Philip's father had such progressive ideas about his responsibilities at the mill. It shocked a good many people, but his view was that if the workers were to be handling something that could kill them and everyone around them in an instant, they needed to be reasonably healthy. And he took it upon himself to look into their welfare. Philip has felt the same way." She smoothed the pretty brocade that covered the arm of her chair, small bunches of cream flowers against a blue background. "My father told him once that coddling people in the village would only give them an exaggerated opinion of their own worth and lead to trouble. It was the only time I saw Philip lose his temper with my father. They never did agree. Not that my father mistreated anyone, no, it was more a question of letting the villagers get on with their own lives, and helping when it was necessary."

The light from the tall windows next to her chair showed only too clearly how tired and distressed she was, and I quickly changed the subject. Before very long she was telling me how she and her husband met—at a ball at Leeds Castle—and about a wedding that was all she could have wished for. "The sun came out of the clouds that morning, and it was the most glorious day. Warm enough, but not too warm. A lovely blue sky. I couldn't believe my good luck. My sister's wedding day had been rain from morning to night." And then she was remembering the evening that Mark had been born, and how pleased everyone was with her for providing the family with an heir straightaway. I listened as she recalled other happier times and watched as the tension around her eyes lessened a little.

Mrs. Byers had just brought in our tea when we heard the house door opening.

Helen Ashton lifted her head, listening eagerly. Nan rose from the hearth rug, her ears alert, also listening. Mrs. Byers, transfixed, the tea tray still in her hands, stared at Clara. And Clara's eyes widened with hope. But all we could hear was one set of footsteps coming down the passage. Nan's tail drooped, and she went back to her accustomed place.

Mark appeared in the doorway. He looked as if he'd been fighting a battle, and I was sure he had been. Verbally, at least. His face was drawn, his mouth set. And then he smiled for his mother's sake.

"Did they allow him to have his valise?" she asked quickly.

"Yes, and the food. This once." He took a deep breath. "Groves was allowed to see him. The police haven't given us all the evidence yet, but this is a start. We'll know more tomorrow."

Mrs. Ashton passed him a cup of tea. I thought perhaps he'd have preferred a whisky, but in deference to his mother he took it, drinking it while still standing.

"I'm sure Mr. Groves knows what he's doing," she said briskly, putting a good face on his news. "And we'll find the best barrister in Kent. In the event your father isn't released by tomorrow."

"I've spoken to Groves about that. The man's name is Worley. Lucius Worley. Groves is arranging a meeting with my father as soon as may be."

"Worley," Mrs. Ashton said pensively. "I know that name. Now from where?"

"Groves asked my father about him. He said he hasn't met him."

She finished her tea and set the cup on the table. "Never mind. It doesn't matter." Looking up, she smiled. "Shall we dress for dinner, tonight? Bess, I'm sure Clara can find something suitable for you. I know how tired you must be, Mark, dear, but keeping up appearances matters most at a time like this."

I saw the flicker of doubt in his face, and then he nodded. "Yes, of course."

We came down to dinner at seven. Clara had given me a lovely gown in pale peach, which went well with my light brown hair and dark eyes. I tried to remember the last time I'd dressed for dinner in something other than my uniform, but I couldn't.

It was not the happiest of meals. I was amazed by what Mrs. Lacey had managed to do, in spite of shortages of nearly everything. Still it didn't lift our spirits, and afterward, sitting in the drawing room struggling to make pleasant conversation felt rather odd, without Mr. Ashton's presence. Nan followed us, as she had done all evening, patiently waiting for her master's return.

I think we were all relieved when Mrs. Aston said with a sigh, "I expect I should go up. I'm rather tired. Bess, do you have everything you need?"

"Yes, thank you, Mrs. Ashton. And my gratitude to you, Clara, for the loan of your gown."

"It suits you," Mark said, lightly. Then he added, "While waiting for Groves to come back to his chambers, I walked over to the railway station. No sign of a train for you yet. The stationmaster is beside himself."

"Mark, how kind of you to think about that." I was both amazed and grateful.

He turned to his cousin. "And, Clara, I must say I've always liked that particular blue gown," he added with a smile. She blushed at the compliment, but thanked him prettily. "I'll take a turn outside before retiring. Good night, Mother." He came to kiss her cheek and then walked with us as far as the stairs. Nan got to her feet, shook herself vigorously, and trotted to the door.

"I'll take her outside," he said. "And put her in Father's room afterward."

"Thank you, my dear."

When I looked back from the landing, I could see the sadness in his face as his gaze followed his mother. And I couldn't believe that Mr. Groves had given him any news that could possibly be construed as hopeful.

My window looked over the high wall and down on the abbey grounds. Even in the light of day there hadn't been much to see. All that was left was the barest outline of what had once been a prosperous community of monks. No tall traceried windows, empty of glass, no great arches and bits of transepts and towers to give a sense of what once had stood there. Not even the stumps of buttresses. Grass had taken over, covering the foundations, which ran as lumpy lines here and there, and an occasional tree growing out of a jumble of stone offered shade. In the distance I could just see flower borders where someone had tried to add a bit of color to the grounds, but the spirit of the place, the heart of it, had long since vanished. All the way to Calais, where the stones had shored up the harbor? Or to some house or shed or pigsty that had benefited? In the dark, there was only a vast emptiness, enclosed by the black line of the wall. I heard a fox bark in the distance, but couldn't conjure up the evensong of the monks.

The cool night air was refreshing, and I left my windows wide.

With a sigh I turned away and undressed, washing my face and hands before climbing into bed. Someone had thoughtfully left several books by the carafe of water on my table, but I wasn't in the mood to read. I set my watch beside them and blew out the lamp.

For a moment my thoughts wandered to London, where I had lived in lodgings in Mrs. Hennessey's house since the first weeks of the war. Had one of my flatmates come in on leave? And where was the Colonel Sahib, or for that matter Simon Brandon?

He now lived in the cottage just through the wood behind our house, and in India he'd taught me to ride and shoot, shielded me from retribution for the worst of my childhood transgressions, and, young as he was, served as my father's Regimental Sergeant-Major. That was, until a few years before the war, when my father had retired from active duty. Recalled to special duty in 1914, they were often off on some mission or other, much of it secret. My mother and I never asked where or why.

Or had my father and Simon spent the evening with my mother? And where was she? In Somerset, or visiting a recent war widow, giving her consolation and support?

With a sigh, I scolded myself for feeling a twinge of homesickness, and instead thought about the evening here at Abbey Hall.

I could commiserate with the Ashtons, trying to keep up appearances as Mrs. Ashton had put it. But it had been even more painful for her and her son, I thought, than just giving in to the moment and dining in our street clothes. It had only emphasized the fact that Mr. Ashton was not in his customary seat at the head of the table. Or his usual chair in the drawing room. And Mark had not presumed to sit in either one tonight.

I turned and tossed for a bit, unable to settle in the unfamiliar bed—even though it was much more comfortable than my usual hard cot. And the soft down quilt over me was a far cry from the rough, harsh blanket I was accustomed to. The pillow was bliss, compared to what might just as well have been a wool sack beneath my head in France. Very different too from the hotel I'd have had to find in Canterbury late in the day when the stationmaster finally admitted that my train wasn't coming through. Assuming even the worst rooms hadn't all been taken by that time. No worries about bedbugs and cockroaches in the Ashtons' house.

I drifted into sleep.

Late in the night, I woke up with a start at the sound of breaking glass. It wasn't in my bedroom, but it was loud enough that it seemed to come from just below my windows. And that must mean in Mrs. Ashton's sitting room.

My first thought was that as a guest in the house, I shouldn't go dashing down to find out what it was. But I wondered if it was another egg tossed into the room for someone to discover in the morning, a sticky smear on the polished floors or the edge of a carpet.

I had just settled back against my pillows, on the verge of drifting off to sleep again, when I sat bolt upright, my nose twitching. Surely what I smelled, wafting up from below through my open window, was a strong whiff of smoke.

Pushing aside the last shreds of sleep, I sniffed the air.

It wasn't the odor of tobacco. Something was *burning*.

Shocked wide awake now, I whipped the covers off, caught up my dressing gown, and ran for the door, not bothering with my slippers.

"*Fire!*" I shouted down the passage as I headed for the stairs. "*Hurry!*"

I was halfway down them when I heard Mark calling, "What is it, what's happening?" He was racing after me, and then I heard Clara's voice asking what was wrong.

"The sitting room," I called over my shoulder, not stopping to explain.

Mark had caught up with me as I headed down the passage, but I stopped him from flinging open the door. "Wait." I reached out and put my hand on the wood. It was cool. "Open it gently."

He did as I asked, and we could see as the door edged wider that the chair that Mrs. Ashton usually sat in, right by the window, was aflame. Not just smoldering; there were licking tongues of orange flame rising higher and higher as we watched. The draft from the door, drawing air in the broken window, gave the flames something to feed on.

I pushed past Mark and shut the door quickly.

In old houses, fire was the dreaded enemy. I ran closer to the chair, saw the tall vase of flowers on one of the tables, pulled out the stems, and threw the water into the seat of the chair, getting as close as I dared to the flames.

I coughed as the smoke billowed up at me, and then Mark was beside me with the bucket of sand that most houses kept at hand. His nightclothes were dangerously close to the blaze as he threw the sand in a careful pattern across the seat of the chair, smothering the flames.

Now we were both coughing.

I turned, realizing that someone had opened the door and was standing there on the threshold. It was Clara, her face as white as the nightgown she was wearing, her robe clutched in her hands. Beyond her, I heard Mrs. Ashton on the stairs, calling to Mark, asking what was wrong.

He was bending over the chair, looking at something. I went to see what it was.

A half-melted candle lay close to the back of the seat.

"Thank God, it wasn't the carpet," he said, and turned to look up at the smashed window. The old glass had shattered, leaving a gaping hole.

I moved forward for a better look at the candle and stubbed my bare toe on a large stone. "Someone broke the window with this," I said, reaching down to pick it up. "Then threw in the candle, hoping it would start a fire."

"Don't come any closer," Mark ordered, and I realized that he was pointing to shards of broken glass littering the floor. And I was barefoot.

Mrs. Ashton had reached the doorway, and I heard the sharp intake of breath as she saw the still smoking chair. "Dear God," she exclaimed.

Mark went to her, saying, "It's all right, Mother, just an accident."

"Accident, my eye," she said furiously. "That window's broken. Someone did this, it didn't just *happen*."

He was trying to calm her down, trying to keep her from hurrying forward to look at the chair for herself. Clara was still by the door, a pale statue with a shocked face.

Mrs. Ashton was saying, "Who discovered it?"

"I heard the window break, Mrs. Ashton," I said quietly. "And then I smelled smoke."

Even in the dimness of the room I could see that she too was pale with horror, and disturbed by what this represented. She turned to Mark. "Bess has the only room on this side of the house," she told him. "The rest of us face the gardens. This would have been a conflagration before anyone knew."

"I'd thought of that," Mark said grimly. He left the room, and in a matter of minutes he was back with a large bucket of water and poured it over the still smoldering seat of the chair. Then he picked the chair up, and trailing the last remnants of smoke, he carried it past Clara, into the passage, and toward the front door. I went after him, got there first, and swung the heavy door wide. He took the chair down the steps and dropped it on the drive, at a safe distance from the house.

Even if the fire wasn't completely out somewhere deep inside the upholstery, it could do no harm now.

He stood there for a moment, staring down at the charred ruin of his mother's favorite chair, then came back to where I was waiting in the doorway. "Someone isn't satisfied that my father is already in jail. It isn't enough."

Chapter Four

We walked back into the house together, Mark and I. In the sitting room, Mrs. Ashton had found matches and lit the lamp. Clara was sitting on one of the other chairs, but her aunt was stooping to scan the floor around the spot where the fire had been. She looked up. "I don't think any sparks flew off onto the carpet."

"No, I think we were in time," Mark agreed.

We were all in our nightclothes. Mark's face was red, where he'd got too close to the flames. Mrs. Ashton, Clara, and I were in our dressing gowns, our hair down our backs. Clara and I were barefoot. But I didn't think anyone had really taken any notice. There were other worries on our minds.

"I'll have the police in, first thing in the morning," Mark was saying. "We'll find out who did this."

"No," his mother said firmly. "Let it go. It will only show how agitated people are about the claims that your father is being held responsible for the explosion. It will only bring more angry people out into the open."

Clara spoke for the first time, her voice strained. "I can't see how burning us alive in our beds would bring any of the dead back."

Mark said bracingly, "Nonsense, they were just trying to frighten us."

"Well, they succeeded," she answered tartly.

"I think it's best to summon the police," I said. "And the sooner the better, before breakfast. Or this will just go on happening."

Mrs. Ashton was about to protest, then stopped. "Why?" she said after a moment.

I took a deep breath. Why indeed? "To do nothing tells the person who did this that the family has something to hide." I pointed to the windows. "Gossip will soon know something happened here. If you bring in the police, it will go a long way toward convincing others that you believe Mr. Ashton is innocent."

There was argument, but in the end, Mrs. Ashton said, "Much as I dislike being the center of gossip, Bess is probably right. Bring it out into the open, rather than behind hands and behind our backs."

Mark said, "I'll go as soon as it's light. I don't want to leave you alone until then."

"Should you walk around the house, to be sure whoever it is isn't out there still?" Clara asked anxiously.

Mark shook his head. "He wouldn't linger. He wouldn't risk getting caught."

"And now, I think we should all go back to our beds and try to sleep," his mother said. She reached for the key that was in the door of the sitting room and ushered us out into the passage. "We'll keep this locked until the police arrive. Clara, my dear, your feet are bare. They must be cold. Would you like a hot water bottle?"

Clara was still very anxious. Mrs. Ashton had been right to draw her attention to her comfort, to take her mind off that frightful image of the burning chair.

"I'll be all right, Aunt Helen," she said staunchly. She and Mark went up the stairs together, and Mrs. Ashton watched them out of sight.

"This isn't the first time we've been a target," she said quietly. "If you would like to go on to London, Bess, I wouldn't blame you in the least. Mark can take you to Canterbury first thing after breakfast."

"I promised to stay and I shall. But do you have any idea who might have done this?"

"I'm afraid I might. A widow, one who won't be satisfied until my husband is dead as well. But proving it? That's quite another matter."

I don't think any of us slept for what was left of the night.

To burn down a house with all the souls sleeping in it, not just the family, but the servants as well—and it could have happened—showed a vicious and determined mind behind the deed.

Thinking about it, I wondered if the candle was an attempt to frighten or an attempt to kill.

And the choice of rooms. Why not the study, which one would think of as Mr. Ashton's? Why the sitting room, where Mrs. Ashton spent much of her day? Was it ignorance of the significance, an any-room-would-do decision?

I got out of bed, pulled on my clothes without lighting a lamp, and felt for the torch I keep in my kit. Then I stole down the stairs. The main door was locked, but opening it was easy enough, and I stepped out into the darkness before dawn.

The chair, its pretty blue brocade dotted with tiny bouquets of flowers, stood like a blackened ruin in the middle of the drive where it circled by the front door. And the odor of smoke and burned stuffing was strong on the night air.

There was a heavy dew, and I was grateful I had put on my nursing shoes, which made up in sturdiness what they lacked in charm. I stood there for a moment, turning off the torch and letting my eyes grow used to what light there was. Then I set out around the house, to my right.

The drawing room. I could tell that quite easily, looking up at the pale linings of the curtains. The study cum library, with its long, diamond-paned windows, was on the opposite side of the house, one of the older rooms. Next, the sitting room. I realized that standing here, I was deeper in the shadow of the wall. Had that helped the candle-thrower to choose his target unseen? He'd been luckier than he knew that the candle hadn't blown out as it flew, and that it had fallen on such fertile ground as the heavily upholstered chair. Had he waited to be sure it was burning? How many candles had he brought with him, just in case his first efforts failed?

I had stayed well clear of the ground closest to the windows and the house wall, where someone must have stood to toss first the rock and then the candle. If there was any chance of finding footprints, I didn't want to ruin it by walking over them in the dark.

I stood there, looking up at the sitting room windows. How many times when the lamps were lit had someone looked in and seen Mrs. Ashton in her chair, or jealously watched the rest of the family as they drank their tea together or talked over the day's events? I had noticed that the curtains were seldom drawn here, as if the wall behind me offered enough privacy. I tried to picture it.

Almost as if I'd wished for it, light bloomed in front of me, and I realized that it must come from the ornate lamp on the table against the wall. I could see the shadow of a shape cast against the ceiling as someone moved about. And then whoever it was came toward the window, almost to where the broken glass lay, and I saw that it was Mrs. Ashton. Even though I couldn't see her face clearly, the aureole of her white hair, back-lit, identified her easily enough.

She stood there, gazing down at the empty place where her chair had sat only a few hours earlier, and at the glass and sand and water all over her pretty carpet.

There was a look of sadness on her face, followed by one of vehement anger.

I felt like a peeping Tom. Looking away, I waited.

But she came closer to the window, unmindful of the glass, and blotting out the light behind her, she stared out into the darkness.

I was sure she couldn't see me where I stood, not with the light in the room spoiling her night vision. And yet I felt naked, vulnerable, as if she were staring straight at me.

I was just uncomfortable enough to step forward and call to her, hesitating only long enough to wonder how to go about it without frightening her.

And then she spoke quite clearly, the words carrying to me where I stood, and I froze, unable to speak her name and identify myself.

"I know who you are," she said. "And if you are out there still, gloating, know this. Touch my family again, and I will do whatever I must to stop you. Hear me. Whatever I must. I have never meant anything more."

And then she turned and walked away, leaving the lamp burning. I could follow the crunching of glass under her slippers and then the shadow gliding across the ceiling before the door was slammed behind her and locked again.

I felt cold. Her calm, icy voice had sent shivers down my spine. I hadn't realized how apt that old expression was until I drew my arms around me as a shield against a chill.

I waited until I was sure she had gone away before I crept back around the house. The night air was cool in spite of my uniform, and I could feel the dampness creeping up from the sea after the warmth of the day.

I'd left the door off the latch, and to my relief, it swung wide, allowing me inside. I shut it carefully, silently, and then started up the stairs, praying I didn't meet Mrs. Ashton in the passage above.

I was halfway up the steps when the door to the dining room on the other side of the stairs opened. The room was dark, but there was a tall figure standing just inside the threshold. As I stopped, staring down at it, Mark's voice spoke quietly.

"Bess? Is that you?"

I could hardly deny it. "Yes, I'm afraid I couldn't sleep."

"Nor could I. There's tea. In here."

I realized he'd thought I was coming down the stairs instead of climbing them. I went back the way I'd come and joined him in the dining room.

As soon as I shut the door, he lit the candles in the sconce nearest me, then gestured. A teapot and a cup were sitting on a tray on the table. I could smell the whisky he'd added to his. "I'll just fetch another cup," he said, and disappeared into the butler's pantry. He was back very soon, also carrying a plate of the sponge we'd had for dinner.

With a grin he set them down on the tray and proceeded to pour a cup for me.

As I took it, he said, amusement in his voice, "I learned to make tea in France. One of my finest accomplishments."

I smiled. "Yes, I'm afraid it's one benefit of the war years."

The smile faded. "And probably the only benefit. No, I've learned to sew on buttons. My sergeant of all people taught me. He was the eldest of six or seven brothers, as I recall. He said he'd learned to be handy in many respects. I'm waiting for first light. I want to see if there are any footprints under the broken window. He'd have had to stand close to chuck the candle in. To make certain it went inside. If there are prints, I'll make sure Constable Hood sees them. A pity it didn't go out. The candle."

"Yes, a pity," I agreed. I noticed that he had used the male pronoun, while his mother believed it had been a woman. "Although he must have brought more than one with him. But who could have done this, Mark? Who hates your family enough to want to see you burn alive?"

He sighed, stirring the contents of his cup, not looking at me. "I'm not sure that was the intent. But it could well have been the result. I seem to apologize to you every few hours, don't I, for dragging you into this, Bess. I had no idea I'd be putting your life in jeopardy."

"No one did," I agreed. "But what matters now is the future. Who could have gone this far?"

"God, take your pick. Over a hundred dead souls? All of them leaving behind wives and sons, even daughters, not to mention grandchildren in one man's case, although I doubt they would be up for this sort of thing. Or perhaps they were, perhaps they were just young enough and shortsighted enough to think a candle through a window was quite clever."

"Your mother said something last night—this morning—after we put out the fire, that made me wonder whether your father's arrest might fail to satisfy whoever is behind these occurrences." I had to tread carefully, not to betray what I'd overheard. "There's also the possibility that the original purpose behind all the gossip and rumors might have been lost as more and more people believed them and acted on what they believed."

He looked surprised. "Independently?" Frowning, he considered that. "It's an interesting thought, Bess. It could explain why we've felt like a fortress under attack. It bears looking into, doesn't it? Whatever Constable Hood has to say, I'll speak to Groves about it. Since it began before I came home, I can't tell him what the first indication of trouble was. But the point is to find why it started."

Changing the subject, I asked, "What does your father have to say to the charges laid against him?"

"Only that they're ridiculous nonsense. Still, he says he'd feel the same if he'd lost members of his family in such a way. Looking for a scapegoat, someone to blame. And most of those victims brought in the only income their families had. The government has done a little, but far from enough. We've done what we could in the worse cases, but charity can only go so far, and sometimes it's rejected out of hand, whatever we offer."

"You mentioned that a witness had come forward, when the Army first began to investigate," I went on, finishing my tea.

"Reluctantly. That's the devil of it. I think what persuaded Rollins to speak up was the strong possibility that this was sabotage. That there were spies in our midst. Do you know how many German students were at Oxford and Cambridge when all this began? Many of them speak perfect English. They could probably pass as English. I think Rollins came forward to stop a witch hunt. Not necessarily for my father's sake or even the Government's."

"It depends, I should think, on his motive. People aren't always altruistic, are they? If it's to their advantage, they're more likely to do their civic duty."

"Which could mean he might have seen *something*— only it wasn't a German raiding party. And so he could do his duty without betraying what else he knew. That could well explain his reluctance," Mark said slowly. "I can see I've been too close to the problem, too personally involved to view the broader picture. Too worried about my father and my mother. Well, that will change, now." Looking toward the windows, he added, "The sun is up. Not quite far enough, but we'll soon be able to take a look." For the first time he noticed the torch in my lap.

"I didn't want to frighten anyone by bumping into things," I said. Truth, yes, but not all of it. Just like Rollins?

"Then I shan't have to go back for mine."

We talked a little until the sun was high enough above the horizon that we could blow out the candles and begin our search. This late in the autumn, I was afraid the household would start to stir quite soon.

As we walked out the door, Mark said, pausing by the sadly burned chair, "I know, of course, that my mother was hardly likely to be sitting there at such an hour. Still."

"Do you think whoever threw the candle into the house knew which room it was?" I asked, testing my own theory. "Or was it random?"

"God, I hope it was random. I can't think why my mother should be a target. But if it was intended to set a fire there, it was where we might not have discovered it in time. And that's rather frightening." He added grimly, "I intend to keep the other possibility in mind."

I went back to the fact that his mother seemed to understand who was behind this business. Hadn't she mentioned the possibility to her husband, if not her son? Or perhaps she had, and Mr. Ashton had discounted it. Mark tended to think of her as his mother. I'd seen a woman made of much sterner stuff in France, when her son's life was in danger. I knew what she was capable of, if they didn't.

We walked in silence around the side of the house as I had done only hours before, skirting the lawn nearest the windows, beginning by the drawing room.

It took nearly three quarters of an hour to search properly. Moving slowly inward, looking for any sign.

Mark found it in the soft earth of the flower bed that ran along this side of the house. The border was wide enough, some three or four feet, that anyone looking out could enjoy it. Then green lawn ran all the way to the abbey wall some forty feet away.

Just beneath the broken window was the impression of a shoe, pressed deep in the loam as its owner balanced on one foot to throw the stone toward the glass.

But not the whole shoe, only the ball of the foot and the toe. That made it almost impossible to judge whether the wearer was a man or a woman.

Mark leaned toward a man, but I was more open-minded. Women could hate just as deeply. There were widows and orphans . . .

We kept looking, but that was the only indication that someone else had been here in the night.

Giving up at last, we walked back to the front of the house. Mark said, "I must find a glazier to repair the window. I don't think my mother will be comfortable in that room again, not for a while, but I want it made habitable as soon as possible. Clara must put the maids to cleaning up as soon as the police leave." He hesitated. "I also need to speak to the police. It's unfair to ask you if you'll go with me. But you were the first to raise the alarm. It might be useful if you are there."

"Your mother mentioned a Constable Hood. Is he here in Cranbourne?"

"He is. But I've decided to go directly to Inspector Brothers."

"Perhaps," I said as diplomatically as I could, "you should begin with the local man." I smiled. "It's rather like the Army, I think. Chain of command."

Mark frowned. "It was Constable Hood who took those depositions to Canterbury that resulted in the arrest of my father."

What he didn't say was, his mother wouldn't appreciate seeing a policeman in her house again.

"Still," I answered, "it's best to follow procedure."

I saw his mouth tighten. But as we walked inside, he went on, "Yes, you're right." He took a deep breath. "Constable Hood it is." Glancing down—he was wearing a shirt and trousers—he said, "I can't appear at breakfast like this. Go on, Bess, I'll join you shortly."

It was a gloomy meal. Mrs. Ashton didn't appear, Clara was morose, and Mark was preoccupied. Nan sat on Mark's feet beneath the table. I toyed with the food on my plate, then pushed it away.

"What did you tell the staff this morning?" I asked Clara, who had been the last to come down.

"I decided on the truth," she replied. "I couldn't think how to explain away the broken window or the burned chair. Mrs. Byers wanted to sweep up the glass straightaway, then send the kitchen maid for the glazier. Bless her, her first thought was Aunt Helen's comfort. But I persuaded her that the police had to see the glass and everything, just as it was. The staff is quite worried, of course, this coming after Uncle Philip was taken away. But they're very loyal to Aunt Helen."

Her fright of the night before seemed to have disappeared in the need to be useful. "Mrs. Byers asked if we knew who might have done this, but I told her it was too dark and too late to be sure. I thought it best to say as little as possible, and leave it to you, Mark, to tell her what she needs to hear."

"Yes, well done." He smiled at her as he rose, and she was pleased by his praise. I wondered how he could miss her feelings, but she was his cousin, and it probably never occurred to him to think of her in any other way. And he was still mourning the loss of Eloise. It had only been a matter of months since her death.

I said, "Mark, where does this constable really stand on your father's guilt or innocence? Do you know?"

He folded his napkin, frowning. He'd eaten very little as well, a pretense at being the good host. "He claims to be objective. Still, he lost a brother in the explosion."

Then Constable Hood was an unknown factor. Well, we'd know soon enough what his views were now.

Mark went up to speak to his mother, and Clara excused herself to have a word with Mrs. Lacey, the cook. But at the door she stopped.

"I've seen to it that all the staff has had a good look at Aunt Helen's chair. I didn't want to mention that to Mark, but I thought it best to have other witnesses than ourselves."

I nodded. "I'm glad you did. Have you looked in on your aunt this morning?"

"I took up her morning tea myself. I don't think she's slept more than a few minutes all night. Even before that stone came through the window. Whoever did that should be put in jail. I'm sorry, but it was cruel."

"Can you think of anyone who would do such a thing?"

She laughed, but not with humor. "The list is a hundred dead men long, I should think. Or count all those out of work because of the explosion. The women who came in on the little trains, the brewery workers. The families who depended on those wages. Many of the women had already lost husbands and sons to the war. It was dangerous work, but it was employment. And the Ashton Powder Mill had always been safe. They counted on that. They trusted my uncle to see them safe."

And broken trust was an emotion that could easily turn to hate.

Shrugging, she added, "Whether it's Uncle Philip's fault or not doesn't matter. He's responsible, isn't he? And he deserves whatever happens to him. That's how people think, you see. They don't consider this family. They didn't see Uncle Philip standing in his study, hands over his face as he wept for the dead. And Aunt Helen unable to comfort him."

The interview with Constable Hood had not gone very well. He listened to what we told him, he looked at the broken window and the shards of glass that

Mrs. Byers had left where they fell, to show him, and he examined the blackened chair. The candle was a twisted lump now, but it was clearly a candle. He even went down on one knee to study the carpet, still gritty with wet sand.

He was a square man with dark blond hair and cold gray eyes. I'd felt an instant dislike the moment I set eyes on him. There was something pinched and shuttered about his features, as if he had no intention of being objective or fair.

I'd given my evidence, and the others had recounted what they had seen and done. He appeared not to have heard a word.

Finally he said, "I'll report this to Inspector Brothers, sir. He may have further questions, of course."

"I hardly think," Mark said stiffly, "he could need any further proof that this house was set afire by someone who didn't particularly care how much harm was caused. This is an old house, Constable, it would have burned rather quickly. If Sister Crawford hadn't awakened and smelled smoke, who knows how far the flames might have reached?"

"But she did smell it, didn't she, sir?" He made it sound as if it had been planned that way. That we had set the fire ourselves and made certain it was put out before more than token damage had been done.

I said, in my best imitation of Matron's most severe voice, "In my experience, Constable Hood, fires seldom follow instructions. From someone outside— or inside—a house. I hardly think after the blow Mrs. Ashton suffered yesterday, she would put her home at risk too. I can't see how it would advance Mr. Ashton's cause."

He had the grace to flush.

Snapping his notebook closed, he said, "I'll speak to the Inspector." With a nod to Clara and Mrs. Ashton, he left the sitting room and walked out to where his bicycle was waiting, leaving the doors standing open.

Watching him go, Mark Ashton said, "I'd have offered to drive him into Canterbury. Now, I'm glad I didn't."

With that he whistled to Nan, crossed the hall to his father's study, and closed the door behind him.

Mrs. Ashton put a hand on my arm, saying quietly, "Thank you, Bess. We weren't in a position to defend ourselves. I'm very grateful. Now I think I should see if Mark is all right."

Clara wasn't very happy to be excluded. She quickly made an excuse about some household duty or other, as if that explained not being asked to join them, and I was left on my own.

Between the visits of Inspector Brothers yesterday and Constable Hood this morning, I could truly see how the people of The Swale region and even as far away as Canterbury were ready to believe the worst about the Ashtons. But that was the trouble; they seemed not to discriminate between the man and his family.

I considered going to sit in the herb garden, but that was Mrs. Ashton's sanctuary, and I didn't wish to intrude. Instead I collected my coat and went out for a walk. The sun had gone behind the clouds, but the day was still warm for this time of year and so I followed the abbey wall, looking for the entrance to the grounds. It led me instead to a street of interesting houses, and that in turn led to the town's square, where there was a market in full swing despite the graying skies.

Wandering along the line of stalls, I couldn't help but think how meager the goods were, compared to an autumn market before the war. God willing it would be over soon, and there would be peace. Still—it could never be 1914 again. Too many men had died or had suffered horrid wounds that would always be there—the lost limbs and the burns and the scars. How long would it be before these market stalls would be full once more, and women would have new gowns and hats and linens for their houses? And the horses were gone, as well as the men, and homes had been turned into clinics, and factories had grown accustomed to feeding the machines of war. Women had been just as patriotic as the men, replacing those needed at the Front, learning to work in factories and drive omnibuses and grow food on empty ground. How was that going to return to what we remembered in the past? Where would the house parties and the summer afternoons on the lawns or in quiet back gardens be held when there weren't enough men to play tennis or croquet or dance with the women who had no one else to make pleasant conversation with and look pretty for?

It was a heartbreaking realization. That we'd fought so long and so hard and at such cost to save something that had been smashed to bits the minute the Germans crossed the frontier into Belgium. What would we replace it with? How would the future look?

Trying to shrug off my sad spirits, I suddenly realized that I hadn't heard the usual banter that made market day more than what was put out for sale. I turned and looked back at the stalls I'd just passed, only to meet the speculative gazes of a dozen pairs of eyes as marketgoers and sellers in the stalls alike followed my progress in silence.

They knew who I was. They knew where I'd come from. I might as well be an Ashton, in their eyes. The enemy. And they would give me no quarter, just as they wouldn't give an Ashton quarter.

It was a revelation. A first look on my part into the chasm of hate that separated Abbey Hall from Cranbourne. It was one thing to turn their backs to the motorcar, and quite another to treat a stranger as if she had been accused of murder too.

It was such an odd feeling that I wasn't quite sure what to do. Walk back the way I'd come, or finish strolling through the square? And I think everyone watching me wondered as well what I would decide.

I was only a guest in the Ashton house, yet Cranbourne's animosity toward the family had spilled over to include me.

Or perhaps they'd already heard that I was the one who'd smelled smoke and prevented the fire from spreading.

No one was going to attack me here in the little square, in front of all these people, but I felt distinctly uneasy. For all I knew, any one of them could have tossed that candle into the sitting room, certain that his actions would meet the approval of everyone watching me.

I took a deep breath. I was wearing the uniform of Queen Alexandra's Imperial Military Nursing Service. And I would not dishonor it by scurrying away like a coward.

Carrying on, I finished my circuit of the little square, head high, a calm expression on my face. My pace was leisurely, and if I inadvertently caught the eye of someone staring at me, I let a faint smile speak for me.

One woman, standing in front of her stall, actually spat at me, and another turned her back, refusing to serve me, even though I wasn't buying.

A man cursed under his breath, just loud enough for me to hear the words he was using. I carried on as if I hadn't heard. Or understood.

At last I came back to the street that had brought me into the square, and with a sense of relief, I put those unfriendly faces behind.

I could leave here—indeed, I'd be leaving tomorrow, and for Dover, not London. But the Ashtons couldn't. And how safe would a household of women feel when Mark went back to France? I couldn't see any way that Mr. Ashton would be freed anytime soon. In fact, he might be safer where he was until there was a trial.

As I reached the abbey wall, I noticed the woman ahead of me. She'd been carrying a basket of things she'd bought in the market. I could see the leaves of sugar beets and the pale color of parsnips. There was even a small aubergine tucked in beside the cabbage, rich dark purple against the dark green leaves. She had set the basket down and was rubbing the small of her back with one hand.

I put her age at close to sixty. There were streaks of gray in her fair hair, and her face was lined from years of drudgery.

Catching her up, I said with a smile, "Let me carry that a little way for you."

There was resentment in her gaze as she turned toward me. "I can manage." Her voice was cold as Arctic ice.

"My name isn't Ashton," I said quietly. "I've come to Abbey Hall because I had helped to nurse Major Ashton when he was severely wounded, and I sat by his bed on long night watches with Mrs. Ashton. I wasn't here when the mill blew up. It's unfair to blame me for what I haven't done."

"You should have let him die," she said venomously.

"You can't mean that. Not if you have children of your own. You wouldn't wish such anguish on another man's mother."

"I lost my only son at Ypres," she said. "And he wasn't nursed in a ward with officers."

I picked up the basket and started walking. She had no choice but to come after me. "I daresay I've attended to the wounds of more men in the ranks than I have of officers. It doesn't matter, you know, who is bleeding. One sees only the need."

It was clear that she didn't believe me. But she hadn't tried to take the basket from me, certain proof that her back was really troubling her. I could see too that she had a slight limp, which surely wasn't helping it.

Without waiting for her to answer me, I added, "I couldn't help but notice in the square. The men and women with stalls and those who were doing their marketing eyed me with dislike. I found it disturbing."

She said nothing for a moment, then she answered grudgingly, "They thought you were the Major's new fiancée."

I stared at her, shocked. "On the contrary. I'll be going back to France in a matter of days. I was on leave, on my way to London, when Major Ashton saw me in Canterbury. The trains were running very late, and he suggested I visit his mother rather than spend the night in a hotel or failing that, the railway station. It was very kind of him."

It was her turn to stare at me.

"It's a great tragedy, what happened to the mill. I didn't even know about the explosion until yesterday, when the Major told me. What I don't understand is why his mother and his cousin should be harassed. How can the villagers blame them for this disaster?"

"It was coming," she said darkly. We had left the shadows of the abbey wall now, and she pointed down toward the River Cran. It was the road that Mark had driven on that first morning, and where I'd walked on my own. We turned in that direction. "It was the nailbourne started it."

"Nailbourne?" I asked, wondering if that was a person or a thing.

"The winter springs." She nodded her head toward the river and The Swale beyond. "It's marshy ground, that is."

"Why did they build the powder mill in a marsh?"

She shook her head, certain now that I was dim-witted. "The powder mill was built on a deep chalk outcropping. But there's marsh beside and below it."

"Ah. And the nailbourne?"

"There's a pond where one of the creeks ran, and the Ashton windmill feeds it. See, just there?"

We could look down on the River Cran now, and the ruins. I hadn't paid any heed to the windmill before, because it was derelict, many of the slats on the bare arms missing.

The woman stopped, pointing. "I live over there, beyond the windmill."

It was a long walk, carrying that basket. I was appalled.

"And the nailbourne?" I asked for a third time. "Is it a creek?"

"I said, didn't I? They're winter springs."

"But you blamed them for the explosion."

"They come up in the winter, those nailbournes. And as the weather warms, they dry up. But a few can run something fierce for a time, and this one did in the winter of 1916, running as hard as any creek, seeking The Swale. More water than any of us ever recalled seeing, even old Harry Barnes, and he's near ninety. And it kept running when the others had disappeared into the earth they come from. They're fickle, these upwellings. Not all appear, and not every year. Then men from the mill came out to have a look at this nailbourne, and they claimed if it kept on widening its channel, it was going to weaken the banks of yon mill pond they needed for making the gunpowder. We *told* them not to mettle, but those men went to Mr. Ashton and reported what they'd seen. And he came out there and dammed it before it could reach the pond. Late March, that was. The next morning, the nailbourne began drying up, all the way back to its spring. Mr. Ashton was right pleased."

I could begin to see where she was going. "But if the nailbourne—the spring—should have dried up of its own accord, but didn't, then was it so harmful to encourage it to stop?"

"You aren't from Kent, so you wouldn't know, but Mr. Ashton was born here, he should have understood.

Such springs must find their own way. And this one couldn't. Some of us tried to tell him no good would come of it, that this one was already a Sign, but he wouldn't hear of such superstitious nonsense. That's what he called it, nonsense."

The bloody battle of the Somme had begun in July 1916. I tried not to think about that as her Sign. To her, the explosion in April was more important. "But how did this cause the explosion? How could this nailbourne have interfered with the powder mill?"

"It was the powder mill caused it to be dammed, wasn't it?" She gave me that withering look again. As if I ought to understand the implications straightaway. "And so the mill had to pay for it, didn't it?"

"But to blow up the mill, with such tragic loss of life—it seems rather—" I was at a loss to find the right word. "Severe," I said finally.

"The nailbournes have always been there, haven't they? Having their own way long before the Conqueror came. And didn't St. Augustine himself cause one to rise where he'd knelt, over Elham way? Besides," she added, with a distinct note of triumph in her voice, "only the men died that day, didn't they? Not the women who worked in the mill of a weekday. Only the men. The woe-water wasn't greedy."

It was a telling argument if you believed in such things. I could now see why the case against Philip

Ashton was so powerful. He'd defied the ancient gods, as it were, and the mill had paid the price, along with the men inside there on that Sunday.

I picked up the woman's basket again, and we walked as far as the banks of the Cran. It was low enough now that one could cross, and she knew precisely where the bank was lowest on both sides. I told her I'd carry the basket to her door, but she shook her head. She'd done this year in and year out and didn't think of it as a hardship. With a nod, she went on her way, and I watched her for some time before turning back to the house.

The door of the shed belonging to the man who built boats was closed.

Chapter Five

When I had a chance later in the day, I tried to explain to Mark what the woman had told me about the woe-water.

He smiled and shook his head, saying, "Local superstition and legend. When my family built the first powder mill here over a hundred years ago, there were people who were against it then. And yet it provided a living for many generations to come."

There was no point in arguing. And lunch was ready. Through the open study door I'd seen Mrs. Ashton and Clara walking together toward the dining room.

Still, I thought he was overlooking one source of the unrest I'd felt in this village. Legend or not, superstition or not, how people felt about such things mattered. Given the nailbourne drying up so suddenly and inauspiciously, and the explosion occurring almost on the heels of that, many would see a connection and come to believe in it, and it would take a great deal of persuasion to move them to change their views—if not a miracle to match a miracle.

The empty chair at the head of the table cast a shadow over this meal as it had all the others since Mr. Ashton had been taken away. Mrs. Ashton must have realized just how demoralizing it was for everyone, including the servants trying to avoid it, and she said, "You know, I think we'll have dinner this evening in my sitting room, if the glazier has finished. I shan't feel up to dressing, and there are only the four of us tonight."

As if we'd been twenty or thirty at each meal, and tonight was a respite from such busy entertaining.

Everyone agreed. And I silently cheered her for carrying it off so well.

In the afternoon Mark went to another conference with his father's lawyers, and Mrs. Ashton asked to go with him in the hope that she might also be allowed to speak to her husband.

Both mother and son returned with long faces. Mrs. Ashton hadn't been permitted to see, much less speak to, her husband. And the solicitor, after the conference with Mr. Ashton's barrister, didn't hold out much hope.

"But they'll send for the witness, won't they? Rollins?" I asked. "If only to refute these new depositions? After all, he came forward at the time, whereas apparently they've suddenly recovered their memories."

"I'm certain they will, my dear," Mrs. Ashton assured me, but I caught the echo of doubt in her voice. So many accusations pointed in her husband's direction. And of course no one quite knew what Mr. Rollins would tell the court.

I said bracingly, "Early days. Once their case is put together, Mr. Groves and Mr. Worley will feel better about what they can do with the evidence."

Her face brightened a little. "Yes. Yes, I'm sure you're right. Thank you, my dear."

Clara spoke, her voice carrying a mixture of anger and anguish. "He's a good man, Aunt Helen. Uncle Philip has always been admired and respected. No one could possibly be convinced that he could commit murder. It's all the fault of selfish people who can't believe they've lost their positions at the mill. Once they've been shown up as vengeful, it will all be over."

Mrs. Ashton's gaze met that of her son, but she said with a smile, "I don't know what I'd do without you, Clara."

Half an hour later, when I went to look for a book to read, I found Mark in his father's study, sitting at the desk, staring into space. I started to withdraw, but he looked up and said, "Come in. I don't think I can stand my own company much longer."

I shut the door behind me and went to the hearth, where Nan was stretched out, drowsing as dogs do. She lifted her head, and I scratched behind her silky ears. Without looking at Mark, I asked, "Is there anything you and the solicitor failed to tell your mother?"

"Only that finding jurors who haven't heard about the explosion and fire will be difficult. God knows what opinions they may have already formed. It's been two years, but Canterbury felt the force of the explosion. As I think I told you, everyone thought the Germans were shelling Kent. People don't forget a fright like that. It wouldn't be surprising if they've already made up their minds."

"Yes, I can understand that."

He roused himself. "But you shouldn't be dragged into this affair. You've had only a few days of leave," he went on with a smile, "and we've hardly done more than talk about our troubles. I'm so sorry, Bess."

"I don't see why you should apologize to me. You couldn't have foreseen your father's arrest, and certainly not the fire. Besides, I'd have spent much of my leave in a railway station waiting for a train if it weren't for you and your family. Instead, I've been here and much more comfortable. It was so good to meet your mother again. And to find you fully recovered."

He took a deep breath. "I should have offered to walk into the village with you, or into the abbey grounds, but remembering the eggs, I didn't think it was advisable just now."

"I've walked on my own into the village," I reminded him. "There are very lovely old houses here in Cranbourne. I enjoyed them."

"You probably haven't seen the Tudor Almshouse. And there's another house similar to the Hall on the far side of the ruins. It was the Abbot's Lodging. It's not as old as the Hall; one of the later abbots rebuilt it after a fire, enlarging it in the process. It's closed now. The Carstairs have lived in London since the start of the war." Smiling ruefully, he said, "We seem to run to fires out here in Cranbourne, don't we?"

"You do. I didn't intend to disturb you—I was looking for something to read. Your mother isn't in her sitting room."

"You didn't disturb me. And Mother is very likely in her garden. It's where she retreats when she's worried. But don't go just yet." He fidgeted with the pen lying on the blotter in front of him, and then said, "I shall have to face the Medical Board soon, Bess. And I've known for the past fortnight that my hearing has been steadily improving. There are some levels of sound that still seem to be in the far distance, but I want to get back to my men. Every day away from them I worry about where they are, what's happening to them, who has been wounded, who has been killed. Captain Hunt has written to me, and Lieutenant Wilmont as well." He grinned. "For God's sake, even Sergeant Edgar has written. I nearly fell out of my chair when I saw the letter. Hunt is a new man—he was brought in after I'd been sent home. I only know him by reputation. Wilmont is steady enough, but Sergeant Edgar runs the show. He's thirty-five now and survived four years of the worst of it. Granddad, his men call him. With affection, I might add, and only behind his back. At any rate, that's where I need to be. Ought to be. But how in God's name can I go back, with half my mind here? Leaving Mother to deal with the lawyers? Leaving my father sitting in a jail cell with, let's be honest, an uncertain future? They won't even call me back to testify. I wasn't here when the mill went up, and so there's nothing I can add to general knowledge."

"Your mother is quite capable of taking on the police and anyone else," I reminded him. "But still, it will be hard on her." And hard on Mark too, in an entirely different way. I knew all too well that men whose attention was divided by worry about something at home—an unfaithful wife, a sick child or parent, a brother just enlisting, even money woes, the list was infinite—were in greater danger of being killed. They lost that sharp edge of attention, intuition, and skill at reading events that gave them a better chance of surviving. A letter on the eve of an attack, even an instant's distraction could make the difference between life and death.

Mark knew that as well as I did. Firsthand, in fact, while my experience came from talking to the wounded. And listening to the Colonel Sahib and Simon go over an action. What went right, what went wrong, how it might have turned out differently. For better or worse.

I think what really troubled Mark was the nearness of the war's end—if all the rumors could be believed. He wanted to be there at the finish, to keep as many of his men alive as possible to see it through. At the same time he needed to be here for his mother—if his father was convicted and condemned. And that last he didn't want to put into actual thought, much less words.

I said, "Ask for compassionate leave, Mark. They won't deny it, surely."

"I've been away too long. It's not right, not fair to my men."

"It won't help your men or your mother if you're killed," I told him bluntly. "Ask for it. As soon as you know where matters stand for your father, you can go back to France."

He put his head in his hands for a moment, then looked at me. "I try to keep up her spirits. But I think she knows I can't abandon her."

I wanted to tell him that it appeared that the war was all but over. That his presence—or his absence— wouldn't change the outcome. But that wouldn't matter to him. It wasn't what drove men like Mark Ashton. Or the Colonel Sahib or Simon or any of those I knew who wore the King's uniform.

"Write the letter tomorrow," I said. "The sooner the better. It won't do to put it off. If by any stretch of the imagination you're refused, then you can face the alternative with a clearer mind. You'll know you've done your very best for everyone, your men, your family. It's not going to be easy for your father, either. Sitting there, knowing he must await events when he'd much rather shape them, knowing you're in France, that your mother is alone. For his sake, and hers, at least ask."

I didn't tell him that it might be a sign of which way the wind blew, depending on whether or not the request for leave was granted. But I was beginning to think it was possible that whoever was behind this torment of the Ashton family might want Mark well out of the way.

"How did you come to be so wise?" he asked.

I laughed. "It's common sense, Mark, not wisdom. Only you're too close to the matter to see it as clearly."

I went to find Mrs. Ashton, and she was indeed in her garden, busily deadheading the blooms, dropping them into the basket at her feet, then picking it up by its long handle to move closer to her next task. It was nearly dusk, but she appeared not to notice. Looking up as I came toward her, she said, "Ah, Bess. I've neglected these rather badly, haven't I?"

"They don't seem to mind. The plants are still blooming quite enthusiastically."

"They're protected here, of course. Even in late winter I can find the earliest bulbs and flowers starting to open. The sun warms the brick and the brick warms the buds. The monks built well." And then she straightened her back and looked up at the fading colors in the western sky. "But I can't protect my husband or my son. Sad, isn't it?"

"None of us can," I told her. "Who was it said it best? Francis Bacon? All of us give hostages to fortune. It's just that right now, yours are very pressing."

"True." She bent to her work again. "I can't ask Mark to stay. He's been fretting to return to France almost since the day he arrived. It's where he belongs, where his heart is, with the men who serve under him. It's a terribly close bond. I've learned that."

We wandered toward the bottom of the garden, where the ponds were dark, secretive now. She set her basket at her feet and looked down the greensward toward the house. The upper windows were reflecting the last of the light.

"Mark is torn," I said gently. "If he goes, you must assure him that all will be well here."

"I can do that," she said, still not looking at me. "I was in France, Bess. I read letters to the wounded and the dying. "

I thought perhaps she was frightened for herself and her husband and unwilling to admit it. Loneliness and fear . . .

"Clara will stay with you, I'm sure."

"Yes, she's a dear." But it was not said with conviction. And then she turned to me. "If only Ellie had lived. I was so counting on her as my daughter-in-law. I think I've mourned her death nearly as deeply as Mark has."

"He talked about her in France. I remember holding his hand one night—oh, it must have been well after two o'clock—as he told me how happy he was going to be."

"She had other suitors, of course," Mrs. Ashton went on. "But she and Mark had been friends since they were ten and twelve. And that grew into love. I was the one who had to tell him that she'd died only hours before he got here. The look on his face was beyond bearing." She took a deep breath. "And so you see, Bess, if Mark chooses to go back to France, I'll be all right. I've faced harder tasks than that."

I wasn't sure whether she was trying to convince me or herself.

As we slowly walked back toward the house, I said diffidently, "I can't help but wonder how this began—how a village could be turned against one man in only a matter of months. From what Mark has told me, for a year or more everyone had accepted the fact that the explosion and fire had been an appalling accident. No one's fault. What could have changed their minds? Who could have started such rumors?"

I had hoped that she would confide in me, that it might help her to unburden herself.

It was almost too dark now to read her face, although I tried.

"I don't know," she said, a deep sorrow in her voice. "I wish to God I did."

In the silence that followed, we walked together back into the house. Who could she choose over her husband and her son? Who would she protect at their expense?

Or was what I'd overheard in the darkness outside the sitting room window an act of sheer bravado, an attempt to stop her family's persecutor by making him or her believe that she knew who it was and would take her own vengeance?

I wanted to believe that it had been an act. A bluff.

Whether that was the truth or not was a very different matter.

I wondered again if she had mentioned a name to her husband—and he'd refused to believe it, making her doubt her own conclusions.

At dinner Mark told me that he'd drive me into Canterbury in the morning, in time for my train. "I have a meeting with Groves tomorrow, and I expect Lucius Worley will be there as well. They'll have spoken to my father."

I saw the longing on Mrs. Ashton's face. She would have given much to be allowed to see her husband. Not even Mark had been allowed to speak to him. I thought it was cruel of Inspector Brothers, even if Philip Ashton was charged with multiple counts of murder.

Thanking Mark, I added, "I'm so sorry to have come at such a sad time, but I can't regret staying. Please, if there's anything more I can do, you have only to let me know."

When we went up to bed shortly before ten o'clock, Mark stopped me on the stairs. I looked up at him as he said, "I told you you'd be good for my mother. And you have been, more than you perhaps realize."

I hoped he was right. Mrs. Ashton had spoken to me as she would have talked to Ellie, and in such a distressing time as this, it had been a way to cope with the weight of worry she carried.

For some reason I couldn't sleep. Part of that was concern for the Ashtons, and part of it was missing my own family. I had never got to London to see or even speak to them.

I sat by the window for an hour or so, looking out into the night. For a time I watched bats dipping and swooping over the drive, for it was still warm enough for them to be out and about. They were fast and graceful, with that little flutter of the wings as they adjusted their flight patterns.

I was still watching when I realized that someone was coming up the drive. A man, walking quietly on the grassy verge, taking his time. I thought at first it was Mark, unable to sleep too, but this man didn't walk like Mark. Mark had a slight limp, and this one was more pronounced.

Whoever he was, he stopped some twenty feet from the front door, as if trying to make up his mind about something. The chair had been removed to the tip; it couldn't have been what he was looking for. Instead I thought he was studying the front door of the house, perhaps even trying to see if a light shone from any of the windows.

I tensed, wondering if this might be the person who had thrown the stone through the sitting room window. If he took another step toward the house or raised an arm, I would find Mark's room and wake him up at once.

But he didn't. He simply stood there in the dark. And then as his gaze swept the house again, he paused, suddenly alert, and I wondered if he could see me by the window, looking down at him. My room was dark, and I was wearing my dark dressing gown. I didn't think it was possible.

And yet it felt as if our eyes had locked, and I realized with a shock that this must be the man I'd seen by the river, working on his boat.

What had brought him to Abbey Hall? In the middle of the night?

Almost in the same moment he made an abrupt, involuntary movement, then lowered his head before turning and walking briskly back the way he'd come.

Had he been set on some mischief here? Or had he simply come out of curiosity, or for some other reason I couldn't understand?

I waited another half an hour, but he didn't come back.

I was wary of mentioning what I'd seen to Mark. And so I was very glad to find Mrs. Ashton downstairs before anyone else. She was sitting at the table, a cup of tea in front of her, but she was staring into space, her mind anywhere but here. With her husband in his cell? I thought it likely.

She stirred as I came in, picking up her cup as if she hadn't been gathering wool.

"Good morning, my dear. I expect you'll have good sailing weather back to France. The barometer in the study is pointing steadily at Fair."

"Good news," I agreed lightly, pouring my own cup of tea, adding honey and—such a luxury—fresh milk. Taking my place at the table, I added, "Who is the man who works on boats down by the Cran?"

Surprised, she frowned for a moment. "How did you come to meet Alex Craig?"

"He happened to be there when I saw the ware-houses."

She nodded. "And Mark didn't think it necessary to introduce you." Before I could tell her he hadn't been with me, she took a deep breath. "Alex was in love with Eloise, you know. Quite madly. But she chose Mark, and there was an end to it. He came here when she was so very ill, half out of his mind with grief.

And I let him see her. I couldn't turn him away. But I never told Mark that. I didn't think it was—he wasn't in time, you know. Mark. And it seemed cruel to say anything."

"I didn't know she was here when she died."

"It was rather terrible, how it happened. We'd had a lovely weekend. Her parents came over from Chilham with Eloise, and we had dinner here on Friday evening. And then on Saturday we went into Canterbury—there was a memorial service for the son of a family we all knew very well. Afterward we decided to walk a bit, down toward houses where the weavers once lived. It was such a beautiful spring day, and the service had been rather sad. I think we all felt better for that walk. We came back to the Hall to dine, rather than trust to what a restaurant might have on offer, and then we sat on the terrace for a time, to watch the sun set. The next morning, as Eloise and her parents were preparing to leave, she fainted as she came down the stairs. She'd seemed very much herself at breakfast, although she'd mentioned a slight headache. We sent at once for Dr. Mason in Canterbury, and he told us she must have caught a spring chill. Forty-eight hours later, she was fighting for her life. Her parents stayed with her to the very end."

"In France I saw the influenza kill just as quickly. There was nothing anyone could do."

"And yet I felt as if I'd failed my son. I'd sent for Mark, he managed to get leave almost at once, but of course it was too late. If I'd lost my own daughter, I don't think I could have grieved any more deeply."

"Was she an only child?"

"Yes. Her parents went to London not very long after the funeral. They couldn't bear to rattle around in that big empty house in Chilham. It was too painful. We correspond, Eloise's mother and I. But I think we both find it very hard. What is there to say but what might have been?"

"And Alex Craig?"

"He wasn't her only suitor—"

She broke off, hearing someone at the door. Clara came in, wishing us both a good morning, and then Mark followed a minute or so later.

There wasn't a chance to explain why I'd asked Mrs. Ashton about Alex Craig.

If he'd loved Eloise so deeply, and had been allowed to say good-bye to her, I couldn't imagine that he wished the Ashtons ill. He was probably drawn to the house where Eloise had died, rather than to a stone in a churchyard. He hadn't seemed too fond of Mark, his rival, but that was more or less expected. And so I told myself I could put him out of my mind.

———————

Two hours later, carrying my kit, Mark walked with me through the crowded waiting room at the railway station and inquired about my train. This time to Dover. It was expected to arrive within the hour, we were told.

"I shan't be able to wait," Mark warned me. "But if this train is delayed as well, and you're stranded again, you must come for me at Groves's chambers." He told me how to find the address, and indeed, it wasn't far to walk. "Promise me?"

It was kind of him, but of course I couldn't expect him to drive me to Dover. Still, I smiled and said, "I promise."

Satisfied, he said, "It was good to see you again, Bess." He bent to kiss me lightly on the cheek. "That's in gratitude for being such a brick."

And then he was gone.

After a few minutes I inquired of the stationmaster where I might find a telephone. It wasn't far, but I hurried, fearing I might have to wait my turn using the one in the hotel.

My parents were there, and it was wonderful to hear their voices.

"Simon is in Scotland," Mother told me, "but I'll be sure to let him know you're all right. And I'll send word to Mrs. Hennessey, shall I?"

"Yes, please. I do wish there had been a chance to come home, but the trains were impossible."

My father said, when his turn came, "I'll leave your motorcar in Dover, shall I? It might be for the best."

I laughed, knowing he was teasing me.

It was after we'd chatted for a while that I told him about the Ashtons.

I had to be circumspect. While my father was listening to me, I had to wonder who else might be on this line, hearing every word. But there would be no time to write before my train departed for Dover. And once in Dover, there would be the usual madness. It was now or never.

Falling back on Hindi, one of the languages I'd learned as a child when my father and the regiment were serving in India, I told him as much as I could, trying to keep to the essential facts, not my own feelings about what I myself had witnessed.

As usual he had a number of questions when I'd finished, and then he told me, "I knew about the explosion. We were quite concerned about the loss of the powder, and what it would mean in France. The Army had to move quickly to find new sources and begin to enlarge them. I was more involved with that than the official report. But I did read the preliminary findings. It wasn't sabotage, thank God, although the officer in charge of the inquiry was convinced it must be. That had been a risk from the start, using the Ashton mill, because it was so close to the sea—so easily reached by a determined band of men bent on destruction. But the facilities were excellent, and the Ashtons' record was impeccable. Gunpowder is a dangerous and difficult business at the best of times, but in wartime, when you need more and more of it, you can't simply double up on production. It doesn't work that way."

He paused. "Let me look into what's happening, Bess. There may be something I can do."

Happy to leave the matter in capable hands, I thanked him and hurried back to the railway station.

The train, long and crowded with men, was just pulling in, and it took me several minutes to find my carriage.

I made my connection to the transport in Dover with only two hours to wait, and then I was at sea. We convoyed with other ships out of Folkestone, and made an easy crossing, for once without alarms of German submarines hunting in the Channel.

Calais was its usual crowded, chaotic self. As I disembarked, I wondered where the stones from Cranbourne Abbey had been used, but it was impossible to tell anything in the murky light. I walked some distance before

I found my next transport, which turned out to be a battered ambulance that had just delivered wounded to a ship returning to England.

The driver and I were old acquaintances, and I asked him how it was at the Front. He was a burly, graying man from Cheshire who had volunteered, found he wasn't wanted, and then volunteered once again, this time as a medical orderly. Because of his mechanical knowledge, he'd been given ambulance duty instead.

"Men are dying still, or being blown apart," he told me with a shrug. "Nothing has changed. It's as if no one up there at the Front believes the rumors. Least of all the Germans."

And he was right. I could hear the guns clearly, pounding away at the opposite trenches as if they might go on firing for another four long years.

The mist in Calais had been the remnant of a heavy rain in this part of France, and the roads were the usual morass of ruts and mud and filth of unimaginable origins. As we bumped and slipped and rumbled our way north, I prepared myself for returning to duty. Just as well, for the forward aid station where I was assigned had just fallen back as a ferocious German counterattack threatened to break through the British line.

Most of our cases at the moment were shell frag-ments, and I thought of the former pilot I'd encountered by the River Cran, with a bit of shrapnel near his heart. Alex Craig.

Shrapnel knew no boundaries. Arms, legs, body, head, eyes—stretchers lined up, snaking back down the communications trenches. Men lay there white-faced, trying not to moan, lips clenched over clenched teeth, putting up a good front. We cleaned and probed and cleaned again, then bandaged, sending the worst cases back, returning the walking wounded to the line wherever possible. And then the machine-gun cases followed as the British counterattacked. Mostly arms and knees, sometimes bodies or shoulders as men crouched as they ran to make themselves smaller targets, and only succeeded in giving the gunners better ones within their range of fire.

There was no time to rest. I reported for duty and two minutes later was working, and went on working through what remained of the night. We had only enough time to gulp down a little porridge for breakfast before the shelling began again, this time British guns pounding the German line.

I thought, listening to the fighting, that it had been the same since the stalemate in the winter of 1915, when both sides in this conflict realized that they couldn't go forward and wouldn't move back, digging in to fight for inches or—sometimes, if they were lucky—a few feet of ground.

The Front had shifted back and forth once more, with pathetically little gain. I talked to the men as I worked, getting a sense of what was going on up ahead of us. Then, miraculously, we made nearly a hundred yards, only to lose it again in a fierce counterattack. Sometimes I needed only to look at the wounds in front of me to know what was happening along the entire line.

There was the briefest of lulls, and someone shoved a cup of soup into my hands. I drank it down, never noticing that there had been no salt to flavor it. We were running low on bandages and other necessities as well.

It occurred to me, standing there talking to a young private, his face green with shock and exhaustion, that I'd seen cavalry give way to trenches, aircraft learning to pursue the enemy or strafe the lines or, when the chance arose, fighting each other high above the battle-field. I'd watched tanks grow from clumsy beasts that killed more men than they preserved to useful battle-field weapons. And always, behind it all, the artillery, able to put a hundred shells in the same sector over and over and over again, until the sky sometimes seemed to rain metal and disemboweled earth. But the infantry still climbed up their ladders at the sound of an offi-cer's whistle, raced headlong across the bloody ground between lines, and died in shell holes, on the lips of the enemy's trenches, in the barbed wire or even the muddy, pitted ground.

With a sigh I changed my apron for a clean one and went back to work, knowing that until such time as victory came, I still had much to do.

There was a letter from Mark Ashton waiting in my tent a day or two later. I opened it, hoping it must bring good news, since he'd had the time to write at all. But nothing had changed. His father was still in custody, the barrister was trying to bring the trial forward as quickly as possible, and he himself had been granted compassionate leave. However, he went on:

There's a new problem. The Army has refused to send home the only honest witness to the explosion. Their position is, he'd given his statement to the Army investigators at the time of the disaster, and that should be sufficient for the purposes of the trial. I've appealed this decision, but it seems that Sergeant Rollins is the best tank officer they have got and they won't hear of him being given leave to testify in person. Mr. Worley has hoped that putting Rollins in the witness box will allow him to cross-examine the man and use that testimony to show that my father couldn't have caused either the fire or the explosion. Still the Army refuses to listen. I've written to the King, but I have very little expectation of my letter ever reaching him.

I could hear the despair in his words.

It was very likely that the Army had questioned Rollins only in regard to the possibility of sabotage. That had been their sole interest in the beginning, their need to hunt down the saboteurs as quickly as possible. Neither the Army nor anyone else would have considered the presence of Philip Ashton at the powder mill as anything to think twice about. After all, he ran the mill. How many Sundays had he walked down from the Hall to see how the foremen were managing? How many evenings, come to that, had he strolled to the banks of the River Cran and simply stood, taking the pulse of the day?

What had been far more worrying to the Government and the Army was the fact that in this part of Kent there was marshy ground where two main rivers emptied into the sea. There were watchers all around the coasts of Essex and Kent, to spot midnight landings or small boats coming in at dawn. But however many watchers the Army had set, no one could guard all the little inlets all the time.

Then, once sabotage had been ruled out, of course the next most likely cause of the explosion had been presumed to be an accident. Fate. A careless moment. Luck that had finally run out. A flash of spark, and the mill vanishing in a roar. No one would be happy with that, but the very nature of gunpowder made an accident not only likely but nearly inevitable as the need for it pressed men to do more and more, faster and faster.

At that stage, the Army had faced a far more important question, whether to rebuild the powder mill here in Kent—or somewhere well out of the reach of the enemy and well away from villages.

Far away had won.

And very likely, Sergeant Rollins, long since back in France, had been forgotten. No one had even thought to ask him what else he might have seen from his little boat out there on the waters on The Swale.

I could see why Lucius Worley wanted to interview Sergeant Rollins.

On the other hand, I could see a point that might not have occurred to Mark at this stage. That the evidence Rollins might give could do more harm than it would help.

Perhaps that was why Mr. Worley had taken the Army's refusal as final, while Mark hadn't given up.

What more could this man add; what questions had never been put to him? Would he clear Mr. Ashton? Or convict him?

It wasn't until much later, as I was collecting myself to try to sleep, that I thought of something else. It had occurred to me before, but in a different situation. If Sergeant Rollins *had* seen something, had information that could clear up the mystery of the explosion and fire, why hadn't he told the Army about it at the time? Even if it had something to do with Mr. Ashton and nothing to do with saboteurs?

I sat up in my cot.

Why had he answered only the questions put to him? Because he hadn't seen anything, because he wanted to protect someone, because he didn't think he'd be believed?

There had been no word from the Colonel Sahib. I'd left the problem of Philip Ashton in his capable hands.

I could do more harm than good if I took it upon myself to meddle.

After a moment I lay back down again and firmly told myself to go to sleep.

Still, it was another quarter of an hour before I heeded my own advice.

In the morning, as I was eating my cold porridge, a runner appeared with a letter. I saw him speaking to the doctor, who was smoking a cigarette and staring out at the gray dawn. The doctor seemed to rouse himself, looked around, and after a moment pointed in my direction.

The mud-splattered runner came over to me.

"Sister Crawford?"

"Yes?"

"Letter for you. Military pouch." He looked me over, wondering how it was my letter shared the pouch with far more important orders and other Army missives.

I smiled and took it from him. From time to time my father or Simon wrote to me by this means in order to avoid having something pass through the censor's hands and possibly be lost. "Thank you, Corporal. I think there's another cup of tea in the pot over there."

He grunted with pleasure and was gone.

Slipping the letter into my pocket, I finished my porridge and relieved Sister Herries, returning to my place in the receiving line of wounded.

When I could take a break, shortly after noon, I poured my own cup of tea—for a wonder it was a fresh brew—and went to my quarters to read my letter.

It was from the Colonel Sahib.

Bess, I've looked into the matter you spoke to me about, and I can tell you that there is very little I can do through my contacts here. Once the question of German involvement had been settled, the Army closed the investigation and set about moving the mill to a similar facility in Scotland. The investigation has now been reopened as a criminal inquiry. The Army will hold a watching brief, to be sure, but it will not interfere in a civilian criminal inquiry unless treason is suspected.

I did my best to find out where and when this reopening of the case had occurred. And who had initiated it. Who had brought the first charges against Ashton. But because it's a current case, this is between the Chief Constable and the Canterbury police, and I have no authority there. I can tell you, however, that despite the charges, no one has contacted Scotland Yard to take over the inquiry. It is being kept at the local level. For Ashton's sake, it would be better to have the Yard handling the investigation into the facts. I think you will understand why.

I must tell you that none of this is favorable to Ashton's chances. I understand there was an eyewitness to events, and that he is presently serving in France. But no request has been made to the Army by Canterbury police or the Chief Constable to release him to testify. Make of that what you will.

My dear, I am not happy about this. If there is any more that I can do, I will. At the moment it seems to be very little.

He went on to say that all was well in Somerset, and that my mother had heard from Mrs. Hennessey recently.

There was a final brief paragraph.

Our neighbor through the woods is recovering from boredom and will be joining us for dinner tonight. I am to convey his greetings and I am to tell you as well that he has met your young American Marine.

The neighbor, of course, would be Simon. Deciphering my father's cryptic comment, I gathered Simon Brandon had been rather busy somewhere, and he'd just arrived in Somerset, intending to sleep the rest of that day before joining my parents for dinner. The fact that he'd met "my young American Marine"—a reference to a man I'd treated some weeks ago as he passed through our aid station—told me that Simon had been involved in some liaison work with the Americans. Possibly the 5th Marines, possibly not. But he might well have encountered the man I'd treated or someone else in the Marine's company.

They were the bravest of the brave, those American Marines, holding out for a month at Belleau Wood in impossible circumstances and setting the Germans on their ear.

Smiling, I was about to fold up the letter when I saw the hastily scrawled postscript. My smile faded.

You should be aware that the local police are adamant that this is a matter for the Kent courts.

Someone was determined to see that Mr. Ashton hanged. Someone had kept the inquiry out of Army hands and out of Scotland Yard's hands as well. But why should that matter if the evidence against Mark's father was so strong?

Was it Inspector Brothers? Or someone with even more authority? The Chief Constable could call in the Yard to take over an inquiry. Especially if Inspector Brothers requested it.

The Inspector's brother had been killed in the explosion . . .

There was no sure way of reaching the Ashtons with what I'd learned. Any letter passing through the hands of the censors could take days or weeks to arrive, and it was never certain what they would consider aiding the enemy or weakening the will of the home front. A friend had written to his mother about an herb garden he'd stumbled across while retreating down the Ypres Road, and that had been cut because it might tell the Germans where this company had found a speedy path south. Another had posted to his convalescent Captain a happy birthday message from his men, only to learn later that the names of the well-wishers had been cut to keep the enemy from knowing who they were.

What I could do was find this Sergeant Rollins and let him know what was happening in Kent. It might be possible for him to speak to one of his officers and give evidence in a new deposition. At least this would assure Mr. Ashton a fair trial. I didn't care at all for the present odds. Guilty or innocent, a man deserved a fair trial. It was the bedrock of English law.

And I had a resource that I could call upon.

My Australian soldier who had helped me more than once to find information I badly needed: Sergeant Lassiter. If there was anyone who knew more about the men fighting this war than anyone else, it was he.

I spoke casually to a sergeant from a Wiltshire regiment, asking if he'd ever encountered an Aussie by the name of Lassiter.

He frowned—I was sewing up a leg wound at the time, and hoping to distract him.

"Name's familiar. Can't say I've ever run across him. But I've heard rumors. An Aussie, you say? It wouldn't be that crazy fool who took out a machine-gun nest because it interfered with his sleep?"

I hadn't heard about that. "It might be," I answered warily, finishing the last stitch and tying off the thread.

"And what do you want with him?"

"Actually, it's a friend in Kent who is looking for news of him. I told her I'd do what I could to see if he's all right. I'm afraid he's not much at writing letters."

"I'll pass the word," Sergeant Wills told me, although he didn't sound too hopeful.

Once his leg was properly dressed, he hobbled back to his lines.

The next person I chose to ask was in the ranks of a Lancashire regiment. Corporal Denton. He'd lost part of his ear to a sniper, and as I cleaned and dressed the wound, I asked again about Sergeant Lassiter. He started to shake his head, then remembered his ear. "Doesn't ring a bell, Sister. But I'll pass the word."

I was always careful that no one else was within hearing as I put my questions. No need to bring trouble down on the sergeant or on me.

We were moved shortly after that, the entire forward dressing station, and I was sent to another sector.

I had to start again, planting that same seed and professing no personal interest in the sergeant. A corporal, grinning at me as I bandaged his hand, wanted to know if the friend in Kent looking to find the Australian was pretty. I assured him that she was quite pretty, although a little on the large side.

"Oh, well, then, I'll help the sergeant along with his romance."

And a few days later it paid off.

A private said to me as I was cleaning his shoulder, "There's someone asking for Sergeant Lassiter. Do you know the Sister who's looking for news of him?"

"I don't," I said, concealing my excitement. "But I'll pass it on."

Private Howell nodded. "The sergeant's a little occupied at the moment, but as soon as may be, he'll send word to Kent that he's all right."

That must mean he was in the midst of a push and couldn't get away. I could wait. But I wasn't sure for how long. It had occurred to me that I could have passed the word to find Sergeant Rollins rather than go through Sergeant Lassiter. But the trouble was, Sergeant Rollins didn't know me; he wouldn't have understood any message I could have made up to draw his attention. I couldn't mention the Ashtons, as it would only cause trouble if the Army had already forbidden any contact.

But Sergeant Lassiter could find Rollins for me, and if he was alive, I could try to contrive a meeting.

And then another letter arrived from Abbey House, and this time it was from Helen Ashton.

After giving me news of Mark and Clara and herself, she added,

I am sitting in my little garden, where I can drop the cheerful face I wear to keep everyone's spirits up. I shouldn't be telling you my troubles, there's nothing you can do, and the last thing I wish to do is burden you with them. That said, I need to talk to someone. Ellie should be here to sit by me and listen to my worries, but she isn't, and I miss her more with every passing day. I don't really know how Mark has managed to carry on without her.

I felt a wave of sadness for her.

Turning the page, I read on.

Someone else has come forward, Bess. Claiming to be a witness but this time with more damning evidence than the earlier so-called witnesses appeared to have. Mr. Groves has been given her name. I don't yet know who it is, but I have the most awful

feeling about this. Why should she speak out now, two years late, swearing she knows Philip is a murderer? If she's so certain, why didn't she tell the Army in 1916? Is she a widow, vindictive enough that the truth doesn't matter? Don't any of them realize that my husband could hang, if found guilty?

I remembered the woman at the market in the square, spitting at me. And the others who'd turned their backs on me. Only because I was a guest in the Ashton house. Many of these villagers must be related to the dead men. And so all of them might be vulnerable to a well-planned campaign of malicious gossip and lies.

Possibly more to the point, how many of them would go so far as to perjure themselves? Even when they knew what they were saying was a lie? I couldn't answer that. I couldn't even begin to guess. And yet I had seen for myself just how deeply their hatred had taken root.

But whose campaign was it? Whose feelings went even deeper? Which family wanted an eye for an eye badly enough to see that they got it?

More worrying was what Mrs. Ashton might do once she learned the name of this new witness.

The last page of the letter had clearly been difficult to write.

I have asked repeatedly to be able to visit Philip, but the request is denied each time. Mr. Groves sees him, and Mr. Worley. But Mark and I are kept from him. It would help us both if we could speak to him, to know he is well and in good spirits, to hear what advice he might give us in regard to his affairs, or anything he might wish us to learn from him rather than Mr. Groves. Mark is beside himself, and yesterday snapped at Clara, sending her in tears to her room. And this morning I fear I nearly did the same myself. We can't begin tearing at each other. Philip needs us. But I'm afraid that's what is happening. And if there is a trial, we will need to be strong, for his sake.

And then she had written,

Philip won't defend himself. Groves complains that he refuses to cooperate with his Counsel, Lucius Worley. I don't like this man Worley, Bess. I don't trust him. Mark and Groves and even Philip feel he's brilliant and so I must put my faith in his judgment. How can I?

I see only darkness ahead, my dear. Tell me that there will be light. Make me believe it.

My heart ached for Helen Ashton.

I was glad I'd put out queries for Sergeant Lassiter. I'd doubted whether it was the right thing to do, but I knew now that it was.

And then I found out what was keeping Sergeant Lassiter.

It wasn't a push, as I'd thought.

He had crossed his commanding officer and was summarily arrested for insubordination.

My spirits plummeted. They would surely shoot him. Or lock him away until the end of the war, and leave me to search for Sergeant Rollins on my own.

Chapter Six

The best I could do under the circumstances, I thought as I accompanied a convoy of severely wounded men to a base hospital, was to beg to take a convoy to England. I needed to speak to the Colonel Sahib.

The ambulances now ran in the dark, without lights, because there was a rogue German aircraft that seemed to be in every part of the Front at once. And the pilot's favorite sport, when he couldn't spot replacement troops marching to the Front, was to play fast and loose with the ambulances.

He flew an aircraft rather like the one that had made the Red Baron a terror in the sky. Except that this one was black, save for its insignia. Everyone could recognize it at first sight and everyone dreaded it. Somehow the pilot managed to escape any British craft, slipping through a cloud, hugging the ground, passing almost over the heads of troops, using the weather to conceal him until he reached our lines. And then he made his presence felt with a vengeance.

He'd never actually shot an ambulance, to my knowledge. But he would fire in front of one, to the driver's side, or just over the bonnet, making the driver swear and swerve, only to meet another burst as he did, forcing him to swerve in the opposite direction.

Needless to say, this pilot was badly wanted by everyone, but he seemed to live a charmed life.

And somehow this night, as we took six ambulances of badly wounded men to the base hospital, he spotted us, making our lives wretched and giving the wounded a bad turn.

Sitting beside the driver, I said in exasperation, "For heaven's sake, don't play his game. Put on your headlamps and drive straight on, straight through to the base hospital. Just as if he wasn't there."

"He'll strafe us, kill half of us," the man said grimly. "I've been strafed before."

"Yes, I'm sure you have. But he's just toying with us. Can't you see? Ignore him and he'll go away."

"Or kill the lot of us," the driver said morosely, his eyes searching the sky above us. He jumped as the aircraft came swooping down again, another burst of fire across our path. And then it was gone, rising up into the blackness like some elegant night bird.

I couldn't convince him, but somehow we made it through without losing any of our patients, and the last I saw of the driver, he was heading purposefully for the nearest canteen.

We finally settled the men, still shaken by their experience and very angry indeed, and after that I was relieved for the evening. I went to the room I'd been assigned to and dug pen and paper out of my kit, intending to write to Simon.

Then I thought better of it and wrote to the Colonel Sahib instead. My mother knew who Sergeant Lassiter was; he'd summoned her to France when I'd been taken so terribly ill with the Spanish flu. She would speak up for him.

I explained that he was in something of a predicament with the Army, but that I needed him to be free to find someone for me. That it was essential that I have his help.

Ending the letter, I added, *Besides, he's more useful in the trenches than he is in gaol.*

His reputation among his men was proof of how good a soldier he was. I knew my father would appreciate that.

Early the next morning, I waylaid one of the couriers and bribed him with the last pot of honey I'd brought to France with me to slip my letter into the military pouch. And made a mental note to tell Sergeant Lassiter what he had cost me.

All I could do now was wait.

The base hospital wanted to keep me, but I was sent back into the field, and spent the next few days wishing I'd also made the courier promise to bring any reply directly to me.

Each night I listened to the shelling, and each day I worked with the wounded. There were fewer gas attacks, although the base hospitals and the clinics in England were still crowded with men whose lungs were burned beyond repair. I was glad not to be sent to those wards, where the sound of coughing and raspy breathing filled the rooms and men struggled to keep air moving through passages that were clogged by scarred and ruined tissue.

Overnight it seemed that the weather had turned colder, the brisk days of autumn behind us, and I blew on my hands one morning, trying to warm them up as I dressed. There would be tea waiting for me, perhaps porridge or sandwiches, and I was already missing that little jug of honey. I'd learned early on to do without milk, but often Army tea was too strong not to have something to sweeten it. I could hardly remember the taste of sugar.

I was just stepping out of my tent when I blundered into one of the night Sisters, just going off duty.

"Oh—! Sorry," I said. "Is it bad this morning?"

"Not terribly," Sister Hancock said. "There's a visitor for you. Over by the water lorry."

My heart leapt. Could it be Sergeant Lassiter so soon? I was feeling unspeakably grateful to my father for managing to free him.

But I should have known—I should have realized that I hadn't heard his distinctive signal, that of a bird famous in the Outback for its strange laughing call.

Instead it was Simon waiting there in the shadow of the tank, for the sun rose late these days.

"Is everyone all right?" I asked quickly as he greeted me. Sergeant-Major Brandon was wearing a khaki uniform with a tear in the shoulder and a streak of what looked like blood across the front of his blouse, black in this light. "Are *you* all right?" I added as that registered. I'd worked to save his arm once, when the Gurkhas had brought him into our station and left him there before melting away in the dark.

"Not my blood," he said briskly. "I haven't much time. But your father asked me to let you know. Captain Maxwell, in Sergeant Lassiter's sector, is very angry with him, and the Colonel Sahib has been hard-pressed to make him see reason."

"Oh, dear. What has the sergeant done?" I had nearly added "This time," but thought better of it. Sergeant Lassiter didn't suffer fools lightly, and I wouldn't have been surprised if he'd struck someone. If it were an officer, then he would be in very difficult straits indeed.

I watched as Simon tried to suppress a grin. "He told his commanding officer that three men just reduced in rank for insubordination were actually trying to keep Captain Maxwell from looking like a fool. And he added that it had been all but an impossible task from the start."

I sighed. "And he was probably right."

"This man Maxwell isn't fit to lead anyone. He'd been a green lieutenant, in the front line barely three days, when his superiors were killed in an action. He was promoted forthwith because his father is something at HQ, and because it was thought he was cut from the same cloth. He isn't."

"What are we to do? More importantly, what is Sergeant Lassiter to do?"

"God knows. Who is this man you need to find?"

"You won't know him—but Mark Ashton's father has been charged with murder, accused of setting the fire that burned everything after the Ashton Powder Mill blew up. It's a long story. But there's a witness, a Sergeant Rollins, that the Army doesn't feel needs to be brought to Canterbury to testify on Mr. Ashton's behalf. He'd already given a statement to the Army, but that testimony dealt only with possible sabotage. No one has questioned him about any other reason for the blast."

Simon frowned. "Cranbourne, in Kent? I recall that explosion. The Colonel Sahib was one of the men suggested to carry out the inquiry. He was busy elsewhere and another senior officer took his place. Soon afterward he was put in charge of finding a suitable replacement for the mill as quickly as possible."

"I don't think I'd ever heard of the explosion."

"It was quickly hushed up. Morale. And to keep such news from the Germans. It was quite a blow to lose that mill at any time. Two months later we were in the midst of the Somme offensive. We were hardpressed to keep up with the demand for powder."

Perhaps the Army held what had happened against Philip Ashton, long before the people of Cranbourne had pointed a finger at him.

"What am I to do?"

"Pray," Simon told me. "The Colonel is doing what he can. But Maxwell is a stubborn prig."

"Can the Colonel Sahib find a way to bring Sergeant Rollins to Canterbury to be questioned by Lucius Worley, Philip Ashton's barrister?" I could hear the sound of heavy boots hurrying across rough ground. I was going to be needed very soon.

"Not if the Army doesn't want him to appear," Simon replied. "I'm told he's indispensable where he is."

It was what I had feared.

Oh dear indeed.

One of the orderlies was shouting for me.

"I must go, Simon. You will take care, won't you?"

"Don't worry about me," he said, smiling as he disappeared into the ground mist that was springing up as the sun tried to rise behind a heavy bank of clouds.

I ran quickly to my post, and was just in time to work with a young corporal whose leg was badly torn. I managed to stop the bleeding, but he would have to go to hospital as soon as possible. He might still lose that leg, but for the moment he was stable.

I'd forgot my breakfast. With one part of my mind busy with what Simon had told me, I worked with the other part, examining incoming wounds, judging what best to do about them, and sending for the doctor in the worse cases while one of the other Sisters dealt with the superficial injuries.

And what was Simon doing in France anyway, covered in blood that wasn't his own? I'd heard a story told in confidence by a Gurkha officer that the little men from Nepal who fought with such courage and skill could run their fingers lightly up the laces of a sleeping man's boots and tell at once whether he was German or British. Laces ran a certain way in the British Army, a different way in the German forces.

They had rescued any number of prisoners that way. No one mentioned how many men they might have assassinated as well.

Had Simon been behind the lines looking for prisoners? He was one of the few men other than the Gurkha officers who spoke the language. He might have been sent out to find information . . .

I forced myself to pay attention to what I was doing, but when there was a break in the number of wounded, I went quickly to find something to eat.

What were we to do about Sergeant Rollins?

Or for that matter, about Sergeant Lassiter?

There was a lull in the fighting, fierce as it had been for almost seven hours, and when I came off duty, I fell on my cot, asleep almost at once.

One of the officers I'd treated had a badly torn knee from machine-gun fire, and he told me with some anger that the Germans had pushed hard enough to retake a good two hundred feet of what they'd lost. There had been a mad scramble on the part of the British to withdraw in some order, but they had had to retrieve their dead and wounded under a white flag.

"How did they break through?" I asked as I worked.

"God knows. Someone said a sector down the line had folded." He tried to keep still as I worked, for any movement made his knee hurt very badly, but it was nearly impossible. "I expect it's probably true. The Germans are quick to find a weakness. We'll retake it in a day or so. But there's no way to bring back the dead who tried their best to stop them from overrunning our position. A waste, a stupid bloody *waste*."

I gave him something for his pain and marked him for the next convoy of ambulances. At a guess he was close to thirty-five, an old hand, his body lean from years in the trenches, his mind filled with strategy and tactics, what worked and what didn't. He wouldn't be particularly happy with me for sending him to hospital, but there was no way he could return to his men. He could barely stand, much less lead them up a ladder in the next charge. And even if he could, he'd have an infected knee for his trouble. That could lead to amputation and even to death.

I was sewing up a man's face when to my astonishment I heard the familiar cry of the kookaburra bird in the distance.

It was nearly dusk, and it had been raining off and on for the past two hours. I had the feeling that both sides had sat down somewhere dry to lick their wounds, for the shelling had stopped an hour ago.

I finished what I was doing and turned my patient over to one of the other Sisters. Stopping in the main tent, I asked the doctor if he needed me.

He looked up, his face tired in the light of the shuttered lamp. "Get yourself a cup of soup, Sister. You've earned it. I'll be along soon."

But I knew he wouldn't. There were too many stretchers waiting for him.

Coming out of the main tent, I heard a noise overhead and looked up in time to see that black Fokker swooping down from the sky and heading for the rear, where the ambulances would be forming up to collect the seriously wounded. I gritted my teeth in anger, wondering why this pilot was bereft of kindness. What had happened to him or to his to make him the way he was? Was he eager to kill because he could, and it gave him something, a sense of power? Or just a feeling that his side was losing the war and there was nothing left for them in the air or at sea. Only here at the Front could bravery and a quick eye allow him to harass the helpless.

I'd reached the water lorry in my search for Sergeant Lassiter when a voice said out of the growing darkness, "Is that you, Bess?"

I turned quickly, and there he was. Filthy, his uniform torn, blood everywhere.

"Are you hurt?" I asked him, just as I had asked Simon.

"Just a little scratch here and there. We held as long as we could."

"But I thought you were on charge for insubordination."

"So I was, but it got hot enough that I was given my rifle and told to do my duty. I got most of my men safely back from No Man's Land. It was touch and go."

"What happened to Captain Maxwell?" I asked, fearing the worst—a shot in the back, perhaps, as he led the charge.

I could see the surprise on Lassiter's face as he said, "He turned out to be a right sort after all. Fussy little bas— fussy little man, always looking for something to nag a soul about, even someone who'd been at the Front for four years. But when it came down to hand-to-hand he didn't blink, and I watched him fall. Nothing I could do, I was rather busy myself. But I got his body back."

"But what about the charges brought against you?"

He grinned suddenly. "Corporal Eustace, now, he's a lovely man. Forgetful as the very devil. He never sent the papers back to the rear. Not for any of us, although he swore up and down that they were on their way to regimental HQ. I doubt anyone will be able to find them now. Or the Germans might have captured them. Good luck to them."

I had to laugh. Only Sergeant Lassiter could make light of what was happening under a man who was all but incompetent.

"So it wasn't your sector that folded?"

He looked offended. "God as my witness, no."

I believed him.

Telling him very quickly why it was I needed his help finding Sergeant Rollins, I explained the reason it was so urgent.

"This Major. Is he someone you care about?"

"Major Ashton?" I stared at him. "Not in that way, Sergeant. Besides, he's just lost his fiancée to the Spanish flu. I don't think he sees me as anything more than a friend."

"And what about you?"

"Sergeant Lassiter," I said, frowning up at him in exasperation, "I haven't given my heart to anyone, not even you. Least of all to the Major. And even if he was the love of my life, I'd *still* expect you to help him and his father."

He put his hands on my waist, lifting me off my feet, and whirled me around. "A man can't be too careful," he said grinning. "All right, lass, I'll find your Sergeant Rollins, and send you word as soon as I do." Setting me back on my feet again, he added, "I've missed you, Sister Crawford, and that's a fact."

And he was gone into the darkness.

I looked around quickly to be sure no one had seen his exuberance. He was incorrigible. But one day he was going to make a young woman a very fine husband. And she would be lucky to have him.

Hastily drinking my soup, I hurried to take up my place examining the lines of wounded. Everyone must have been too busy to notice my encounter with Sergeant Lassiter, for no one mentioned him to me. I was very glad of that. We were told over and over again not to encourage any officer or man in the ranks to think about us as anything more than a nursing Sister.

Sergeant Lassiter, alas, had needed no encouragement at all.

The night wore on, my apron so spattered with blood that I had to change it at midnight.

It was late the next morning that I heard that call of the kookaburra bird again and looked up to see Sergeant Lassiter stalking toward us beside a stretcher bearing a very badly burned man.

I quickly made my way toward them.

"He was in a tank that took a hit," the sergeant said, touching his cap to me as if we were strangers. "I told them they'd do better to bring him here to be cared for."

Looking up at him, I said, "Is it . . . ?" and stopped without saying the name.

Sergeant Lassiter shook his head. "Meet Sergeant Overton, from Hampshire."

Unable to question him further, I followed the stretcher bearers to the tent and called to the doctor to come and have a look. Then I took out my scissors and began very carefully to cut away Overton's blouse, giving the doctor a better view of the man's wounds. He was awake, gazing at me with pain-filled eyes. I spoke soothingly to him, telling him what I was doing and asking him where his mates were, for tanks carried a full complement of men.

"They got out. The pigeons too." Every tank carried a cage of pigeons, their only method of communicating with the rear. "I—I was the last. Shell bowled us right over and set us alight. Poor old girl, she'd done well by us."

The Army had male and female tanks, depending on their armament.

"You're all very lucky," I assured him. And then the doctor was there, working with him, and I had no choice but to return to my own duty, judging the new arrivals. I'd finished the line when a hand was thrust into mine, and Sergeant Lassiter's voice said, "It's hurting just there, Sister. I don't think you got it all."

And under his breath as I held his hand and looked at the healed wound I'd dressed some time ago, he added, "Rollins wasn't aboard. But he's in the same company. I've got people keeping an eye out. You'd better wrap the wrist, Bess. I told our new Lieutenant that I'd sprained something."

"I will do just that. Gratefully." I set about washing the hand and then bandaging it. "Does this man Overton know Sergeant Rollins?"

"He does. I thought you might find him useful."

I suppressed a smile. Depend on Sergeant Lassiter to make the best of a bad situation.

I finished his wrist and watched him walk away, carefully cradling it. Then I went back to the wounded awaiting transfer to a base hospital, and knelt beside the man with the burns.

"Have you been in the tank corps for very long?" I asked as I counted his pulse.

"From the start. The Mark I. Can't say what drew me to the silly things. I expect I thought it was better than being shot at."

I smiled. "And found yourself to be a much larger target, I expect."

"You're right there, Sister."

"I was in Canterbury not long ago. Someone mentioned a sergeant in the tank corps. Roland? Ralphson?"

"There's a Sergeant Rollins. He was in it from the start as well, even worked on the first designs. Rumor says he met Mr. Churchill, when he came down to see a demonstration."

"Did he, indeed?" The Colonel Sahib had remarked that Mr. Churchill was one of the earliest proponents of the tank, working hard to settle on a design and start production. And he had also brought the Admiralty in on design, for they understood hulls in ways the Army didn't. "Sergeant Rollins must be a very good tank man."

"One of the best we've got." My patient moved restlessly, and it was time to give him a little relief. It would also let him sleep until he was back at a base hospital. Still, this would be my last opportunity to question him. "He named his first tank after his sister. Agatha. Said he couldn't stand her, mind you, and thought if anything went wrong with that tank, he could blame it on her."

I laughed. Mark had mentioned a sister . . .

"Inside a tank is a wretched place to be. Loud, smelly, jarring every bone. I've seen men's knees buckle when they step out into the fresh air after only a few hours inside."

I tried to think of a way to bring the conversation back to Sergeant Rollins. "Was Sergeant Rollins at Cambrai?" It was the first use of tanks, during the Battle of the Somme. "Were you?"

He shook his head. "Not me. But Rollins was. Said it was a bloo—a disaster, but they learned from it."

I took pity on him and let him drift into that quiet realm where, for a while, pain didn't exist. He nodded as I rose to leave. "Thank you, Sister," he said drowsily. "I'm glad there was someone like you here. Kind. I wasn't sure I'd make it."

"You will," I assured him. "Not quite as handsome as you were, not until your eyebrows grow in again. But that's a small price to pay."

He quickly put up a hand, discovering that his face wasn't bandaged. Only his arms and chest. Grinning at me, he said, "I'll pay it. Gladly."

It was hard to say how much help Sergeant Overton had been, but I could at least be sure of two things, first that Sergeant Rollins was still alive and well, and second that the man Sergeant Lassiter was trying to find for me was in fact the man I needed to speak to.

As it happened, I met him sooner than expected.

I'd taken a convoy of wounded to the base hospital, once more dodging that black aircraft, and when we arrived, I reported to Matron what had happened.

Incensed, I said, "Can nothing be done to stop that pilot?"

"The Army assures me they are preparing to deal with him. I'm told they are encouraging anyone in the line who spots him to shoot him down. There's a reward."

It had been rumored that the Red Baron had been brought down by men in a trench.

"Now, then, Sister Crawford. Your report on the men you've brought us?"

Clearing my mind of the black aircraft, I sat down and gave Matron the information she needed to continue the care of the wounded from our sector.

When I'd finished my report, when we'd got every man into a bed, his needs addressed, and his body as comfortable as possible, I was free to walk across to the canteen and have a hot meal for the first time in days.

I was just finishing the last of bit of bread on my plate when the canteen door opened and a man came in.

He stood there, scanning the room, and then crossed to the cluttered table in the rear where another man was sitting, hunched over a cup of tea. The newcomer joined him.

I was taking my tray back to the counter when there was a crashing of cutlery and silverware, and I turned, like everyone else, to see what it was.

The man who had been sitting with a cup clenched in both hands was on his feet, his body shaking, his eyes wide. The table before him was swept clean, and broken crockery lay scattered across the floor.

The newcomer had touched his arm, trying to calm the distraught soldier, but he shook off the hand and went staggering across to the door like someone who was blind.

I left my tray where it was and went after him.

He'd made it halfway across the compound. There was the stunted trunk of a tree near the line of ambulances, and he had reached it before collapsing against it, as if his limbs couldn't support him any longer.

I reached him to find him crying in great gulps of air and tears, his head pressed so hard against the tree's rough bark that I could see a thin line of blood beginning to trickle down.

He was a corporal in the tank corps. I knew better than to put my hand on him, and so I stood there beside him, blocking the view of people who had stopped what they were doing to stare in his direction, trying to give him what little privacy I could in this very open place crowded with wounded and nurses and orderlies.

I was aware that the other man had come up behind us, but he stood there, keeping his distance, letting the corporal weep. It was several minutes before the gulps and choked cries began to subside. Not, I thought, because the man's pain had subsided but because his body could stand no more grief. Now he simply leaned against the tree, as if for support. His eyes were closed, his breathing still ragged, and that trickle of blood was garish against his pale skin.

"Corporal?" I said quietly. "May I escort you somewhere more private than this? I think it might be more comfortable for you."

I didn't think he'd heard me at first, but then he turned and stumbled after me as I led him to one of the small rooms the hospital chaplain used to speak privately with anyone needing his care.

The other man followed us. I wasn't sure whether he was a friend or the corporal's sergeant. I hesitated, and then held the door for him to join us.

The corporal sank into a chair, buried his face in his hands, and said nothing. I could hear him breathing, shallowly at first, then more deeply with time. It was the only sound in the small room.

I sat across from him, wondering if I'd miss my transport back to the Front lines. But his need was desperate, and the other man didn't seem to know what to say.

After a bit, I asked, "Corporal? Is there anything I can do?"

He shook his head.

Behind me, the other man said softly, "They were killed. The others in the tank. Shot while climbing out of the burning vehicle. His sergeant made it this far, but succumbed to his wound before they could take him into surgery."

And as far as I could tell, this poor man hadn't a scratch on him.

He'd survived. By some miracle, he'd made it out of his burning tank and through a hail of bullets, and the others hadn't. They had died at the scene, save for one who had not lived long enough to reach an aid station.

I said to the man by the door, "Find the chaplain, please. And bring him here."

He nodded and was gone.

I sat with the distraught man until the chaplain arrived. He was alone, thinner than he should be, with a tired face and circles beneath his eyes. I found myself thinking that he too needed help. He took in the state of the man in the chair, then nodded to me in understanding.

"My son," he said in a steadying voice. "I have just prayed for the soul of your sergeant. And I think now he would wish me to pray for yours. It is no small thing to lose so many good friends at once."

I slipped out of the little room, leaving the chaplain to his duty. The other man who had been with us had disappeared. I hurried to the line of ambulances, but they were still being cleaned. I took this extra time and went back to the wards for a last look at my own patients. They were doing well, except for a private who was in great pain, and I sat with him for several minutes, cheering him on, telling him that I would be thinking about him. But I could smell the early stages of gangrene in his foot, and I felt a sweeping sympathy for what was to come for him.

It was less than twenty-four hours later when I brought more wounded back to this same base hospital. Only a handful this time, but critical cases that couldn't wait. Once more I spoke to Matron, and then helped settle my patients.

Aching for something hot to drink after the cold drive in, I went across to the canteen again, and the first person I saw was the chaplain. He was sitting alone, staring into space, a cup between his hands as if to warm them. I collected a bowl of soup and went to join him.

"May I?"

"Yes, of course," he said without looking up, but as I sat down, he said, "Ah. Sister."

"How is the man I left with you?"

He took a deep breath. "He tried to kill himself last night. But we stopped him in time, and I think now he might be the better for it."

He had made the gesture. He had salved his conscience. Perhaps now he could heal . . .

"I was worried about him. How sad."

He shook his head. "It was Sergeant Rollins who suggested the suicide watch. And of course he was right. Corporal Haines is sleeping now, Matron prescribed something to allow him to sleep."

I'd heard the words *Sergeant Rollins*, and was busy trying to take them in. Surely that wasn't the Sergeant Rollins I was searching for? But it must be.

He'd shown such compassion for one of his men. Perhaps he'd be willing to help Philip Ashton as well.

"I'm glad," I said, referring to the corporal. "I couldn't leave him. Not like that. But you said Sergeant Rollins?"

He roused himself. "Yes, that's right. The sergeant who was with Corporal Haines when you first sent for me. Do you know him?"

"Only by reputation. I would have liked to meet him. Speak to him. But he'd left by the time I could look for him."

"Several of the tank corps have been brought in. Losses can be high sometimes. He must have come to look in on them, then gone straight back to the lines."

I tried to remember his face. But Rollins had one of those ordinary faces, the features unremarkable and yet, as a whole, pleasant enough. Short-cropped dark hair, pale eyes—a light blue, I thought—and only of middle height. But then tall men didn't fit into tanks quite as well. Good shoulders, a quiet manner. He hadn't panicked when Corporal Haines had fallen apart. And he'd listened to me when I suggested going for the chaplain.

An experienced soldier who took good care of his men.

My spirits lifted.

Chapter Seven

After talking with the chaplain, I went back into the wards to find the Sister in charge of the beds where Corporal Haines was sleeping away his fear and anxiety. But she had been dealing with an emergency and hadn't spoken to Sergeant Rollins. She had no idea whether he would be coming back.

The Sister who had worked with Matron to calm Corporal Haines was off duty and very likely sleeping.

I could of course speak to Matron herself. But that was a very different matter. One of the ward Sisters would take my questions in stride. Matron would want to know why I was asking questions about a man in the ranks. And that would mean telling her about the Ashtons.

By that time, my transport north was about to leave, and I had to hurry out to the ambulance line to find the one assigned to take me back.

There was a good bit of excitement at the forward aid station when I arrived.

The black aircraft had come back, and someone in the lines had been shooting at it. It had turned back to its own lines trailing black smoke, and speculation was rife that someone had not only hit the machine but possibly brought it down behind German lines.

Safely behind German lines. Those were the words used. Back with his own.

It was all rather bloodthirsty, but then this single craft had been annoying ambulance drivers and patients alike. There wasn't much sympathy for him on our side of No Man's Land.

Two days later, I found myself face-to-face with Sergeant Rollins again. This time he was a patient.

He had burned his hand rather badly, and I was assigned to cleaning and treating it.

How do you start a conversation with someone about what they witnessed when an explosion ripped through a small town?

I chose the least pressing way I could think of.

"I'm told you're from Kent," I began. "I took a convoy of wounded to Canterbury recently." I mentioned the clinic where I'd been sent. "Do you know it? They do good work there."

He simply stared at me with those light blue eyes. I'd been right about them. They reminded me of a china doll I'd played with as a child. I couldn't tell what he was thinking.

I wasn't the sort to rattle on inanely. But I found myself doing just that. "I'm told that the police have arrested Philip Ashton for murder, accusing him of being responsible for the fire if not the explosion at the Ashton Powder Mill."

He was watching my hands now as I worked.

I was suddenly possessed by the horrid fear that his sister had written to him about Sister Crawford, and he already knew what I was about to ask him.

Well. In for a penny, in for a pound.

"A pity," I went on. I kept my voice low. "I know his wife. And his son. I can't imagine that he would want to wreck his own property, much less be responsible for so many deaths."

From somewhere behind me the doctor called, "Sister Crawford, how much longer with that hand?"

I was needed elsewhere. It was time to be direct. "If you are the Sergeant Rollins who witnessed the disaster, your testimony could help avert a miscarriage of justice."

He looked straight at me then. "Why do you think it would do any such thing?"

I stared at him. "Are you telling me that you saw something that day? That whatever it was, it would hurt Mr. Ashton rather than save him?"

"I have no interest in the Ashtons. What happens to them is no concern of mine." He started to pull away, but I hadn't finished tying off the bandage around his hand.

I said hurriedly, "How sad. If it were your family facing such a blow, you might feel differently."

"I'm a soldier," he said tightly. "And my duty is here, not in a courtroom."

He rose and walked away.

I washed my hands and went to help the doctor. He said as we worked, "Was that the famous tank man? I thought I recognized him. What were you two talking about?"

"Kent," I said truthfully. "He's from there, I'm told."

"Is he indeed," the doctor said, and lost all interest in Sergeant Rollins as he concentrated on saving the arm of the man on the table in front of him.

I really don't know what I'd expected.

Certainly not that Sergeant Rollins would feel compelled to rush back to Kent and give his evidence just because of our brief conversation.

Nor that he would tell me something that could be used in Philip Ashton's defense.

I had simply wanted to tell this man what was happening in Cranbourne.

Which brought me back to his sister, Agatha.

Was my news old to him? Had she already written to him, telling him of the arrest of Philip Ashton? Sergeant Rollins was no fool. He must already know whether or not what he'd seen while fishing in The Swale would make a difference to the police or to the court or to Mr. Groves and Lucius Worley. Whether it was valuable information or useless.

I'd wanted to find him, to make him aware of the fact that he could do something for someone in trouble. If the Army wouldn't bring him home, if Canterbury wouldn't call for his evidence, then at least he might consider his own duty in the matter and offer to give a new statement.

And instead he'd turned his back on the Ashtons.

Did he believe Philip Ashton was guilty? Or had he believed the rumors and tales his sister might have passed on to him?

There was no way to tell.

This man I'd watched show such compassion for one of his own tank corps had spurned any suggestion of concern for a man facing hanging.

It was a shock. I'd been brought up to duty. I'd watched my father serve his country and his men without regard to self. I'd been taught in my training that my duty was to my patient, and that I must use all my skill to help him. Whether I liked the man, his uniform, or his side in this war was immaterial. If he was wounded, he was my concern.

Well.

So much for Sergeant Rollins.

The question now was, should I tell Mark what I'd encountered? Or would that do more harm to his father's cause than good?

In the end I decided that discretion was best.

What I knew about Sergeant Rollins I would keep to myself. For now.

I threw myself into my work as the lines of wounded passed through my hands. But Sergeant Lassiter hadn't forgot I wanted to speak to the sergeant, and late one evening as I was trying to wash out a uniform apron, I heard the call of the kookaburra bird.

The sergeant came sauntering in, spoke to the Sister on night duty, received a packet of bandages from her, and then came my way.

I brushed a loose strand of hair behind my ear and said, "What brings you to us in the middle of the night?"

"We were short of bandages. I volunteered to fetch more."

I had to smile. He was just as likely to have hidden all the bandages his unit had possessed in order to proclaim a shortage.

"Still looking for yon sergeant? The tank man?"

"I've spoken to him," I said, trying to keep any hint of anger out of my voice. "He didn't seem to be inclined to help me."

Sergeant Lassiter frowned. I could see his brows draw together. "I don't like the sound of that, lass. Shall I have a word with him, d'ye think?"

I could imagine what having a word with the reluctant sergeant might mean to this man.

"No, it won't help. He knows *something* about an event that happened two years ago, and I don't know whether his knowledge would help Mr. Ashton fight the charges brought against him, or if his evidence would condemn the man."

"And this worries you, does it?"

"What worries me is that if this man isn't guilty, he should be set free. And the people who nearly burned down his house while I was in it need to *see* that he has been set free, and stop harassing the family." I hadn't intended to tell him that. I was tired, although that was hardly an excuse, and we'd lost two men who shouldn't have died, and I felt that very strongly. It was hard to keep my feelings in check at the moment.

"Burned the house—Bess, were you hurt in that fire?"

"No, it was put out in time. But it might not have been. That was the worrying part. It could have caught the carpet, and then the floor. It could have done serious damage, and it was only sheer luck that it didn't. This was after Mr. Ashton had been arrested. That's what is troubling. Someone wanted to hurt that family very badly, and they've succeeded. And it makes me angry. They aren't satisfied with what they've accomplished, and that makes me fearful that worse could happen."

He was staring off toward the German lines. I could hear singing, and I realized that it was a Sunday evening. These were hymns.

"I wish the war would end," I said wearily. "For all our sakes."

"I'm doing my best, love," he said, and I smiled at his arrogance, but it was comforting in a way too. "It's yon Major whose family you're worried about?"

"Yes, it is. And no, I'm not in love with him. I told you."

He grinned. "Leave it to me. I'll have a word with this man Rollins."

"No, you mustn't! Leave him alone, Sergeant. That's an order."

"Whatever you say, lass." And then he was gone in the darkness, and I had the feeling he hadn't listened to me any more than Sergeant Rollins had.

Exasperated, I hung up my apron to dry and crawled into my cot. My blanket felt good, the night was chill, and I was almost too weary to sleep. But in the end I did.

The next news I had of Sergeant Rollins was very different from what I'd expected.

Sergeant Lassiter hadn't taken his fists to the man in order to make him more cooperative. That was a blessing.

Instead, word came down that someone had tried to kill him.

And apparently it wasn't the Germans. This had happened behind our own lines. What's more, no one seemed to know who was responsible or why Sergeant Rollins should be a target at all. It was shocking, and I was told the Army was trying to hush it up.

I couldn't learn any more than that. Not until days later.

And the word then was that the sergeant had been struck in the head by a stray bullet.

That was even worse news.

188 · CHARLES TODD

I knew that he'd survived, but head wounds could vary from simple grazes to serious damage.

When I went back to the base hospital with our next convoy of ambulances, I asked one of the Sisters on the wards if she'd heard any news of Sergeant Rollins's condition.

"Bess, don't tell me you know him? Surely he's not a beau?" she asked, her eyes twinkling.

"Alice, don't be ridiculous," I said, laughing with her, even though I didn't feel like it. "What would the Colonel Sahib have to say about bringing home a *sergeant*?"

"I'm told he has many admirers."

"I'm not one of them. But I met him once. I'd like to know he was all right."

"He is, although he had a thundering headache when that bullet creased his forehead. Any deeper and it would have burrowed along his skull. Or cut a groove through it. A lucky man. But they say he's the best tank man ever. The doctors have already cleared him to return to Agatha."

For an instant I thought she meant home to Kent and his sister, and then I realized she was speaking of his tank.

She went on to sing his praises, but all I could see were those expressionless blue eyes staring at me as the sergeant refused to do anything for Philip Ashton.

"Did he say anything about being shot? Was it really an accident, or were the first reports right, that someone had tried to kill him?" I asked, hoping to learn the truth about what had happened.

Alice shook her head. "We were told not to talk about it with him. And all he seemed to care about was getting back to his men as quickly as possible. Still, there was a lot of coming and going from the Army, officers talking to him quietly. It made you wonder."

And that was all I could discover.

The next day I was sent to England with a convoy of wounded.

It happened quite by accident. The Sister in charge had had word that her brother was badly wounded and in the base hospital in Rouen. She asked for leave to visit him, and I was ordered to take her place on the journey to England, since I'd done it so many times before.

I hadn't seen my parents in weeks. I wanted nothing more than to spend a day sleeping in my flat at Mrs. Hennessey's house in London, then travel on to Somerset and my home.

It was a wet crossing; we believed we were being shadowed by a submarine, although neither the captain of the *Louisa* nor the watch had seen any verifiable signs; and the harbor in Dover was full. We waited our turn, and then I spent the next hour making sure that the unstable cases were fit to be transported by train to London. By the time the train pulled out, I had begged a lift as far as Canterbury from a Lieutenant who was on his way to Rochester in his own motorcar, and I found myself in Canterbury in the middle of the night.

There were no trains to London until the morning.

The Lieutenant was concerned when I couldn't find a hotel room anywhere, and he agreed to run me on to Cranbourne.

I disliked appearing in the wee hours asking for a bed, but it was the only alternative to sleeping where I could in the railway station.

I had to hammer on the door to be heard, and the Lieutenant, standing by his motorcar, said, "Bess, why don't I simply run you up to London?"

It was tempting, but I shook my head. His family must be waiting anxiously for him in Rochester, and his leave was brief enough as it was. Just then the door opened a crack, and Mrs. Byers said, "Who is it?"

"Bess Crawford," I said with a surge of relief. "Do you think you could put me up for the night, Mrs. Byers? There's no train until the morning."

"My dear," she said, opening the door wide and peering out at the motorcar in the drive. "And the young man?"

"He's on his way to Rochester, I'm afraid. He was kind enough to stop here for me." I waved at Lieutenant Jamison, and he lifted a hand as he let in the clutch and went on his way.

"I'm so sorry to come in so late," I said softly, following her toward the stairs. "But I had nowhere else to go."

"Think nothing of it, Sister. Your room hasn't been aired, but the sheets are fresh. You'll be all right for what's left of the night."

"Yes, thank you, Mrs. Byers. I'm so grateful."

"Shall I fetch you something from the kitchen? A sandwich, perhaps? And I believe there's even a little soup."

It sounded heavenly but I was too tired to swallow a bite of food, and thanked her for being thoughtful.

She opened my door for me, and I set my kit down by the armoire. "It needs a fire," she said, going at once to the hearth. "There's a chill tonight."

"Don't bother," I began, but she was already kneeling to make sure that everything was as it should be. I handed her a match, and she carefully lit the bit of rag that acted as tinder. Watching it catch properly, she got to her feet. "There, that should see you through the night. And I'll fetch a pitcher of water for you. Those towels are fresh. Are you sure you wouldn't care for a cup of tea, at least?"

I'd have loved one, but I shook my head. "Thank you. A comfortable bed is all I need."

By the time she had got me settled, I was feeling the weight of my fatigue, and I was asleep, I think, before she'd climbed the stairs again to her own room.

The next morning when I came down I could see that Mrs. Byers had spread the news. I was welcomed by Mrs. Ashton and Mark. Even Nan lifted her head and wagged her tail a thump or two.

Mrs. Ashton looked worn, as if worry about her husband had been slowly taking its toll. Mark too looked very tired. Clara came in shortly after that and greeted me warmly as well.

"What is the news?" I asked eagerly as I helped myself to toast and eggs. "I have thought of you so often, and hoped that all was well."

"Philip is still incarcerated," Mrs. Ashton said slowly. "They refuse to set him free. Multiple counts of murder, they say. He could flee to Ireland, or even to Canada. But Mr. Groves remains optimistic that he'll be cleared."

Mark looked up at that. "I wonder sometimes. They've postponed the trial again. I think it's rather malicious on the part of the K.C., but I'm told it's the number of cases before the justices at the moment. You'd think Kent was suddenly a hotbed of crime."

"I saw Sergeant Rollins while I was in France," I began, and added quickly before their hopes rose too high, "He's not interested in returning to give a statement. And he didn't offer to give one to me. Of course," I went on as their faces fell, "I'd just bandaged his hand, you see." I took my plate across to the table. "Does his sister still live here in Cranbourne?"

"She does," Mrs. Ashton replied. "There's a cottage on the other side of the abbey ruins, down near the water."

I also gave them the rest of the information my father had given me about Scotland Yard and the determination of the local courts to try the case in Canterbury. "I'm so sorry I couldn't bring you better news," I added.

"But how did you come to meet the sergeant?" Clara asked, frowning. "I don't understand."

I had no intention of mentioning Sergeant Lassiter.

"I see so many wounded," I replied. "Occasionally I recognize a face or a name. Mark had mentioned Sergeant Rollins, and the man I was treating was in the tank corps. And so I asked if he came from Kent."

"It was so kind of you to try," Mrs. Ashton said gratefully. And her gratitude stung because I'd wanted so much to help. "We are in need of news. There has been so little of it."

"But what is Mr. Groves actually *doing*?" I asked. "Or this man Worley? You tell me he's one of the best in the county. Surely he's looked into what happened? He can use the investigation done by the Army to show that the authorities were satisfied that this was an accident, tragic though it was. Gunpowder mills do blow up. It's not as if this is a first. What about the men on duty that day? I'm not accusing them of carelessness, please understand that, but were they the best trained? Were they new to the process? Had there been changes in that process? Did they have any personal worries that might have made them forget to do something? Or was it the weather that day, making it more likely that a spark might happen? Was it too hot for April?" I stopped, suddenly conscious of overstepping the bounds of friendship. "I'm so sorry. It's just that I've had time to think about this. I'm sure Mr. Groves or Mr. Worley has done the same."

Mark and his mother exchanged glances.

"Mr. Worley," Helen Ashton said after a moment, "feels that it would do no good and possibly a great deal of harm if he sets about interviewing people and calling their 'evidence' into question. They've already made up their minds. He feels," she added, "that this case rests on my husband's reputation in the field, and his integrity."

But that's what a barrister does, isn't it? I wanted to ask her, but stopped myself in time. *Examine the evidence for flaws and prejudice? For a pattern that might indicate witnesses are being coached or coerced? Anything that will allow an opening to challenge the charges. Most particularly if the jury is already predisposed to find his client guilty.*

Whose side was Mr. Groves on? And what sort of defense was Lucius Worley planning to mount?

"Mr. Worley is an experienced barrister," Mark said, a little stiffly, I thought. "His record is impeccable."

"No doubt that's true," I agreed. "Does he believe in your father's innocence? Have you asked him?"

It hadn't occurred to Mark to ask. I could read the answer in his face. He'd assumed this was the case, and trusted that Mr. Worley wouldn't have taken on his father's defense if he hadn't believed.

One gentleman to another.

Trying to make some amends, I said, "I'm sure you're right about his record. Mr. Worley's. Mr. Groves must have handled your family's affairs for many years, and he would certainly choose the best."

"As a matter of fact, this is his son. Our Mr. Groves has had to retire for reasons of poor health," Mrs. Ashton said. "That was two years ago. As I remember, it was just after the explosion." She turned to her son. "Mark?"

"Yes, that's right," he said. "His heart. We were all so afraid it was the work of saboteurs. And we didn't know at first whether they were German or German sympathizers. Mr. Groves's mother was German. *Our* Mr. Groves, I mean. Her father had come over to work in the brewery. His family had owned a very large brewery outside Berlin. I know there were whispers. But of course there would be. Nothing came of it. Still, it was very stressful for him."

Disentangling this family tree, I deduced that "young Mr. Groves" was the great-grandson of the German brewer. And his grandmother had been German as well.

Oh, dear. Was this the first time there had been a conflict of interest between Groves and his son and the Ashtons? Would a willingness to help defend Mr. Ashton revive any unpleasantness about their German background?

I could say no more.

I replied, "How interesting." And let it go at that.

Clara said, "I never knew the Groves family had a connection to the brewery."

"I expect it never came up. That was so long ago. But some people did remember the story, when the mill blew up. Our Mr. Groves had come down from London and joined his other grandfather's firm in Canterbury," Mrs. Ashton said. "He earned a partnership before Timothy Groves retired, and now his son is head of the firm. They've been in the same chambers for nearly seventy years."

Our Mr. Groves. Young Mr. Groves. A household like the Ashtons, very like the royal family, kept connections over the generations. One had one's boots made at the same shop that had made one's great-grandfather's boots, and ordered one's clothes from the same tailor in London, one's hats from the same hatmaker, one's wines from the same wine merchant. Mrs. Ashton's calling cards and stationery would have come from the shop where her mother had ordered hers. And the merchants who supplied them would keep to the same high standards as their own forebears. It was a part of country life. My mother had her favorite dressmaker, and my father ordered his uniforms from the same London tailor that had made his great-great-grandfather's before Waterloo. To change—short of gross mismanagement on a supplier's part—was unthinkable. My grandmother had even had her favorite chocolatier, who knew her tastes and never failed to please her.

Casting doubt on Mr. Groves senior or junior would not be wise. But my cousin Melinda Crawford also lived in Kent, and she might know more about him.

Changing the subject, Mrs. Ashton said, "They aren't allowing me to send in Philip's meals, but I have been able to see that he's well dressed when he has an interview with Mr. Worley. That has mattered, I know."

Keeping up appearances . . .

I was glad for her; I knew how much this meant to her.

After breakfast, Clara went into Canterbury with Mark to call on a friend from school who lived there now. She was happy to have this outing with him, and we saw them off before retiring to the sitting room.

I had intended to go with them, to take the train up to London as I'd planned. But when we were alone for several minutes, as Mark and Clara went up to change, Mrs. Ashton had begged me to stay with her for "a day or so."

"I need someone to talk to, Bess. Mark and I try, but he wants to believe his father will be safe, and I am so afraid he will lose this battle. I'm so afraid we're being lied to, lulled into accepting whatever we're told. Something is wrong, and I can't speak to Philip, I can't ask him to tell me what he thinks. Does *he* trust the lawyers? I'd feel so much better if I knew the answer to that."

And so, reluctantly—though I managed to hide it well—I agreed to stay.

In the sitting room, there was a new carpet on the floor and a new chair under the window. I said nothing about them as we sat down.

Mrs. Ashton sighed as she picked up her knitting. Like so many women, she had volunteered to make scarves and gloves and stockings for the Army. "I keep up a good front for Mark's sake," she began, "but I haven't been sleeping well, Bess. I wish I could take something to help me, but I'm afraid of that sort of thing."

"And you should be. You're safer letting sleep come when it will."

"I sleep in that big empty room, in that big empty bed, no one to talk to at the end of the day, to share my life with or plan for the morrow. I feel like a widow— and my husband is still very much alive."

I could understand her feelings. "I'm so sorry," I said, and meant it. "This has been very trying for all of you." It was trite, but there was no other way of expressing myself.

"Thank you, dear." She gave me a tentative smile.

"And you've had no more trouble in the night? Since the fire? I've been worried about that."

"A few breaches of walls, a dead rat in Mark's motorcar one morning, someone outside my window in the middle of the night shouting 'Murderer.' Eggs thrown at the house door—quite rotten, it took Mrs. Byers two days to rid the steps of the smell. And Mark will have to request more leave. His time is nearly up. They didn't see fit to extend it indefinitely, and I think that was partly Mark's eagerness to get back to his men. He chafes at our wretched circumstances. But he says nothing to me."

I remembered the man I'd seen by the river and again in the drive near the door.

"And that reminds me. I never had a chance to tell you when I was here the last time. I saw Alex Craig on the drive in the middle of the night. He never came to the door, he seemed to stand and stare up at the first-floor windows."

"I expect that's because Eloise died in a room facing the drive. I've never seen him here, but it doesn't surprise me." She smiled wryly. "I mustn't think about the past. I must see to Philip's shirts and the pressing of his coats. It's the only thing they'll allow me to do for him. I ask Mark, but he swears Mr. Grove says Philip hasn't lost weight. That he's taking care of himself. But I can't see how that could be possible. He doesn't exercise, and this is a man who walked all over his lands, thinking nothing of it. And I can't imagine how he finds an appetite for the meals brought to him."

"If you want my opinion, Mr. Ashton will make certain that his gaolers never see a moment's weakness. If he has to, he will pace his cell to stay fit, and he'll eat what he's given without a word of complaint."

Her face brightened. "Do you know, I think you're absolutely right? That's precisely what Philip will do. I've fallen into such a habit of worrying—wives do— that I haven't considered *his* views on being in jail." She put aside the knitting and rose. "Now, will you be all right on your own for a bit? It's time for me to confer with Mrs. Lacey."

"I'll be perfectly fine." A thought occurred to me. "I wonder. Would you mind if I called on your former housemaid, Betty, I think her name was? Mrs. Byers mentioned her to me once. If she lives in the village, she may know more about the source of these rumors than anyone in this household."

"Betty Perkins," she said, frowning. "I was sorry to lose her. But she couldn't seem to find her way after her brother and her fiancé died. One more victim of that tragedy. Yes, that's rather a good idea, Bess. I've thought of calling on her to see how she was getting on, but Philip felt it would only open old wounds."

She gave me directions, and then at the door, she turned. "If you would like to call on Agatha Rollins as well, you'll find her direction there on the desk. I'd been wondering whether she could contact her brother for us. But I don't know what her feelings were about Philip. It would have been—unpleasant—if she happened to be among his accusers." She gave me a wry smile. "It might be construed as attempting to work my way into her good graces to reach her brother. Which of course would be the truth. You, on the other hand, have no reason to feel embarrassed. But I do want to warn you. She's not an easy woman to approach. Still, she and her brother were always at odds."

Surprised, I said, "Thank you." I'd wondered how to discover where Miss Rollins lived, if for no other reason, to find out what she might have told her brother about events in Cranbourne, and if her version of them had helped turn him against the Ashtons. And if he had told her anything about having been shot.

"And would you mind taking Nan with you? Her lead is hanging on a hook in the hall. You can't miss it. I'm afraid Mark hasn't had time to walk her properly, and somehow I haven't had the heart to drag her away from the study. If the door's ajar, she's in there before we can stop her."

"I'll be happy to."

I found the directions, and studied them for a moment. I didn't know Cranbourne well, but I thought perhaps I could find my way to both women without too much difficulty.

But what was I to say to either of them?

Setting out with Nan on her lead, I found my first quarry easily enough.

Betty Perkins lived on a side street not far from the village square. It was an older house, already showing signs of needing a new coat of paint and new steps at the door. Another of the war's victims, I thought. There were not enough painters or plasterers or carpenters or thatchers or roofers or chimney sweeps left to keep such houses in good condition. The tradesmen were at the Front, recovering from wounds, or doing other war work instead. I mounted the steps carefully, knocked, and waited for someone to answer my summons.

Finally a young woman came to the door, opened it narrowly, and said, "What is it you want? If you're collecting for the wounded, there's nothing to give you." Her hair was a stringy brown pulled tight to her head, and she looked very tired, circles beneath her brown eyes. Her hands were red, as if she'd been doing washing. There was a faint yellow tinge to her skin. I'd heard this was the price of working with cordite.

"Betty Perkins? My name is Bess Crawford. I'm a friend of the Ashtons. Would you mind terribly if I came in and spoke to you for a bit?"

"What about?" she asked warily.

"About the explosion at the powder mill. About the whispers circulating that blame Mr. Ashton. I'd like very much to know why these rumors ever got started."

She glared at me. "You weren't here, were you? You didn't send your brother off to work, and then have someone tell you there wasn't enough of him left to bury. I don't know how he died. Nor the man I was to marry. Was they blown to bits, as I was told? Or was they badly hurt and left to burn alive, with no one to save them? You tend the wounded. How does it feel to have your legs blown off, and not be able to move as the fire comes toward you? How long does it hurt?"

I had no answer for that—it would only have made her nightmares worse. But I said, "I would be surprised if anyone survived the blast. They wouldn't have known about the fire."

"You don't *know*. I dreamed about it for the longest time. Terrible dreams, where I could hear them calling, and I couldn't help them. I would run through the fire and not be in time—all I'd find were blackened bits, like a roast left too long in the oven. But I could see their eyes, pleading with me, even though it was too late."

"Do you blame Philip Ashton for what happened?"

"I don't know," she said wearily. "But if it wasn't for the war, the mill wouldn't have been running flat out. They wouldn't have tons of TNT waiting to be sent to the munitions factory. It was very hot for an April day, and the leaves hadn't fully come out on the trees that were put in to shade the mill. My brother said it wasn't like the old ways, it was harder to make the cordite. So many stages. Everyone had to learn the new methods. It was easy to make a mistake. I work now filling shells over on Sheppey. Killing Germans in the only way I can. It's better than housework any day."

But very dangerous. Those women were extraordinarily brave, I thought, to take such risks. They wore garments that were unbecoming, nothing metal, even their hair in a cap. Hardly stylish, but who was there to see them? Only the other women and a handful of men.

"Have you heard the rumors about Mr. Ashton?"

"I have. But they don't do me any good, do they? They won't bring Joey back, nor Bobby, will they? At least I can have a taste of revenge, filling shell casings. That's more satisfying."

"But who started these rumors? Where did they begin?"

She shrugged. "How do I know? I just hear them from time to time, and then whoever is telling me the latest gossip remembers I worked for the Ashton family, and they stop."

"You've never wondered who could hate your former employers so much?"

"If you're asking if I'm curious, the answer is no. I don't really care. It's no longer my business, what they say about the family. The Ashtons let me go, after all. I don't owe them any loyalty now, do I? Besides, I have more important things to think about than whether the grates are cleaned properly or the beds tidy and smooth, a room aired. I put the bands on every shell, and I think, 'This one's for Bobby. That one's for Joey.' And it's important to get it right, to see the shell isn't a dud. I don't want to make duds. They don't kill anyone."

I thanked her for her time and left. Betty Perkins had moved on. The fate of Philip Ashton didn't weigh with her. She would not go out of her way either to help him or to condemn him. It was her feelings about every shell that mattered, and I thought that must explain the fatigue taking its toll on her body and her spirit. She hadn't died in the explosion, but it had killed more than her brother and her fiancé.

I turned back the way I had come, reached the abbey wall, and followed it toward the part of Cranbourne where Agatha Rollins lived. But it took me several minutes to put Betty Perkins and her pain out of my mind.

Stopping to let Nan sniff a particularly interesting clump of grass by the abbey gates, I forced myself to think about my next approach.

Should I tell her that I'd encountered her brother in the course of my duties? Like Mrs. Ashton, I had no desire to make matters worse by alienating her. I knew her brother avoided her, but I had no way of knowing how she felt about him.

I was suddenly reminded of a woman I'd known in our village in Somerset. Surely Miss Rollins couldn't be any more ferocious than Mrs. Clegg—I remembered as a child believing she must be a witch, poor woman.

Waiting for Nan, I looked through the abbey gate at the ruins. It must have been a small monastic church compared to the extensive ruins I'd seen elsewhere. Nothing to match great cathedrals like Canterbury or Winchester or Salisbury. I wondered if it had been a way station for pilgrims, a place where the poor could find alms and the wealthier travelers could find lodgings on their way to pray at the shrine of Thomas à Becket. Pilgrimages had not only been popular, they had also brought money into the coffers of the church. And Chaucer had made Canterbury famous as a destination.

Nan, finally satisfied, turned and trotted politely by my side, quiet and well behaved.

Thinking about Chaucer, I didn't notice a group of young boys standing on a street corner watching me from a distance. It was Nan's low growl and pricked ears that made me look in their direction.

Ages twelve to fifteen, at a guess. They made me uneasy, staring at me. Having already run the gantlet of their elders on market day, I had the feeling they might prove to be more troublesome. Like dogs that minded their own business when trotting down a street alone, only to turn dangerous when in a pack of four or five.

They were of an age, too, to have heard their parents talking about the Ashtons, and then consider it something of a lark to tear down pasture walls or throw rotten eggs at a house door in the middle of the night. Constable Hood had referred to high spirits, and he might have known what he was talking about. Although high spirits in this case was little more than pure vandalism.

Speaking softly to Nan to calm her down, I was debating what to do if they crossed the road.

And then Alex Craig turned into the same street, slowed as he saw them, and with a few words, scattered them about their business. I couldn't tell if he'd seen me or just the prospects for trouble of some kind.

I came to the end of the abbey wall, where it turned down toward the water. A long drive went in through a plantation of trees that obscured the house at the end, and I thought it must be the other surviving building from the abbey, whose present owners were living in London. Indeed, there was a heavy chain across the drive farther along. I walked on, staying on the main road until I'd come to a pair of lanes, one running back into the village and another snaking through high grass toward a row of cottages leading down toward the distant blue of water. I thought these might belong to fishermen, because one or two had nets spread to dry on racks and left there to rot when the fishing fleet found itself shut in by the German raiders and the men who manned it went off to fight in France. In the distance now, beyond a line of what appeared to be sheds, I could see the sturdy fishing boats themselves pulled up out of the water for the duration and left like driftwood along the shoreline. High grass grew up their sides and caught in the rudders, even as vines had run up and over the gunwales.

The fifth cottage in was a little larger than its neighbors, and I wondered why the Rollins family had prospered enough to build on. The addition had settled, indicating it was probably a good thirty years old, but it had nearly doubled the size of the original cottage and could well have cost more than a fisherman earned.

Nan and I went up a walk set off by seashells and the dying stalks of marigolds and petunias on either side, and I knocked lightly on the door.

Chapter Eight

No one answered at first, and I thought perhaps Miss Rollins wasn't in. Then the door opened a crack and a woman's face peered out.

"And what may you be wanting, Sister?" she asked in a cold voice.

"Miss Rollins? May I come in?"

I didn't expect her to let me set foot through the door, but to my surprise, after a moment she stepped back. I looped Nan's lead around a boot scraper, and followed Miss Rollins inside. I had to bend my head a little to pass through the door, and I thought with amusement that Simon would have had a narrow miss with the lintel, even ducking to pass through.

The smile was still there as I straightened up, and I met with a scowl, as if she thought I was judging her home.

The room was immaculate. Colorful rag rugs carpeted the floor, and the furnishings, while of another generation, gleamed with polish. There was a lovely old nursing rocker by the hearth, and through a doorway I could see the glow of copper pots hung on a rack above the cookstove. A spinning wheel stood in a corner, and all the chairs had lace antimacassars where one's head and hands might rest. There were lace curtains at the three windows, and several pots of herbs sitting on the ledges.

House proud was the expression that came to mind.

Nor was there even a hint of masculinity, as if Miss Rollins refused to acknowledge the fact that her brother also lived here.

Leaving the door open to indicate that she expected the interview to be brief, she grudgingly offered me a seat. As I thanked her and took it, I had my first really good look at Miss Rollins.

She must have been quite pretty when she was young. She had good bones, as my mother would say, the kind of structure to her face that would carry over well into age. But disappointment and bitterness had soured her, her mouth turning down, her hazel eyes hard now. And the lines bracketing her lips were deeper than they should be at what I guessed to be her age: thirty-five, although that might be off by a year or so either side. She was still slim, but I guessed that she no longer cared about her appearance, for the dress she was wearing was tight at the waist and across the shoulders, as if she had gained weight since her brother's enlistment.

"I've just arrived in Cranbourne last night," I said. "I was told you lived here in the village. I thought you might wish to know that I saw your brother while I was in France. He'd burned his hand, but otherwise he was well. He's in the tank corps, I believe?"

She stared at me. "Is that what brought you here?"

It was unexpected.

"Knowing a loved one is safe is good news to many."

"And you went about the village, did you, spreading this cheer?"

"I'm afraid you misunderstand me, Miss Rollins. I treat any number of patients, and I do what I can for all of them. Whether they live in Cranbourne or not."

"And what are you to him, might I ask?"

"The nursing Sister who dressed his hand," I replied, in Matron's no-nonsense voice. "He passed through the forward aid station where I was posted. He's quite a hero, and everyone seemed to know him." A slight exaggeration, but it didn't matter.

"And so you have come to call."

Through the open door I could see Nan from where I sat. She had stretched out with her nose on her front paws.

"I'm afraid so."

That gave her pause. She hadn't expected me to agree with her.

When she said nothing, I added, "I'm told in the village that your brother was the only witness when the Ashton Powder Mill went up."

"To his sorrow."

"I'm curious. What did he see?"

"He didn't see Germans, if that's what you're asking."

"I didn't suppose that he had. My father is in the Army. He knew a little something about that inquiry into the cause of the explosion. He told me so."

She hadn't expected that, either.

Sitting down across from me in the other chair, she said, "What really brought you to my door?"

"I told you. Curiosity. The explosion, coming just before the First Battle of the Somme, cost the Army dearly. Every shell and cartridge we could make was sorely needed. For the artillery, for the rifles, for the machine guns. Not even taking into account the loss of life."

"The Army concluded it was an accident."

"Yes, I'm sure it was. Manufacturing gunpowder of any kind is dangerous work. A dropped tool setting off a spark, a moment's lapse in concentration, can make a difference. It's just that the Ashton mill had been luckier than most. Over the years it hadn't had a serious accident, much less a calamity, to mar its record. I'm told that was because of the stringent rules regarding each step of the process. But it was a Sunday, of course." I left it there.

"What does a Sunday have to do with it?"

I shrugged. "Some people enjoy their Saturday evening a bit too much. You never know."

Goaded, she said, "There was another witness. Just come forward."

I raised my eyebrows to let her see I was shocked. "Was there, now?"

"Oh yes. Closer than my brother. She saw the whole thing. Start to finish."

"Why didn't she speak up at the time?"

"She did. The Army wasn't interested in what she had to say. They only wanted to hear about the Germans. Besides, she was a woman. What does she know about such matters?"

Was that true about the Army? "Women worked in the mill."

"They did. Her sister was one of them. Only she wasn't working that Sunday."

"What is her name?"

Miss Rollins gave me a sly smile. "It's for the police to know. You don't even live in Cranbourne."

"Well, if it wasn't saboteurs, then it doesn't matter what she saw, does it?" I said.

"The *police* listened. This time. And there were other depositions before she spoke up."

"I can't imagine why. It's been nearly two years, for heaven's sake. A little late to be bothering them with such stories now."

"That's what you think. They were that eager to hear what she had to say."

"I don't see that it would do anyone any good to rake it all up again."

"That's what the Ashtons would like to believe. Well, they've had it their own way for long enough."

"Surely you aren't saying she saw the owner do anything wrong? I can't think why he'd blow up his own source of livelihood."

"That's just it. The Army wasn't paying him enough. He wanted more. It was one thing when they made the original agreement, he and the Army. They thought the war would be over by Christmas, didn't they? But when it dragged on, he thought he'd have the Army over a barrel. That they'd give him what he asked. And when they wouldn't, he arranged for the fire. Only it didn't go as planned, did it? All those men died."

"Oh, I'm sure you're wrong. It's unthinkable."

"Unthinkable or not, that's what happened."

Putting suspicion in my voice, narrowing my eyes, I said, "And how is it that you know so much about it?"

"I was the one who encouraged her to go to the police," she said triumphantly.

"What did the Ashtons ever do to you that you should make so much trouble for them? You don't pay them rent, do you? This isn't their land?"

"My family has lived in Cranbourne as long as they have. Longer. My family served the abbey for generations. They manned the fishing fleet that brought in the fish the abbey salted and dried. They owned the coasters that traded up and down the shore, from here to Norfolk and all the way round to Hastings and beyond. They even made a foray now and again to the coast of France and brought back goods. Salt, French wines from Normandy and cloth from Nantes, and even gold coins that could be melted down for collars and rings. The abbots liked fine things. And they were grateful to us. Until King Henry brought down the abbey and gave the Hall to the Ashtons—hangers-on at Hever Castle, the Ashtons were. Nobodies. Jumped-up connections of the Whore. Anne Boleyn. For her sake they turned out the monks and the lay brothers, and burned the boats to the waterline. They took away our livelihood without a thought for what might happen to us."

That was when? Nearly four hundred years ago. Surely the Rollins family hadn't nursed such a grievance for hundreds of years?

Then what had stirred up this ancient history, and made Agatha Rollins so bitter about her family's ruin? Hardly ruin, I realized, looking about me. But then who was I to judge what it was that Agatha Rollins wanted? And if she had been convinced that the Ashtons had wronged her, it would take more arguments than I could muster to change her mind.

Still, I said, "It wasn't an Ashton who turned out the monks and burned the ships. It was Henry VIII. If you have a quarrel with anyone, it's the Tudors, although I don't think there are many of them left today. Henry would have given the property to someone in his retinue. Better, I should think, for it to be someone from Kent, than an absentee landlord who lived in Leicestershire or Hampshire and simply collected the rents. Besides, the Ashtons themselves built the powder mills, and through the years employed a good many people. That had nothing to do with the Crown."

"That's what you'd like to think, isn't it?" she retorted darkly. "I know better."

I rose. "It's none of my concern, anyway. Holding grudges is a tiresome business. All the same, I can't help but wonder what your brother would have to say about this new piece of testimony. Have you even asked him? Perhaps he knows more about the witness than you do."

I could see from her face that she hadn't told him. It had very likely never occurred to her. A shadow of uncertainty appeared in her eyes.

"It's none of his business," she said stoutly, but with less conviction than I would have expected.

"And coming so late in the day, one does wonder if it's trustworthy. What this new witness might have to say. It was a pleasure meeting you, Miss Rollins."

She got to her feet with alacrity, and followed me to the door. "Your kind always stick together. I shouldn't have let you in, to start with."

"My kind? I'm a nursing Sister, Miss Rollins. I'm trained to care for the wounded, as I cared for your brother. I don't ask where he came from or how much money he has on deposit in a bank, or what connections he might have socially. When a man is bleeding and in pain, such things don't matter, do they?"

With a smile, I gathered Nan's lead in one hand, turned, and walked up the path to the lane. Nan seemed to be as glad to go as I was, trotting beside me with no

desire to linger. But I could sense Miss Rollins standing there in the doorway, uncertain what to make of
my visit—and whether she might have said more than
she had intended to.

But as I reached the lane and turned to look back the
way I'd come, she shut the door smartly. I didn't look
back again.

Miss Rollins hadn't mentioned her brother's head
wound. And so I had decided against saying anything.
It was very likely the Army hadn't notified her yet,
which meant it was not my place to meddle. Still, I
found it very curious.

However good the grammar school in Cranbourne,
I couldn't quite believe that the lessons taught there
included such a detailed history of Henry VIII's assault
on Cranbourne Abbey and the Ashton family's connection to Anne Boleyn's career—even if the stories
were true. Even if Hever Castle, the Tudor home of
the Boleyns, was not all that many miles away from
here. Of course some account could have been passed
down in a few of the families, but it was oddly complete, down to naming the Ashtons as throwing out the
monks and burning the boats. *Personally.* If such hard
feelings had existed for centuries, surely the Ashtons
would have been seen as the local villains long before

1916, and it wouldn't have taken such an intense campaign of lies to draw the attention of the police to their latest crimes?

Then who had filled Agatha Rollins's head full of such tales?

It was a very good question, but one I had no answer to.

What appeared to be a concerted effort to bring down the Ashton family had to have its roots somewhere. But I didn't think it was the Rollins family that had started the lies.

Who could hate them so much that even someone like Miss Rollins had been drawn into the fray? Or her brother?

I walked back toward the Hall, thinking about this.

The instigator would have needed a surrogate. And yet someone from the police or Canterbury or even a neighboring village would have stood out as a stranger here in this poorer part of Cranbourne. There would have been gossip, talk about whoever it was. Arguments over whether to believe him or not. As I was sure there would be gossip about my visit to Miss Rollins.

Constable Hood? Would he have been a willing representative of someone intent on making life wretched for the Ashtons?

Possibly. He'd been determined not to find the culprits who had been wreaking havoc around the Ashton property. He'd blamed it on high spirits, which could be true—I'd seen that group of young boys, looking bored and ready for any mischief. How many more were there like them? Harmless until fed by what they'd heard at the dinner table or around the schoolyard and finding an outlet for their boredom in the Ashtons. Still, even they couldn't be held accountable for all of it.

I was back to the main point. It all had to start somewhere.

And it must have begun with a hatred that would be satisfied only by the destruction of a family.

Who had Mrs. Ashton believed to be responsible for the candle that burned her chair? I didn't think it was Miss Rollins, for Mrs. Ashton had helped me find my way there.

Alex Craig? Did he hold them responsible for Eloise's death, or was it just the fact that Mark Ashton had won her hand?

A servant like Betty? Unlikely. A tool, perhaps, but not the originator of all this trouble.

What had Philip Ashton done to incur such enmity? Was it the explosion at the mill, followed by a fire? Or something much deeper? Although I was hard-pressed to think what could be worse than killing more than a hundred men in a matter of seconds.

When I reached the house, I found a calfskin valise standing just inside the door. It was one of those used to take Philip Ashton's clothing to and from his prison cell. Mrs. Byers, just coming through from the nether regions, was carrying an armful of undergarments, and I held the valise open while she tucked them in. Nan sniffed the valise with interest, but when I removed her lead, she trotted to the study door and dropped down against it.

"There," Mrs. Byers said with satisfaction. Looking down at the valise, she added, "How many more days will we be doing this? I wish I knew." Glancing at me, as if hoping I hadn't heard those last words, she politely asked, "Did you enjoy your walk?"

"Very much so."

"Most of the female staff is afraid to venture far. It's a shame. Mrs. Ashton is in her garden, if you're looking to find her."

"Yes, thank you, I'll step out there."

I found Mrs. Ashton sitting in one of the chairs at the far end of the garden, her head in her hands. She straightened up at once, her face flushed, as she heard the sound of the door opening.

Hesitating, I stopped on the threshold.

"I thought it was Clara," she called. "Come and join me, Bess." I could see her struggle to regain her composure but I pretended I hadn't noticed.

She had seemed to be at peace when I'd left her earlier. Now as I approached the chairs I could see she was very upset, even close to tears.

I sat down beside her and took her hand. "What is it? What happened?"

She moved her other hand, and I saw there was a stone in her lap. Next to it was a crumpled twist of paper.

Pushing the stone away as if it burned her, she held out the scrap of paper.

I smoothed it out across my knee and looked at the figure drawn in heavy black ink.

It was a crude sketch of a man hanging from a gallows. The face was black, the eyes white and staring, the tongue grotesquely hanging down the chin. Very ugly, but very effective.

Printed in rough letters at the bottom of the sketch were two words:

VERY SOON.

"It was the shock. I shouldn't have picked it up—the thing was lying just there, a few feet from the wall."

Angry, she pointed to a clump of pinks, now just a mat of tiny silvery green stalks. "I shouldn't have touched it, I should have walked by and left it there. It's what it deserved. But before I quite knew what I was doing I picked it up. And I couldn't miss the drawing. It hurt. As it was meant to do." She shook her head. "Well. At least they couldn't see my pain, could they? That's my only satisfaction."

Taking a deep breath she started to tear the ugly thing into bits, but I put out my hand to stop her. "It must go to the police. It's evidence," I said.

"I don't want anyone else to see it. I won't have people staring at it and wondering how I felt about it."

"Still. You must give it to Mr. Groves, if not to the police. You're being harassed by someone, and perhaps it will count, a little, toward showing that there must be more to this business than the police want to believe."

"They tried to burn us alive. If the police won't believe that happened, then this drawing won't move anyone," Mrs. Ashton said bitterly. "No. Better that whoever sent this wonders if it was ever seen." And she ripped the drawing into halves, then half again and again until bits were the size of confetti. She turned and dropped them into the fishpond, watching them soak up the water, the black ink blurring, vanishing in rivulets that had no shape or form. Finally the wet bits began to sink with the weight of the water, vanishing one by one.

"There. I shouldn't have shown even you. Promise me you won't say anything to Mark or Clara."

"No, of course not," I said. "If that's what you want."

"Thank you, my dear." She gave me a smile that wavered and then steadied. "Did you see Miss Rollins? Or perhaps I should ask, did she let you in the door?"

"She did. Much to my surprise. She talked about an old grievance—how her ancestors had been cheated after the abbey had been pulled down. I can't think she's always believed such a thing, but then the question is, who told her the Ashtons had profited at her family's expense? That they had done Henry's dirty work? Or that the Ashtons were connected with the Boleyns?"

Mrs. Ashton frowned. "I've heard that before. Now, where? Was it Philip who told me? Or perhaps his mother. No, it wasn't like her to boast about such things." Her face cleared. "I have it now. It was in an article in the Canterbury newspaper, oh, years and years ago. 1906? The Astors were living at Hever at the time and there was a lavish party to show off what had been done with the gardens. Mention was made of a local connection with the Boleyns and Hever. Only it wasn't the Ashtons, it was another family. Philip's mother had kept the cutting for the descriptions of the gardens, thinking we might wish to do something similar here at the Hall." She smiled wistfully. "There was no place on the grounds for a lake and mazes. Although we did put in the borders under the windows there by the abbey wall using some of the same perennials. Mary, bless her, lived to see the first blooms."

"Still, someone else must have seen the same story, and either confused the names or purposely changed them."

"But why stir up envy in the Rollins family?"

"In the hope of preventing Sergeant Rollins from speaking out on behalf of Mr. Ashton?"

"Oh, I find that hard to believe. Although I wouldn't put it past Agatha Rollins to do something of the sort. Not telling him the whole story, of course, but leading him to think that we had always been liars and cheats."

"Where did they find the money to build the extra rooms on the cottage?"

"I shouldn't be surprised if Freddy Rollins and his father before him indulged in a bit of smuggling. It used to be a cottage industry here in Kent. Philip was a magistrate for many years, and while he didn't actually turn a blind eye, he left it to the police to decide when and where to bring charges. If Freddy or his father came up before him, he set the fine, and there was an end to it for a few weeks. The Rollins father and son had a boat built by the Craig family, and it was faster than most."

And where had they found the money for that?

As if she'd heard the thought, Mrs. Ashton said, "One of the Craig boats was damaged in a storm. Beyond repair, it was thought. Rollins bought it for the wood—he said—and made it seaworthy again. Alex Craig's father wasn't best pleased by that. Nothing he could do of course, but it didn't sit well for a Rollins to be tooling about in a boat that others paid hundreds of pounds for."

She began to walk toward the house door. "Mark should be home very soon. We'll have tea in the sitting room, shall we, and wait for him there."

But the pot was barely lukewarm by the time we heard Mark's footsteps in the passage.

His face was grim as he opened the door, and that was the first thing I saw, looking up.

Glancing over his shoulder just as he closed the door, he said, "Clara has gone up to take off her coat. I must tell you. Groves had finally got the name of this new witness everyone has been so secretive about. Her name is Florence Benning. She lost her husband in the explosion. She's also the sister of one of the women who worked in the mill. And the sister's husband was one of the men who died. Tate, George Tate. I've tried to persuade Groves that her testimony must be tainted, but he tells me that she appears to be an honest woman and the jury will probably believe her."

His mother's face lost its color. "Mark—what could she have seen?"

"She claims she saw my father hand the foreman a packet of cigarettes. And later she watched as my father struck a match on his thumbnail and dropped it where he stood. I don't know why Groves feels she has no ulterior motive."

"He hasn't looked very hard, has he? After the explosion her widowed sister came to live with her, with five little ones. I expect it has been overwhelming for Florence Benning to have six more mouths to feed, in addition to her own three. And the house is hardly large enough for so many children. A house damaged by the explosion. They'll be under each other's feet. By now I should think Mrs. Benning could be persuaded to blame the archangels for her circumstances, much less my husband. Her life must be wretched."

"I haven't told Clara, by the way. She's already upset. She'd said good-bye to her friend, and unaware that Groves had kept me waiting, she came to his chambers. When his clerk told her I was still closeted with him, she decided on her own to see if she would be allowed to visit my father." He hesitated. "They refused, of course. But then one of the men in the room, she's not sure who it was, told her that it was likely that my father would be sent to London, that Canterbury doesn't have facilities to hold him until his trial."

"Dear God. Mark, we mustn't let that happen. He must stay here, where we can at least see to his needs. Surely Mr. Worley is pushing for an early trial?"

"He tells me he has been." Mark ran a hand through his hair. "I've never been involved in a murder trial before. There's much I don't know about such things. It just seems to me that not enough has been done toward preparing Father's defense. When I ask about interviews, I'm told it's difficult to convince people to talk to Groves's clerks. I'm told Worley doesn't intend to interview you, since you were at home that morning. He feels that a statement from our bank manager would only appear to reinforce the position that my father was pressing the Government for more money out of greed. Moneygrubbing, he called it."

"It was nothing of the kind," Mrs. Ashton said, outraged.

"I've suggested calling on an expert who can speak to the explosion and the fire. This isn't the first blast in a powder mill. The Americans have had some experience with that as well. But Worley feels that under cross-examination, the expert might well express a view that would serve the prosecution. With no survivors to tell us what happened, it would be guesswork on his part, not based on interviews and fact. I reminded him that granaries and flour mills have been known to go up, even with those machines designed to control the dust. He tells me there's no comparison."

I could read the frustration in his face. And I had to agree with him. But people often needed someone to blame, to explain the sudden deaths of so many people. And from all I'd learned, Philip Ashton wasn't the sort of man who drew people to him, not the way Mrs. Ashton did. It would be easy to cast him in the role of villain.

I remembered suddenly how Mrs. Ashton had stood in this very room and dared someone to touch her family.

She had told me afterward she feared it was a widow, jealous that *her* husband was still living, who was behind what was happening. Now, in a sense, Mrs. Ashton was proved right. But there were a hundred grieving widows out there. Had that been no more than a convenient answer when I'd pressed her? It occurred to me that it was Mark who had attended all the conferences with Philip Ashton's solicitor and K.C. Alone.

And Mrs. Ashton hadn't trusted either of them. Was this why she was unwilling to speak up, knowing she would be ignored? As strong a woman as she was, she just might be biding her time, waiting to find out who had told this twisted pattern of lies, before taking matters into her own hands. It was an unsettling thought.

Not ten minutes later, there was a loud knocking at the door, and Mrs. Byers hurried up from downstairs to answer the summons.

She came to the sitting room, where we were waiting with some anxiety to discover who it was. The last time there had been such a knock, the police had taken Mr. Ashton away.

It was Constable Hood. Mrs. Byers announced him with the same formality with which she'd have announced a duke, but there was a coolness in her voice that told me—and no doubt the constable as well—that she was not pleased to be the one who let him cross the Ashton threshold.

Nan had risen from the hearth rug, the ruff around her neck bristling a little, but she didn't bark.

Constable Hood said, "Ah, there's the creature."

He started forward, and Mrs. Ashton rose, saying, "What brings you here today, Constable?"

"The dog, ma'am. I've come to take it away."

"Have you indeed?" she asked coldly, stepping between the man and the dog. "And why is that, pray?"

"She was running wild this afternoon, and got into the pen where Mrs. Branch keeps her chickens. She got three of them before Mrs. Branch could chase her out of the pen. It's not the first time, I'm told. She went after the goat that Mrs. Hailey keeps."

"Nan?" Mrs. Ashton asked. "Surely you're mistaken. She doesn't leave the house without one of us walking with her."

"Mrs. Branch has registered a complaint. I shall have to take her away. She wants the animal destroyed."

We stared at him.

People depended on their chickens for meat and for eggs in this time of austerity. Losing part of a flock could mean going without.

Still, this was Nan.

I was the first to recover.

"I'm afraid you can't do that, Constable," I said as he made another move toward the dog. Nan didn't care for him, and I worried that she might bite if he tried to force her to come with him. "I was walking Nan on a lead this afternoon. And a number of people can vouch for that. Mr. Craig, for one. Miss Rollins, for another. I have no idea where this Mrs. Branch lives, but I can assure you that we met no chickens on our way."

I wasn't certain that either of my "witnesses" would confirm the fact that Nan was on a lead, but I could see that this gave Constable Hood pause.

"Mrs. Branch says—" he began after considering me for a moment, as if weighing whether I was telling the truth or not.

"Forgive me, but I should like to speak to Mrs. Branch. Shall I come down to the station with you, and wait while you bring her there? It would be no trouble. I can vouch for Nan. I should like to question Mrs. Branch about what she actually saw. I expect you've inspected these dead chickens for yourself?"

It was obvious that he hadn't.

"I'm sure Mrs. Ashton would reimburse her for them, if it had been Nan. But if Mrs. Branch is expecting payment for the loss of her hens, she will have to produce the chickens and identify the animal."

Flustered, he said, "Mrs. Branch came to the station not half an hour ago. She described the dog in question. She said she recognized her."

"Of course she would know Nan," Mrs. Ashton said tartly. "She's seen her with my husband I don't know how many times. And she lost her brother and her son in the mill explosion, poor woman. But I'm afraid Nan has had nothing to do with her hens."

"There aren't that many liver-and-white spaniels in Cranbourne," the constable said, trying to find firmer ground to stand on. But it was evident that he hadn't investigated the claim, he'd simply taken Mrs. Branch at her word. Because he was eager for an excuse to harass the Ashtons again?

It took ten minutes of argument before Constable Hood beat a retreat, leaving without the little dog.

As the housekeeper saw him to the door, I said, "Perhaps I shouldn't have taken Nan out."

"On the contrary, it's as well you did. The nerve of that woman! But who put her up to it? If a word of it had been true, she'd have brought the dead hens to the station with her, demanding justice straightaway. She'd have followed the constable to our door, ready to quarrel with me. But she did none of these things. She was lying, start to finish. They aren't satisfied with Philip. They want to kill his dog as well."

Mrs. Ashton was very angry. I understood that feeling. Nan was too well behaved to have attacked chickens or anything else. And she had never left my side. Even when her lead was wrapped around the boot scraper at Miss Rollins's cottage, she was in full view. Had someone seen her waiting for me on Miss Rollins's doorstep and decided to make trouble? But who could it have been?

"I'm going to fetch my hat, Bess. *And* my purse. I want to see these dead chickens for myself."

With that she smoothed Nan's silky ears and hurried away upstairs. Not two minutes later she was back, and we left the Hall, walking briskly along the abbey's wall, retracing my steps a little earlier.

"Is Mrs. Branch one of those who has fed the rumor mill?" I asked as we turned the corner of the wall.

"I shouldn't at all be surprised. She wasn't a very pleasant woman to start with, and her loss has made her bitter."

"Did she come up with this story about Nan on her own, do you think? Or did someone put her up to it?"

"I expect someone had only to drop a word in her ear. She would like nothing better than to cause trouble."

"But who could have been that mean-spirited? I mean to say, Nan!"

She shook her head. "My dear, the list would be unpleasantly long. It's all of a piece with Philip's arrest." She fell silent until we had turned into the lane that ran by the Rollins cottage, but the Branch cottage was farther along, toward the sea.

It had seen better days. The roof needed repairs and the garden by the door had gone to seed a year ago, if not two.

Mrs. Ashton went ahead of me up the path and tapped briskly on the door.

A woman opened it, recognized the person on her doorstep, and would have shut it smartly if Mrs. Ashton hadn't shoved her foot into the opening.

"Yes, Mrs. Branch, I have come to see your dead chickens."

Flustered, Mrs. Branch stared at us.

She was in her late thirties, I thought, with thinning hair and the red face and hands of a woman accustomed to working in all weathers. There was dirt beneath her nails, and her apron wasn't the cleanest. I realized she must have had a rough time of it since the deaths of her son and her brother. There was a tightness in the line of her mouth that spoke of bitterness and disappointments.

"Mrs. Branch? The dead chickens?" Mrs. Ashton pressed when the woman in the doorway didn't move.

"I gave them away," she said finally, daring Mrs. Ashton to disprove it. "What was I to do with three dead 'uns, and only me to feed? I couldn't take them to market, the way they looked."

"I'm sure they haven't been plucked. Give me the names of the people you gave them to. You've accused my husband's spaniel, Mrs. Branch. You sent Constable Hood to my door to put her down as a rogue animal. I have a right to see the chickens."

Her eyes lit up. "The constable came and took her away, did he?"

Out of the corner of my eye, I saw movement in the house behind her. Someone standing in the back of the room, in the shadows by the stairs to the upper floor. I couldn't tell who it was, and before I could say anything, whoever it was had stepped into deeper shadow.

"Give me the names, Mrs. Branch," Mrs. Ashton said firmly. "I shall need to see the evidence if I'm to offer you compensation." She held up her purse, and Mrs. Branch's gaze was riveted on it. I thought for an instant she would turn and ask the person behind her what to do now.

Was it Constable Hood I'd glimpsed? But then I realized that he would have had to tell her that the spaniel was safe. And she hadn't known that.

Who then?

She wavered, then gave us two names. "I kept the smallest one for myself. It's in the sink. Dead as dead can be.

"I shall have to see that one too."

Mrs. Branch did glance over her shoulder then before saying, "Stay here. I'll bring it to you." Using her own foot, she shoved Mrs. Ashton's out of the way and, before either of us could move, shut the door with what amounted to a slam.

Mrs. Ashton turned to me. "Well. There appears to be a dead hen after all."

Before I could answer, Mrs. Branch was back with a red hen, limp and very dead.

I inspected it. "There's no indication that it was killed by a dog," I said, touching the smooth feathers. "I rather think you'd already decided on this one for your own dinner."

"It was a dog," she said stubbornly. "I saw it with my own eyes."

"You're a liar," Mrs. Ashton said, unable to stop herself. "And you know you are. Enjoy your dinner, Mrs. Branch. I shall tell Constable Hood what I've just seen. And while I'm there, I shall bring charges against you for falsely accusing Nan. I hope whoever put you up to this has paid you well. You will need it to cover your fine."

She turned and walked away. Mrs. Branch, looking from me to Mrs. Ashton's retreating back, said hurriedly, "Here! I may've been mistaken about the dog. I saw it through the window. I may've been wrong about whose it was. I'll speak to Constable Hood myself and tell him so."

"It's too late," I said and prepared to walk away myself. "The damage has already been done. You might tell your visitor for me that he has overstepped himself. I saw him over your shoulder just now."

And I too left her standing there.

"I'll find you another dog," she called, her voice anxious. "I swear I will."

But we didn't stop or look back.

Chapter Nine

Catching up with Mrs. Ashton, I said, "I'm nearly sure there was someone else in the house with Mrs. Branch. It's why we weren't invited to come inside."

Mrs. Ashton glanced at me. "Can you describe whoever it was?" There was a note in her voice that told me she was more interested than she appeared to be.

"I can't. It was the merest glimpse. A shadow moving away, toward the stairs."

"Constable Hood?"

"That was my first thought. But she didn't know, did she, that Nan was still at the Hall and safe? It must have been someone else. Who would prefer not to be seen? Do you have any idea?"

She was looking straight ahead now. "I don't. One of her brother's friends? Or her son's? They must look in on her from time to time. And it would be just like one of them not to want to be involved."

"Why would anyone wish to see Nan put down? Unless it was done to torment Mr. Ashton."

"I don't know. Why would someone wish to torment any of us?" There was despair in her voice. "I dare not let my guard down ever, because there's no way of knowing what will happen to us next."

I turned to look back at the Branch house. Was there someone at the window watching us, making certain we were gone? I wouldn't have been at all surprised.

All around me the land was flat, with nowhere for me to stand and wait for whoever was in that house to leave. I tried to recall precisely what I'd seen. But there was nothing to distinguish the figure in the shadows. Perhaps it was a friend, come to buy eggs or borrow a cup of flour. But my first impression had been a man, not another woman standing there, and I wanted very much to know who it was.

Mrs. Ashton was already at the head of the lane, turning toward the abbey wall. She glanced over her shoulder to see what was keeping me. I waved her on. "I think I've dropped my little watch. The pin has been loose for some time. I'll just retrace my steps and look for it."

"I don't think you were wearing it this afternoon," she said.

She was right, it was lying on the dressing table in my room.

"Still," I said. "I just want to make sure. I won't go as far as the cottage."

"I can't go back there. I'll walk on, shall I? Will you be all right?"

"Yes, of course."

She hesitated, and then went on.

Pretending to search for the little watch, I scouted about until she was out of sight, and then, as if giving up, I too walked on.

But when I came to the corner of the abbey wall, I stopped where the spreading limbs of a tree gave me a little protection, and waited.

Half an hour later, I was about to give up my post and return to the Hall when the door of Mrs. Branch's cottage opened and a man stepped out.

I stood very still, fearing that even at that distance he might spot me waiting.

But he didn't come my way. Instead he walked down to the water, where the fishing boats had once put in, and stood there, looking out toward the sea.

He wasn't wearing a cap, but he was in uniform. An officer, I was sure of it. And I could see that his hair was cut like that of an officer. What's more, there was a noticeable limp in his gait.

I needed to ask Mrs. Ashton or Mark whose son or husband or brother this might be. But Mrs. Ashton hadn't waited for me.

By the time I reached the Hall, Mrs. Ashton was not in her sitting room. I couldn't be sure whether she had gone upstairs or out to her private garden. Either way, it was clear she didn't want company just now.

Mark, on the other hand, was in his father's study, and I put my question to him.

"An officer?" He had poured himself a glass of whisky, and he took a drink before he answered me. "Why do you ask?"

"I hadn't noticed anyone else in an officer's uniform in Cranbourne. Until today. I wondered who he might be. Were there many officers from this village?"

"Sadly, no. Let me see. Hobson was killed at Mons. Ford and Aubrey died of wounds on the Somme. Meredith and the solicitor's elder son, Barry, were killed in the second battle for Ypres. Craig survived a crash but was invalided out. The Vicar's brother is a chaplain. He's visited a number of times. The solicitor's younger son lost a leg at Passchendaele." He smiled ruefully. "I'm not quite sure how I've managed to survive this long."

Officers led their men in attacks. Easily recognized, easily identified by a sniper or hit with the first round of machine-gun fire. I hadn't meant for Mark to dwell on his own good fortune. He could so easily have died of his own wounds. But what interested me more was the reference to a solicitor's two sons, one of whom had died. *Groves?*

I must have said the name aloud, for Mark answered my question. "No, a man by the name of Snelling. He had chambers here before the war, but he's retired to Brighton to be nearer his younger son."

Clara came into the study just then, and there was no opportunity to ask Mark any more questions.

"I heard about Nan," she said, going to the hearth to pet the spaniel. "Silly man, Constable Hood, to think she could do such a thing." Nan rolled over, and Clara rubbed her stomach. Nan sighed with pleasure.

"What's this about Nan?" Mark asked, his voice sharp. "Tell me."

I did, reluctantly. Mark's face was dark with anger. "I'll have something to say to Constable Hood."

"No, please don't," Mrs. Ashton said, coming into the room. "She's safe, nothing happened. Let it go." Catching my eye, she gave me a straight look, and I knew she didn't want to tell him about Mrs. Branch. "It was all a mistake, anyway."

Mark glanced from his mother to me and back again. "If you're sure. I don't like this. They're growing bolder, more personal with each attack."

"We won't stop it by complaining to Constable Hood."

"That's true enough," Clara put in. "I think he's hand in glove with whoever it is."

But Mark was still angry when we went in to dinner.

Could it have been Alex Craig in the Branch cottage this afternoon? He had no love for the Ashtons. Still, I'd only seen him in dusty corduroys and a flannel shirt, even on the street today. But he must have his uniform still. And he limped, just as Mark did.

I glanced toward Mrs. Ashton at the foot of the table.

Mark was right about the boldness of the attacks. And he wasn't even aware of the figure of the hanged man.

Surely she would speak up now. But she didn't.

Sleepless that night and unable to make myself comfortable in that comfortable bed, I got up a little before six in the morning, dressed, and went down to Philip Ashton's study. Books lined the shelves, and after lighting the lamp, I walked along them, looking for something to read. For the most part the subject matter was history, voyages of discovery, biographies, poetry—the classics—and atlases and maps. Even a few books in Greek—Homer, Aristotle, Plato, Euripides, Sophocles, Socrates—the sort of titles a well-educated man would possess. But I persisted, preferring something lighter that would keep my attention until breakfast was served at eight.

I found what I was looking for on the middle shelf near the window. Dickens, Jane Austen, Wilkie Collins, and other authors. I took out *Pride and Prejudice*, went to sit by the lamp, and opened the book to chapter one. I'd read a dozen or so pages before I drifted into a light sleep. I don't know how long I might have slept there, but the book slid from my fingers and went down on the floor with a thud. It woke me, and at first I wasn't sure where I was. Then, remembering, I reached down for the book and lifted it.

A folded sheet of stationery fell out and drifted to the floor. I picked it up and, out of curiosity, unfolded it.

It was part of a letter, a middle page, because there was no salutation and no signature. More importantly, no date.

In regard to the question you raised, I can find out nothing of interest. If there is a fault, it's ambition. But that isn't necessarily a bad thing, is it? Much depends on how that ambition is expressed. And you will know more about that than I do. I am sorry I can't give you more. I do know how

worried you have been and how much you were
counting on what I could discover. Sadly, far too
little.

The following paragraph contained a brief account
of a visit to a friend who had been ill for some time.

I realized, looking at the sheet in my hands, that
this could have been abstracted from a letter without
making it obvious that a page had been removed. And
then this sheet had been put into a book that neither
Philip Ashton nor his son would be likely to pick up
and read. Hidden, in fact, where no servant would be
likely to stumble over it either.

But who had written the letter? And to whom? This
was a woman's hand, I thought. The little flourishes
were more feminine than masculine. And when was it
written? Before the war? Later? Who was the subject
of the inquiry?

It was the sort of letter a mother might receive if
her son had formed an attachment to a young woman
who was not suitable, and she'd asked a friend for con-
firmation of her suspicions. But Mark had been in love
with Eloise for some time, and her background was
known.

Then who would Mrs. Ashton be seeking information about?

Was it Lucius Worley? That was my next thought. But was I right? The answer in this letter had been carefully worded to give nothing away. If Mrs. Ashton had been worried enough about the man to make inquiries, surely she would have told her son what she had learned? Or encouraged him to look elsewhere for someone to represent her husband.

I remembered Mrs. Ashton's expression at the window when she had called out to someone in the night.

She was searching for answers. Proof. And so she might not have been certain enough of her facts to do anything about it. It appeared she'd asked a friend for help, rather than her own family. I wished I knew when this letter had arrived. When this search had begun.

But why an outsider rather than her own husband or her son?

And why, after all that had happened, had she kept her suspicions to herself?

I carefully replaced the page in the book, and put the book back on the shelf. Then I went through all the Jane Austen titles, looking for more hidden pages. But this was the only one.

Had someone come in as Mrs. Ashton was reading her letter, forcing her to hide the page? Very likely she could have read the rest of the letter to anyone without giving away her query.

It was a problem I couldn't quite unravel. But it was beginning to worry me. Surely she would do anything to help her husband's cause. Surely she wasn't planning to do anything foolish with whatever information she had.

No one was in the best of spirits that morning. A sea mist had rolled in, draping everything in long tendrils of wetness that seemed to cling to everything.

Restless, I walked into town, not toward the square but toward the church towers I could see above the bare trees. The man delivering the milk touched his cap to me and went on his way as I turned into the gate through the low stone wall around the churchyard.

The board told me that this was the Church of St. Anne, and that a Mr. Gardener was the Vicar. Looking up, I saw that the towers were lost in the mist. The rectory stood next to the church, set back to one side of the churchyard, and it loomed like a ghostly edifice until I was close enough to realize it was a pretty stone house with flower pots by the door and a knocker in the shape of a lamb. I smiled as I lifted the knocker to let it fall against the plate.

A housekeeper answered the summons, and I asked if the Vicar was receiving callers.

He was.

I followed her into the hall, and down a passage to a closed door that led into the rectory parlor.

It was a large room with dark furniture and antimacassars and a Sansevieria that was thriving in the light from a pair of windows. The mantel was marble, with blue tiles surrounding the hearth. There was money in this living, apparently, and I wondered if it had come from the powder mill.

The door opened a moment later and a tall, thin man stepped into the room. He had a kind face, but his chin was weak, and I wondered if I'd made a mistake in coming here.

"Good morning, Sister. Which of course is an expression of hope rather than a description of the day."

"Indeed," I said, smiling, as he gestured to a chair and took his own seat.

"And what brings you to the Vicarage? Is all well with Mrs. Ashton?"

So he knew who I was. But to my knowledge he had never come to the house while I was visiting, not even the day Philip Ashton was taken into custody, when presumably the man's wife would be in dire need of comfort.

"She is a strong woman with a strong faith," I said. "She believes her husband will be exonerated."

"I have kept him in my prayers every day. And Mrs. Ashton as well."

"Then you don't believe that Philip Ashton deliberately killed all those men in his employ?" I asked bluntly.

"I find it hard to believe he could do such a thing. And yet the police have seen fit to take him into custody."

"The police are sometimes wrong."

"That's true."

I couldn't tell whether he was guileless or devious. Or if he was trying to sit astride the fence and not alienate any of his parishioners, whichever side they were on.

"Can you tell me who is behind this campaign of slander and accusation that has caused the family so much grief? I know two things already: that people willingly lie to make trouble, and that there must be someone who persuades them to do it. A man, I think. Possibly even an officer. But I'm only a visitor in Cranbourne. I can't find the source without help."

"I don't know," he told me, and I thought he was probably telling the truth. "I've tried to speak up on their behalf, but no one listens to me. When people are angry and hurt, they'll believe anything that makes them feel better. The explosion was only two years ago.

Many are still grieving. It's easy to use that grief to make someone hate."

"The Army has looked very thoroughly into the possibility of sabotage. They didn't find a shred of evidence to support that. But surely in their search for answers, they'd have found *something* to connect Philip Ashton to the fire, and they'd have made an example of him. Instead they concluded that it was an unfortunate catastrophe."

"I know. I've talked with the officers the Army sent down to Kent. I've spoken with Captain Collier, their liaison in Cranbourne, who knew the men who were killed. No mention was ever made of Philip Ashton's role in events."

I couldn't be sure what he was telling me. "You're saying that the Army wasn't interested in simple murder?"

"I'm saying that they were satisfied that it wasn't sabotage. By anyone."

There I had to agree. Not by Germans, and not by Philip Ashton.

"Then what are we to do?"

"I don't know that there is anything we can do. For one thing, Philip Ashton refused to defend himself when the first rumors began to fly. He seemed to think it would all blow away of its own accord. And so the whispers grew louder. I think we've reached a point where he must stand trial to answer his accusers once and for all."

"Is that why you haven't been to call on Mrs. Ashton, to offer comfort?"

He flushed slightly. "Mr. Ashton asked me not to take sides in the matter."

"I hardly think visiting a frightened woman is taking sides. What if he can't prove that all these accusations are false? If worse comes to worst, will you call then?"

"God will provide an answer, Sister."

"You hear confessions. Has anyone come to you and admitted to persecuting the Ashtons?"

"I couldn't tell you if they had. But the truth is, I don't think anyone trusts me. They don't confide in me. Not even in the confessional. Either that or they feel they have nothing *to* confess."

So all his efforts to appear unbiased had gone for nothing. But then he was the Vicar, and like the squire and the doctor, high in the hierarchy of any village. Socially he stood with the Ashtons. And people knew that.

I looked at him. "What will you say to Mrs. Ashton if her husband is found guilty? In spite of your prayers and the best efforts of Mr. Worley?"

His face was drawn. "It won't come to that. It can't."

"But it could," I persisted. "That's why I've spoken to you. The attacks now are vicious, personal—trying to burn down the house, accusing the spaniel of killing Mrs. Branch's hens, threatening Mrs. Ashton directly. It's got out of hand. However it started, for whatever reason, it's like a witch hunt now. And that's frightening."

"There's nothing more I can do. I tell you, no one trusts me." There was anguish in his voice now.

"Not even the Ashtons?"

Shaken, he said, "I've gone to Canterbury, I've spoken to Groves. I've told him this is a farce, that it's vindictive. He thinks I'm exaggerating, that we attribute every small incident to hatred of the family. I don't know that Mark has talked to him about what's happening at home. The Ashtons have always dealt with their own problems, you see. They've never needed anyone else to fight their battles for them. For a start, he *must* speak to Groves."

But later that evening, when I broached the subject to Mark, he shook his head. "I've consulted Groves. He doesn't believe it will help us to be seen as victims. The prosecution will twist it, like everything else, and claim we set the chair ablaze ourselves, for sympathy. That we've torn down our own stone walls and cut the hop vines and let the sheep run to show that we're the ones being persecuted."

"You didn't kill Mrs. Branch's hens," I said before I could stop myself.

He smiled wryly. "No. But so far there's been no real damage done, you see. It's all been"—he searched for the right word—"superficial."

"Or a matter of sheer luck."

"That too."

"And so until someone actually attacks you—or your mother or Clara, or one of the staff—and you can show the physical bruises to Mr. Groves, nothing can be done?"

"I think Groves would tell you that it will never go that far. Not if whoever is behind this wants to see my father hanged. The person who is in real danger is my father."

"But you went to the police. When there was trouble."

"And it stopped there. No one cared to look into any of the allegations. For the very reason I've given. No harm done."

I took a deep breath. What game was Young Mr. Groves playing? But I thought I knew. He didn't want to defend Philip Ashton, for fear that people would bring up his German background if he succeeded in having the case dismissed or helped Worley win in an open trial. That they would turn on him, just as they'd turned, whoever they were, on the Ashtons. He was *afraid.* It was the only explanation I could think of. Spy fever had declined from those first mad days of September and October 1914. But there had been any number of people arrested—London waiters in restaurants, students attending University, importers who had done business with German firms, the list went on. It must have put the wind up many people with German ties. And it wouldn't easily be forgot that such people had suffered, whether they actually favored Germany or not.

It was on the tip of my tongue to ask Mark about that German connection, but he changed the subject before I could.

The next morning I was back in Dover, on my way to France.

There had just been time to put in a telephone call to Cousin Melinda. She was happy to hear my voice, and she asked half a dozen questions before I was able to answer even one of them, mainly hoping all was well and that I could come to her for a few days. As soon as I was able to say more than two words, I asked if she knew of a solicitor in Canterbury by the name of Groves.

"Yes, of course," she said. "That's to say, not personally. Only that he's reputed to be a good solicitor.

Why? Are you in need of a solicitor? Or is it someone you know, my dear? Whatever his problem, I'll do what I can."

I smiled at the telephone. "I was wondering. Do many people know that the Groveses, Père and Fils, are German in background on one side of the family?"

"Oh, dear. Don't tell me someone is trying to bring that up. That was two generations ago. Although I must tell you, Carlotta—the grandmother—was the loveliest young girl. I've seen a miniature of her by an artist in the Royal Academy. It's in a private collection. But it was the talk of London the year it was shown. Apparently he'd seen her in Canterbury and asked her father permission to paint her. Of course that was when the Germans were allies. Even Prince Albert had German connections."

"Do you think anyone remembers the painting now?"

"I've no idea. But someone would only have to go to Somerset House to find out about the past of the Groves family. They needn't have seen the painting. You remember how mad it was, after the Kaiser invaded Belgium. A friend took all the German authors out of his library and burned them in the back garden. Quite ridiculous. But I'm sure the Groves family must have known more than a moment's anxiety at the time."

And I couldn't ask anyone in Canterbury about those early days of the war, for fear I'd remind them of things best forgot, like Carlotta, the elder Groves's German mother. Most especially if I was looking in the wrong direction. But I couldn't believe that I was.

We talked for a few minutes more, and then I had to rush back to the quay.

I was just preparing to board my transport when I spotted a familiar face in the throng of men behind me.

Calling out to Simon, I stepped out of the queue and waited for him to make his way to me.

"I was hoping I might catch you," he said, smiling down at me. "I was ordered by your mother to see that you had this." He handed me a small satchel, and I heard the clink of jars inside.

I could feel my face lighting up. "Jam? Honey?" I asked eagerly.

"And Branson pickles," he told me. "There's a tin of tea as well, and another of milk."

"Bless her!" I said, torn between laughing and crying. I'd so missed seeing my parents, and Mrs. Hennessey, and all the familiar faces of home. "And you, for bringing them all this way."

He grinned. "I was beginning to wonder what to do with the lot of them if I didn't find you. Luckily, I'm a passenger on the *Sea Maid* myself. I'm carrying dispatches for your father."

"Are you indeed?" I couldn't help but think luck had nothing to do with our taking the same transport.

"Yes, and we'd better hurry, or there will be no place to sit."

He shouldered my kit, took my hand, and led me the rest of the way aboard. We found a sheltered spot on the lee side where we could watch the crew casting off. The wind had increased since I'd left Canterbury, and I could feel its bite as we pulled out of our berth and headed slowly into open water. The first waves picked up the ship, and the first of the men crowded into every available space made a dash for the railing and hung wretchedly over it, staring down into the gray and roiling sea.

I felt for them, although I'd always been a strong sailor. Simon watched them for a moment too, then said, "Tell me about Cranbourne."

I looked over his shoulder, but he had chosen well; we were out of hearing of almost everyone, tucked into a space under the ladder to the bridge, giving us a modicum of protection.

I told him what I knew—and after that, what I guessed.

"What worries me most is that whoever is behind this terrorizing of the Ashton family will stop at nothing. Simon, they even tried to have Philip Ashton's little spaniel put down. There's a cruelty in that, and it means that whoever it is doing all of this isn't afraid of the local government, the police, or the court."

"What about enemies?"

"The relatives of the dead men, of course. They've been led to believe that Mr. Ashton is guilty of causing the fire, if not the explosion. And that's the problem, you see. Whoever started these rumors may have lost control of those he—or she—stirred up."

"Was Ashton responsible?"

"I don't know—I find it hard to believe. But whether he was or not, the family is at risk too. Besides, Simon, there's the fact that someone tried to kill Sergeant Rollins. Why? I can only wonder about the connection with Cranbourne. He's refusing to come back to testify and he won't give a statement. If he won't help Philip Ashton, then why attack him? It doesn't make sense."

"It would if someone is afraid that Rollins knows more than he's willing to tell. It could explain why he won't come back to England. I should think that if he believed he would damn Ashton with what he saw, he might jump at the chance to do just that."

"That's a very good point," I agreed. "Except that most of the people who are attacking Philip Ashton are civilian. We'd have to look for someone who has relatives serving in France. But you can't simply write to your brother-in-law and ask him to arrange a quiet little murder for you. You'd have to be sure, wouldn't you, that he could be trusted to do it without getting caught. And it would have to be murder. If Rollins was only wounded, he'd be sent home to England anyway."

The bow wave was sending a spray of cold gray foam over the railings now as we moved into deeper water. Simon took my hand and we made our way toward the nearest watertight door. As it shut behind us, cutting off the roar of the wind and the sea, I could hear myself think again.

"And that," said Simon, leading me toward the canteen, "might have been the intent, not murder. Perhaps someone *wanted* him sent home to testify."

It was a very different way of looking at what had happened to Sergeant Rollins.

Had someone intended to kill him? Or only to make certain that he did in fact reach England before Mr. Ashton's trial began? Or was I leaping to conclusions? Even on a battlefield, one could make enemies.

"That opens up a new list of suspects," I said ruefully.

"It does. You told me Mark Ashton had loyal men in the ranks. Could he have asked one of them to wound Rollins?"

Shocked, I said, "Mark? No, I can't believe that of him."

And in the same moment I realized that there might not be anything he wouldn't try to save his father's life. To protect his mother . . .

Simon managed two cups of tea for us and found a place where we could sit down to drink them, although we had to step over several men stretched out asleep on the carpeted salon floor.

"I'm convinced that Mrs. Ashton knows more than she's telling. But why would she keep to herself anything that would help her husband?"

"Because she can't prove it. And she's afraid that if she gives them a name, and she's wrong, it will cause more harm than good. Which puts her in danger. You realize that, don't you?"

Thinking about his question, I asked, "Was that the reason to try to have the spaniel put down? Nan would raise the alarm if someone tried to slip into the house. And someone could, there are any number of doors. Not all of them would be proof against a housebreaker. I wish I'd thought of that sooner."

"Either that, or to lower Ashton's spirits. Remember, he's in a cell, helpless to do anything for his family. The Colonel Sahib has looked through all the records regarding the destruction of the mill. He could find no reason to charge Ashton. That means all of this is coming from someone locally. And those same people are now the ones who believe he's guilty, and are coming forward with 'new' evidence that the Army didn't have at the time."

I looked away, my mind coming to terms with the new possibilities Simon had brought up. "I don't think Mrs. Branch or Miss Rollins or even Constable Hood have the ear of enough people to start such a ground-swell of suspicion. They've been used, of course. And they might have added their bit without urging. But I don't see how they could have brought off such a coup as having Philip Ashton arrested."

"Where there is smoke," Simon replied.

"True. But nearly all of the people involved lost someone in that explosion And because of the fire, no one could hope to find survivors. That's the key, Simon, that nothing could be done for the men buried under all that rubble. It's rather like a disaster in a mine. People are concerned for those still underground, not for the men who escape in time. They couldn't save anyone, they couldn't get at the truth, they couldn't even bring the bodies out for a funeral. And so it's still *unfinished*. Anyone could prey on that feeling."

We'd come to the same conclusion, Simon and I, that there was very little to be done. And yet it rankled. I felt as helpless as the Ashtons.

I asked for news of home, and learned that my father had been summoned to London on Army business while my mother had taken on yet another charity.

"And you? Why are you on your way to France? It isn't just dispatches, is it?"

"This time it is," he said. "No one wants these messages falling in the wrong hands."

"To do with the end of the war?"

"I wasn't told what was in the messages."

A counteroffer to help speed the end of the war? I didn't ask, I knew better, but I was glad it wasn't another foray behind the lines or acting as an observer for the American forces.

We settled into a companionable silence. And then I remembered the black aircraft that had been toying with ambulance convoys.

Simon had heard of him. He said, "They've sent over a special team of marksmen to bring him down."

"Whoever he is, he's a superb pilot. They'll have their work cut out for them."

Simon saw me to my transport, and then went off to find his own. I'd been glad to see him, a bit of home. I'd given up two leaves to help the Ashtons, and while I had no regrets, I missed my parents and Mrs. Hennessey and my flatmates.

We rattled and bounced across the quagmire that passed for roads, dodging reinforcements and lorries laden with cases of ammunition and other gear. I didn't know what we were carrying—the canvas flap was across the back. But I discovered later that it was a shipment of wooden coffins moving north toward the Front.

I was posted this time at a field hospital well behind the lines. As darkness came down we could see the muzzle flashes of the big guns in the distance, and hear the steady thunder that followed.

How many months and weeks and days had I traveled these roads? I'd lost count long ago.

The driver, a taciturn Scot, had little to say, but he was a good driver and spared me the worst of the ruts and gullies when he could. All the same, my back felt as if it had been used as a washboard.

I reported to Matron, who gave me ten minutes to wash my face, change my apron, and take my place in the surgical unit, where I'd had previous experience. An orderly showed me to my quarters and waited to point out where the various parts of the hospital were located. The overworked Sisters in the wards welcomed me with relief, for it seemed that there had been no reduction in the number of patients coming in from the forward aid stations. And then I was turned over to the surgical team, where a Dr. Lytton was dealing with a variety of conditions.

We cleaned a shrapnel-torn leg and a lacerated arm, set two fractures, and dealt with five cases of trench foot, cleaning and binding the toes, before an ambulance delivered a half dozen machine-gun cases with badly damaged knees. It was dark when I was finally relieved and allowed to stumble back to my cot. I expected to fall asleep at once. Instead I lay there reliving each patient, my eyes wide and staring up at the ceiling.

The next thing I knew someone was shaking me awake. It was the doctor, calling my name and telling me to come with him at once.

I'd been too tired to think about undressing, and so I found my shoes, laced them quickly, and followed him to one of the surgical units.

But there was no patient on the table. Instead, seated in a chair by the door was one of the nurses I'd replaced last evening. Her name, I thought, was Morris, Sister Morris.

She was choking and coughing, her face streaked with tears and her hands shaking so badly she was sloshing hot tea all over her apron. I saw that one hand was badly scratched and bleeding. There was another long scratch on her face.

I looked at Dr. Lytton standing beside her chair, not sure whether she had fallen or had had a severe shock of some kind.

The doctor kept his voice low. "She was attacked in her sleep. Someone covered her face and nearly smothered her. The sentry making his rounds heard something and rushed into her quarters, but he himself was knocked to the ground as someone shoved him to one side and disappeared. He's having his head looked at in another room. Possible concussion, and a gash from hitting the corner of a chest."

"Is she hurt, other than the attempt to smother her? I see blood on her fingers."

"She clawed at the person holding her down. Partly his blood, partly hers."

"But who would do such a thing?" I asked.

"That's what you're to find out. I have a chest wound to deal with."

And he was gone.

I knelt beside her chair and took the cup of tea from her, holding it to her lips.

But she was unable to drink, and I set it aside. "Did you see who it was? If you did, you must tell me, and we'll begin a search."

She shook her head, saying huskily, "I don't know. It was dark in the room."

"Tell me what happened," I asked gently. "It will help."

"I was asleep, and suddenly there was something pressed against my face. I couldn't breathe, and I tried to push it away. But it wouldn't move, and that's when

I realized someone was holding it down. I kicked out wildly, trying to call for help, and the bed was creaking—I thought it would break under our combined weight and I'd be hurt. Then someone else was in the room, and the pressure lifted. I heard the sentry cry out as he fell and struck his head. I was already struggling to light the lamp, but I knocked it over instead. By that time the sentry was back on his feet, and he asked if I was all right. I was in tears, I couldn't answer him, and he took me by the arm, pulling me after him. Dr. Lytton was just going into the surgical unit, and he saw us. He sent the sentry away with one of the nurses, and went to find you himself."

She seemed a little calmer, and I held the cup for her once more. This time she managed a few sips. I bathed the cut on her cheek and the scratches on her hands, cleaning them and putting an antiseptic on them. She winced as I worked on her face, but let me do what needed to be done.

Looking up at me, she said, "You're Sister Crawford, aren't you?"

I'd seen her the previous evening but we hadn't been introduced. A nod as we passed, she on the way to bed, myself on the way to where the ambulances were turning in.

"Yes. Bess Crawford."

"I arrived three hours before you did, and Matron gave me your room because mine wasn't ready. She said it wouldn't matter, they were alike, and you could take mine when you got in. I couldn't help but wonder—whoever it was—could he have been looking for you?"

She was searching my face, waiting for some sort of answer. She didn't want to be the intended victim, and she didn't want this to be a random choice, something she would have to fear happening again.

"I don't know that the change in rooms mattered. I've only just arrived as well. I can't think why anyone should wish to harm either of us."

Another sentry stuck his head in the doorway. "Whoever he was, he's gone now, Sister. I'll post a guard by your door, shall I?"

Sister Morris said quickly, "Oh yes, please."

I got her to drink the rest of her tea, then urged her back to bed. She didn't want to go at first, but when she saw the sentry by the door, smiling down at her, she went into her room and I helped her right the lamp and make up the cot again, smoothing the sheets and settling her. It was then I saw the bedraggled cushion, its covering a heavy burlap roughly sewn together. It had fallen to the floor and been kicked to one side.

"Is this yours?" I asked Sister Morris, holding it up.

"No." She swallowed hard, frightened again. "I never saw it before—it wasn't in the room when I came in."

"Not very decorative, is it?" I asked lightly, to distract her. I tossed it toward the half-open door. "Shall I leave the lamp burning? Would that help?"

"Please. And will you stay with me for a few minutes?" she asked. "I don't want to be alone."

I found the camp stool and sat down. "You're safe. Try to sleep—tomorrow will surely be another long day, and you will think more clearly if you are rested."

But it was nearly three quarters of an hour before she drifted into sleep and I could go. I picked up the cushion, closed her door, and then went to find Dr. Lytton. He was just coming out of surgery, his face grim. "Touch and go," he said in explanation. "Is Sister Morris resting? I couldn't be sure whether she'd had a nightmare or if something had really happened. Still, the sentry claims there was someone else in the room."

I could tell he wondered if she had invited someone in and then panicked.

I held up the cushion for him to see. It was large enough that it would have covered her face completely, smothering her even as it smothered her cries. "I think it was real. Not a lover's quarrel."

"It's not hers?"

"She says it isn't, and I believe her. Nor was it there when she walked into that room for the first time."

"We've never had any problems with the Sisters before this," he said. "Someone drunk, I expect."

I didn't tell him what Sister Morris had said about switching rooms. I wasn't completely convinced about that. After all, I'd just arrived. Who would have known where I was posted, much less which room was mine? It was far more likely to have been a random choice.

I said, "I don't think he'd been drinking, whoever he was. I didn't smell it as I helped Sister Morris back into bed."

"The sentries are alert now, that's what matters. All right, I have another patient to see. Go back to your bed, Sister. Morning will come soon enough."

He was right. I thanked him and went to my own room, taking the ugly cushion with me.

Where had it come from? And why should anyone attack Sister Morris? Or me?

Sister Morris avoided me the next morning. She seemed convinced that having taken the room set aside for me had put her in jeopardy. I overheard several people asking her about the cut on her face, and she hesitated before answering that she'd bumped into something in the dark.

272 • CHARLES TODD

I arose early enough to go and speak to the sentries who had been on duty during the night. They hadn't seen anyone who could be described as an intruder. They'd searched the area carefully after the alarm had been raised, but whoever it was had vanished.

Nor could the aide in charge of cleaning our quarters recall ever seeing the cushion in either room, mine or Sister Morris's.

I was increasingly certain that whoever attacked her must already be here, assigned to the hospital in some capacity, not an outsider breaking through the perimeter of sentries.

There were the doctors, of course, and the nursing Sisters, orderlies, the burial detail, the people who worked shifts in the laundry, the sentries, the ambulance drivers, those who worked in the canteens and prepared the patients' meals, aides who did the housekeeping, the patients themselves, and those in the pharmacies dispensing medicines. A veritable small city of those who kept a hospital running.

I went to the board that listed staff, and found my name there as a replacement for a Sister Nelson, invalided home with appendicitis. And my room was still listed as the one Sister Morris now occupied. So far no one had changed it.

The hospital laundry here employed seven Chinese laborers who for one reason or another were no longer

fit for repairing roads and other tasks. Many like them
had come to France to fight our war and to make money,
and some of them had died of disease, the shelling, the
influenza, and the occasional accident. During the time
allotted for my lunch, I went to the building where
they worked. It was noisy, steamy, hot, and smelled of
disinfectant. I watched the men doing this menial but
essential work, then stepped through the door. Most of
them, I learned, spoke very little English, depending
on a single person to translate for them.

They were very unlikely to come in as far as
Matron's office, much less read the listing for my post-
ing. I bowed to them as they bowed to me, and left
them to their work.

The canteen staff also had almost no access to the
board outside Matron's office, but still I looked at the
duty roster there for familiar names.

The roster for orderlies was also posted by Matron's
door, and I scanned that as I was hurrying on to report
to the surgical unit.

More than a hundred men had died in the destruction of the Ashton Powder Mill. I didn't know most
of their names. Only Branch and Rollins, Hood and
Brothers, possibly Groves and even Worley. And of
course those Mark or Mrs. Ashton had mentioned. I
could have passed over dozens of other names. It was a
hopeless task.

That evening I pulled out the cushion from the corner where I'd tossed it, and took a better look at it. It could have come from anywhere. And yet I thought it must be something that someone had sat on for a very long time.

A lorry driver, to ease his back over the impossible roads? An ambulance driver, for the same reasons?

Or had someone made a rough pillow of it?

I took my nail scissors and unpicked the stitching that had sewn the burlap into a cover for the cushion. Roughly done, but sturdy enough to last. Underneath was a canvas covering, worn threadbare. I unpicked the stitching on that as well. And now I was at the original cover of the cushion. It was wool, a dark gray, possibly, or even a faded black, it was hard to tell. I turned it over.

Someone had embroidered the face of the cushion. Although most of the threads were loose or missing altogether, I could just recognize the pattern.

The white cliffs at Dover and beneath them the word *INVICTA*.

Unconquered. Undefeated.

The ancient motto of Kent.

Chapter Ten

I told myself that this did not necessarily mean that the cushion belonged to someone from Kent. It could have been found or taken away by anyone in need of a better seat. From a transport ship, from the wreckage of a lorry, from someone's kit. It could have been wandering around the battlefields of France since the BEF landed and marched north to Mons, passed from one hand to another.

And yet . . . Someone had made an effort twice to replace the worn covering over the pillow. First with canvas and then with burlap. Someone hadn't intended for the pillow to be used until the stuffing had fallen out, then tossed aside. It meant enough that it was kept in use.

When the furor died down, would the owner of the cushion come looking for it? I really should have considered that possibility last night.

I picked up first the canvas covering and then the burlap, sewing them back in place, trying to match the awkward, untutored stitches that had held them together this long.

Could someone tell what I'd done? Would he—or even she—look at the stitching to see if the cushion's secret had been discovered?

I thought not. Most people wouldn't have tried to take that cushion apart looking for evidence. Although my mother, who had taught me to make tiny, almost invisible stitches, would raise her eyebrows at my poor workmanship.

I got up from the camp stool by my bed and tossed the cushion in a heap just outside my door, as if I'd taken it from Sister Morris's room but had not wanted to keep it.

I undressed and went to bed but hardly slept, one eye on my door, in case whoever it was came in—with that pillow. But close to morning I fell into a deep sleep and nearly missed breakfast.

I got up and hastily prepared for my day with a clean uniform and apron, laced up my boots, and put up my hair after brushing it.

It was only then that I realized that the cushion was no longer lying there just outside the passage door.

The cases of trench foot were moved to a base hospital to allow their damaged toes to heal. They had been gone for two days when one of the ward Sisters said, as I helped her make up a fresh bed for a shoulder surgery case, "I was glad to see the back of them. A cheeky lot. Not ill enough to lie there and simply moan. Not well enough to help out with feeding some of the other patients. But I did catch one of them sleepwalking, when he'd been told to stay off his feet."

"Sleepwalking?" It did happen, but it was rare. Most of the men we cared for were recovering from serious wounds that kept them in their beds.

"Oh yes. It was around two in the morning. He came limping back to his bed. I startled him when I asked him what he thought he was doing. 'Sister, you'll give a man heart failure if you frighten him like that.'" She mimicked his voice, grinning up at me.

I'd worked with the trench foot cases. "Are you sure he was sleepwalking?"

She shrugged. "What else could it be? I ask you. Limping down the rows with his arms outstretched, and his eyes closed?"

But that wasn't sleepwalking. I'd seen a patient do just that when I was in training. He'd got up from his bed, his eyes open, and walked down the passage toward the hospital door. I'd followed him, uncertain what to make of him. But he couldn't manage the bolt, and he stood there, trying to pull the door open for several minutes. And then he'd turned and walked back to his bed, lying down as if nothing had happened.

"Which of the trench foot cases was he?"

"His name was Private Britton. Charley Britton."

"Do you know where he was from?"

She shook her head. "A Kent regiment. I saw the badge."

But at this stage in the war, a man could be assigned to any regiment needing to make up numbers. He might be from Kent or Lancashire or Hertfordshire.

I changed the subject as we finished the bed, asking about another patient that Dr. Lytton had been concerned about.

"The incision is draining well," she said. "If his fever breaks, I think he'll be all right."

"Good news," I told her, and went back to the surgical unit to help transfer the shoulder case to the ward.

But I made a mental note of the sleepwalker's name, and that night I wrote a letter to Mrs. Ashton, asking her if she recognized it.

And as I set the letter out to be collected for the morning post, I wondered if it was Private Britton who had come for his cushion before being transferred.

I'd asked around the wards, but no one remembered seeing it. Still, if it had been in his kit, it was possible no one had.

Three days later I was sent to a forward aid station, replacing a Sister who was due to have leave.

It was Mary, one of my flatmates.

She saw me step out of the ambulance and ran over to embrace me. "Bess! I can't believe it. I'd just written to Mrs. Hennessey to ask for word of you. How are you?"

"I'm fine," I told her. "And you?"

"Tired, but aren't we all?" She made a wry face. "You'd think, wouldn't you, that with all these rumors of an end to the war, the fighting would have slowed down a bit, but they seem to be just as eager to kill each other now as they were in 1914."

"We've been busy back at the hospital," I agreed, and shivered as a cold wind swept across No Man's Land and made its way behind the lines to swirl around the tents behind Mary. We spent another five minutes catching up on each other's news, and then the ambulance driver called to her, and she had to go.

I waved her out of sight, and looked up at a sound overhead. It was the black aircraft I'd seen before, swooping down toward the convoy heading south. I shook my fist at it and hoped that Mary would be all right.

I was busy for twenty-four hours, and then there was a lull in the fighting. I sat on a low stool by the surgical tent, finishing a sandwich.

In the distance I heard a familiar sound, and looked up to see Sergeant Lassiter coming toward me.

"They told me you'd returned," he said complacently.

"They? Who?"

He grinned. "The lads who keep an eye on you. You'd be surprised how fast news travels."

"I would indeed. Sergeant, do you know a Private Britton? He's from a Kent regiment, I'm told. Out with a case of trench foot. Have you heard anything about him?"

"I don't know the name, lass. But I'll keep an ear to the ground. Any particular reason you want to know about him?"

"I want to know where he's from. I think he may have tried to kill one of the Sisters back at the hospital, thinking she was me."

His fair brows twitched together in a frown. "That makes a difference," he said. "Is she all right?"

"A good fright. One of the sentries got there in time, but he couldn't hold the man."

"Why should he want to kill you?"

"The truth is, I don't know. There was trouble in Kent on my last leave, but I can't see how he might be connected with that. It might even be that Sister Morris was his target after all. She's quite pretty. He might have gone into her room to speak to her and when she started to scream, he tried to smother her." But why had he taken that cushion with him? I shook my head. "It's strange, Sergeant. He had a cushion with him. Small, but large enough to do what he set out to do. It was covered in burlap."

"I don't like the sound of this." He rose. "I hear the Sergeant-Major was back in France. On a peaceful errand this time."

My eyebrows flew up. "Indeed?" How on earth had Sergeant Lassiter learned that?

"One of the lads saw him. Something to do with that black bas—black craft flying behind the lines. There's a reward out for bringing it down. Did you know? Three of my mates had a go at him the other day. But he knows what he's doing. He comes over the lines too high for us to touch him."

"What's the reward?" I asked, curious.

"A weekend's leave in Paris. So they say. All expenses, and all you can drink."

I laughed. That would appeal to more soldiers than coin, which would smack a little of blood money.

Sergeant Lassiter got to his feet. "Well, lass, I've seen your fair face and assured myself that you were still alive and well. And still unmarried."

He was irrepressible.

"No thanks to the Australian Army. I've had ten proposals a day when an Aussie is in hospital."

"Only ten? I'll have a word with my mates. They're slackers."

He reached out and touched my cheek, and then he was gone.

I finished my tea, washed my cup, and put it back on the tray. With a sigh I went back to work.

Two days later a soldier with a splinter of shrapnel in his shoulder asked my name, and when I told him, he turned his palm a little to show me a scrap of paper. I pocketed it when no one was looking. He was in great pain, but he smiled lopsidedly at me and said, "I'll pass the word."

At my first break I went into my tent on a pretext, and sat down on my cot to read the message.

It was brief.

B is from Devon. Served an officer as batman for the first two years of the war. Then transferred to K R and sent to France.

I stared at the message. A Devon man? Transferred to a Kent regiment. I couldn't imagine how he could possibly have had anything to do with Cranbourne or the explosion or even with me.

I'd hoped to learn just the opposite. That there was some connection—that possibly he'd even been the person who attacked Sergeant Rollins.

More disappointed than I cared to admit, even to myself, I struck a match and burned the fragment of paper, then ground the ashes underfoot.

Assault on a Sister with the intent to rape was not unheard of, though mercifully rare.

It appeared that Private Britton's connection with the cushion was slim indeed.

The letter that arrived from Mrs. Ashton only confirmed what Sergeant Lassiter had found out for me.

I don't recall anyone by the name of Britton. Nor is that name on the list of the dead. If he's related to someone on that list, I'd have no way of knowing. I did ask Mark, and he said he thought it was familiar, but he wasn't sure why. Perhaps someone he knew in France? Alas, there have been so many.

She was right, an officer would have had hundreds under his command, many of them killed in their first week at the Front. Many officers had told me that they could remember every face, each name. Others swore they could not.

The rest of the letter was a recounting of efforts to visit her husband and to find evidence that would free him. Sadly, in neither case had she or Mark been successful.

I set the letter aside with a heavy heart. Sleepwalker or not, it appeared that Britton had no connection to Cranbourne. And we still had no idea why Sister Morris had been attacked.

Much to my surprise, I encountered Sergeant Rollins again when I took a convoy of wounded back to the field hospital. He'd been brought in with a badly blistered arm and face where he'd pulled men out of a burning tank. They too were being cared for, their red, peeling faces oozing fluids and their eyes dazed from the pain.

Rollins was in a hurry to rejoin his men, but the doctor insisted on keeping him for a few days. I'd heard much the same argument before from other patients, but as I passed by the burn ward, I'd recognized his voice.

The doctor beckoned to me to come in and help him put salve on the wound, and I saw recognition in Rollins's eyes as I came forward.

This wasn't my ward, but when a doctor summons a nursing Sister, she answers that call without question.

I didn't speak to the patient, keeping my attention on the arm I was working with. The burns weren't as deep as those of the others, but infection always lurks close by when the skin is open.

I finished lightly bandaging the arm, just enough to protect it, and a Sister appeared with something for his pain. But Rollins refused it, glaring at both of us as if we were personally responsible for his situation.

Dr. Fields said, "Nonsense, take the powder, Sergeant. You'll be out of here all the sooner if you don't fight us."

After a moment Rollins took the cup of water into which the other Sister had stirred the powder and swallowed it down, grimacing a little at the end.

"All right, Sister," Dr. Fields said to me. "Get him into bed. He can have a normal diet as long as he isn't running a fever. But I want to know if he does."

"Yes, sir," I said, and pulled back the sheet on the cot, for Rollins to swing his feet underneath. I thought at first he intended to sit up, but he thought better of it, and gingerly stretched out on the bed, edging the arm onto a soft pillow.

The other Sister turned away, following the doctor to the next bed. I too prepared to go back to my own patients, well aware that the ambulances were waiting to return to the forward station as soon as I'd logged them in.

Rollins reached out with his good hand and caught my wrist. His grip was so strong it hurt, and I turned at once to face him, prepared to call the doctor back if I had to.

"You spoke to my sister," he said in a fierce whisper that wouldn't carry.

"Of course I did. I'd seen you, you were safe and well. I thought it would give her a little peace."

"You told her I'd refused to help the Ashtons."

"Yes, I did. I had the feeling she was quite pleased about that."

"You shouldn't have drawn her into that business."

I shook my head. "She was already drawn into it. She's quite vocal about her feelings, is your sister. And she encouraged another witness to step forward. One who has no qualms about telling what she saw."

It was clear he hadn't heard that bit of news.

"There *was* no other witness."

"Miss Rollins claims there was."

"Damn it. I was there. I ought to know."

"That may well be, but the police seem to be delighted with the news." I felt a surge of excitement, thinking this information might make him change his mind about his own testimony. But I should have known better.

He released my wrist and lay back against his pillows. "She's a fool to get involved," he said. And I realized then that his concern was only for her. "It could cause trouble in the end."

"Why should you care? You don't want to help."

But he didn't answer me. He lay there, staring up at my face while his mind was busy elsewhere. "Who came forward?" he asked then. "Who was it?"

"A Florence Benning. Her sister is the widow of George Tate. Perhaps she's lying."

I took a chance then, and asked a very different question. "Was it Private Britton who tried to kill you? I'd like to know, you see, because he also tried to kill me."

That got his attention straightaway.

"I didn't see who attacked me. Why do you think it was Britton?"

"Because he'd been brought in with a case of trench foot. And one of the other Sisters saw him coming back to his bed afterward." I made no mention of sleepwalking.

He digested that, then asked, "Why should he care, one way or another?"

"Do you know him?" I asked, with an effort keeping the eagerness out of my voice. But he caught it anyway.

"You're lying," he said with something like contempt in his face. "It's a trick, that's what it is. Go away."

"You still refuse to help the Ashtons?" I said, ignoring his words.

"Why does everyone think I can save them?" he demanded querulously. "For all you know my testimony will damn them."

And he closed his eyes, effectively shutting me out.

One of the ward Sisters was standing in the doorway, beckoning me. I had to go.

But I said softly before I left, "Still, someone wants you out of the way. I'd be careful if I were you."

Turning, I walked away, and I didn't look back to see if he was watching me.

By the time I'd reached the forward aid station, everyone there was abuzz with excitement.

Someone had nearly brought down the black German aircraft. Three witnesses had seen it streaking for home with dark smoke billowing out of the engine. And a Yorkshireman had come forward to say he'd fired the shot that hit it.

It was the second time the aircraft had been hit by ground fire. The pilot appeared to lead a charmed life.

Still, the Yorkshireman was vociferous in his certainty that it was his shot. But there was no proof that the aircraft had crashed. For all anyone knew, it had made it safely back to its airfield once again. Or to another, where it could land and make repairs.

And witnesses agreed, however reluctantly, that the pilot was still alive, because it was evident that he was still in control.

There was much debate over the Yorkshireman's claim. Even the seriously wounded in hospital asked us if we'd heard any news. As if HQ would inform us first. All the same it was good for morale, and we let the arguments rage around our ears as the pros and cons were weighed, and the question of whether or not the reward should be given to the Yorkshireman was hotly debated too.

The general feeling was, the reward was still to be won.

In the midst of all this uproar, Simon appeared, bringing me a letter from home and reminding me that I hadn't written for some time.

"Is there any news about Philip Ashton's trial?" I asked.

"Nothing has changed, as far as I know. Your father has looked into the matter again, but there's nothing in Sergeant Rollins's earlier statement that condemns or exonerates Ashton. In fact, he didn't mention him at all. Which can be taken to mean he didn't consider Ashton as a suspect at that stage."

"At the time, he couldn't have known that Mr. Ashton would be accused. He was only asked about acts of sabotage."

"You're right. But the woman who has come forward now is hard to refute. She was in a house closer to the mill. Rollins might not have been in a position to see her, although from there she could have seen what Ashton was doing, even though his back was to everyone on the other side of the Cran. Still, the question is, why didn't she speak up in 1916?"

"It means if she gives evidence, he'll be convicted. I spoke to Sergeant Rollins again. But he isn't interested in helping. He's made that clear enough."

"It doesn't bode well for the Ashtons, does it?" Simon asked.

"Will you do something for me?" I told him about the pillow that was used to smother Sister Morris, and about Private Britton. "Sergeant Rollins seemed to recognize the name, but he also appeared to think this man had nothing to do with Ashton or his own shooting."

"He could have met him in France, Bess."

"Yes, I know, but all the same, I'd like to learn more about him. If only to eliminate him from any list of suspects."

"I can't promise you I will learn anything about a pillow," he said with a smile, "but I'll look up Britton's whereabouts. You do know, of course, that there may be more than one man by that name." And then he was gone.

When I had a moment, I read the letter from my mother. It was the usual chatty missive, and for a few minutes I could hear her voice and see the faces of those at home. The Vicar was planning a Thanksgiving Service if the war ended, and there was a feeling that the news could come at any moment, even though it was still only rumor. The last of the apples had been picked before the weather changed, and my mother had helped dry slices for winter pies and sauces. The frog in the pond at the bottom of the garden hadn't been seen for more than a fortnight, and it was thought he had hibernated deep in the mud at the bottom. And there had only been two cases of influenza reported this autumn, both of them on one of the outlying farms.

I finished the letter and returned it to its envelope. Somerset seemed a very long way away. With a sigh, I put the envelope in my correspondence box and went back to work. For the wounded and dying, the war's end wouldn't come soon enough.

To everyone's chagrin—most particularly the Yorkshireman's—the black aircraft returned two days later, flying low and catching a half dozen new recruits out in the open.

I accompanied a convoy back to the base hospital—
this time without the attentions of the black aircraft—
and found Matron waiting for me when I got in.

"Sister, you're taking wounded back to England.
I've sent a runner for your kit. We have a number of
very bad cases. They'll need further surgery when
they reach London. That's why we're sending an experienced nurse with them. Make your report about the
men you've just brought in, and as soon as your kit
arrives, we'll load the ambulances for Calais."

I settled my patients and then with Matron visited
the men who would be traveling with me. Gray-faced,
their eyes barely registering my presence, they lay in
drug-induced stupors. We went over their histories,
where they were wounded, what had been done, and
what the prognosis was: in most cases, grim.

When the ambulances pulled out of the hospital,
they moved with care, trying to avoid the worst of the
ruts, keeping a steady but gentle pace when we reached
the main road.

Mercifully the ship was in, and I was able to arrange
immediate transfer of my cases, handing the second
officer the forms Matron had already completed.

I knew this man—Lieutenant Harcourt—and
together we watched as the orderlies unloaded each
stretcher and brought it aboard with great care. My
seven cases were not taken below decks but to the

former salon of this ship. It would save them a painful jostling. Ten more such cases were brought in from another base hospital, and I recognized the Sister in charge. We had worked together many times before.

The rest of the wounded were brought aboard, and as soon as the last of the ambulance drivers and orderlies had stepped ashore, ropes were cast off and we began to move slowly out into the roads. At first the gentle movement—it was a clear, calm day—seemed to be comforting to my patients, but the increasing roll began to take its toll. I had to be watchful, to be certain they didn't vomit and breathe it in. A very real danger for anyone lying on his back and helpless.

We made it to Dover without losing anyone, and I stood there, watching my patients being carried off to the waiting ambulances that would see them on the London train. Lieutenant Harcourt, once more standing beside me, his duties done for the moment, looked down.

"You're tired, Bess. Get some sleep if you can in London."

"I'll try," I promised, and he bent down to kiss my cheek as I made to follow the last man off the ship.

"Stay safe," he said, and was gone.

I'd met such good men while serving with Queen Alexandra's Imperial Military Nursing Service. And lost a good many friends as well. It was the cost of war, of course, but now I wished them safe at home at last. Lieutenant Harcourt had a fiancée in Oxford, and the Captain had recently been blessed with his third child, a little girl. A future, if God granted them one.

Boarding the train, I ran into Diana, another one of my flatmates, who was also bringing patients back. We only had time for a brief embrace and exchange of news, and then we were busy with our charges.

Diana was not staying in Canterbury. She was taking the next available train back to Dover, where her fiancé was stationed at Dover Castle.

When I arrived in London, my charges were carefully offloaded and taken once more to waiting ambulances, and I was occupied for nearly three quarters of an hour with Matron from the London hospital taking charge of their care. I was pleased to hand them over alive—there had been a very good chance that I would lose at least one on the homeward voyage. That done, I collected my kit and started toward the exit from Victoria Station.

And there, to my surprise, stood my mother and the Colonel Sahib, waiting for me.

No end pleased, I greeted them and was swept up in my father's arms, with a jubilant "It's time you were here in London. I was beginning to think that it was Major Ashton's charms keeping you in Canterbury."

"I had very ill patients this trip. They're to be treated here in London. But how on earth did you know I'd be here, and on this train? There hadn't been time in Dover to telephone you."

"I've been reduced to bribing the Royal Navy," my father said, laughing.

My mother added dryly, give me a huge hug, "That nice Lieutenant Harcourt sent us a telegram. We only just had time to jump in the motorcar and drive like madmen to London."

"How kind of him!" I exclaimed as my father took my kit from me, and we began to walk toward the waiting motorcar.

They took me first to Mrs. Hennessey's so that I could wash my face and leave my kit before going to a late supper somewhere.

That was the plan. Only it didn't work out that way.

Chapter Eleven

Mrs. Hennessey heard footsteps in the hall, and peered around her door.

"Bess, dear!" she exclaimed, and then saw my parents just behind me.

"Hallo, Mrs. Hennessey," I said cheerfully. "Is anyone else here? My father has volunteered to take my kit up to the flat for me. Is that all right?"

Mrs. Hennessey was very strict about the good names of her young ladies, as she called us. No male above the age of seven was allowed to go up the stairs, not even my father, not even Simon (whom she credited with saving her life not so very long ago).

She stood there in her doorway, looking flustered and confused.

"Is everything all right?" She looked over my father's shoulder. "Is it that nice young man? Simon? Has something happened?"

It was our turn to stare.

"Simon?" my mother asked quickly.

"What is it? What's wrong?" my father put in at almost the same time.

I went to her and took her hands. "What is it?" I asked, trying to keep the alarm from my voice.

She gestured over her shoulder to her sitting room. "I didn't know—it came not ten minutes ago. I was afraid to open it."

I walked past her into the sitting room and saw a telegram lying on the tea table.

I picked it up. It was marked *URGENT*, and it was addressed to me in care of Mrs. Hennessey.

I went back out into the entry and held the telegram up for my parents to see.

All the while my mind was busy. Simon was in France. Had something happened to him? But if it was Simon, surely the War Office or the Army would have contacted my father at once . . .

"Open it," the Colonel Sahib commanded.

I tore it open and looked first to see who had sent it.

"It's from Diana," I said in surprise. I went back to the message, reading it aloud.

"*Went to Canterbury to dinner. A Philip Ashton attempted suicide this morning in his cell. Felt you should know. Is this the Ashton you treated in France?*"

Depend on Diana to remember the name of an attractive man. She had met Mark when she had brought wounded to hospital, and she had told me later that he was the perfect match for me. She had made a face at me when I pointed out that he was engaged to be married.

Diana, happy with her own future, was delighted to arrange the affairs of others.

But this wasn't Mark. It was his father. What had happened?

I looked up at my father. "I must go," I said. "I must find out if this is true. Mrs. Ashton must be out of her mind with worry."

The Colonel Sahib frowned. "I can't drive you. I'm taking the train—er—north tomorrow morning. I left my luggage at my club. Still, a train will get you there faster. I'll see what I can do."

He thanked Mrs. Hennessey and turned to go.

"I'll stay here, shall I? Until you bring the motor-car back." My mother walked over to Mrs. Hennessey, who was still looking alarmed and uncertain. Taking her arm, she added, "We'll have a small glass of sherry, shall we?"

My father picked up my kit while I said good-bye to Mrs. Hennessey and my mother, then hurried after him.

"What if there's no space?" I asked, climbing into his motorcar.

"Let me worry about that." He turned the crank, got in beside me, and drove back the way we'd come.

The station was crowded, as I'd expected it would be. But the Colonel Sahib took no notice. He found the stationmaster just coming out of the little café, and said, "Colonel Crawford. This Sister missed her connections. It's imperative that she reach Canterbury as soon as possible."

Looking over my father's shoulder at the crowded platform, the stationmaster shook his gray head. "There's no room to be had, sir. With the best will in the world."

"I'm sure someone will sit on the floor, if necessary, to give this young woman his seat."

"If you find him, sir, I'll be happy to give her a ticket."

My father walked toward the crowd. The train hadn't come in yet, but people were milling about, saying good-bye, looking for friends, staring into space as they wished the train would arrive and be done with it.

Making his way through the throng, men saluting and stepping aside as he passed, he spotted a young corporal in The Buffs.

Making for him, my father tapped him on the shoulder.

The young corporal turned to see who it was, then squared his shoulders and saluted. "Sir," he said.

"Heading for Dover, are you, Corporal?"

"Yes, sir."

"This young woman needs to be in Canterbury as soon as possible. Will you give up your seat and make the best of the journey, so that she can travel?"

Glancing at me out of the corner of his eye, the corporal said at once, "Yes, sir, be happy to, sir. A Sister saved my foot after the Somme. My pleasure, sir."

"Good man," my father said, just as we heard the train's whistle followed by the engine's roar as it came into the station. To me, he said, "Stay here. I'll bring your ticket."

I nodded and he disappeared into the crowd. I turned to my savior.

"What's your name, Corporal?" I asked, smiling.

"Miller, Sister. From Huntingdon."

"Thank you, Corporal Miller. I hope you won't be too uncomfortable."

"No, Sister. I'll be fine."

My father was back with my ticket, handing it to me and saying, "Godspeed," as the stationmaster blew his whistle and everyone headed toward the train. Corporal Miller saw to it that I had a seat by the window in a first-class compartment, although there were already several officers in occupation.

"Call me if you need anything," he said. "I'll be in the corridor just there."

I thanked him again, then turned quickly as the train began to move, waving to my father, who was standing to one side, watching to be sure I was settled.

And then we were pulling out of the station, and for the first time I could think about what might be waiting for me in Canterbury.

We sat on a siding for a quarter of an hour to give a train full of wounded the right of way—that was just outside Rochester—and then we were pulling into Canterbury. I said good-bye to Corporal Miller, who had managed to find me a cup of tea and a bun as well as giving me his seat.

Two of the officers were disembarking there—I'd discovered that they were on leave—and one of them carried my kit as far as the street. They found a cab for me, and I gave the address of the police station.

I had no way of reaching Abbey Hall, but I hoped I could find out something from Inspector Brothers.

I went up the steps to the police station and opened the door.

The sergeant at the desk looked up, and got to his feet when he saw me.

"Sister," he said with a nod. "What can I do for you?"

I expect he was thinking that I'd been addressed by someone in the street and had come to report it.

I said, as firmly as I could, "My name is Crawford. Inspector Brothers knows who I am. I understand my cousin tried to kill himself this morning. I've just arrived from France, and I've come here for the latest word before going on to Cranbourne."

He couldn't disprove that I was a cousin. I didn't think Inspector Brothers would know any better, either. And it was clear that I already knew what had happened. He chose discretion over valor and said, "You must speak to Inspector Brothers." I wasn't sure that the Inspector would appreciate the decision.

"Thank you."

I waited while he walked down a passage and opened a door. After a moment he came back and ushered me into the Inspector's office.

There was only one chair in front of the desk, and I took it without invitation, as if by right. I had learned, dealing with Authority, that the best offense was to appear to be perfectly comfortable and in control.

"I remember you," he said, frowning. "You were at the Hall when I took Ashton into custody."

"I was," I said, without explaining how I'd come to be there. "Can you tell me if my cousin is still alive?"

"He is." His mouth twisted in a grimace. "He tried to cut his wrists."

"Where is he now?"

"In hospital. Under guard."

"As you can see, I'm a nursing Sister. I should like permission to look in on him and make certain he's been given every care."

"The doctor has already seen him."

"That may well be. But it is your doctor, Inspector, and I am with Queen Alexandra's Imperial Military Nursing Service. I'm trained to inspect wounds. The man's family has a right to know that these—injuries— are indeed self-inflicted."

"He tried to kill himself," he expostulated. "What more proof do you need than that?"

"Has his wife seen him? Or his son? Mr. Groves, perhaps? No? Then I shall have to insist that you allow my visit. The news of what happened is common knowledge, Inspector. It will not look good if you refuse to let Mr. Ashton's family see for themselves that all is well. It will appear that you have something to hide in this matter." I wasn't at all sure of my legal grounds, but I hoped the Inspector didn't know that.

I could see that he was on the fence, uncertain what to do with me. I crossed my fingers in the pocket of my apron, and waited.

But it looked as if he was going to refuse. Time for the next salvo. "I should think that you prefer not to have it said at my cousin's trial that he'd been driven to take his own life while in your custody. Or that he was perhaps—helped—in that direction. After all, you've refused to allow his family to see him. There is no certainty that his health hasn't deteriorated in the time he's been in this place." Still no sign of capitulation. Beginning to worry now, I went on. "A newspaper account of his condition would be useful in procuring him a fair trial in another jurisdiction."

I could see from his eyes that I'd made my point, and I sent up a silent prayer of gratitude for my father's advice. As we'd driven to Victoria Station, he and I had hammered out the best arguments I could use in gaining access to Philip Ashton.

"All right," Inspector Brothers said grudgingly. "I'll give you a pass to see him. No more than five minutes."

"Fifteen," I amended. "I have no way of knowing how long it will take for me to assess his condition."

"Fifteen," he agreed against his will. "Not a second longer."

He scribbled something on a piece of paper and handed it to me. I read it before I stood up.

Sister Crawford is allowed fifteen minutes and fifteen minutes only with the prisoner.

"If there are other wounds or signs of bruising or abuse, I will report this at once to the doctors in charge. Is that understood, Inspector?"

"You won't find any," he said sourly.

"I sincerely hope I shan't." I nodded and left the little office, walking down the passage, expecting at any moment to hear Inspector Brothers call me back and tell me he'd changed his mind. But I nodded to the sergeant at the desk and stepped out the door without any trouble.

Sighing with relief, I shifted my kit to the other hand and hurried to the hospital, opening the main doors and walking to Reception. The orderly behind the desk gave me directions, and in a matter of minutes I was making my way to the first floor, where Mr. Ashton was being kept under guard.

I could see the uniformed constables as soon as I came up the stairs and turned into the corridor. They were sitting in chairs outside a private ward.

To one side was a small room where families could wait for news, and as I walked past it, Mark Ashton said, "Bess? My God, where did you come from?"

He was on his feet, coming toward me, but I raised a hand to stop him and slipped into the room before he could step out into the passage. He looked drawn, tired to the bone.

"I can't stay," I said quickly. "I have permission to examine the patient. Have you seen him?"

"No," Mark said. "They won't let us near the room. I took my mother and Clara home not half an hour ago. They've been here most of the afternoon, since the news first reached us."

"How did you hear about what happened?"

"It was Mrs. Lacey. Our cook. She came into Canterbury to do her marketing, and she overheard someone talking about it. He'd seen the ambulance arriving at the police station, and someone in the crowd told him what was happening."

"Wait for me downstairs. I'm allowed fifteen minutes with your father. I'll meet you when I've finished. It might not be wise for us to be seen leaving together. Inspector Brothers could still send someone to stop me."

"Let me go in with you—"

"You can't." I held up the slip of paper that gave me permission. "If you try, they might stop both of us."

He nodded reluctantly. "Yes, all right. At least someone will see him, speak to him, find out what really happened."

He stood aside and I went back into the corridor, walking briskly toward the guarded room.

When I got there, the two constables on duty blocked the door as I started to enter.

I handed them my permission, and said pleasantly, "Good evening. I've just seen Inspector Brothers. If you have any questions, you're to contact him."

That seemed to reassure them, for they stepped aside, and one of the constables opened the door for me.

When he started to follow me inside the room, I said, "You're to remain on duty while I examine the patient."

He stepped back and allowed me to enter the room alone. I thanked him.

Philip Ashton was lying in bed, covered by a sheet. His face was gray with fatigue and he seemed much thinner than when I'd last seen him. I thought he might be asleep, because his eyes were closed.

I touched his shoulder gently, and his eyes flew open, staring at me with alarm. He relaxed when he saw the uniform, and then he recognized me.

"Bess—how on earth did you get in here?"

"With great difficulty. What happened? There isn't much time."

"I tried to slash my wrists." He pulled an arm from beneath the sheet and showed me a bandaged wrist. "But I was careful not to cut very deeply. Still, there was a good deal of blood, and they were frightened enough to bring me here. I thought they might allow me to see Helen or Mark. I've had no news of my family at all."

"They're well and quite worried about you. Mark is here in the waiting room downstairs, but they won't allow him to see you. And they won't let Mrs. Ashton visit you. It's Inspector Brothers's doing, but I don't think Mr. Groves has pressed him too hard." I unwrapped the bandages as I spoke, and looked at the cuts on his wrists before carefully rewrapping them. He was right. He'd done what he could to maximize the amount of blood with several shallow cuts, but none of them was deep enough to be life-threatening. "Why are you still here? Why haven't they returned you to your cell?"

"The doctor was worried. I've lost several stone. I've been refusing to eat."

"But you need your strength. For the trial."

"Bess. They can't beat me, it would show. But the food has been nearly inedible, and I've refused it. That didn't work, and so I managed to cut my arms. I can't bear that cell any longer. I have no exercise, I have nothing to read, I can see the sun for only a matter of minutes each day, when it shines over the wall outside my window. I'm going mad, and I must listen as my guards make macabre jokes about the hangman. Groves and Worley tell me to throw myself on the mercy of the court, that the evidence against me is too strong to fight, that I must convince the jury that I kicked over a stone and it lit the spark that started the fire. That I didn't see it until too late. Or some such."

"Is that what happened?" I couldn't conceal my surprise.

"God, no. No. I was standing there, listening for any signs of life in the rubble, and I heard the shouting behind me. When I turned, there were men coming with shovels and pickaxes to dig for survivors. I went to tell them that it was too dangerous, we'd have to do it by hand. Before I could reach the Cran, the fire was suddenly visible. I still don't know if there was a fire before the explosions began or if it was spontaneous afterward. But of course it must have appeared that I was running from it."

Were these the same men who now claimed he was gleeful as he left the ruins, the fire already showing behind him? If not, why hadn't at least one of them stepped forward?

Philip Ashton hadn't spoken about what he'd seen in nearly two years—not since he'd given evidence to the Army. And now, as if having been trapped in a cell with no one to speak to, day after day, he couldn't stop. "Have Mark and Helen agreed to that plea? I need to know. Groves tells me they feel it would save my life. I can't believe that's true. I can't believe they would be willing to take such a risk. Because that's what it will be, Bess. If the jury has a taste for a hanging, they won't hear what I have to say, and if there's an appeal after conviction, then it's on record that I've confessed. It's one of the reasons I did *this*." He nodded toward his other wrist as I finished rebandaging it.

"I don't believe anyone at the Hall knows about this plea. But they're as unhappy with what's happening as you are. Please. Don't listen to Groves. Or Worley. I don't think either of them has your best interests at heart." I put a hand on his arm. "There's so little time. Let me tell you what else we've learned." And I explained what we knew about Sergeant Rollins and his sister, Agatha, and about Florence Benning, the woman who had come forward so late in the day. "Even Sergeant Rollins doesn't believe her. We've got to find a way to prove all these people are lying."

He lay there, taking it in.

I said urgently, "Can you think of anyone who could be behind this? Someone who wishes you ill?"

"No. Not that kind of hatred. It doesn't make sense."

"But you're seen as a murderer. All those men. And whoever it is, he—or she—is believed. That's what's worrying Mark. It's like fighting in the dark, to try to counteract that kind of venom."

He shook his head. "I didn't kill them. If anyone is to blame, it's the way the Army pushed for a higher and higher output of powder. I understood the need, I knew how the war was going, but it's dangerous work, it can't be rushed or steps skipped. Men make mistakes when there's someone urging them on, telling them they must increase output. The Army kept telling *me* there was a war to fight, and it was essential that we win it. That we'd have to take the risk. That's what I was arguing with the foreman about just that morning. He told me the men were tired, and I needed to speak to Captain Collier about giving them more time to rest. I felt it was better to hire more people, so that we could keep to schedule. I'd already written to London, asking permission to do just that."

I had hoped he might know something or have seen something that could be used in his defense. Instead he'd kept silent because he thought people should know him well enough to believe he would never do anything that would harm the mill or the people who worked in it. Philip Ashton, the man with the impeccable record at the mill. The man everyone looked up to and trusted. And ought to trust still.

He didn't seem to understand that such a fall from grace—being arrested—made enemies born of disappointment and grief turn on him like hyenas on a wounded antelope. I could see he still found it hard to believe that they could do such a thing.

And he was tiring. I could see that as well. The loss of weight was catching up with him.

I said, "Is there anyone who could speak on your behalf? Anyone with the Army or the Government who might explain to the court just what they believed had happened? Surely there must be someone who could point out just how hard the War Office was pushing those men."

"Captain Collier, although he's probably in France somewhere, if he's still alive."

But he sounded doubtful, and I could understand why. If the Captain was tasked with keeping output as high as possible, he might be reluctant to come forward and admit to having any responsibility for what had happened. It was very unlikely that his view of events would ever be the same as Philip Ashton's. Friend or not.

We were nearly out of time.

I still had several more questions to ask—about Corporal Britton, about Mrs. Benning, even about Young Mr. Groves, but I decided on the most important one. "Can you tell me why Sergeant Rollins refuses to come back to England to speak on your behalf? Or at least give someone a statement that could be used at your trial? It might help refute some of these more recent accusations. If I knew what the problem was, I might be able to persuade him to change his mind."

The door opened before he could answer. I now had only seconds left. I laid a hand on his forehead, as if judging whether or not he had a fever. And bending over him, I spoke softly so that only he could hear me. "Please, if you think of anything, tell Mr. Groves to pass it on to Mark. You must *try.* And don't give in. Mark is doing all he can."

And then I turned and walked briskly out of the room.

I went to find the doctor to ask what was to be done about their prisoner patient.

"He's been refusing to eat," the doctor told me, annoyance in his voice. "I can't say I blame him, I can't imagine that the food brought in to him is anything he's been accustomed to."

"It isn't a matter of what he's accustomed to, is it?" I suggested. "I believe he's abandoned hope."

"It's the weight of his guilt."

"Is it? Did the police tell you that? Or is it a very real fear that he's been abandoned by the law? He hasn't been allowed to see his family—no reading materials—no exercise. He might as well be a condemned man."

The doctor seemed surprised. "Are you telling me the truth?"

"Ask Mr. Ashton yourself. Speak to his gaolers. I've only just been informed myself. It's—troubling."

"So many men died in that blast. It's inconceivable that something didn't go wrong."

This was exactly the frame of mind that made it possible for so many people to believe the worst about Philip Ashton.

I swallowed what I'd have liked to say, that he wasn't being very fair. I already knew that fairness didn't enter into it.

"I'm sure something did go wrong. And the Army came to the conclusion that it was a tragic accident. *They* didn't put the blame on Mr. Ashton."

"Yes, well, they demoted their own man."

This was news to me.

"I'm sorry?"

"They demoted him to Lieutenant and put him behind a desk in London. Someone told me that. I don't recall who it was, but he'd been a brevetted Captain for the duration." A nurse was walking down the hall toward him, and he said, "I must go, there's a patient in surgery. I'll do what I can for Ashton."

I put out a hand to stop him. "Where is Captain—Lieutenant—Collier now?"

"I have no idea."

And then he was gone.

It was late, but I hoped to find the telegraph office to send a message to my father. And then I remembered that he was leaving on the morning train. Most likely it wouldn't reach him.

And where was Simon? Still in France? I could use his objective viewpoint. I needed information, information I didn't think Mark would have.

I was on my way to meet him when I discovered the hospital had a telephone and I begged the use of it.

My mother wasn't at home. She was still in London. I left a message. And another at my father's club.

Mark was waiting outside for me. He must be eaten up by anxiety by now! I hurried out the door and saw his motorcar in the shadows at the corner of the building.

He got out at once and ran toward me.

"How is he? What happened?"

I told him. "The doctor will do what he can," I ended with more optimism than I actually felt. "But he's in no danger. I promise you."

Even in the light spilling out from the hospital windows he looked grim.

"It's true then, that they're pressing him not to fight."

"Yes, I think Worley must feel that it's impossible to go forward, and he's going to lose if he does. That it's best to hope for mercy. But I'm not ready yet to believe that. Mark, what happened to the officer who was the liaison between your father and the Army?"

"Captain Collier? I've no idea. He was recalled during the investigation. Well, there was nothing for him to do in Cranbourne. I seem to remember some possibility of sending him north to oversee the expansion of the Scottish mill that was to take over from Ashton Mill."

I said, wanting to pace in my frustration, "Yes, but I need to find him."

"Do you think he knew more than he told the authorities?"

"He might be able to tell a jury that your father couldn't have caused the deaths of those men. He can give evidence for the defense, explain how difficult it was to keep up production, the pressure on the workers, the dangers they faced. He was your father's opposite number. That would bear weight. It would help."

"Is there any chance I'll be allowed to see my father?"

"Not tonight," I said, trying to soften the blow. "But he's all right. Just—discouraged. As you'd expect."

"Come on, then. Into the motor. We'll sort this out at Abbey Hall."

It was the invitation I was waiting for. An opportunity to speak to Mrs. Ashton.

"Thank you, Mark." He took my kit and carried it to the motorcar, and in a matter of minutes we were on our way. But he had looked back at the hospital wistfully, as if he could see through the very walls into his father's room.

Mrs. Ashton was delighted to see me. Clara perhaps a little less so. I was given my old room and offered a late supper when they discovered that I hadn't eaten since breakfast.

They were all eager to hear what I could tell them about Philip Ashton. Mrs. Ashton had been fretting about her husband all day, and I could see that she had tried to put a good face on her worry and it had given her a thundering headache instead.

I repeated what I'd told Mark, leaving out only what the doctor had said about the liaison officer.

And then the questions began. How the patient had looked, how he felt, how serious were his wounds, asked in endless variations, as if to elicit some small comforting fact that I might have forgotten or left out. I repeated myself a number of times, trying to give them a little hope.

"I told everyone I was a cousin," I said ruefully. "A lie, but Inspector Brothers had seen me here in the house, and so he was willing to accept it."

"Never mind," Mrs. Ashton said. "It's a very small lie compared to those being told about *us*. What's more, it worked." She put out her hand. "I'd be glad to call you cousin, if the Inspector comes prying. But tell me . . ."

The round of questions began again.

"I knew I should have sent him food from the house," she worried. "I knew it must be better than what the police could manage."

"They wouldn't allow it," Mark reminded her.

"How much weight has he lost? Are you sure it's not serious?"

It was nearly midnight when Mark called a halt to the questions and sent us all to bed. I climbed the stairs gratefully, and my eyes were closing even as I blew out my lamp.

The quiet room, the quiet night, played their part, and it was nearly seven when I awoke.

It was difficult to get Mrs. Ashton alone. Clara was there, and if not Clara, Mark, debating whether or not to return to the hospital waiting room in the hope of catching a glimpse of his father.

In the end, he and Clara went off to Canterbury together, although I knew it to be hopeless.

Grateful for this opportunity, I turned to Mrs. Ashton as we walked in her enclosed garden. The day had turned decidedly chilly, and we wore wraps against it, even though we were protected from the wind.

"What happened to the officer who was the liaison between Mr. Ashton and the Army?" I asked, not knowing any better way to broach the subject.

She stared at me, then walked on. "I have no idea. The Army recalled him."

"But you don't believe that," I said. "You think he's still here, somewhere, in Cranbourne or else in Canterbury or one of the nearby villages."

"No, truly, he was recalled. To London. They felt he was too close to the situation to take part in the Army's inquiry into what happened," she said. "I expect he's in France somewhere by now. If he's still alive. Philip didn't keep in touch with him, so I have no idea."

"Then why did you stand at the window on the night of the fire, when you thought everyone had gone to bed, and threaten someone if he hurt your family?"

Surprised, she walked on a few steps, and then turned.

"Bess. How did you hear that?"

"I had walked outside, hoping to find footprints or something else, to show Constable Hood in the morning."

"I wanted to lash out at whoever had done this. I thought perhaps it was one of the women who had been widowed, and she might be frightened off if she could be convinced we knew who had started the fire. But I don't really believe that all these people making our lives so wretched are acting on their own. I've lived in Cranbourne since Philip brought me here as his bride. I know these villagers. And so I've been looking for whoever it is who began this business. But I can't find him—or her. Every time I think I might be getting close, I realize I'm wrong again. I tried to persuade Philip that it was all a conspiracy, but he never wanted to believe his own people had turned against him."

I didn't know whether to believe her.

"Why were you out there?" she asked, as she realized the implications of what I'd told her. "Was Mark with you? Clara?"

"No one was with me." And then, goaded by disbelief, I said, "I saw your face, Mrs. Ashton. You believed you *knew*."

She walked on, and I followed her. I was about to ask again, even if she threw me out of her house, when she stopped.

"Yes, all right. At one point I was afraid it was Alex. Alex Craig. Well, no, that's not quite true. I didn't want to believe it could be. But I was frightened too, you see. Not thinking clearly. I knew he sometimes came to the house late at night, when he couldn't sleep. He loved Eloise the way I'd loved someone once, when I was very young. And he lost her twice. First to Mark and then to the Spanish influenza. I had hoped letting him say good-bye to her would help him. And so I felt betrayed that night, when we had the fire. I was upset over Philip, and seeing the sitting room alight was the last straw. And I couldn't tell Mark what I feared, could I?"

Some of the tension went out of her face, as if she was glad to have told someone what she believed at the time. But I still wasn't sure I believed *her*. Yet, in a quick search in my memory of all the people I knew of who might be involved, I couldn't think of anyone else she might feel so intense about. And until the incident with Nan, the dog, the personal attacks had actually seemed to stop.

"Tell me about the liaison officer," I asked, attempting to turn the conversation now. "Do you think he would speak on behalf of your husband if we could find him? It might go a long way in the trial if he explained to the jurors what working in the mill was like."

"Captain Collier? I didn't like him very much." She walked over to the border and snapped off a seed pod. It fell apart in her hand, and she looked at it in surprise, as if it had hurt her.

"You didn't?"

"He was always on about what should be done to increase production, and Philip had enough on his mind without that constant pressure," she said, slowly, as if trying to put her feelings into words. "He was ambitious, anxious to prove himself. To keep that temporary rank."

Ambitious. I was suddenly reminded of the portion of a letter I'd found in the study, secreted in a Jane Austen novel. Had Mrs. Ashton asked questions about Collier of a friend in London, because she was worried about her husband? Possibly even before the explosion? I thought it might be likely. Who else could it have been? And, of course, she wouldn't have wanted her husband to know about her query.

She was still talking about Collier. "And yet he had very little experience with gunpowder. Or at the Front, for that matter. He'd worked in Stores—he'd had some experience with manufacturers; boots, blankets, that sort of thing. And so it was thought he could learn about cordite as well. He wanted to be seen as the Army's man in Cranbourne, and it was a constant battle to rein in his enthusiasm for new methods that hadn't been tested. Philip was always trying to keep him focused on what was possible or realistic. I don't think he realized what a pest he'd become. Even at social gatherings he was always looking for some advantage to himself. I learned to avoid him. But to answer your question, I don't think his testimony would go very far in helping Philip. Even if he willingly came forward."

"I've heard you and Mark mention several times that Captain Collier pushed the workers too hard for greater output. Does Mr. Groves know this? It could be important."

She shook her head. "Not hard enough to make them careless. That was the last thing he'd want to happen. It was Philip he pushed. And it made Philip appear old-fashioned, uninterested in progress or improvement. Which was unfair, when he had so many lives to consider."

"Did the Captain blame Mr. Ashton for what happened?"

"He was as stunned as everyone else. He'd gone into Canterbury the evening before, to have dinner with a friend on his way to the Front, and that morning they went to early services before Captain Collier saw him off on his train. He was just leaving the railway station when the explosion occurred. People were shocked, wondering if Dover was being shelled by a German cruiser or if there had been an earthquake, or a zeppelin raid, and it was an hour before the Captain could find someone to take him back to Cranbourne. By that time, it was too late, the fire was well and truly burning, and there was nothing anyone could do. To his credit, he sent men straightaway to The Swale and all along the coastline to look for German boats and saboteurs. The Army commended him for that. But of course there weren't any." She let the seeds sift through her fingers, watching them fall. "In some ways we'd have been better off, all of us, if it had been Germans. Even the Captain. He might well have gained a promotion out of it. Have you said anything to Mark about finding Collier and asking him to appear?"

"Briefly. He didn't know what had become of the Captain."

"Not surprising. Mark barely knew him." She smiled wryly. "Except through my letters, complaining about the Captain's latest peccadillo." We stood for a moment by the fishpond, watching the wind ripple the clear surface. "I'm afraid, Bess. I don't know where to turn for help. Philip had so many friends. And so many of them have fallen away since the troubles began. Or had already moved to London for the duration. I've thought of writing to several of them, but I never quite found the courage. I was afraid they might reject my plea for support. I've had enough of rejection now."

She turned to stare unseeing at the house. "There's something else that could be looked into. The women who worked at the mill were terribly upset. For one thing, of course, they'd just lost their livelihood and many of their friends if not relatives. A number of them had breakdowns. It haunted them that if it had been a Saturday or a Monday, they'd have been killed as well. For another, there's the fact that we found so few remains. The ruins were searched as soon as they were cool enough. There had been talk about a mass grave. But there wasn't enough to bury, Bess. If you go into St. Anne's, to the nave, there's a large brass memorial plaque to the dead. We had that put up, listing every man's name. But the women who survived the dead, and the women who might have been killed if the explosion had happened on another day, felt it was not enough. They raised the money themselves to put up a stone in the churchyard." She cleared her throat, as if it was suddenly tight. "It was as if they felt our money was tainted. That the brass plaque was erected to salve our consciences."

I hadn't seen either of the memorials.

"They can bear grudges, these village women. They might even want to see Philip hang."

I didn't have the heart to tell her that they had also turned their backs on the Vicar.

"Well," she went on. "That's water under the bridge, is it not? I can't bear to think about it any longer. Are you absolutely certain that Philip's wounds weren't life-threatening? That he didn't at least try to kill himself? You aren't holding back something, are you?"

But even as I tried to reassure her, I knew it wasn't enough.

Chapter Twelve

Mark had no luck at the hospital. He was refused permission to speak to his father, or even to see him.

Angry and worried, he went to call on Mr. Groves, and as he related the meeting to his mother and to me, it was clearly not a pleasant one.

"It's true what Father told Bess—that they want him to throw himself on the mercy of the court and claim that the fire was an accident. They're suggesting that when he went over to see the extent of the damage, he inadvertently set off a spark that started the blaze. Groves and Worley feel it's the only way to avoid a far worse outcome."

I said, "But I thought no one was certain whether the fire caused the explosion or followed it. Besides, if your father admits culpability, he could be held responsible for the deaths of workers who might have survived the blasts."

"No one could have survived," Mrs. Ashton said.

"But there's no proof of that, is there? He could find himself faced with endless claims for wrongful deaths—loss of income—whatever someone wants to accuse him of. Even the Army could come back to you and demand money because they couldn't rebuild in the ruins."

Mark said, "I know. It would break us financially. But the alternative could well be a hanging."

"Philip will never agree to such a plea," Mrs. Ashton said.

Clara, who had been silent for a time, spoke up. "What if he does agree? And the court refuses to accept his plea? And they insist on trying him anyway? He'll be seen as doubly guilty. By his own admission and by the findings of the jury."

"She's right," Mrs. Ashton said. "Is Mr. Groves so certain that such a plea would be accepted?"

"He can't promise anything. Feelings have run high, there have been comments made in the newspaper."

"Then we have no choice but to agree to the trial. And hope for the best."

"It's difficult to change a trial to another town," I said. "But it would be worth trying. That is, if the police or the Chief Constable would allow it." I wanted to tell them instead that a change of briefs would be much wiser. Finding someone who believed in Philip Ashton and would fight for him.

But all of us, sitting there in that pleasant room, knew that the trial would very likely end with a conviction.

Unless something was done soon.

Mark got up and paced the floor. "I can't believe this is happening. Not to my father. I feel *helpless*."

"Sit down, my dear, I'll pour you a whisky. We'll think of something."

But of course none of us believed we could.

Later that afternoon, I walked as far as St. Anne's and found the large stone in the churchyard marked with a cross and the words *Our Loved Ones*. Followed by the date. Very simple and possibly all they could afford, the survivors and the women who worked in the mill. But it brought tears to my eyes.

The church door was unlocked, and I slipped inside. It was cool and dim, the way churches so often are on weekdays. My footsteps echoed, and I was glad to find that no one else was there.

I walked first down the side aisle to my right, looking for a large brass plaque. There were small ones here, clusters of them, memorials put up to the dead buried in France. An officer here, a private soldier there, giving their rank and the date and name of the battle in which they'd been killed. Others gave the name of the battle below the date of death, and added, *Died of Wounds*. It was a sad array.

I found the larger, more ornate plaque set between two lovely stained glass windows. It depicted a simple cross at the top with engraved lilies to either side.

This was followed by the words:

IN MEMORIAM
THE VICTIMS OF THE ASHTON MILL
EXPLOSION AND FIRE

There followed the date and then, in four rows, the names of all the men who had been killed that day.

And below the list was a final line: *Oremus pro invicem.*

If I remembered my Latin, it meant *Let us pray for one another.*

A very touching tribute. I thought it must be Mr. Ashton's dearest wish, that they comfort one another, the dead and the living.

It occurred to me that grief sometimes divided people rather than drawing them together.

I was just leaving the church when I encountered the Vicar coming in, a hymnal in his hand.

"Sister Crawford," he said in some surprise. "I didn't know you were back in Cranbourne."

"I came to look in on Mr. Ashton."

"Is he free? I hadn't heard."

"According to the police, he tried to cut his wrists."

"Dear God." He stared at me. "I must go to him. If the police will allow me to visit with him? I've heard that they are very strict about this."

"I don't know. They seem to be unwilling to put themselves out."

"But surely if he's in need of comfort? A man in such despair? I'll travel to Canterbury this evening. And Mrs. Ashton? How is she holding up?"

"Quite bravely. I think events have been hardest for Major Ashton." Changing the subject I added, "I've wished to ask you. By any chance do you know where I can find Captain Collier?"

"He was living in the former foreman's house on the far side of the mill. It was refurbished for the Army's use. While the Army was investigating what had happened, Captain Collier was reassigned. To London, I believe. I never had his address there. But I doubt he stayed in the city for long, given the need for men in France."

"He hasn't come back to visit since he left?"

"Not to my knowledge. Oddly enough I did think I caught sight of him in Canterbury one day. But that was nearly a year ago. You know how it is; you see someone you believe you recognize, but when you catch him up, he generally isn't. There are so many men in uniform."

"Do you get to Canterbury often?"

"Sadly no, my duties have kept me closer to Cranbourne and the Swale villages. Without the mill for employment, there have been hardships. My fellow priests and I do what we can to alleviate it. And then there are those of our parish who receive bad news."

I remembered the Vicar at home in Somerset telling us when he came to dine that his duties had trebled since the war began. Often without the resources necessary to help those in need. My parents had been generous. I wondered if the Ashtons also gave freely.

"Do you remember a Corporal Britton? I'm told he was from Devon, but he appears to have been serving in a Kent regiment."

"The name isn't familiar. And I expect I'd have remembered someone from Devon. They have such a queer accent, don't they?"

I had to smile. Kent had its own accent. And Somerset too, for that matter. I could understand it, having spent a large part of my life there, but to some people it was incomprehensible.

I thanked him and went on my way.

I was aware of the stares as I walked back, and the snubs by those I passed. The mist was beginning to lift, and I hurried, not wanting to deal with a confrontation.

Halfway to the Hall as I turned a corner near the abbey wall, I literally ran into Alex Craig.

He caught my arms to steady me, then recognized me as he released me and stepped back.

"Sister," he said, touching his hat.

"Hallo," I said. And then before I could think better of it I asked him, "I wonder. Do you by any chance know where I can find a man named Britton?"

His mouth twisted. "Still trying to save the Major's father? He's guilty, you must know that."

"There's been no trial," I replied. "Legally, Mr. Aston is still only a suspect."

He considered me for a moment. "You must love him deeply to fight so hard for his father."

Exasperated, I said, "I don't think you realize how self-absorbed you sound. I have no desire to replace Eloise in Major Ashton's affections. Now or at any time in the future. You remind me of his cousin, Clara, leaping to conclusions because you're so filled with jealousy you can't think about anything else." I hadn't meant to mention Clara, but it came out before I could help it. And remembering Mrs. Ashton's fears about this man, I wondered for a frightful moment if he'd tried to burn down the house just because he believed Mark had brought his new fiancée home to meet his parents. It never occurred to me that Alex Craig might have leapt to such a conclusion about my visits. But logic doesn't always enter into the picture where love is concerned.

"I'm not *jealous*," Alex Craig told me, as angry as I'd ever seen anyone. "I wouldn't have replaced Eloise so quickly. I couldn't have. She deserves more than that."

"If you think Mark Ashton hasn't mourned her as fiercely as you appear to have done, then you're sadly mistaken. Whatever else Eloise was, she seems to have touched you and the Major very deeply. I can't imagine what kind of woman she must have been, to be able to do that. But you dishonor her memory if you judge the grief of others and measure it by your own. Now answer my question, if you please, or go away."

"I have no idea who he might be," he said tightly. And with that he brushed past me and limped on down the path by the wall toward the center of Cranbourne.

A PATTERN OF LIES · 335

Watching him, I felt a sudden *frisson* of unease. Alex Craig was certainly in a position to make life unbearable for the Ashtons, as punishment for Mark having won Eloise's heart. He was angry enough to feel many things besides jealousy. I could easily picture him meddling in the Ashton family affairs to salve his own wretchedness at losing Eloise. Even though Mrs. Ashton had been kind to him when Eloise lay dying. Ungrateful man!

Perhaps it wasn't the ghosts of the dead he saw but the ghost of what might have been.

Then I turned away and scolded myself for being quite so fanciful. But that very odd feeling was slow to go away.

Since Alex Craig was definitely not down by the river this morning, I decided it was safe to explore a little on my own. I wasn't quite ready to go back to the Hall.

I walked briskly through the thinning mists toward the river. And when I reached the Cran, I saw that the tide was out and I could cross almost dry-shod.

I scrambled down the embankment and chose my footing carefully. It was a little more difficult to climb the other side because an outcropping of chalk made it very slippery just there. But used as I was to the mud of France, I made it up to the grassy verge of the river.

Careful of the marshy bits, I walked down toward
The Swale, watching the long grasses of late summer
blow in the wind. The Swale was a cold steel gray, and
beyond I could just catch the ripples of current in the
estuary as the sun came out and sparkled across them.
The Isle of Sheppey was still partially floating in mist,
but close in I thought I could pick out sheep idly graz-
ing. In the distance on this side of The Swale I could
see where the fishing fleet lay waiting for the war to
end, and in between lay the abbey, of course, and closer
to that, the land belonging to the Ashtons. There were
the sheep meadows, there the plowed land for the hop
gardens.

Turning, I walked toward the ruins of the gunpowder mill. At first I felt only a scattering of stones
beneath my boots, and then they were large enough to
trip me up. By the time I could see the broken foundations I stopped.

Men were buried here. I wouldn't intrude.

In the distance to my right, I could see a straggling village, and nearer to, the house that must have
belonged to Captain Collier, situated very close by
where the tracks must have come in from the other
Swale villages. They were still shrouded in mist.

The extent of the ruins gave me some feeling for
the size of the mill. After all, during the week, three

hundred or more souls had been employed here in the manufacture of cordite. Now I could identify the ragged, blackened foundations of several dozen smaller buildings grouped by tasks and the broad crater where perhaps a larger one might have stood. The pond that had fed the operation was now shallow and algae covered, as if it had been neglected, but a pair of mallard ducks floated in the small clear pool where it must still be deep enough for them.

I wondered if this winter the nailbourne would rise again, and feel triumphant that there would be no interference with it now.

And throughout the site stood those shattered and broken trees, some of them struggling to put up new shoots, for a leaf continued to cling to the branches here and there, as if desperate to hide the still raw wounds of this place.

I could believe the ruins were haunted. The way the wind whispered in the tall grass sounded like muted voices, and at night there would be a black and shapeless jumble that belonged only to hunting owls or prowling foxes. No one in his right mind would wander here after dark, for no other reason than fear of breaking a limb among the scattered and only half-visible stones.

I turned away, crossing the field of grass toward the river. The tide was just turning, and I made my way back to the far side before my boots were soaked. It was with a feeling of relief that I reached the lane that ran down to Abbey Hall.

Mark was preparing to return to Canterbury. I met him just coming out the door on his way to the motorcar.

"There you are," he said with a smile. "I'm going to have another word with Groves. There has to be something we can do. I can't wait here while they sort it out. Somehow I have to convince Lucius Worley to put up a fight. Do you want to come?"

"Yes, I'd like to. I can stop in the hospital and see what I can learn there."

"Good, yes, that might work." He held the door for me and I stepped in, realizing as I did that my boots were muddy from crossing the river and there were burrs on my skirts from the high grass.

Oh, well. It didn't matter.

We made good time into Canterbury, and found the city nearly empty this morning. Mark dropped me at the hospital, asking, "Do you want me to wait for you?"

"Go on to the solicitor's office. Why don't I meet you later by the cathedral gates?"

"That would be even better. All right, then. Good luck!"

But when I reached the first floor, where Philip Ashton had been under guard, I found the room cleaned, the bedclothes changed, and a new patient lying there with his eyes closed.

I went to find Matron, and waited for her to lock up the dispensary after the morning medicines had been set out for the ward Sisters. I asked if I might speak to her for a moment, and she looked at my uniform and said, "I wasn't informed that we were to have a new Sister this morning." I followed her back to her room, and she gestured to the chair in front of her desk.

I smiled as I sat down. "My name is Sister Crawford, Matron. I was here the other evening, to attend Mr. Ashton, who was brought in by the police after a suicide attempt. I see he's no longer in that room." I hoped she wouldn't probe further and discover I was on leave from duties in France, not posted in Canterbury.

"Ah, yes, Doctor Scott mentioned you to me. He tried to persuade Inspector Brothers to allow us to treat the patient for another few days, but the police refused, since the patient is accused of multiple counts of murder and an escape attempt was feared."

I was surprised. "Escape?"

"So Inspector Brothers insisted. As a result, Mr. Ashton has been returned to his cell."

"Then I should be speaking to Inspector Brothers," I said, swallowing my disappointment.

"I would advise you to do just that," she replied. "Doctor Scott was concerned enough to bring Mr. Ashton's condition to my attention."

I rose and thanked her, moving toward the door.

"Your shoes, Sister. They leave much to be desired."

In the motorcar, I had picked off the burrs on my skirts and even tried to clean my boots before entering the hospital. But Matron's sharp eyes had seen what my efforts had missed.

"Yes, Matron, thank you," I said, and made my escape.

I left the hospital without speaking to anyone else and risking having my identity questioned. But as I stepped out into watery sunshine, my spirits plummeted. Even if I hadn't been able to see Mr. Ashton, I would have been happy to hear he was being kept in hospital a little longer. And it was useless to try to speak to the Inspector again.

I walked toward the gates of the cathedral, knowing I would have to tell Mark my news. But it would be some time before he'd finished his business with Mr. Groves.

My spirits low, I passed the shops with barely a glance at the windows. I stood by the gates for a quarter of an hour, judging by the cathedral's bell, but there was no sign of Mark. I wandered out into the street again, walking aimlessly, unable to stand still.

On a side street, I passed the recruiting office without noticing it, and stopped in the middle of the street, nearly colliding with two women chatting as they strolled along.

It was a very unlikely place to look for information, but I'd tried everything.

I turned and stepped through the open doorway. The officer behind the desk looked up.

"Sister?" he said, getting to his feet.

He was perhaps thirty-five, fair, slim build.

"I'm looking for a friend," I said pleasantly. "I wonder if you can tell me if he's still in Kent."

"I'll try," he answered, "although I don't have records of all the men in Kent serving in various regiments."

"Yes, I do understand that. But Captain Collier was here in this part of Kent for two years. I seem to have lost track of him."

He blinked in surprise. "Captain Collier?"

"Do you know him?"

"I met him several times when he was in Cranbourne. But I'm afraid I haven't heard from him in some time."

"Where did he go when he left Cranbourne?"

"Scotland? I seem to remember hearing something about that."

Disappointed, I said, "Thank you, Lieutenant."

He came around the desk. "Have you known him long?"

"Not very long. But while I was in Canterbury, I thought I might look him up."

"What brings you to Kent?"

"I'm on leave," I answered. "Visiting friends."

"I hope you enjoy your stay," he said. "If I hear from Captain Collier, I'll tell him someone was inquiring after him."

I thanked him before he could ask my name, and left.

It was time to find a telephone and put in a call to my mother. Surely the Colonel Sahib had returned from his latest duty.

But he was still away, Iris, our maid, told me. And my mother was in Chester, calling on another recent widow.

"Where is the Sergeant-Major?" I asked, hoping that Simon at least was at home in Somerset.

"I don't know, Miss. I haven't seen him."

I left messages for my parents and for Simon, most particularly asking for information about Captain Collier and Corporal Britton. "I'll be in Canterbury another two or three days," I said. "At Abbey Hall, the home of the Ashtons. If they learn anything about either of these men, please, let me know as soon as possible."

"I'll be sure to tell them, Miss. Are you all right?"

"I am," I said. "Just worried for the Ashtons."

Putting up the receiver, I hurried back to the cathedral gate, hoping that I hadn't kept Mark waiting.

But he still wasn't there, and after another quarter of an hour, I turned and made my way to the solicitor's chambers.

Chapter Thirteen

The solicitor's clerk welcomed me without enthusiasm. He was a middle-aged man with glasses and thinning iron-gray hair. I asked if Major Ashton was still here.

"Major Ashton is closeted with Mr. Groves. If you'd care to have a seat in Reception, I'll let him know that you're here, Sister . . . ?"

"Sister Crawford," I told him. I couldn't judge from his expression whether he recognized the name or not. He offered me a chair and refreshment, which I politely declined, and I sat there after he'd gone away, listening to the raised voices coming from one of the inner rooms. I couldn't hear the words, only the angry tones.

And then without warning, an inner door slammed and the door into Reception was thrust open with such force that it banged against the wall. Major Ashton came through the room at speed, only stopping with his hand on the outer door as my presence registered through the haze of his anger.

"Bess. The cathedral. I'm sorry, I've kept you waiting." He sounded distracted, as if only half his mind was on me.

I was already on my feet and following him to the door. Outside, the sun had tried to strengthen, and I blinked in the unaccustomed brightness.

Without speaking, Mark strode down the street for nearly a full block before he calmed down.

Turning to me, he said, "I've done it, Bess. I don't know what Mother and my father will say, but I've sacked Mr. Groves."

I didn't know how to answer him—whether to tell him he'd done the right thing in my view, or to ask him to speak to his mother before he did anything rash.

While breaking off the connection with a solicitor whose chambers have represented a family through several generations was not precisely unheard of, it wasn't common either. And generally it was done when there was misconduct or a strong disagreement. I could see that Mark's anger met the criterion of strong disagreement.

"He wouldn't hear me out. He was too busy telling me that my father refused to listen to reason and predicting that he would find himself regretting it. I asked Groves if Lucius Worley was of the same opinion, and he said that Worley was, that he had felt very strongly about my father's case from the start, and held the view that there was only a very slim chance that he could defend my father successfully."

It was what they'd been saying for some time, only not as openly or as forcefully.

Mark was still talking. "It's late in the day, but I'll find another solicitor and another barrister. Someone who believes in my father's innocence and will try to keep him alive so that my mother won't spend the rest of her life as a grieving widow." His motorcar was just down the street. "Can you drive, Bess?"

"Yes, of course I can."

"Take me as far as the railway station, and then drive on to Cranbourne. Tell my mother and Clara that I had business to attend to in London. But not that I've sacked Groves. I'll tell her as soon as I've found someone else."

"Mark—you have nothing with you. A change of clothes—"

"At my club. Time is short, Bess. It will be easier to explain to Mother when I have a new man to take over." He was holding the driver's door for me.

I thought he was underestimating Helen Ashton. But I got in behind the wheel while he cranked the motor.

It was only a short drive to the station, and I waited while he looked into the availability of a ticket. But he was a Major, so it presented no problem at all, as far as I could tell, and within minutes he was waving to me from the station door.

I returned the wave, let in the clutch, and set out for Cranbourne.

In her sitting room, Mrs. Ashton listened to what I had to say, and then gave me a skeptical glance.

"My dear, I'm sure that's how he asked you to explain his absence to me. Thank you. It's very kind of you. Now tell me what actually happened."

I smiled ruefully. "He asked me not to tell you any more than that."

"Yes, I'm sure he did. Very well, then. Let me guess. He's sacked Groves. I don't know why, but I expect he was fed up with the man's timidity. And by extension Worley's as well. And he's gone up to London to find someone to take over Philip's case."

I said nothing.

"Well, if he hadn't sacked Groves, I was on the point of doing it myself. Enough is enough. The question is, do you think my son will be successful in finding someone suitable? At this stage in the proceedings?"

"I believe he will. If they are agreeable to coming down to Canterbury."

"Good. I'd have probably found someone before dispensing with Groves's services, but what's done is done. I never cared for him, he was never the man his father and grandfather were, but we'd inherited him, and we made the best of it for two years. It's almost a relief to be done with him."

Clara was less hopeful. She said to me a little later, as we were going up before dinner, "Are you encouraging Aunt Helen because you believe it's the right step to take, or are you supporting Mark whether it was the wisest choice or not?"

I was surprised that she would doubt Mark.

When I took my time about answering, she added, "Mr. Groves knew the local feelings about Uncle Philip. How long will it take a new man to understand all the problems here?"

I found myself imagining how to explain a nailbourne to a London barrister or his clerk. Much less the difference between the two memorials in St. Anne's nave and churchyard.

"Perhaps he'll see the issues more clearly because he's not involved," I suggested.

"There's that," she agreed, turning toward her room. "I'm just so afraid that this won't turn out well. That feelings run too high against the Ashtons for my uncle to receive a fair trial, whoever is representing him. I can't sleep, sometimes, worrying about that."

"I think all of us are haunted by that."

In my room, washing my face and hands, pinning up my hair beneath my cap, and smoothing my skirts, I listened to rising wind outside my window and felt the cold draft that came in gusts down the chimney, sending the flames shooting higher in a shower of sparks.

And then, putting on a brave face, I walked back down the stairs and into the sitting room, where the first course was just being served, a potato and leek soup.

Mrs. Ashton smiled cheerfully as Clara came in behind me, but the smile was belied by her eyes. I wondered if she'd been crying, although her voice was calm and steady as she asked Mrs. Byers to bring all of us a glass of wine.

But even that couldn't lift our spirits very far.

It was close on three in the morning when we heard someone at the door to the house.

Roused from a deep sleep I hurried across the cold floor in my bare feet to peer out into the night.

There was a cab from Canterbury standing in the drive, but I couldn't see who was at the door. Whoever it was must be just out of my line of sight.

I heard the door open an inch or two, and Mrs. Byers's voice asking who was there.

The rest was muffled.

Not Mark then.

I found my slippers and my robe, and hurried out of my room to the top of the stairs.

There I met Mrs. Byers just coming up toward me. The door behind her was closed, and she held a telegram in her hand, as if it were a bomb ready to go off in her fingers.

"Sister Crawford," she said in astonishment. "It's for you. A telegram. I hope it isn't bad news."

I held out my hand for it and she gave it to me, then stood there at the head of the stairs, waiting for me to open it. Holding the lamp in her hand high enough for me to see, she watched as I tore open the flap.

My heart was in my throat. Mother? The Colonel Sahib? Simon?

I fumbled at the sheet inside. Mrs. Ashton had heard our voices, and she was coming down the passage toward me.

"Is it Mark?" she was asking. And then she saw that I'd opened the envelope, not waiting for her, and she said at once, "My dear . . ."

I flattened the sheet. It was from my father.

News has just reached me. The sergeant you were seeking in France has been killed. Word says in action. Not confirmed.

My first thought was that he meant Sergeant Lassiter, and I felt cold at the possibility. And then I realized that he must be referring to Sergeant Rollins, the tank hero.

Dead.

I stared at the sheet in my hands, then looked up.

Whatever she read in my face, Mrs. Ashton put her hand to her throat, a protective gesture against bad news.

"It's from my father," I told her. "Sergeant Rollins has been listed as killed. It's probably true. My father would know. The sergeant won't be able to testify for either side."

I could see the sergeant's face in my mind's eye. Adamant that he wouldn't make a statement or come to Canterbury to give evidence.

What had he known? Would it have damned Philip Ashton? Or saved him?

And then another thought on the very heels of that.

If he'd given Canterbury a statement, would he still be alive now? Or would he have died anyway?

Was it the Germans? Or was it murder?

Chapter Fourteen

Mrs. Ashton was silent, shock in her eyes.

I hadn't realized just how much she had still hoped that Sergeant Rollins would relent in the end and somehow help her husband clear himself. She hadn't spoken to him in France as I had done; she still believed that by some miracle, he would change his mind.

But he wouldn't now. Whatever he'd known had died with him.

Mrs. Byers, still holding up the lamp, looked from one to the other of us. "It's bad news, then."

"I'm afraid so," I answered.

"I'll put the kettle on. You'll be needing a cup of tea."

She turned to go down the stairs, and without a word we followed her. Not just to the sitting room but down to the kitchen below stairs.

It was immaculate in the light of her lamp. She lit another to chase away the shadows, and then went to test the stove and to put the kettle on. We sat down at the long table where the staff usually took their meals. Butler and footmen, housekeeper and maids. Only it was a much reduced staff these days.

Mrs. Ashton said, "He was famous, wasn't he? Rollins? The best tank man we had."

"Yes. His tank was named for his sister. Agatha." I could have bit my tongue as soon as the words were out of my mouth.

Mrs. Ashton said quickly, "What else did you know about him?"

"Not much. He took very good care of his men. He'd been in the tanks almost from the start. He was respected by everyone."

She nodded. "Yes, he's been called a hero. Here in Cranbourne. What do you think he could have told the court?"

I shrugged lightly. "Your guess is as good as mine. I'd hoped he could tell us whether he'd seen flames from his vantage point on The Swale, well before Mr. Ashton reached the ruins. It was possible. And it would have helped."

She sighed.

"I couldn't be sure whether he refused to testify or give a statement because he knew it would help—or send your husband to the gallows. I don't think he liked Mr. Ashton, particularly. Perhaps that's why he wouldn't help. But it's even possible that he hadn't seen anything of importance, just as he'd said in his first statement. He hadn't seen any Germans, and he hadn't seen anyone else."

"Well," she said as Mrs. Byers set cups in front of us, "there is nothing we can do, is there? No, Mrs. Byers, sit here, at the table with us," she added as the housekeeper turned to leave us to speak privately. "Thank you for the tea. I badly needed it. And I think Sister Crawford did as well."

I smiled. "Yes, thank you."

"But what, if I may ask, does this change?" Mrs. Byers wanted to know, speaking diffidently. "If he wasn't going to testify at all, Mr. Ashton's situation hasn't changed at all, to my way of thinking."

"There was hope," Mrs. Ashton said gently.

"Yes, hope, there's that. But if he didn't absolve Mr. Ashton, at least he didn't bury him either."

Mrs. Ashton put down her cup. "It's true. We're no better nor worse off than we were before." But however bracingly she said the words, I knew how much the news had hurt her.

Hope taken away could be a very painful loss.

We sat there in silence for quite some time, sipping our tea, our thoughts far away from this tidy room with its cream walls and brown floor, the lamps casting shadows into corners and the silence somehow reminding us of the cheerful voices that usually filled this space.

Our cups empty, we set them in the sink for the morning, and Mrs. Byers blew out the kitchen lamp, leading us back up the kitchen stairs into the hall.

We had just turned toward the steps when the outside door opened and Mark came striding in.

He stopped short at the spectacle of three women in their nightdresses standing at the bottom of the stairs and staring at him as if he were the ghost of Sergeant Rollins.

Mrs. Ashton was the first to recover, smiling at her son and then breaking into a nervous laugh. "Mark," she said, as if she barely recognized him.

"What the devil—! Has something happened?" He looked around, as if expecting to see smoke or flames billowing out of one of the rooms to either side of the staircase.

Mrs. Byers said formally, "Major Ashton. We weren't expecting you tonight."

"Apparently not. My father?" The door was standing wide behind him, and I could just see the headlamps of a motorcar lighting up the night outside.

"He's all right, my dear. As far as we know. But there's been a telegram about another matter." She held out her hand, and I passed the telegram to her. She in turn gave it to her son.

Mrs. Byers brought the single lamp forward so that he could read it better. As it shone on his face, I could see the lines of fatigue around his mouth and the deep shadows beneath his eyes.

Scanning the telegram quickly, he said, "Well. I'm glad I got rid of Groves."

Then, remembering, he added, "You won't know about that, Mother. I'll explain later." He gave her the telegram, turning to Mrs. Byers. "I've brought a houseguest down from London with me. He has—er—special needs and has his valet with him. Sorry to ask you to wake up a maid and prepare two rooms, but it's important."

I said, before the astonished housekeeper could think what to do, "I'll help her, Mark. I'm sure there are rooms ready, Mrs. Byers? A change of sheets or a fire lit on the hearth?"

She looked at me, and I knew what she was about to say, that I was a guest.

Mrs. Ashton spoke. "And I'll help as well. We mustn't keep our guest waiting. And I'm not dressed to receive anyone. At breakfast, Mark?"

"Yes," he said, clearly relieved. "Thank you, Mother. Bess. Mrs. Byers."

But we were already hurrying up the steps, Mrs. Ashton deciding on which rooms to assign to the guest and his valet, Mrs. Byers nodding as she considered the state of each one. Mrs. Ashton and I continued down the passage while Mrs. Byers went to the linen closet for fresh bedding. Mrs. Ashton chose a room several doors down from mine, hurrying to open a window a crack while I knelt at the hearth.

"Mrs. Byers was right," I said. "It only needs a match." Rising, I found one in the container on the mantelpiece, thinking to myself that despite the war and the lack of staff, here were two bedrooms with fires ready laid and sheets sprinkled with lavender, in the event someone arrived without notice. Just as my room had been ready for me.

Mrs. Byers came in with the bedding and the three of us made short work of changing the linens. The fresh ones also smelled of lavender. The window was closed, we checked that the fire was drawing well, already taking a little of the chill off the unused room, and then we hurried next door. It was smaller, but just as well prepared. We repeated what we'd done a matter of minutes before, and then nodded in satisfaction. When Mrs. Ashton wasn't looking, Mrs. Byers ran a finger over the wood of a table by the window. It brought no dust with it.

"Thank you, Mrs. Byers," Mrs. Ashton said as we closed the door behind us and started down the passage. "And will you tell Mrs. Lacey that we will have two more guests for breakfast, one in the dining room and the other with staff downstairs? Indefinitely?"

"I will that. Good night."

She walked on toward the servants' stairs at the end of the passage, while Mrs. Ashton and I went on toward our rooms.

"I hope whoever it is that Mark brought with him is a better man than Mr. Groves," she said as she opened her door. "We're going to need him. Good night, my dear. Thank you."

I went the dozen more steps to my own door, and was just closing it when I saw a strange man coming up the stairs and setting down an invalid chair at the top before disappearing down them again.

It was an unexpected sight.

I closed my door smartly as voices came up the stairwell, Mark's among them.

The next morning the Hall had a feeling of bustle about it. As I walked into the dining room, I saw that Mark was already there, and at his side at the table sat a thin, bespectacled man in an invalid chair—the chair I'd glimpsed last night.

Mark rose and presented me to Theodore Heatherton-Scott.

"She's a houseguest at the moment, but I can't tell you how much she has done for all of us. It was Sister Crawford who received the telegram I spoke to you about. The one informing us that Sergeant Rollins had been killed."

I walked around to his chair and he took my hand. "Good morning, Sister." His voice was strong and deep, and behind the spectacles intelligent gray eyes met mine. "I'm sorry for the midnight arrival, but we wanted to be in Canterbury as quickly as possible."

I wasn't sure just who this man was, but Mark quickly enlightened me.

"Mr. Heatherton-Scott has come to represent my father in his upcoming trial. He'll dispense with a local solicitor at this stage. There's a man in London who will act on our behalf, as necessary."

Mrs. Byers came in just then, carrying a fresh rack of toast. She greeted me, and then said to Mr. Heatherton-Scott, "Your valet has finished his breakfast, sir, and has asked me to tell you that he's ready whenever you ring."

"Thank you, Mrs. Byers."

I filled my plate from the buffet and sat down. "I don't know whether it's bad news or good that Sergeant Rollins has been killed. I intended to go into Canterbury this morning and send a telegram to my father, asking for further details."

"Yes, your father is Colonel Crawford, is he not? I know him by reputation. A cousin served under him in India. A Lieutenant Scott."

I remembered him. A very pleasant officer who was not only popular with the men under him but with the ladies as well. Everyone liked him, and we were sorry to lose him to a virulent fever he'd picked up while in Lahore.

I told Mr. Heatherton-Scott that.

"Indeed. We were all devastated. But as to the sergeant, we will manage quite well without him." He smiled, his eyes suddenly twinkling. "I have the disadvantage of being chair bound, but Henry is mobile and very useful. Would you be insulted if I asked you to tell him all you know about this affair? We will put him to good use, and he has the advantage of not being known in the community."

"I'll be happy to."

"I'm grateful. Ah—" He broke off as Mrs. Ashton came in. "I'm sorry to have arrived like a thief in the night," he said to her as she came to greet him. "I'm replacing your Mr. Worley. I hope you won't mind."

Charmed, she walked over to his chair as I had done, and he took her hand. "I am grateful, Mr. Heatherton-Scott. I can't tell you how grateful."

In the course of their conversation he asked her about speaking to Henry, and by this time I was curious about the valet. I'd only glimpsed him briefly at the head of the stairs.

After we'd finished breakfast, I was summoned to the study, where Mr. Heatherton-Scott sat in his chair behind Mr. Ashton's desk, papers spread out around him. I looked for Mark, but he wasn't present.

Another man was, who rose politely as I entered. This time I had a very good look at him. He was tall, but not noticeably so, quite broad in the shoulder, and, I had a feeling, quite strong as well. His hair was thick and brown, well cut to the shape of his head, and his eyes were the blue of a summer sky, the most notable feature about him. It occurred to me that Henry could walk anywhere and not draw attention to himself unless he wished to.

Mr. Heather-Scott presented him, and he came forward, bowing slightly, the way a well-trained valet would have done.

It seemed that he looked after Mr. Heatherton-Scott in more ways than one, personally and professionally.

He said quietly, in a very pleasant baritone, "Sister."

"Now that that's out of the way," Mr. Heatherton-Scott went on, "I should like you to tell us what you know about the Ashtons and about the people connected to this explosion. Please speak frankly. Nothing you say will leave this room. But it may help me to fill in the blanks of my knowledge."

I started to sit down in the chair in front of the desk, but he was already rolling his chair out from behind it, moving toward the grouping of chairs by the hearth. It changed the atmosphere from formal to comfortable. Henry went to stand by the hearth. I expected him to take out a notebook, but instead, he simply stood there, looking out toward the double doors to the terrace, where the wind was battering at the bare trees. I had the distinct impression that he would not miss a word.

I began with my arrival in Cranbourne, and slowly told Mr. Heatherton-Scott everything I had known and done. He was most particularly interested in the embroidered cushion I'd discovered when Sister Morris was nearly suffocated.

"We may be dealing with more than one person here," he said thoughtfully. "In France and in Kent."

That had occurred to me as well, but I couldn't think of anyone who might be a strong enough candidate for masterminding both Kent and the trenches.

When I said as much aloud, Mr. Heatherton-Scott glanced at his valet and then turned his gaze back to me. "Leave that to me to untangle. I have resources that you don't, although your connections with the Army may be very useful to us in discovering precisely what happened to Sergeant Rollins. Are you certain you've remembered everything?"

I had—except for the remarks Mrs. Ashton had made to the night outside her broken window. That was too personal, and I wanted to be sure of my ground before mentioning it.

"You've been most helpful, Sister Crawford. And very concise, very clear. That's even more helpful. Who do you think is behind the troubles that have faced the Ashtons?"

"I wish I knew."

He nodded. "With luck we'll soon find that out. Do you believe that Mr. Groves had intentionally tried to dissuade his client, Mr. Ashton, from standing trial?"

"He felt strongly about Mr. Ashton throwing himself on the mercy of the court. I don't know why. But I sometimes had the impression, judging from events, that Mr. Groves was a man of limited imagination. I have not met Mr. Worley."

"Cautious," he said, surprising me. "Worley has made his reputation taking only those clients whose trials he believed he could win. He takes great pride in winning."

"Then why did he agree to represent Mr. Ashton?" I asked.

"I can't answer that question. It might well be that he has other reasons for taking on this case."

I knew that Mr. Worley had relatives connected with the explosion. An interesting thought.

Was it possible he was behind what was happening? It was a chilling idea, and I wondered what he would do now that he and Mr. Groves had been dismissed.

It occurred to me then that no one had informed Philip Ashton about the change in representation. And that was worrying. I said as much to Mr. Heatherton-Scott.

"Not a concern, Sister. I intend to visit him after I've spoken to everyone and have formed a clear picture of what I'm facing. Meanwhile, I have a favor to ask of you. Could you draw me a rough map of Cranbourne? It needn't be perfectly accurate. There's a large sheet of paper on Mr. Ashton's desk. I'd like to know where to find Mrs. Branch or St. Anne's or the riverbank."

I rose and went to the desk. Cartography wasn't my strong point. Still, I'd watched the Colonel Sahib and Simon redraw maps from reconnaissance reports, setting out new information in relation to what was already known. What mattered was having reference points that put the new information into proper perspective. I thought for a moment and then picked up the pencil lying beside the blotter. I began to draw in the abbey grounds. After all, they were central to the town that had grown up outside them. Next the village square, and the River Cran. Given those landmarks, I could put in Abbey Hall, the warehouses, the ruins, the far side of the grounds where Miss Rollins and Mrs. Branch lived. By the time I had finished, there was a fair amount of information on the sheet of paper.

"Well done," Mr. Heatherton-Scott said. He had wheeled himself across to the desk to watch what I was doing. "That will serve nicely. I could have asked Mrs. Ashton or the Major to help us with this, but I rather thought you might be more objective. And you are. You have made no excuses for including any place or for leaving any out. Again I must thank you, Sister Crawford." I rose, taking that for dismissal. I was half-way to the door when he added, "Oh, yes, another matter. Henry, here, would be much happier if you didn't acknowledge him if you happened to meet out-side this house."

Which meant, I thought, that he was planning to do a little reconnaissance of his own. Why wasn't he in the Army? He looked fit enough. And young enough. How had he escaped conscription?

I was beginning to find Henry more and more interesting. It occurred to me that I didn't know his surname. And valets were generally called by their last names, not their Christian names. Curiouser and curiouser . . .

"Yes, of course," I said, my hand on the doorknob.

"And if you'll ask Mrs. Ashton if she has a moment to speak with me?"

Two hours later, after he'd interviewed everyone in the house down to the lowliest kitchen maid, who had—I was told later by Mrs. Byers, who had been present—stared at him as if he had just landed from the moon, Mr. Heatherton-Scott was lifted into his motorcar and driven away by Henry. I went to find Mark.

He was in the study, writing a letter at his father's desk.

"How did you find Mr. Heatherton-Scott?" I asked. "And how did you persuade him to represent your father?"

Looking up, he grinned at me. "I'm not precisely sure," he said. "I asked a friend whose father is a K.C. where I might find someone I could trust. William has been invalided out of the Army after losing his leg, and it seems he'd met Heatherton-Scott in his doctor's surgery in Harley Street. William never hesitated, he sent me round to Heatherton-Scott's house with a note introducing me, and the next thing I knew we were driving down to Cranbourne with Henry at the wheel."

"But what persuaded him that he could help your father?"

"I'm not quite certain whether it's helping my father or besting Lucius Worley. Apparently there's bad blood between them. But to his credit, Heatherton-Scott listened to everything I told him about the situation, and then he said, 'It's been mismanaged. From the start. How did you come up to London?' I told him I'd come by train, and he replied, 'Good, good. I'll drive you down and you can tell me more on the way.' That's when I met Henry."

"But what are his credentials? How good is he?"

"According to William—and he should know—Heatherton-Scott has one of the finest reputations in London. But he's considered unconventional, and apparently that's how he manages to win so often. And to tell you the truth, I liked what I saw."

"Yes, I agree. You appear to have been very lucky."

"Don't I know that! I expected to interview a dozen men before I found one who cared about the situation and expressed any hope of saving my father. Heatherton-Scott has made no rash promises, but I have the feeling that he will make sure he wins. If only to annoy Worley."

"And Henry?"

"God knows where Heatherton-Scott found him. I did hear him say that Henry had been with him for some twenty years or more."

I'd put the barrister's age at somewhere between forty and forty-five, well aware that his affliction, whatever it was that confined him to his chair, could also age a person. If only from the struggle to do the ordinary things a whole man would take for granted, and not taking into account any pain that followed in its wake.

Henry's age I'd put as mid-thirties. Which meant that Heatherton-Scott had taken Henry on at a very early age, long before he could have been trained to be a competent valet. And that told me something else, that the lawyer had found someone he could trust implicitly, which was more important than skill and training. Henry had become his eyes, his ears, and most importantly, his legs. And that meant that Henry was not only trustworthy but also very intelligent.

It wouldn't pay to underestimate either man.

As I was leaving the study, Mark asked, "How did my mother take the change in lawyers? Was she very put out with me this morning?"

Turning at the door, I smiled at him. "I think if you hadn't got rid of Mr. Groves, she would have done it for you."

He laughed—the first time I had heard his laughter in a long while.

I wanted to walk, cold as it was, and escape the confines of the house for a little while. But I was also wary of running into any of the local people. Nor did I feel free to take Nan for a run. After what nearly happened to her, we walked her in Mrs. Ashton's private garden, throwing a ball for her or racing down the garden toward the pond. Not all the exercise she needed, but enough to keep her healthy.

I hesitated to invade Mrs. Ashton's privacy as well, using her garden for my own pleasure. In the end, I borrowed a heavier coat from Clara, and a red cap to match, and walked down to the Cran. With the wind off the sea, no one was lingering there except the expectant gulls looking to see if I'd brought their dinner.

I walked along the river, in full spate just before the tide turned, the boats still at their anchors, and the surface of the water very smooth, except where the wind ruffled it as it passed.

The door to the shed where Alex Craig worked on his boat stood wide, and I debated turning around before he could see me out here. And then I decided that it didn't matter, he was probably too busy with his sanding or staining or varnishing to pay heed to me.

I walked quietly past the opening, and if he glanced up, he must have taken me for someone else, without my uniform to set me apart. Glad that I had not hesitated, I walked to the end of the broad dock, looking out to sea, where there were whitecaps on The Swale and the Thames out beyond. In the distance I could pick out the shape of a frigate. I wondered if it was on station, patrolling the entrance to the river that led straight up to London.

The wind seemed to blow right through the cloth of Clara's coat, warm as it had seemed when I had started out. I turned to walk back the way I'd come, and saw Henry standing at the far end of the lane, looking my way. I almost waved, but remembered his request to be ignored. I glanced around to see who might be watching, and realized from this position I had a perfect view of the ruins, better even than where Mark and I had stopped that first day and looked down on them.

Had anyone stood here the day of the explosion?

But that was impossible. Whoever it was, he or she would have been killed by the physical force of the explosion. It had shredded doors and roofs, for heaven's sake, and flesh couldn't have withstood it. And yet . . .

There was a street of older houses that ran along above the river. A few trees, the back gardens. I hadn't really noticed them before, they were well away from the water.

Who lived in them? Their windows had been blown in, for one thing, and their roofs and walls must have suffered too, a chimney toppled here, a tree there. Surely the Army had interviewed those people?

I would have to ask Mark who they were.

When I turned back to the river, Henry had gone. I walked back the way I'd come, busy with my thoughts.

Alex Craig stepped out into my path.

Surprised, I said, "Hallo."

"I didn't recognize you in those clothes."

"Indeed."

"Is it true that Philip Ashton tried to kill himself? Rumors are flying."

I debated how to answer him. It was Mark's place, and his mother's, to decide what the local people knew or were told. But I could see that Alex Craig badly wanted an answer. To gloat? I decided to test that possibility.

"It's true," I said, without elaboration.

"For what reason? Remorse? His conscience?"

"Despair," I told him. "Because he's innocent, and no one will listen. They've all decided he's guilty, and they're howling for his blood."

"They?"

"The police. His lawyers. Everyone, it seems, in Cranbourne. The Swale villages. I shouldn't be surprised if half of Canterbury also felt the same way."

When he didn't respond, I added, "They might as well hang him and be done with it. Even if he's acquitted by some legal miracle, what sort of life can he expect to live here? No one will believe it was a fair trial. They'll say that because he's influential, the jury was afraid to convict. Or that his defense was too clever. There's always a reason why the verdict didn't run with popular sentiment." There was contempt in my voice, although I tried to keep it out. "The *punishment* will go on and on."

"And Mrs. Ashton?"

"Have you not seen her lately?"

"No."

"Perhaps you should make a point to see her. I'm told she was kind to you once."

And I walked on.

He didn't try to stop me.

Chapter Fifteen

Having encountered Henry down by the river, I wasn't surprised to find the Heatherton-Scott motorcar standing in the drive as I came back to Abbey Hall.

As I walked into the house, I could hear voices from the open doorway of the study. Mrs. Ashton responded to a question, and I took this to be a family conference with Mr. Heatherton-Scott. I turned toward the stairs and was just starting up when Mark called.

"Bess?"

"Yes?"

"We're in the study." He came to the door and added, "Join us, please."

I couldn't tell from his expression whether the news was good or bad. I stopped only long enough to remove the red cap and Clara's coat, draping them over the curve where the banister ended at the foot of the stairs.

Mr. Heatherton-Scott was by the hearth in his invalid chair, Mrs. Ashton and Clara seated before him. Henry was nowhere in sight.

He looked up as I walked into the room. "Sister," he said, acknowledging me with a nod. "I was just telling Mrs. Ashton that I was able to visit her husband. Inspector Brothers was bent on thwarting me, but I was not to be thwarted." He smiled. "I don't think he believed that such a pitiful creature in a chair could be the new lawyer, and once I'd proved that I was, he took heart, certain that Mr. Ashton had gone from bad to worse when it came to representation. And so I was allowed, finally, to see him."

"How was he?" I asked, having had no news since he left hospital. "Have his bandages been changed?"

"Apparently they have. I made a point to look at them. I was just about to tell everyone about my first words with my client. Mr. Ashton was quite surprised to find me admitted to his cell, and I explained the change in management, as it were. His first question, as soon as the gaoler had walked away, was, 'Are you here to convince me to admit I was responsible for the fire, if not the explosion? If you are, call that man back and tell him I have refused to receive you.'"

Mrs. Ashton smiled. "That sounds just like Philip."

"It took very little time to persuade him that I had no such intentions, and that if I'd agreed with anything Groves and Worley had done, I wouldn't have bothered to leave London for Canterbury. He was pleased to have word of you, Mrs. Ashton. As neither Mr. Groves nor Mr. Worley had seen you recently, they hadn't been able to give him truthful news of his family. You, Sister Crawford, had set his mind at rest during your visit to his hospital room, and that counted for much. He was in better spirits."

"Will I be able to visit Philip now?" Helen Ashton asked eagerly.

"No, sadly, but I shall be happy to take your letters to him, and his to you. That will help a little, I think."

A little . . . but not enough. Mrs. Ashton tried to school her face to hide her disappointment, but I saw the pain in her eyes.

"This was my first conference with my client," Mr. Heatherton-Scott told her gently. "We shall see what inroads we can make in the next one or two. But I have made it official now. Groves and Worley are struck off the list. We will go forward from that."

Clara spoke up then. "I'd like to know what keeps the agitation at such a high level. It never seems to fade away, does it? Just as it seems about to calm down again, something else stirs it up."

It was the question I'd have liked to ask but didn't feel free to bring up. Mr. Heatherton-Scott had gone to great pains to reassure the Ashtons, and I could tell he was not best pleased.

But he answered Clara with a smile. "That's in hand. It's all I can tell you at this stage, but I think I will have more to say on that subject later."

When Henry had made his report?

Mark said, as we left the study and closed the door on Mr. Heatherton-Scott, "Did you want to run into Canterbury to put in a call to your father?"

We needed to know more about what had happened to Sergeant Rollins.

"Yes, please. Thank you, Mark."

I went to fetch my own coat, returning the borrowed one to Clara, and we set out in the motorcar. The wind whipped around us, and I could feel my cheeks stinging from the chill in the air.

As we passed through the square in Cranbourne, I glimpsed Henry standing outside the tobacconist talking to several men. He didn't react when the motorcar passed by, but he must surely have seen the expressions on the faces of the men beside him as they turned their backs.

That was a good thing, I thought. He would see for himself what the Ashton family had had to endure for months.

When we had left the square behind, I asked Mark if he knew what Henry's background was.

"No idea," he told me. "I was told that his name was Henry, and I could see that he was valet-chauffeur and general dogsbody, enabling Heatherton-Scott to do his work despite his disability. Even on the drive back to Cranbourne, when we stopped in Rochester for petrol, Henry appeared to be just that. But after my mother's interview with Heatherton-Scott, she asked me the same question."

I smiled. "If her interview was anything like mine, I'm not surprised. I drew a map for Mr. Heatherton-Scott, but it was Henry who put it to use, I think. He was down by the river earlier."

"Was he indeed?"

I had to wait three quarters of an hour for the use of a telephone. Seven officers had been given day passes from a clinic outside Canterbury, and they were eager to speak to their families. Such leaves were often a final test of a man's return to full strength. I watched their high spirits, smiling at the general laughter and sense of well-being. When my turn finally came, I met with disappointment.

My mother was on her way into London to meet the Colonel Sahib's train. I inquired after everyone, but it wasn't the same as hearing their voices.

Simon was still away. And that was worrying too. I wondered if my father knew where he was.

Asking Iris to pass on my request for more information on Sergeant Rollins, I put up the receiver and stepped aside as another eager officer thanked me and took my place.

When I came out of the hotel to where Mark and the motorcar were waiting, he asked, "Any news? No?"

"No." I was to leave for France tomorrow. There was nothing for it but to ask Sergeant Lassiter what he could find out about Sergeant Rollins's death. "I'm sure my father will find a way to reach me when he has something to tell us."

We turned a corner back toward the square before the cathedral gate, and there was Henry, chatting with a man who looked very much like Mr. Groves's clerk. I touched Mark's arm and pointed. But there were others in the way before he could turn his head, and he couldn't be sure who it was.

I couldn't help but wonder how Henry had managed that encounter.

As we drove back toward Cranbourne, I said to Mark, "I've been meaning to ask. Who lives in that street of houses just above the river? Those you can see from the end of the dock?"

"Mostly town merchants. It's an older part of town, of course, and many of the houses were built when wool was king. Merchants who dealt in wool after the abbey was slighted made their own fortunes and wanted to live above the river. Times have changed, of course, but many of the houses have been renovated, and they were in great demand after the turn of the century. The branch manager of the bank lives there, and the greengrocer who once lived above his shop moved there in 1911. The doctor, of course. I expect the Vicar would prefer it to that drafty pile that's the Vicarage now."

"Which means, if the inhabitants saw anything out their windows two years ago, they aren't telling anyone. Their livelihood depends on the villagers, doesn't it, and so they will cater to them politically just as they do professionally."

"Exactly. Nicely put. The doctor has been distinctly chilly since the troubles began, and the bank manager as well. Not to mention the greengrocer and all the rest. You very quickly learn who your friends are, in circumstances like ours. At the moment, I could count them on the fingers of one hand."

"How sad."

"I have every hope that Heatherton-Scott will change that. Although once a friend has turned his back, it's impossible to trust him afterward."

I was posted this time to the hospital where influenza patients were taken. I'd survived my own case, and it was felt that I had the immunity now to work with the more seriously ill. I had served in such a hospital before, and it was heartbreaking to watch a strong man sink into unconsciousness and die before the night was finished. Or hear others coughing and struggling to breathe, knowing so little could be done to help them. It was a dreadful disease, and it had taken a terrible toll on everyone, not just the British and French lines.

On the third day, a Sister came down the row of beds and said quietly to me, "There's a man by the ambulances who wants to speak to you. Don't let Matron see you go, she doesn't care for fraternizing."

I finished bathing the face of the officer I'd been sitting beside for what seemed hours. He was as stable as we could make him, but I could see how quiet he was, and I didn't like it. In spite of the cool cloths, his fever was still very high.

"Keep an eye on Captain Thomas for me, please," I asked Sister Harris, who was working with the patient in the next bed.

She nodded, and I hurried out to the ambulance line, expecting to meet Simon there. But it wasn't, it was Sergeant Lassiter.

"I heard you were back in France," he said, welcoming me with a grin.

I was certain he could find me wherever I was, so far-flung was his network of watchers. I found myself thinking that if British Intelligence had anything to match it, we might have won this war in six months.

"I'm glad you came. I need your help in a very important matter."

"It may well be that I've already done what you're about to ask. It's to do with Sergeant Rollins, I expect."

"Yes, the report of his death reached me in Kent, but there were no particulars. What happened to him, do you know?"

"The first report claimed that a sniper got him. He was out of his tank, trying to rescue three men from another that was on fire. He was very close to the lines, well within range. But when the men he pulled out of that tank were able to talk, they told another story. It was murder, pure and simple. From our side of the line. But they never found the man. He got away while everyone else was watching the tank burn and the men who were on fire rolling on the ground trying to put out the flames. Several other men rushed over, using blankets to wrap them, then dragged the sergeant and the others back to safety."

"Then no one knows who shot him?"

"That's as may be, lass. But Rollins was still alive when they got him to the doctor. And he was reported to have said he was happy to die for Britain. But that's not how it was."

"What do you mean?"

"He kept saying 'Britain. Britain.' Three times he said it, and then he was gone."

"Britton," I said slowly. "He meant *Britton*. Bless him, he left us a clue. It could very well be the same man who shot at the sergeant before and missed. I can't believe *two* people were stalking him! Did the sergeant see him just as he was firing? Is that how he knew? Because I was nearly sure Sergeant Rollins knew who Britton was. Or did one of the men with him see who it was? I do know for a certainty that Britton was the 'sleepwalker' the night Sister Morris was attacked. The night our rooms were switched. All this is too much of a coincidence not to be true. And here I'd nearly convinced myself that Britton had nothing to do with Cranbourne. But it makes more sense now that the owner of that cushion did intend to smother me in my bed. Sister Morris just happened to be in it instead of me."

"Then I'll have to be looking for this man Britton," he said harshly. "Know his rank, lass? It would help if you did, but I'll find him one way or another."

"He's a corporal. From Devon. He's serving with The Buffs, I think. Unless he's been reassigned. But, Sergeant—I want him alive and able to answer questions. Do you hear me? There's more to this than getting my own back here, or even avenging Sergeant Rollins. I think he knows something about what's going on in Kent—otherwise, why would he try to kill Sergeant Rollins *and* me? The only connection between us is Cranbourne."

"If that's how you want it," he answered me. "I'll even tie him up in a bow, if that's what would make you happy. Red or blue?"

"Getting to question him before the Military Foot Police find him would be satisfaction enough."

"I'll see to it. Never fear." There were people down by the hospital doorway, well within sight of us. And so rather than kissing me on the cheek as he generally did, he winked at me, then said in a low voice, "Mind yourself, lass. He may find you before I find him. But only if I miss him."

"I promise. Be careful, please. He won't hesitate to kill you, if he suspects you're after him."

He grinned, but there was no humor in it. "Be safe, luv."

And he was off, moving swiftly to where a messenger's motorcycle was ticking over. Where he'd found it or what had happened to the driver, heaven only knew. But he was gone in a roar of sound, scattering earth and dust behind him as he headed north.

As I walked toward the hospital, I heard in the distance that familiar sound of the kookaburra bird, even over the engine's growl.

When I got back to the wards, the Sister who had given me the message was waiting. "He's quite attractive," she said.

"He brought me family news," I said. "I'd been worried." And I walked on to the chair where I'd been sitting.

As I wrung out another cool compress for Captain Thomas's head, he opened his eyes and smiled. I was so pleased to see him better that I wanted to embrace him, but that would never do. Instead I said, looking down at him, "Nice to have you back, Captain."

He was too exhausted to respond, but as he closed his eyes again, there was a glimmer of relief in them.

My next visitor arrived very early in the morning, just as I was crossing to the canteen for my last meal before finding my cot. It had been a long night, and I had lost a patient. My spirits were sunk well down into my boots as I walked through a light drizzle toward the canteen door.

"Bess."

I turned. It was Simon. I was so glad to see him I didn't at first know what to say.

Hurrying toward the large tree where he was standing, I realized how very tired he looked.

"Are you all right?" I asked, suddenly worried for him. This influenza could find any weakness in the body's defenses, and fatigue was one of the worst.

"I haven't slept in three days," he said ruefully. "I was sent over to find out who killed Sergeant Rollins. Did the Colonel not tell you?"

I shook my head. "Come and have some tea. And a biscuit. We can talk inside. The canteen is almost deserted at this hour."

I took his arm and we walked side by side toward the door. There were only two other people in the room, not counting the sleepy night staff behind the counter. Choosing a table by one of the back windows where I thought we might not be disturbed, I asked for two cups of tea and a plate of sandwiches.

We sat down in silence, waiting until they were brought to us. The tea was fresh and hot, but the sandwiches were dry. Nevertheless, Simon tucked into them with the appetite of a hungry man.

"I haven't been able to reach my father," I said quietly when we were alone. "He's been in the north. At least that's what he told me. I received one telegram telling me only that Sergeant Rollins had been killed. Nothing after that. When I telephoned Somerset, Iris told me that Mother was driving into London to pick up my father at the station."

"He sent you a second telegram. I expect it was delayed for military traffic or is still waiting for you in Kent. The doctor who examined the sergeant's body told his commanding officer that it was not a sniper's shot that brought him down. It was a regular issue Army rifle cartridge. And someone from his tank swore that he'd been shot by one of his own men. But no one knows who."

"I think I do," I said, feeling a little better as I sipped my tea. I was hoping Simon felt the same. "It was Sergeant Lassiter who told me that very likely the shot had come from our own lines. And then he told me that the sergeant had spoken just before he died."

"Yes, that message was relayed to London. It will be sent to the King in due course."

"But it's not what they thought it was, Simon." I put down my cup. "He said the word three times. *Britain.*

Everyone took it to mean that he was dying for Britain. A very brave last word from a hero. They didn't know what I did. That a man named Britton had tried to kill me—"

Simon's head came up, his eyes intent on mine. "You never said anything about this to your father. I'd have heard."

"He attacked the wrong Sister. She was given the room that was listed as mine, because she arrived earlier than expected and her own room wasn't ready. They're all alike. Ordinarily it wouldn't matter. This night it did. She screamed and fought, and one of the night guards heard her. When he got there, she was scratched and coughing but very much alive. It was put down to a drunken orderly, but no one ever found him, as far as I know." I went on to describe the cushion that I'd discovered and dissected, then explained about the sleepwalking trench foot case. "I suspected then that he had some connection with Kent. Corporal Britton. He was from Devon but he was serving with The Buffs. He once served as batman to an officer. At a guess, when that officer was killed, he went back to his regiment and was eventually promoted in the field."

Simon had once been my father's batman, his military servant.

"Yes, that sounds logical. But what has he to do with Sergeant Rollins?"

"I suspect he'd already attempted to kill the sergeant, but missed his shot. I tried to warn Rollins to be careful, but he felt he could take care of himself. Apparently when the first attempt failed, someone tried again. Sergeant Rollins was the only witness when the Ashton Powder Mill went up and then burned. The Army interviewed him. But now Philip Ashton is about to go on trial for murdering the men who died in that explosion and fire. And no one wanted to bring Sergeant Rollins back to question him again. The Army was only interested in saboteurs. Rollins himself refused to return to Kent when I proposed that he ask for leave to testify." I gave Simon an account of what the sergeant had told me. "So it's very likely that Sergeant Rollins's death and the attack on me are connected, and the only possible connection is the Ashton family."

"I'm confused. Why should Britton be involved with that? Did he ever work for the mill?"

"According to Mrs. Ashton, he didn't. I don't know his connection. Not yet. But if you can find him, you can question him about it. It might be the only way to learn why Rollins had to die."

"That's very helpful, Bess. It should make my task much easier."

"You'd better hurry," I told him. "Sergeant Lassiter has put out word that he wants Britton rather badly."

Simon said grimly, "He'll have to find him before I do."

"What has happened with the black aircraft? I haven't heard anything about it since I got back to France."

"He's down. Crashed behind his own lines. Word has it that his leg was broken in the crash, and he won't be flying again. A pity. He was a fine pilot."

I thought about Alex Craig, who wouldn't fly again either. "Why is it soldiers always respect the abilities of their enemies?" I asked, already knowing the answer.

Simon grinned. "That's how we came to have the Gurkha battalions. They were such fine enemies, we decided to recruit them for our own ranks."

I'd been brought up on the stories.

Simon finished his tea. "Thanks for this. I feel much better." He looked better as well. "I must go." He got to his feet.

We walked to the door, and as we opened it, Matron came in. She looked at me, at the tall man beside me in his uniform of a Sergeant-Major, and she frowned.

I had to think fast.

I smiled. "Matron. May I present Sergeant-Major Brandon? He's just brought me word from Colonel Crawford. I haven't been able to reach my father for some time. It was worrying."

She knew, of course, who my father was. I had never kept it particularly secret, but I hadn't used it to my advantage either.

"Indeed," she said, smiling up at Simon. "Give the Colonel my regards, please, Sergeant-Major."

"Thank you, Matron. Sister Crawford, I'll escort you to the hospital before leaving."

"Thank you."

We escaped without a lecture from Matron. Out of earshot, I said, "Between you and Sergeant Lassiter, I shall have no reputation left by the time the war ends."

I expected him to smile with me. Instead, his eyes were bleak.

"It will be an Armistice, Bess. Not a victory."

An Armistice. After all the bloodshed and the suffering. It hardly seemed worth four years of fighting to end in a draw.

Well. It would be over. That's what mattered.

"Keep in touch," I said as he prepared to leave. "And find Britton."

And then he was gone, my connection with home and my parents gone with him.

I was the attending Sister in surgery when they brought in a man who had been battered almost beyond recognition.

The doctor working on a shattered leg was cursing under his breath as he looked at the incision he'd just made.

"He'll never walk again," he said grimly. "Not with this leg."

But I wondered if he would survive at all, whether whatever had happened to this soldier was too traumatic to survive. There must surely be severe concussion . . .

We worked well into the night before the doctor straightened his back and said, "All right. Take him to recovery. We'll just have to wait and see."

I removed my apron and went to wash my hands. Another Sister came to wheel away the stretcher on which the patient was lying.

The doctor turned to me. "Get yourself some food, Sister. It's well after dinner."

I thanked him and took his advice, crossing through the cold, clear air to the canteen. For some reason I was reminded of sitting here with Simon, and I went to that table with my meal. I was too tired to eat anything, instead letting the quiet seep through me and trying to summon the strength to take my dishes back to the counter.

Sister Anderson came in just then, asking for tea, and then bringing it over to where I was sitting. I really didn't feel like talking to anyone, but it was clear that she needed company.

"Captain Taylor died." It was a stark comment.

"I am so sorry," I said. I knew how she felt. That sense of helplessness in the face of death. "He seemed to be better this morning."

"Yes, that's what's so hard, isn't it?" She put her head in her hands for a moment. "You'd think, wouldn't you, that it would be easier after a while. But it isn't." After a moment or two, she raised her head and reached for her cup. "What has kept you up this late?"

"A surgical case was brought in earlier." We were an influenza hospital, but we couldn't turn away emergencies. "I don't know if he's going to live."

"The corporal? I saw the ambulance that brought him in. What happened to him?"

"I wasn't told."

"I looked at the chart earlier. Someone found him in one of the communication trenches, but it wasn't his own sector. No one quite knows how he got there."

"It looked as if someone had attacked him. Bruises and cuts and a badly broken leg. A concussion."

"He had enemies," she said.

"How do you know? Who was he?"

"The name is Britton. Charles Davis Britton. But wounds like that aren't from fighting. It's retaliation."

I stared at her. "Are you sure?"

"His name was there on the chart."

But that wasn't what I'd asked.

I rose, starting toward the counter. I needed to speak to Britton straightaway. And then I remembered: the surgery. He wouldn't be awake for some hours.

I stopped, turning back to Sister Anderson. "Sorry, I just remembered something I have to do."

"Then go to bed. Do you know how late it is? I'm going myself in a bit."

I took her advice, setting my internal alarm clock to wake me in two hours.

But it was nearly three before I opened my eyes. I bathed my face, dressed hastily, and went back to the wards.

Matron had put the corporal in isolation, where he was less likely to contract influenza before he could be moved to another hospital. I stepped in and looked at the patient.

If I could have recognized him before, I surely couldn't now. I leaned closer in the dim light to be sure.

Yes, I thought it was the Corporal Britton I'd treated for trench foot and who must have tried to kill Sister Morris.

He was moving restlessly. The doctors had been wary of giving him too much to ease his pain until they could determine the extent of his concussion.

I thought perhaps he was rousing up from the surgery, and I waited. After a time, he opened his eyes and said, "Am I alive?"

"You are," I answered. He was trying to see me, but his eyes were swollen and I expect my face appeared blurred to him.

He lapsed into unconsciousness again, then roused once more. "Who are you?" he asked.

"I'm the Sister who assisted the doctor during your surgery. Your leg—it has been splinted. You must leave it that way for a while. But it's still there." I didn't add, *At least for now.* But that's what his chart indicated.

He lifted a hand and put his arm across his eyes. "My head aches like the very devil," he said, more a statement than a complaint.

"We can't give you too much to ease that until we know whether you have a concussion or not."

"Everything hurts. But the head is worse. Worse even than my leg."

He drifted again. I said, "What happened to you?"

"I was set upon. Out of the blue. That's all I remember. The next thing I knew, I came to here. I don't know where *here* is."

I told him, then I asked, "Why did you hunt down Sergeant Rollins?"

"Who is Sergeant Rollins?"

I couldn't judge whether he really didn't know—or if he was awake enough to try to confuse me. I said, "The tank man you killed."

His mind had clouded again. It was still too soon after the ether to expect him to make sense.

"Did you see who did this to you?" My fear was, he'd tell me it was Sergeant Lassiter.

"I don't know."

But I thought he did. I got nowhere, although I tried several more times to find out if he was the man I thought he must be. To find out why he had wanted to kill Sergeant Rollins.

"Do you know anyone in Kent? In a village called Cranbourne?" I asked finally.

And the bleary eyes stared sharply at me. "Why do you want to know?"

"Just curious," I said.

He turned his face to the wall then, and wouldn't speak to me.

I stood there for a moment longer and then quietly left the little room.

The next morning he was gone.

I got up early to look in on him, and found the room cleared and cleaned.

"What's become of our surgical patient?" I asked Matron later in the morning. "Surely he hasn't been put in one of the wards, with the influenza cases."

"You were in the theater with Dr. Browning, weren't you? Yes. We had an ambulance going on to Rouen. We sent him with it. He didn't belong here, they'll manage his care better in Rouen."

More disappointed than I could say, I nodded. "Thank you, Matron. If there is news of him, I'd like to hear it. I watched Dr. Browning attend to that leg. I'd like to know if the surgery was successful."

"Yes, of course, Sister Crawford. I'll keep that in mind." And she went on her way.

Frustrated by my missed opportunity, I sought out Dr. Browning, and asked him what had happened to our patient before he'd been brought in.

Dr. Browning shook his head. "I was told he was found in that condition and we were the nearest facility that could deal with that leg."

It was later in the day, almost dusk, when I heard the sound of the kookaburra bird.

Sergeant Lassiter.

I had a number of questions to put to him. And I was worried about the answers I was going to receive.

I was just crossing to the tree where I'd first seen Simon when a line of ambulances appeared in the distance, and I heard an orderly call out for a Sister to evaluate the incoming patients.

There was nothing I could do but turn and await their arrival.

Out of the corner of my eye, I saw Sergeant Lassiter just stepping into the meager shelter of the leafless branches. I could only hope that he'd wait.

Chapter Sixteen

It was well after dark before I'd finished, and rain was coming down in buckets as we got the last of the new arrivals settled in cots. Three of them were critical, another five were in the early stages of contagion, and ten of them were already showing signs of heavy lung congestion.

I washed my hands, settled my cap into place, and walked toward the hospital's main door. I could see the tree from the doorway, and there was no one standing beneath it.

Where was Sergeant Lassiter?

I considered crossing over to the canteen, but one look at the heavy rain, and I decided against it. Where then would he go, if not the canteen? The small chapel?

I went there to look, and found him asleep on one of the benches.

Waking him with a light touch, I said, "Sergeant?"

He leapt to his feet, ready for action, then relaxed when he realized who it was. I had seen more than one soldier come out of a deep sleep in just this way.

"I'm sorry," I began, but he shook his head.

"I didn't intend to nod off. Not here. But it was warm and dry, and nobody about."

"Have you come about Corporal Britton?"

"Aye, I have. Where is he? Word was, he'd been brought here."

"Someone gave him a nasty beating, Sergeant. There was surgery on his leg, for one thing, and worry about concussion for another."

"Well, I'm not feeling sorry for the bas— for the bloke. Not after what he did. I reckon he thought it was near enough to the end of the war for it not to matter if our best tank man was killed. But it hurt morale, Bess. Rollins had been at Cambrai. The Old Man."

It was a common term in the trenches for someone who had survived impossible battles and charges and hand-to-hand fighting, used with reverence. Whether he was barely twenty or pressing forty didn't matter.

"Is that what you're telling me, that Britton was beaten senseless for shooting Sergeant Rollins?"

"He swore it was a mistake. That's what I was told. But of course it wasn't. You know that as well as I do."

"But was it you and your mates who taught him a sharp lesson?"

Sergeant Lassiter drew himself up to his full height, his face suddenly stern.

"Lass. You surely aren't thinking that I had a hand in this business."

"London has sent someone out to look into what happened. I have to ask," I said soberly, hoping he would understand. "It's Simon Brandon, Sergeant. He won't stop until he knows the full story. And he knows I've turned to you for help, that I told you about Sister Morris. I have to ask. For my sake and yours."

"You must ask Britton."

"I can't."

"Is he dead?"

"Not dead. They moved him to Rouen, because this is an influenza hospital."

He relented. "I can see your dilemma."

"I don't want to see you and Simon clash. Not over something like this. Not if it's not needed."

"Word has it that when the rumor spread about who shot Rollins—that it was one of us, not a sniper—some of the men in the tank corps went looking for answers when they were taken out of the line for a rest.

They looked up to Sergeant Rollins. He kept them safe, and when they weren't safe, he pulled them out of their burning tanks. I don't know how they got on to Britton. Someone claimed Rollins himself had seen who shot him and told his mates. Another story was, his mates recognized the man and cursed him all the way to hospital. I also heard that his own company turned Britton in. However it was, I expect Agatha's crew wanted to teach him a lesson, as you said, and got carried away. They saw that he got medical attention afterward. Someone had a conscience."

I'd witnessed, over and over again, the odd way information made the rounds of the Front. I'd used this bush telegraph myself to find people. Britton had pushed his luck too far, and somehow word had got out.

More relieved than I wanted to admit, I said, "Then what do we do now?"

"Find Brandon and tell him where to look for Britton. He'll have learned the rest by the time he reaches Rouen."

Simon was very good at putting two and two together.

"Can you put out the word?"

"If that's what you want."

I realized what he was saying.

"How did you come here, Sergeant?"

"I borrowed a motorcycle."

"How far is it to Rouen?"

"We could make it tonight. If we started now."

"I'll speak to Matron. Stay here."

"Lass, I should stay with the motorcycle, not here. Out beyond the ambulance lines there's what's left of a cattle byre. I'll be there."

I knew the place. The roof was gone, but part of the wall still stood, an ugly reminder of what war did to people and places. This had been someone's farmhouse, stone built and old, but sturdy and good for another hundred years. A ranging shell had put paid to that.

"Give me a quarter of an hour."

He nodded as we made our way from the chapel toward the outer door.

Apparently my question still rankled. As we were parting company, Sergeant Lassiter put a hand on my shoulder. "Did you seriously believe I'd done that to Britton?"

"I could think of only two reasons for such a beating. His killing Sergeant Rollins, and the fact that you knew he'd tried to kill me. I had to ask."

It was the third time I'd said that. And he looked off into the distance, as if weighing the words.

After a moment he turned back to me. "I think I understand. And I'm grateful you cared enough to ask."

I didn't want him to mistake my intentions. I tried for lightness. "You're far too tall for a firing squad, and you're too big to hang. Neither would be a pretty sight."

He laughed then and, without another word, walked away.

But as he disappeared behind the ambulance lines, I heard that cheeky call of the kookaburra bird. It sounded quite pleased with itself.

I had only minutes to think of an excuse to ask for a brief leave. I knew several of the nurses at the American Base Hospital, and I knew a houseful of nuns and orphaned children. Neither would weigh very heavily with Matron, faced with wards full of ill and dying men and only half the staff she truly needed to cope with all of them.

In the end, I decided on honesty.

Running her to earth in her office, I simply asked if I might have the day off.

She looked at me for a moment, and then to my astonishment, she said, "That surgery was long and exhausting. You need a break before resuming your duties, Sister. We can't have you collapsing with this influenza. It would be bad for morale and it would prove that immunity isn't very lasting." But she smiled as she said the words. A tired smile, and I found myself thinking that if anyone needed or deserved a day of rest, it was this woman. I felt a surge of guilt for even asking.

"Go on, take your holiday. And come back refreshed."

It was hardly going to be refreshing to ride a motorcycle through this rain as far as Rouen, but I returned the smile and promised that I would do just that.

Another few minutes I spent digging out my winter boots and a jumper to go under my coat. I found a knitted cap as well, took off my uniform cap, and carefully folded it before putting it into my apron pocket. I looked at myself in the mirror. With my hair hidden, no one would mistake me for Sister Crawford now. I didn't want word getting back to Matron that one of her supposedly exhausted staff was on the back of a motorcycle with a man from the ranks flying down the Rouen road. And then I went to find Sergeant Lassiter.

From somewhere he'd liberated a length of canvas, which he fashioned like a cloak around me, to keep out the worst of the rain and the mud.

"I wish I had a sidecar, but this was the best I could do at the time, and the need for a lady's carriage hadn't occurred to me."

He got into the saddle in front of me, and asked, "Are you set, lass? Then hold on tight. I don't want to lose you on the road somewhere."

I was chuckling to myself as I put my arms around his middle and hooked my fingers together as best I could. I could feel his body shaking with his own laughter.

And then we were off in a shower of muddy rainwater. If Sergeant Lassiter hadn't been as good as he was with this machine, I was sure we'd have skidded into the nearest puddle. He steadied us with practiced ease, and soon we were indeed flying down the Rouen road.

We arrived in Rouen with my arms aching from holding on as tightly as I could, and my fingers permanently turned into claws from attaching themselves to the sergeant's coat.

We stopped at a small café not far from the cathedral to have a coffee and to give me a chance to restore a more respectable appearance. And then we went to the gates of the American Base Hospital.

It had been set up in the famous Rouen racetrack, and had put the space to good use. The man at the gate looked me up and down and demanded my pass.

"I don't need one," I said firmly. "A patient of ours was brought in here and I have come to inspect his quarters. He shouldn't have been brought here in the first place. We intended to invalid him back to England."

It was the best excuse I could think of, and it worked.

"Patient's name and rank?"

"Britton. Corporal. Buffs."

"Says here he's with a Wiltshire regiment now."

"I'm sorry. I was given the most recent data we had. He was unconscious when he was brought in."

"It happens. All right, Sister, you'll find him in the surgical ward."

"Yes, I know where that is," I said briskly, and marched past him. The sergeant waited for me at the gate. I found the tent, looked for the Sister in charge, and once more explained my errand.

"The doctors are with him now. You'll have to wait. There's tea in the canteen, if you'd like a cup. Or coffee, if you'd prefer it." She smiled. "I've grown quite fond of the coffee here. My parents will be shocked."

I went to the canteen and was surprised to find sugar for my tea and fresh milk in a pitcher. Such luxury. But the Americans hadn't been at war for four long years; they still had all the necessities we lacked. I even chose a small raisin bun, for the pleasure of it.

Ten minutes later I was back at the surgical ward.

Corporal Britton was barely awake. And he'd just been prodded and examined by a phalanx of doctors. He looked up at me with pain-ridden eyes. "I've had my powders," he said. "They aren't working yet. So if there's more?" His voice was thick from the swelling in his face and around his nose.

"Not this soon, I'm afraid," I told him. "I must complete your chart. Where were you attacked, and by whom?"

"None of your business, Sister, begging your pardon."

"Was it for shooting one Sergeant Rollins of the tank corps?"

He scowled at me. "Who says it was?"

"That's the rumor," I said. "The Army will be here shortly to confirm it. And I need to complete your chart."

He turned his head away. I didn't think he recalled my questioning him in the middle of the night. He had more on his mind than one Sister Crawford. And I thought his sight was still blurred. His eyelids were still thick and purple.

"Please, I'll be in trouble with Matron, if I don't fill out this chart," I said, a whining note in my voice. "I've seven more patients to speak to."

He turned back to face me. "I'm alive, and I intend to stay that way. I fell into a trench, Sister, and nobody caught me."

Men did take flying leaps into trench lines, during a retreat across No Man's Land, to avoid getting shot. And it was common practice for those already safely out of harm's way to catch those still inbound.

It could be true. But the extent of his injuries belied his story.

What's more, he persisted in his refusal to say more than that.

I couldn't stay much longer. The ward Sister would come to see why I was still with this patient, or an orderly would come by and tell me not to badger him.

I tried one final time. "I can't just write down that you fell into a trench. I can see for myself that you have two black eyes today, swollen lips, and what appears to be a broken nose. Not to overlook that leg. And your chart indicates there is additional bruising on your body as well. It speaks of fisticuffs, Corporal. Tell me again how you got those falling into a trench?"

"You've never been in a trench, have you, Sister? You can't tell me what happened when I was there."

But I had been in trenches, both German and British. When I told him as much, he stared at me, his gaze intensifying.

"I've seen you before," he said, his voice beginning to rise.

"Of course you have. Who do you think sat with you the better part of the night? And now I'm on record duty."

He turned his face away and this time ignored me completely. The ward Sister was coming this way, and so I had no choice but to leave. Smiling at her as we passed in the aisle between beds, I said, "Number Eleven is sleeping. I expect he's had a long night."

"Yes, I had a look at that leg when the bandages were changed. Poor man."

"Indeed," I replied dryly, but she had already stepped in to speak to a patient with bandaged eyes. A gas case, I thought as he coughed as if his lungs were on fire.

Outside the gate I found Sergeant Lassiter waiting in the rain.

"Any luck?" he asked quietly.

"None. He tells everyone he'd taken a flying leap into a trench. Not true, of course, but he refuses to say more." As the sergeant helped me back on the motorcycle and draped the canvas over me once more, I added, "No one will believe him, not the way he looks." I described what I'd seen. "But if he tells that story long enough, after a while, when he's begun to heal, people will have forgot what he looked like when he came in."

"Best to find the Sergeant-Major, then."

Despite the heavy rain, the state of the roads, and the traffic trying to get through them, we reached the hospital before I was to go on duty in one of the wards. And that was thanks to Sergeant Lassiter's skill with a motorcycle. My heart was still in my throat as I dismounted—and nearly fell on my face when my limbs refused to hold me up. A laughing Sergeant Lassiter held on to me until the circulation returned, and then I stamped about vigorously until all the feeling was back again. The constant jarring and the tenseness of holding on regardless of the machine's gyrations had taken their toll.

It would require a bath and a complete change of clothes to remove both the mud and the smell the ride had left in its wake.

I thanked the sergeant for his help, and he in turn told me he'd see that word was passed to Simon.

"Don't worry that you couldn't get what you needed from Britton, lass. Leave him to the Sergeant-Major. He'll know how to go about it."

Which made it sound as if Simon would use the rack or the iron maiden to make Britton talk.

I smiled. "Let us hope."

But it was three days before Simon appeared at the influenza hospital. I found time to sit down with him in the canteen and tell him what had happened to Corporal Britton and that I'd spoken to him twice without any luck.

"I'm glad. I've been chasing rumors over half of Flanders."

It was rather late, and the canteen was nearly empty. I was keeping an eye out for Matron all the same, even though I'd seen her go to her quarters some forty-five minutes ago. Her face was drawn, and I suddenly worried that she might be coming down with influenza herself. She worked as hard as any of the staff, and sometimes even harder, I thought. And the number of deaths hadn't begun to decline. It was heartbreaking to lose a patient to a disease before which we were so completely helpless. Like some ancient plague brought back from the hot sands of Mesopotamia or Egypt to devastate the modern world.

"Have you news of home?" I asked as I finished my tea.

"Not since I saw you last. You?"

"No. We've heard so many rumors. Do you really believe this war will end soon?" I asked. "Everyone seems so hopeful. It would be sad indeed to disappoint them."

"I expect by Christmas," he told me. "I've heard rumors that Germany is in a terrible state, lacking just about everything. Their troops still have the courage to fight on, but even they're finding it hard to defeat the Americans as well the French and the British."

"I just want the killing and maiming to stop. I want to stop worrying about you and the Colonel Sahib and all my friends—those who're left. I want my mother to have a little time to herself, instead of traveling around England comforting widows and families of the dead. Or visiting hospitals to cheer up the wounded and the dying."

He put his hand over mine where it lay beside my cup. It was warm, strong, comforting.

"You've done wonders yourself, Bess. Are there no scars to take home with you?"

"A good many scars," I admitted. "Sleep will never be quite the same for any of us. Peace will never be quite the same, with so many gone."

And then it was time for him to leave for Rouen.

I walked back to my quarters and sat down on my cot, knowing that it would be a while before I could rest.

Simon was back within forty-eight hours. His face was grim, lined with fatigue, and there was anger there as well.

"He's been transferred to England," he told me straightaway. "Britton. His doctor was concerned about that leg, where the surgery was done. About infection. And so he sent Britton back to England."

"Where?"

"I don't know. Not yet. But I'm leaving for Calais at once. The sooner I'm there in England and can find him, the better."

I held out two envelopes. It had occurred to me that he could carry my letter home for me, without the delays of censors and the erratic mail. "Will you see that this arrives in Somerset? And that this one reaches the Ashtons in Cranbourne? I told them about Britton, and even though he's been moved from Rouen, it's still information they need to know."

"I'll see to it."

"Sergeant Lassiter swears he hadn't touched Britton, and I believe him," I reminded Simon.

"I expect Britton is in something of a quandary. If he tells anyone that he was beaten by some of the men in the tanks corps, it will be tantamount to confessing to the murder of Sergeant Rollins. They won't admit to beating him, or they'll be up on charges. This will be a crime that goes unsolved."

"Yes, I thought of that when I tried to question him. Still, it was worth the journey to Rouen. Sometimes after anesthesia or strong sedatives, one's guard is down."

"A pity it didn't work. All right, I must be on my way. Take care, Bess."

I watched him out of sight, then went back to my duties.

We lost three more men that night, and two the night afterward, all of them to pneumonia, one of the risks in influenza. But more were brought in each day to take their places.

I had almost no sleep the third night, as several more patients reached their crisis, then in the morning, a messenger brought me a letter from Simon.

It was brief.

I've been delayed. Storms. Leaving tonight.

I told myself it wouldn't matter. Corporal Britton would be sedated for the journey back to England and then the first day or two after his arrival to be sure he rested and that the limb stayed quiet while the bone knit and the stitches healed. It would be examined several times a day to be certain there was no infection, neither the purpling nor the odor of gangrene. The staff wouldn't let him be distressed by questions.

It wouldn't matter.

But I had an uneasy feeling that it would.

I'd been there during the surgery on his leg. I knew the risk of infection.

Chapter Seventeen

We had a large number of patients who had survived the influenza and were no longer conta-
gious, but who were suffering from the weakness and
malaise that often followed, leaving the body exhausted
and unable to cope. It was decided—I think because
of the rumors of peace—to transfer these patients to
England to be cared for in a hospital in the country,
where fresh air and exercise would restore them to
health. And of course, duty.

I had suffered that weakness myself, unable to lift
my hand to feed myself, even to turn my head on the
pillow. I knew how humiliating it was for grown men
to be as helpless as small children, and sometimes they
pushed themselves too hard and suffered a relapse.

When the convoy was arranged, Matron asked if I
should like to take it in charge.

I was grateful for the opportunity. I hadn't heard from Simon or from the Ashtons and I longed to see my parents. And so I walked the convalescent wards with Matron, assessing the condition of patients.

Two days later, I was coming down the gangway to meet my counterpart, Sister Cameron, who was arranging transport to London.

"Good evening, Sister Crawford," she said, walking up to greet me as I was watching the preparations for unloading my charges. "Let's begin, shall we?"

We sent the stretcher cases to the London train first, haggard men with sunken, dark-rimmed eyes, followed by seven men in invalid chairs pushed by orderlies. They gazed at the white cliffs rising beyond the harbor with amazement, as if unable to believe what they saw. One soldier hadn't been home in three and a half years.

"Died and gone to heaven," he murmured, shaking his head.

Heavy clouds hung over the castle ramparts, and a cold drizzle was falling. We hurried to get our charges under cover as quickly as possible.

As I worked, I looked for Diana or Mary, hoping that they might be passing through. But no such luck. An orderly waiting for the next ship back to France promised to send a telegram for me, letting my parents know that I was on my way to London. There was no assurance it would arrive in a timely fashion, but I could hope.

We reached London, and there was my father, chatting with the stationmaster. I finished arranging for the last patient to be sent onward, and as I signed the last papers, he came striding toward me.

"You're in London," I said in surprise. "Is Mother here as well?"

"She's in Somerset, but she managed to reach me." He looked tired. "I've just arrived from Paris," he added, "but that's for your ears only. I got in two hours ago, and her message was waiting for me at my club."

He took up my kit and we walked toward the exit to the station. "She's well," he went on. "And sends her love. How much time do you have?"

"Not a lot, sadly."

"Simon is in a convalescent hospital outside Folkestone. Your man Britton was taken there as soon as he landed. As I understand it, his fever spiked, and there was some concern about sending him on to Hampshire."

"That's worrying," I told him. "Has he spoken?"

"I don't know that Simon has been allowed to see him. I expect you want to reach Folkestone as soon as possible."

"Yes, if you don't mind." I smiled ruefully. "I seem to be dashing away almost as soon as I arrive. Did you discover anything about this man, Corporal Britton?"

"Unfortunately, very little that would help you or the Ashtons. I did learn that he was in France in late May of 1916. That's when he was promoted to corporal. Half his company was killed in an attack that went wrong, and he got himself and the rest of the men back safely. With that information I sent one of my people to Devon to find his recruiting officer. Sergeant Hull told us that Britton had enlisted just after war had been declared and one step ahead of the police. He was wanted for questioning in a housebreaking case where the owner was badly hurt. But no one would name him, everyone was too afraid of him, even though the local man was certain who it was. In fact, Constable Lake was happy to let the Army take Britton off his hands just to get him out of his patch. Britton went through his training with high marks. The officer in charge called him a natural soldier. Then he was injured on the last day of exercises, and had to be pulled from the ranks. I expect that's how he came to be assigned as someone's batman. I also wonder if that injury might have been contrived by his mates. He was not particularly liked by the men he trained with. Since 1916, there have been a few blemishes on his record, mostly insubordination, but never severe enough to strip him of his rank or report him for discipline."

"A natural troublemaker."

"So it would appear."

"And someone who might have no qualms about killing," I said. But it could also mean that Britton and Rollins might have a history we didn't know existed. Still, that left Sister Morris to be accounted for.

I was on the point of mentioning this to my father when I saw Simon's motorcar waiting just outside the railway station.

"He left it in London," the Colonel explained. "And I've commandeered it. However, he needs it in Folkestone. Shall I act as your chauffeur as far as Rochester?"

"What is in Rochester, that you're traveling there?" I asked.

"A staff motorcar that will return me to London."

I laughed. "You should have joined the Army. You're very good at organizing transport."

He laughed in his turn, and we set out for Kent.

His staff motorcar was waiting at the railway station in Rochester, and I said good-bye to him there. I had enjoyed our journey. The qualities that had made the Colonel Sahib such a good officer had made him a good father as well, and I missed his reassuring presence beside me as I turned the motorcar toward Folkestone. It had been busy as a port through most of the war, relieving the pressure on Dover to handle all the traffic to and from France.

It was nearly dawn and still drizzling when I reached Canterbury. And I was very tired by that time. I decided that Simon wouldn't mind if I went out of my way very briefly, both to rest and to call on the Ashtons.

The maids and the kitchen staff were up and busy with their duties when I arrived at six. Mrs. Byers, smiling to see me, took me at once to the room I was accustomed to using, got me into bed with a minimum of fuss, lit the fire, and brought up a hot water bottle to put at my feet until the room warmed a little. I barely remember seeing her shut the door.

Accustomed to managing on very little sleep, I was awake by nine. I bathed and dressed before going down to Helen Ashton's sitting room.

She was there with Clara, but Mark was in Canterbury, seeing the military board about extending his leave. Mr. Heatherton-Scott was still in possession of Philip Ashton's study, but no one knew quite where Henry was.

"He's a miracle worker," Mrs. Ashton said as she rang for a belated breakfast for me. "According to

Heatherton-Scott, Henry has managed to speak to quite a few people, and he reports that most of them never saw Philip near the ruins of the mill that day. But they had all heard from someone else that he was behaving suspiciously, and that the fire began while he was standing there. He waited until it was sufficiently alight before telling everyone who came to rescue any wounded to stay away. And Henry learned that the Benning woman claimed in her statement to have seen Philip hand the foreman something when they were talking earlier that morning. It was thought he'd given the man cigarettes."

"And they still believe that? In a gunpowder mill?" I shook my head. "Mr. Ashton doesn't smoke. Did anyone think to ask if the foreman did?"

"According to the ever resourceful Henry, the foreman's widow claims he'd never smoked in his life because of his work in the mill. Still, it's interesting to see just how many people are willing to believe something they've been told when they're already looking for a reason to dislike someone. It's all a pattern of hearsay and rumor, a pattern of lies, and yet it's accepted as truth."

"But what good will this do at Mr. Ashton's trial, if you still don't know how these rumors started?"

Her enthusiasm faded. "That's been troubling. Even Henry hasn't found a name. People remember all the accusations, but when he asks who told them such and such a story, it's a neighbor or someone at the greengrocer's or overheard as they're walking out of church on a Sunday. One man claimed it was a woman standing in a queue at the post office in Canterbury who told him Philip Ashton had wanted more money from the Army, and had even threatened to blow up his own mill if he wasn't given it."

"Mrs. Branch, she of the chickens," I said, gesturing to where Nan lay curled up on the hearth rug. "There was someone with her when we were there to confront her. Has Henry looked into that?"

"She vehemently denies it."

"I saw him. I watched him leave her house."

"She talks vaguely about a friend's son bringing her a jar of cherry preserves. But she can't remember who it was or when. She says we frightened her, and it went out of her head."

"Frightened her?"

"We threatened her, according to Henry."

"How does he manage to make these people talk to him?" I asked.

Clara said, "He has a *knack*. According to Mr. Heatherton-Scott."

"Does he indeed? But with Sergeant Rollins dead, you have very little hard evidence to use in a courtroom," I pointed out.

"This man Britton who killed the sergeant—we asked Henry to find out what he could about him. But people shake their heads and claim not to know anyone by that name. And Mark consulted Philip's records. There isn't a Britton, male or female, on the rolls of the mill. I didn't think there was."

I didn't tell them what my father had discovered about the corporal's troubles with the police. I wanted to talk to Simon first. But I did say, "I'm on my way to see Britton. I've learned he's in a hospital outside Folkestone."

"Is he indeed?" Her eyebrows rose. "Then we must tell Henry. The Beaufort House? Yes, it must be. They offered it to the Army as a hospital after they'd lost a son at Ypres. The first time gas was used. Mark remembers him. There was a party there before the war, on the occasion of the son's engagement. A lovely house, with views down to the Channel."

I asked to speak to Mr. Heatherton-Scott, and he listened intently to what I had to say about Corporal Britton.

"The question we must ask now," he said, "is how to connect Rollins and Britton and the explosion. Otherwise the prosecution will claim it was a personal quarrel between the two men. Beaufort House, you say? I'll put Henry on it."

"There's the matter of Sister Morris. If we can show that someone intended to attack me instead, it should go a long way toward providing a link. I'd been trying to convince Sergeant Rollins to give the police a statement. And generally talking to people in Cranbourne. Someone could have been worried about that. It's the only conclusion I can draw."

"There's that. And I tend to agree with you. Still, it would be better if there was definite proof. See if Corporal Britton will talk to you about Sister Morris. He's back in England, now. He can be brought to testify." He paused, playing with his pen. "Henry did say he has encountered any number of faulty memories in the course of his inquiries. Britton could be a name that people prefer *not* to recall."

"I'm on my way to speak to him now. If I learn anything, I'll let you know."

"Yes, thank you. That would save time. The trial is next week."

Stunned, I stared at him. "But you have almost nothing to show that Philip Ashton is innocent."

"We have a few things. Sergeant Rollins's original statement to the Army doesn't mention Ashton. Surely if he'd seen something suspicious, he would have told the Army straightaway? The Army was seeking answers, and if Rollins had known it was Ashton rather than German saboteurs, it would have changed the direction of their inquiry immediately. Surely they wouldn't have spent so much time on searching for Germans if they'd had their miscreant in the beginning."

A good many *surelys* there, I thought. Mr. Heatherton-Scott was probably absolutely right in his assumptions, but would a jury accept them as facts? Still, added to the clear explanation of the rumors and the lack of supporting evidence behind them, it just might work.

"And, of course, Inspector Brothers had relatives killed in the explosion, which affects his objectivity. He would naturally wish to see their deaths avenged. And then there is the financial point of view, that a small explosion or fire in one building would have achieved Mr. Ashton's purpose, if that was to draw the government's attention to his demands."

"Unless that small explosion got out of hand."

"True. But he knew his mill."

It was a very carefully constructed defense, far more effective than anything Groves had attempted to draw up. But was it enough? Without Rollins there?

Mr. Heatherton-Scott must have read the doubt in my face. He smiled. "Even bricks are made of straw, but put together they can hold up a house."

"I thought I had more, that Sergeant Rollins could provide mortar at least. But it wasn't to be."

"Juries are strange creatures, Sister Crawford. When they see me in my invalid chair, they're amused. A great barrister is like Mr. Worley, tall, imposing, with a shock of white hair that makes him look rather like Beethoven. Or a Sistine Chapel vision of God. A puny man in a chair can't amount to much. But they listen to me because they're curious. And when that happens I know I have them."

I smiled. "I wish I could be there to see it."

He laughed, a deep chuckle. "You would stand amazed."

I found I liked him.

"I must meet a friend. I have his motorcar, and he's waiting for it to travel back to London."

I said good-bye to Clara and to Mrs. Ashton, and asked her to thank Mrs. Byers for putting me up last night. Mrs. Ashton had written out directions to Beaufort House, and I was soon on my way. It was only just going on ten. I heard the church clock strike as I passed by.

When I arrived, Simon was waiting in what had been the small drawing room in the lovely old Beaufort House. His expression in repose was grim, but he

428 · CHARLES TODD

smiled in surprise when I walked through the door.
An orderly had told me where to find him.

"I didn't think the Colonel would be here much
before noon."

"He met my train in London and told me he'd commandeered your motorcar. I simply relieved him of it.
But I had to stop outside Canterbury and rest a little.
Have you spoken to Britton? Will they allow me to see
him?"

"He's dead, Bess."

"Dead?" I stared at him. There were others within
hearing, and with a hand at my elbow Simon led me
to a small room in the back of the house where men
exercised during recuperation. We had it to ourselves
at this hour. "Was it a clot? That was a very difficult
surgery. I shouldn't be surprised if that's what happened. Infection? Or gangrene?"

"He was murdered. Someone held a pillow over his
face."

I sat down on the nearest chair. "But who could have
done such a thing? A hospital like this is always busy,
day and night. Who could just walk in here, kill a man,
and walk out again?"

But even as I said it, I knew from my own experience that these wards were very different from a real
hospital. This was a house, after all. The rooms were

used to the best possible advantage, with six to eight men in each one, and only so many critical care or surgical wards, depending on the need at the time. And there were half a dozen doors going outside, with no reason to lock or even guard them.

"There were only the two men in the critical ward. The other soldier hasn't regained consciousness," Simon was saying, as if he'd heard my thought. "When I was trying to question Britton, it was for all intents and purposes a single room."

"When was he killed?"

"Last night. Since dawn I've been talking to everyone in Beaufort House. At first the staff were reluctant to report what had happened. More than half must have feared it was another patient. But there are no head wounds that need to be restrained here, and no tank men. I can tell you this: as his fever rose and Britton was increasingly delirious, he talked about the war and his past. And then the night before he died, his ramblings grew more coherent. That's when I began taking notes. He mentioned Rollins a number of times. It was difficult to understand most of it, something to do with a burning tank."

"A tank was on fire when Rollins was shot."

"Yes. After that he began to talk about Cranbourne. Apparently he didn't think much of the people there and had as little to do with them as possible. But he appeared to know more about what happened than could be accounted for by just reading a newspaper."

"Are you saying *he* might have been responsible?"

"More along the lines of considering the search for Germans foolhardy when they should have been pointing the finger at the men running the day-to-day operations. He thought them incompetent." He drew a sheaf of papers from his tunic. "You can look at these later, but the main facts are that he must have known Rollins and the Ashtons, and a man named Collier. He also said something about you, which I omitted from my notes. He cursed you."

Ignoring that last, I said, "But Captain Collier was the Army's liaison man in Cranbourne. What on earth was Britton doing there?"

And then I remembered. Britton had been an officer's batman. We'd assumed the officer he was assigned to must have been killed in France and Britton carried on with his old regiment. That was the usual course of events. But what if his officer had been reassigned and no longer needed a servant?

I told Simon what my father had learned about Britton's past, put together with what I'd already discovered on my own. "There's the connection we've been searching for, Simon. Britton, Collier, Rollins, the Ashtons. All of them here when the mill blew up. But Britton has been in France since May of 1916. He couldn't have been behind the campaign of whispers."

"Where is Collier?"

"No one seems to know. London? Scotland? France? Except that he isn't on the active duty roster."

"Britton had no visitors, Bess. But the other man in the surgical ward had an unexpected one the second day after Britton arrived. And the day after that. His name was Henley. Lieutenant Henley. I was later told that he sat with the other patient for an hour or more, even though the man was unconscious. He would have heard everything that Britton was saying. To someone who didn't know the man, it would have made almost no sense. To the right person, it would have been a warning."

"Where did this Lieutenant come from? And how did he discover that Britton was here?"

"He claimed he'd just been posted to Folkestone. But no one in charge there knows anything about a Lieutenant Henley. I expect he'd seen the casualty lists, and managed to find out where Britton was taken. If it had been Yorkshire or Dorset, no one would have known what he was saying in his delirium. Here in Kent, it was too great a risk. In fact, one of the Sisters asked me if Cranbourne was Britton's home."

"If Henley doesn't exist, then who was the man? And why would he wish to silence Britton?" I answered my own question. "One, someone who'd served with Rollins? Two, an old enemy of Britton's from before the war? Or this elusive Captain Collier?"

"The tank corps had already got its revenge in France. An old enemy is always a possibility, but too much of a coincidence, I think. Which leaves us with Collier. As for Henley—or whoever he might be—he wasn't here earlier, when Britton was going on about the tanks and his past in Devon. By the time he *was* sitting in that room, Britton was already talking about Cranbourne. And Henley must have heard enough to put the wind up."

"I even asked the recruiting officer in Canterbury if he knew where the Captain had been sent, but he didn't. It's possible he really did go north with the newly expanded mill there."

"If he's at the mill, we'll be able to find out if he took leave this past week."

"Who will handle Britton's death? The Army? The local police?"

"It hasn't been decided."

"You know, it's likely the corporal would have been dead very soon anyway from the infection in that leg. Henley needn't have drawn attention to himself by resorting to murder. He could have simply waited. Unless he was afraid he couldn't afford to."

The trial was set for next week. Had he found that out?

We spent the next hour talking to the Sisters in charge of Corporal Britton's care, but they couldn't help us very much. Yes, they'd seen Lieutenant Henley sitting by the unconscious man's cot. One of the orderlies had admitted him, but he was an officer and passed through without question. Had he returned in the night? No one could say for certain whether he had or not.

As for when Henley had last come to Beaufort House, no one could answer that. As one of the Sisters commented, "Most of the convalescent men are in uniform. Some of them volunteer to read to the bed patients, and others walk the passages for exercise. We have men who are allowed to walk on the grounds. If this Lieutenant was cleared to visit a patient, no one would take particular notice of him."

"But you'd recognize a stranger? Surely?" I asked, but I already knew the answer.

"We're run off our feet, Sister. We could use a dozen more staff, and they send us new patients every day. We weren't supposed to take Corporal Britton, but his fever was very high, and we were the nearest hospital with a surgeon. In case."

In case they'd had to remove that leg.

We did get a description of sorts. Medium height, fair. Nice face. And probably blue eyes as well. Which would fit half the British Army.

After speaking to the Inspector from Folkestone, who had just arrived, we walked out into the house grounds, Simon furiously angry beside me.

"No one saw fit to tell me about Henley, even though I had left orders that no one was to visit Britton. This could have been prevented."

"A determined man . . ." I said. "Still, everyone thought he'd come to see the other patient in the ward. He was even seen sitting by him. It wouldn't have occurred to the staff that he was actually listening to the delirious ramblings on the other side of the room. What will you do now?"

He took a deep breath. "Britton is dead. They wouldn't allow me to go through his belongings—not without permission from his next of kin. I'm not sure it would have changed anything. If Britton killed Rollins, it's too late to do anything about it. I did suggest to the local man that he insist on looking in Britton's kit for that cushion you'd told me about. He didn't seem to think it important. He feels that whoever killed Britton is well away. I've questioned everyone, I've done what I could to help the local man take over the inquiry.

I've asked that a final report on Britton's death be sent to the Colonel. I have no more authority here." But I could tell he was unhappy about the situation.

"The Ashtons will be grateful for any information," I agreed. "Then if you're on your way to London, you can drop me in Canterbury or Cranbourne. I go back to France tomorrow."

Half an hour later, as we turned west out of Beaufort House's drive, I told him about Heatherton-Scott and his man, Henry.

"I recognize the name," Simon replied. "I've never met him. Interesting man."

"And Henry has gleaned a great deal of information in his forays. Intelligence could use a man of his skill."

"He could be a conscientious objector," Simon answered thoughtfully.

"I hadn't considered that. Then why isn't he serving in a hospital or as an orderly?"

"Heatherton-Scott must have friends in high places."

As we left the coast behind and made our way into Canterbury, I said, "I wish you could meet Mark Ashton."

"I must get back to Somerset. There may be new orders waiting."

I had hardly mentioned Mark's name when I looked up to see Mark just crossing the street, walking with another man in uniform.

"Simon—wait. There he is."

When I hailed Mark, he turned, smiled, and made his excuses to the other officer.

"I didn't know you were back in England," he said, coming up to the motorcar where Simon had pulled to the verge, "until Mrs. Byers told me this morning. You were still asleep when I left. The medical board has given me another ten days of leave."

"I'm glad. For your mother's sake." I made the necessary introductions, and went on, "There's something else you should know, Mark. Corporal Britton is dead. He'd just been sent home from France, to Beaufort House. Simon was there to question him, but he had a fever and was raving. And someone must have been worried about that. He was smothered in the night."

Mark said grimly, "There's no end of it, is there? First Rollins and then Britton."

"But Britton mentioned Collier in his ravings," Simon told him. "Bess thinks Britton must have been his batman."

Frowning, Mark looked away. "There *was* a batman. I never met him. But my father must have done. He'd know who it was."

"But Mr. Heatherton-Scott is the only person who can speak to him," I said.

"Then we'll bring him to Canterbury." Mark looked around. "My motorcar is by the hospital. If you'll run me out to the house, Brandon, I'll speak to Heatherton-Scott straightaway."

"Yes, of course."

I said, "You'll need more room. I'll stay here in Canterbury. There's a telephone here, and I can put in a call to the Colonel Sahib to see what else he can discover. If he's available," I added almost under my breath.

"A good idea," Simon agreed. "Ask him about Henley as well. If he exists, it's possible the Colonel can find out what his connection to Britton may be, and if he's on his way to France or still in England."

"I shall."

Mark gave me a hand down, and took my place beside Simon. "We'll meet you by the police station," he told me. "Wait there for us."

I set out to the hotel where I'd used the telephone before, and as before, I explained that it was war related, my call. The hotel policy was strict about public use.

I tried my father's club first, but I was told he'd left. I put in a call to my mother next, and she said, "My dear, it's so good to hear your voice. Where are you? In Dover or Portsmouth?"

"Actually I'm in Canterbury. I ran into Father at Victoria Station, and I brought Simon's motorcar down to Folkestone for him." I changed from English to Hindi, and explained as best I could about Corporal Britton and his death. I didn't want the operator to hear what I was asking. "It's important that I reach Father. Do you know where he is? I've tried the club."

"He's on his way abroad," she said, and I remembered then that he had come from Paris. "Is it truly urgent? What you need to know?"

"Very."

"Can you wait? His papers are on his desk. There might be something that will help you."

But there wasn't. More disappointed than I wanted her to know, I said, "Will you tell him, when you hear from him, that I need to find any connection between these four men? Sergeant Rollins, Corporal Britton, Lieutenant Collier, and Lieutenant Henley. And if I'm back in France, a telegram to Mr. Heatherton-Scott at Abbey Hall will reach the right person."

"I'll see to it. I do wish you could have come home, my dear. We've missed you."

"As much as I've missed you," I said, and then regretfully told her good-bye. I could see the hotel's manager standing outside the glass doors of the telephone closet, his pocket watch in his hands.

Opening the doors, I said, "I'm so sorry. My business took longer than I'd anticipated."

"What was this urgent matter?"

"It's about a murder," I said. "The Military Foot Police are involved."

He stared at me. "I expect you not to say anything about this to the hotel's guests."

I had to promise before he would let me go.

I walked on to the police station, and stood nearby for a quarter of an hour. Restless, I turned and went to find myself a cup of tea. There was a shop not a dozen doors down the street. I could see through the window that it was filled with soldiers and their families. Hesitating, not certain how long it would take to be served, I recognized the man just leaving.

It was the recruiting officer.

I said, "Hallo. I don't know if you remember me. Not long ago I asked you about Captain Collier, and a corporal by the name of Britton. I've learned since that Corporal Britton was Captain Collier's batman." I was fishing for more information.

"Have you indeed? Is it helpful? I think you said you knew the Captain?"

"Only casually, through friends," I said with a smile.

"Walk with me. I'm so sorry I couldn't help you find the man. Have you been able to locate Collier? Is this how you learned he had a batman?"

"I'm still looking for him. Apparently he's not in France. Very likely this means he's up in Scotland. At the mill that replaced Ashton's."

"Surely the Ashtons would have kept up with him?"

"I don't believe anyone locally has. Which again leads to the supposition he's in Scotland."

"Yes, I expect he doesn't get down to Kent very often."

I could see the cathedral gate at the end of the street, and through the arches the church itself, the spires of the towers soaring above.

"Well, again, I'm sorry that I haven't more information to give you. Good day, Sister. I'll leave you here."

He touched his cap to me, and strode off.

Another dead end, I thought, watching him walk on.

I debated finding another tea shop, then decided instead to go on down to the cathedral and step inside. The sun was just coming out after what felt like days of drizzle and downpours, and I thought the stained glass would be at its best just now. I had been about to go inside when first I'd encountered Mark.

I passed through the high gate, feeling the chill of the shadows, and came out into the sunlight again. Ahead was the west front, and the doors were closed against the weather. Not that it helped—these great churches were never warm, even in high summer.

I was reaching out to push open the heavy door when for some reason I turned to look back the way I'd come. Someone was standing there, in the deeper shadows of the gate.

My first thought was, *Simon has come to fetch me.* But whoever it was didn't look at all like Simon. He wasn't tall enough, and he didn't carry himself the way Simon did. What's more, the way he was staring in my direction made me uncomfortable.

Was it Henry? Waiting there for me to go inside so that he could pursue his own affairs for Mr. Heatherton-Scott?

And then whoever it was turned and disappeared around the corner, as if he'd changed his mind about visiting the cathedral.

All the same, I was uneasy. I opened the heavy door and went inside. But instead of letting it swing shut all the way, I held it open just enough to have a clear view of someone walking down toward the west front. If someone *was* following me, I wanted to know.

I could hear footsteps coming toward the entrance, and then a man in uniform with a girl at his side shoved the doors wide, and I had to step hastily away out of their path.

It was a corporal in a Shropshire regiment, and his sweetheart. I could tell by their smiles. Had he been waiting for her by the gate, and then changed his mind and gone to meet her? I felt rather foolish.

While I moved on to enter the sanctuary, they didn't follow. Behind me as I walked on, I could hear them laughing, then a moment of silence while they must have kissed. And then, laughing once more with the excitement of what they'd just done, they went out the doors again. It struck me that they'd just become engaged, and there was probably nowhere else they could snatch a private moment but here.

Smiling, I stared up at the soaring roof of the nave, so delicate and airy that it still had the power to amaze, no matter how many times I'd seen it. The great windows splashed colored light on the stone floors and the clustered pillars, and there was a serenity here that was a breath of peace. And I had it all to myself.

The church was silent—even my own footsteps echoed as I went forward, looking up at the magnificent stained glass. The richness of the blues, an occasional deep green in a robe, a dash of yellow in a shoe, red for drama, but overall those wonderful blues that filled the church with glory. I knew about the quire, the tombs, the chapter house, the zodiac set in brass polished by so many feet. It was the glass I loved.

Once, when we'd come back from India on leave, my cousin Melinda Crawford had brought me here on an outing. My father was in London, conferring with the Army and the War Office, and my mother had gone up with him. It was an odd choice of entertainment for a restless five-year-old. I couldn't appreciate the architecture or the tombs—indeed, even on tiptoe, I could hardly see over the tops of them. I couldn't have told anyone what stories the glass had been created to tell. But the colors had enthralled me. India was gaudy with color; the temples and the gods and the women in their saris brightened the hot, dusty landscape with dazzling, almost garish life. This was somehow different. Brilliant but subtle, soothing but vibrant. When it was time to go, I hadn't wanted to leave.

Behind me I heard the door scrape open, and I turned, thinking that this was a fine place to be trapped. I don't know why that thought popped into my head, but I moved to a point where I could see whoever it was just coming into the nave.

An elderly priest stepped through the doors, his face blotched with age, his arthritic hand holding tightly to a cane. I watched as he came down the north aisle, and I thought he might be going to the place where Becket was martyred, but he made his slow and painful way to the chapter house and disappeared from view.

Quiet descended once more, and I walked on to the crossing of the transepts where the tower of Bell Harry rose high over my head. I could look up into the shaft and see the ornate ceiling there, like embroidery on a ball gown, intricate and delicate and quite beautiful.

There was the scrape of the door again, but I'd got over my anxiety, and didn't hurry back to the nave to see who was there. I wandered on, looking up at the glass.

Brisk footsteps came into the nave, then slowed. Starting up again, they seemed to be exploring, for they moved this way and that, as if admiring all that was on offer.

I had gone into the apse, the chapel where the tomb of Becket had stood before the Reformation, where the blue of the glass seemed to surround me in the curved wall above my head. Absorbed, I lingered there. Then, remembering that I was to meet Simon and Mark at the police station, I turned and started back the way I'd come. And I ran straight into a man standing beneath the shaft of Bell Harry, looking up.

Chapter Eighteen

He seemed startled to see me. It was the recruiting officer.

"Hallo," he said, smiling. "I come here sometimes to get away from the bustle of the town. I've just been to the railway station, seeing off a company of men I'd persuaded to enlist. I try to do that when I can."

"I'm sure it's appreciated."

"I like to think so." He fell into step beside me as I continued to walk toward the nave. "Actually, I'm rather glad I've run into you again. I know we haven't been properly introduced, but I was wondering if we could have lunch together. It's early, I know, but my responsibilities are dealt with, and I don't have to be back at the recruiting office until two o'clock. I'd like it very much if you would say yes."

"I'm so sorry. I have to meet friends, and they're been delayed. That's why I came here to see the stained glass."

"My loss," he said with a wry smile. "Another time, perhaps? We seem to make a habit of running into each other unexpectedly." We had reached the nave again, walking side by side. "Are you in Canterbury for very long?"

"I leave for France tomorrow."

He took out his pocket watch to check the time, and stopped dead. "I've lost the fob." Glancing around, as if it were somewhere underfoot, he said, "My father gave it to me. It's in the shape of a frog. Passed down through the family from a great-great-grandfather. I wonder where it could have got to." He felt in his pocket, then turned to stare back the way we'd come. "I took out my watch in the transept just before I saw you. It's not keeping proper time, and I need to have it looked at. I say, you wouldn't mind helping me search, would you?" An embarrassed note crept into his voice. "My eyesight isn't the best. Which is why I'm recruiting soldiers instead of leading them."

I hesitated, knowing I was probably already late meeting Simon and Mark. But I could hardly walk away.

"Yes, all right, let's have a look."

We walked briskly down the aisle toward the transept and the tower crossing.

"You're sure it was there at that time? You didn't lose it on the street or in the recruiting office?"

"God, I hope not," he said fervently. "But yes, I think it was still there when I took out my watch. It may have caught on my clothing as I put the watch back into my pocket."

We walked past the quire, the tombs, the long beautiful windows, and came to the transept once more. He began looking, staring down at the floor with fixed attention, and I moved a little beyond him.

There was nothing on the floor that I could see. Certainly not something as large as a watch fob.

Still, I kept looking. I could hear him behind me, swearing under his breath, and just then I saw a glimmer of gold in the dark shadows where the light from the transept windows couldn't quite reach it.

"Over here."

I went down on one knee and put out my hand to grasp a handsome little gold frog. No wonder he'd feared losing it.

I had it in my hand and was just turning my head when something soft and white came slipping over my face, settling around my neck. I had a fleeting moment to realize that it was the long silk scarf pilots affected, and to think about Alex Craig, when the scarf began to tighten viciously.

I was still on one knee, but I struggled to get to my feet and succeeded finally, even as the silk tightened again.

"I'm not good at this," he said through clenched teeth. "Stand still, damn you, and it won't hurt as much."

It was hard to breathe now, and I knew very well how little time I had. He was behind me, I couldn't reach his face or his eyes, and even his hands, drawing the scarf tighter, were beyond my fists, though I scrabbled over my shoulders trying to reach them.

I knew that the pressure on the great arteries in the throat would make me pass out, and after that he could finish his work without interference.

But I had my boots, those sensible, sturdy boots that could withstand the mud and rains of France. I made an effort to pull my body away, walking my feet away from him as the scarf tightened again. And then balancing myself on one foot, I stretched my leg out and brought it back against where I judged his kneecap to be, using all the force I could muster.

The flat of my heel must have caught him squarely.

He howled with pain and rage, dropping one end of the silk cloth as he fell back, away from me.

I was very dizzy as I pulled the free end of the scarf away from my throat. The strength needed to kick him had taken the last of my physical energy. I dropped to my knees, gasping for air, trying to clear the darkness from my sight, and all the while my brain was screaming at me to run.

Getting up, I staggered, then found my footing, racing toward the north aisle. I could hear him struggling to follow me, cursing his knee.

I cast one glance over my shoulder, then hurried on, knowing I had to reach the outer door before he could catch up to me. The pain and the numbness would not hold him for very long.

I nearly ran straight into the aged priest. I don't know which of us was more startled.

"Sister?" he stammered.

I saw the cane in his hand, and gently took it from him.

"Please, Vicar—"

Just then my assailant came into sight, dragging one leg, his face flushed with anger and something else I didn't want to think about.

Elderly he might be—he could have been ninety for all I knew—but the Vicar drew himself up to his full height as he took in the situation at a glance.

He was thinking rape, not murder, but I didn't care.

"Here," he bellowed, in a voice that could reach the back of a church from the altar. "What's this about, then?"

Swiftly collecting himself, the Lieutenant stopped and said furiously, "She's stolen my watch fob. It's gold. Worth a pretty sum."

The Vicar turned to me. I realized suddenly that it was still in my hand, that even in my struggles, I hadn't let go of it.

"Show him." The Lieutenant's voice was almost a growl, deep throated and rough.

I opened my fist, and there it lay, in a small pool of blood where I'd clutched it so hard.

"He tried to strangle me. With a scarf. He claimed he'd lost the fob, and I'd gone with him to look." It sounded weak in my own ears.

The man opened his arms wide. "Do you see a scarf?"

"This is a matter for the police," the Vicar said firmly. "You'll both come with me. Now, if you please."

But I knew he wouldn't. That the frail old man was not going to stop him. I knew too much, I couldn't be allowed to speak to the police.

He surprised me. "Lead on."

Nodding, the Vicar took my arm, turning to guide me up the aisle, turning his back on the Lieutenant.

I whirled in time, the cane still in my free hand, and lifted it high just as the Lieutenant raised his clasped fists and was about to bring them down hard on the back of the Vicar's neck.

He saw it coming, and tried to deflect it with one arm, thinking I was aiming for his head, but before he could react, I swung the cane like a cricket bat. It caught him across the throat and chest just beneath his raised hands.

He went down, and a little to one side, and this time I felt no mercy toward him. As his right hand touched the cold stone of the pavement, I lifted the cane again and cracked him across the head with it.

He collapsed and was still.

Beside me, the Vicar was crying, "Here, no! You mustn't."

He reached for the cane in my hands and with surprising strength wrenched it through my fingers.

"Please, we must find the police. He was trying to kill me—he'd have killed you as well if I hadn't stopped him."

Instead the Vicar turned to the man lying at his feet, and he reached a hand down to feel for a pulse. "He's breathing. We must find help for him."

"He's unconscious," I said, "but he'll be rousing up shortly. Please, before that, we must find the police."

I think my urgency got through to the Vicar. Straightening with an effort, he said sternly, "You will stay with me, Sister. I have your description, if you try to run. We will find you."

"My name is Elizabeth Crawford," I told him. "I live in Somerset with my parents. At the moment, I'm staying with the Ashtons in Cranbourne."

His brows rose at that, white tufts of wiry hair above surprisingly sharp gray eyes. "We'll soon see if you're telling the truth."

He took my arm again, although I could have knocked him down without any effort at all, and I meekly let him lead me up the aisle and through the heavy doors to the bright sunshine outside.

Both of us blinked after the dimness of the church. He turned toward Christ Church Gate, and again I followed without demur. The sooner we found the police, the better we would both be.

I cast a glance over my shoulder just as we reached the tall, lovely gate, and I saw the Lieutenant standing in front of the church, swaying, blood on his face. I wondered if I'd broken his nose, or if it was his head.

And then we were outside, in the busy street, where there were people in every direction. I sighed with relief.

Still gripping my arm—I knew I'd have a bruise tomorrow—the Vicar led me the shortest way to the police station. As we approached, two men came out the door and stood for a moment in the road, talking. It was Simon and Mark, and judging by their expressions they'd had no joy of Inspector Brothers. Or perhaps they'd had to wait, and he still hadn't shown his face.

It was Simon who turned, as if he sensed my presence, and said, "Bess."

Mark turned as well, and both of them came striding toward me.

"What's the matter?" Simon asked, his gaze moving from me to my escort, who was breathing a little hard from the pace he'd set us. Then his eyes fell to my throat.

I reached up. The stiff collar of my uniform was crushed and pushed to one side, and my cap was askew. I thought, chagrined, that I must have looked as if I had been drinking, not like a Sister in good standing. I reached up to set them to rights.

The Vicar regarded the two tall men, one in an officer's uniform and the other in that of a Regimental Sergeant-Major.

"Do you know this young woman?" he asked.

"She's my Colonel's daughter," Simon replied shortly. "What's wrong, Bess?"

"The Vicar has rescued me from a man who accosted me in the cathedral. We managed to get away from him, although I think he's got a very sore head and a very painful knee. Mark—Major Ashton—would you do me the greatest favor? Would you go to the cathedral and just there under Bell Harry, see if you can find a white silk scarf? The kind pilots often wear?"

"I won't go anywhere until you tell me what's happened to you."

"Please? Before he remembers it and goes back for it. It's the only proof I have."

The Vicar stared from me to Mark. "The proof is the gold watch fob she's got in her hand."

It was in my pocket now, and I couldn't remember just when I'd dropped it there. When I clutched at the Vicar's cane? As he took my arm?

It didn't matter. I put my hand in my pocket. "Here's the fob. In the shape of a frog. It belongs to that man. He accused me of stealing it, which isn't at all the truth."

Mark said, brooking no argument, "The motorcar. It's the fastest way back to the cathedral. Sir, if you'll come with us now?"

The Vicar clung to my arm. "The police . . ." he began.

"Inspector Brothers isn't in his office just now. If we are to speak to him, we must be sure we have all the evidence."

Confused, the Vicar followed him to the motorcar some ten feet from where we'd been standing, but he insisted that I must sit in the rear seat next to him, where apparently he could keep a close eye on me.

Simon went to the crank while Mark got us into the vehicle, and then we were driving through the busy streets back to Christ Church Gate. As he drew up in front of it, Simon told him, "Stay with the motorcar, sir. I'll have a look."

I knew what he intended. He hoped the man I'd mentioned might still be there. His mouth was drawn in a tight line, and although I couldn't see his eyes, I knew they were angry.

He got down, and strode briskly toward the cathedral.

The Vicar called after him, "If you find the wounded man in the north aisle, give him what help you can."

Simon didn't turn.

We watched him walk through the shadow of the gate and continue to the cathedral doors, disappearing inside.

The Vicar stirred restlessly. "I wish someone would tell me what's going on. We should be speaking to the police. This young woman—I tell you, I was a witness."

"We will, as soon as we have all the facts," Mark assured him. "If Be— Sister Crawford believes there's additional evidence still to be had there in the church, then we have an obligation to find it before we take her to the police."

"You say you know this young woman?"

"She's a guest of my mother's. Mrs. Ashton."

"Your father is charged with that terrible explosion at the powder mill."

"Yes, that's true," Mark answered stiffly. "But we aren't convinced of his guilt."

He turned to me. "Who is this man—the one the Vicar is so concerned about—the one you tell me accosted you?"

"The officer in charge of the recruiting office here in Canterbury."

Mark's eyebrows rose. "Why should he attack you?"

I didn't know. But I was beginning, now that I was feeling less shaken, to pull the pieces together. "We met in the cathedral. In hindsight, I don't know if it was accidental or on purpose. We were just leaving when he realized he'd lost that fob—or claimed he had—well, at any rate, I did find it where he'd said it might be—and the next thing I knew he had a scarf around my throat and was choking me." I told him the rest, while the Vicar listened, appalled, and I watched as Mark's face changed.

"I'm going after the Sergeant-Major. If the man's still there, by God, we'll bring him out."

"I don't believe he is. I saw him leaving the cathedral as we walked through the Gate. He was bleeding."

The Vicar said, "Just what is going on, Major?"

"If Sister Crawford says she was attacked, I believe her, the gold watch fob notwithstanding," he answered harshly.

Just then Simon came striding out of the cathedral. If he had the silk scarf, I couldn't see it.

We waited in silence for him to reach the motor-car, and as he got in, I said, worried, "Did you find it, Simon?"

He put a hand into his tunic and pulled out the silk scarf. "It was where you said it would be. What's more—" He unfolded it, and lifted out his handkerchief. I could see the dark stains in the center of the linen. "*This*," he went on, gesturing to the blood, "was on the paving stones in the north aisle, very close to where I was told to look for an injured man."

"It's the young officer's blood," the Vicar said. "She was beating him about the head with my cane."

"What should we do?" Mark asked, cutting across the Vicar's words. "I don't trust Brothers any farther than I can see him. He'll find a way to twist this, just as he's twisted the evidence in my father's case."

The Vicar spoke up. "If you don't trust the police, may I suggest the Church?"

It was Simon who settled the issue very simply. "It's an Army matter. After all, a serving officer has attacked a member of Queen Alexandra's Imperial Military Nursing Service. But that can wait. First we'll find this man."

The Vicar agreed. "He could be gravely injured. She struck him. Twice. I saw it with my own eyes."

Simon turned in his seat. "You saw the final events, sir. Not the start of this business. Look at Sister Crawford's throat."

I'd done what I could to make myself presentable again. Depend on Simon seeing the marks. But the Vicar, leaning forward, was peering at my throat.

"There are red streaks that could be the beginning of bruising," he said, surprised.

"They are just showing up," Simon told him. He turned to Mark. "Who would know the name of this recruiting officer?"

In smaller towns and villages it was usually a sergeant, but here in Canterbury there was a Lieutenant in charge . . .

Before Mark could answer him, I said, "The recruiting officer is Lieutenant Collier."

Mark and Simon turned to stare at me.

"Are you certain?"

"No. But it's the only explanation. I've asked him about Captain Collier, you see. And he claimed not to know where to find him. What if the Captain's been here from the start? Not in London or Scotland, as everyone thought. What if this was his punishment for the explosion at the mill? We've been told he was demoted in rank."

"But we'd have seen him," Mark said. "Someone from Cranbourne would have recognized him."

"Perhaps someone did, and he saw his chance to take revenge on your father? If he could convince whoever it was to keep his secret, because he was being punished by the Army while your father went free, it would go a long way toward making whatever he said credit-able. After all, it was all too clear that he was telling the truth."

The Vicar said, "Will you please tell me what's going on?"

Mark hadn't cut the motor. He took off the brake and let in the clutch. "If Collier, or whoever he is, is bleeding, he will go to the nearest doctor or hospital."

"I don't know that he will," I responded. "He won't want anyone to know he was in a brawl. I'm sure that's how it would look." I gave him directions to the recruiting office, adding, "He'll go to ground as quickly as possible." As Mark carefully turned the motorcar, I said to the Vicar, showing signs of stopping him straightaway. "Please, there's a good reason for our concern. I didn't steal the watch fob. And I didn't mean to hurt the Lieutenant. You couldn't see—he was on the point of attacking you. Knocking you down." I tried to give him a brief account of what had been happening in Cranbourne for months. And as I did, I thought it might be too much for him to absorb. But he kept nodding as he took it all in.

"It's very different, what occurred in the cathedral, from what I believed at the time. I'm willing to suspend judgment until I know the whole. But I think you ought to give me the watch fob, for safekeeping."

I couldn't tell if it was a test of some kind or not. But I reached into my pocket and brought it out, holding it in the palm of my hand. A stray flash of sunlight as we turned a corner struck gold fire from the little frog.

"Please, take it. I'd rather not have to be responsible for it." And I handed it to him.

Nodding, he slipped it into his pocket. "Thank you, my dear. Now what can I do?"

We were just up the road from the recruitment office. Simon signaled Mark to stop where we were. "He doesn't know me, sir. Let me have a look."

"Yes, good idea," Mark agreed. He pulled to the side of the road, and Simon got out. We watched him walk up to the door and try it. Next he put his hand up to cut out the back light as he peered through the window. Then, stepping back, he looked up, as if trying to see if Lieutenant Collier lived above it. He shook his head and came back to us at a trot.

"He's not inside. The door is shut and locked. Someone gives music lessons in the flat above. I could hear the piano, someone doing finger exercises."

"Where do you suppose he lives?" Mark asked.

"Not on this street," I said. "He wouldn't want to live here." It was a street of lower-middle-class shops, with flats above, and the people I could see walking by us were not the most prosperous. "Bad enough to serve out the war here. He'd want better accommodations elsewhere. Out of pride, if nothing else."

Mark began to drive randomly up that street and then down the next as we considered what to do. "I don't know that I'll recognize him. Even if we pass him."

"I will. Besides, there was blood all over his face. He will try to hide it," I said. "He won't want anyone stopping him to ask questions."

"We aren't likely to find him by chance," Simon put in. "If he's smart, he's at home and out of sight for the time being. Very likely we've lost him."

We had turned down the next street when we saw a cluster of people blocking it ahead of us. There was a good deal of shouting as well. We slowed as a constable arrived at almost the same moment, and began trying to sort it out.

Behind us, others were hurrying down the narrow street, effectively blocking us in both directions now.

"Do you think it's Collier?" I asked quickly. "Trying to find a policeman?"

Mark said, "Sergeant-Major, will you see what this is all about?"

Simon got down and walked swiftly toward the center of the commotion. I could follow the progress of his cap as he made his way through the growing crowd, for he was taller than most. People were coming out of shops now, drawn by the uproar.

We sat there in strained silence, waiting. It was several minutes before Simon came back.

As he got into the motorcar, he said, "A man in uniform, his face bloody, stopped a driver, demanding his motorcar, telling him it was official Army business, and urgent. The man refused to give up his vehicle, and the officer pulled him down and struck him with his revolver. Then he drove off."

"But where to?" I asked, thinking aloud. "Why should the Lieutenant require a motorcar? At a guess he walked to and from his work every day. Or he'd have his own if it was too far to walk." And then almost in the same breath, I answered my own question. "Mark. The house. He's on his way to Cranbourne. He's still looking for me."

Simon got down again and cleared a path for the motorcar. At one point I heard him telling people that the Vicar was on his way to a sickbed. Sometimes he claimed we were on our way to hospital with the Sister and the Vicar. Slowly, reluctantly, a path opened, and Mark reversed through the staring crowd, some of them close enough to touch Mark's vehicle. And then we were clear, and Mark was able to turn back toward the road to Cranbourne. Simon got in and said, "Fast as you can. Sir."

But Mark didn't need encouragement. As soon as we'd reached the outskirts of Canterbury, he drove like a madman. He knew the road, he knew every curve and dip, but we held on nevertheless, and said nothing.

I said into the tense silence, "Mark, you'd gone to fetch Mr. Heatherton-Scott. Is he—was he planning to ask permission to speak to your father?"

"He was waiting for Henry to return. I offered to drive him to Canterbury, but he's used to Henry assisting him. He may be there by now, waiting for Brothers just as we did."

Mr. Ashton could identify the recruiting officer, if he was indeed Lieutenant Collier. All we needed now was to find the man and take him back to Canterbury.

Coming down the hill into the little village, Mark slowed, but not by much. He stood on the horn as he made to pass a slower cart bringing coal into the square, and then he pulled hard on the brake as a crocodile of schoolchildren crossed the road ahead of us, on their way, I thought, to the abbey ruins. They were muffled to the eyes against the wind coming in off The Swale and the Thames Estuary. Finally we were free to run as fast as we could down Abbey Lane.

But there was no motorcar in the drive before the house. We slowed, staring at the empty half circle.

"I don't want to disturb my mother," Mark said sharply. "But where is he?"

"The ruins," I suggested. "The powder mill ruins," I amended. "If he's not there, then it's possible he went to Mrs. Branch's cottage."

"He may have gone to Dover," Mark countered, his anxiety showing in the tension in his voice. "We could be losing time here."

"I can't think why," I answered. "He doesn't have a pass to board a transport. Unless of course he intends to claim you attacked him, Mark." And I felt a *frisson* of worry. If he did that, would he be believed? Would the evidence of his injuries speak for him?

"Try the river," Simon told Mark, omitting the obligatory "sir."

"Why there?" Mark demanded.

"Because it's where this began."

Mark drove out of the circle and turned the bonnet back down the lane, cutting toward the water when he reached the turning.

And there, as we rounded the corner of the first of the warehouses, was a motorcar standing by the open doorway where Alex Craig worked on his boat.

"Stop. Mark? Please," I asked quietly.

But he moved up another ten feet before drawing to a halt.

"Does that motorcar belong to Alex Craig?"

"No. He runs a Sunbeam," Mark answered. "I think we've found our man." I reached for the handle to the door. "Wait. It's not safe, Bess," Mark said urgently. "He's armed, remember?"

"Let her go," Simon told him. "I'll be right behind her."

"Here—" the Vicar began, but he was ignored.

"You aren't armed. Neither am I." Mark put out a restraining hand.

But Simon was out his door, turning to help me down. "Go on. I'll be behind you."

Simon had fought Pathan warriors hand to hand. He didn't need a weapon. I walked briskly toward the

466 · CHARLES TODD

door that was open, and as I came nearer, I could hear voices. Without looking back, I dropped my hand and made a tamping-down motion, and Simon flattened himself against the nearest door.

I reached the end of the opening next but one to Alex Craig's, and listened.

"—I tell you, I want your boat. I can't sail those." He must have gestured toward the small craft floating now in the incoming tide. "You can carry me across and say nothing. You owe it to me."

"And be shot for my troubles as soon as you've landed on Sheppey?"

"Why should I shoot you?"

"Because I know something no one else does. That you were in Canterbury and drunk that Saturday night before the explosion. I saw you stagger out of that pub. And you were too hungover Sunday morning to drive back to Cranbourne. You told Ashton you were in Canterbury for the morning church service. If the Army had known you'd lied about where you were and what you were doing, you'd have been cashiered on the spot. Dereliction of duty, it's called."

"How do I know that you haven't already told someone? Why else was I stripped of my captaincy and sent to handle enlistments? Instead of going to France. I'd have been given an increase in pay, I'd have been able to hold my head up."

"Put the revolver away, Collier. You won't shoot me. You can't handle this craft on your own. Not against the incoming tide."

"I'll take one of the smaller craft, then."

"It won't work, I tell you."

"You can't refuse to help me. I've nowhere else to turn. They won't think to look in Sheppey for me." There was rising fury now in Collier's voice. "You're just like the Ashtons, you've never had to scratch for a living. Looking out for yourself first, thinking about no one but yourself. Well, I won't be caught because of you."

"Don't—" Alex Craig said sharply, and in almost the same instant, a shot rang out, echoing loudly in the enclosed space, and I heard someone grunt in pain.

Chapter Nineteen

I ran toward the sound, into the small space between the boat Alex Craig was building and the wall, and the first thing I saw was Collier with his revolver still pointing at the fallen man. The side of his face was swollen, and there was blood crusted in his officer's mustache. His voice was thick from a puffy nose. The handle of the cane had done quite a bit of damage, and I thought it must hurt like the very devil, which made him even edgier. I found that I felt no remorse.

Collier was saying, "You aren't that badly hurt. Get up and take me where I want to go, or the next time, I will shoot to—" He broke off as he heard me, realizing that he and Alex Craig were no longer alone. Whirling, he leveled the revolver in my direction.

"The Sister. All right, then, you can help me with the bloody boat."

There was no way to take him. I was in Simon's path, and the revolver was steady.

I said, "I'm not alone, Lieutenant. The Army is here. You're surrounded." I raised my hand, as if in a signal, and at that same moment, Simon came in behind me.

"Surrender your weapon," he said sternly, the voice of authority, as if he had half a hundred men at his back.

"I'm damned if I will." He put one hand on the hull of the boat, vaulted over it, and was out the door as Simon wheeled in pursuit.

I ran to Alex Craig, and he looked up at me rather ruefully as the fire in his shoulder registered. "How he thought I could manage her in this state—" he began, and fell back, unconscious. I knelt beside him, paying no heed to the shouts outside. I tore at the simple shirt he was wearing to work on the boat, but it was a clean wound, I didn't think it had struck the lung or embedded itself in bone. Feeling around on his back, I found the exit wound, and then began to tear the shirt in strips to bind it up and stop the bleeding.

I moved swiftly, efficiently, and then laid him back gently on the ground. He was already coming to, frowning as the pain hit in full force.

"I'll be back," I said as I heard the revolver firing again.

I reached the door and looked out. The Lieutenant was wading across the Cran, nearly chest deep, struggling against the current. His revolver was still in his hand. Simon was standing on the embankment, holding his arm. I could see the blood darkening the khaki of his uniform.

Mark was shouting, "Upstream. We can cross there."

Meanwhile, Lieutenant Collier had reached the wet, slippery opposite bank and as he scrabbled up, his feet skidding, his hands finally grasped the tufts of grass that hung above his head. By sheer effort he got himself up the slope, knelt in the heavy growth of two years, his head down, catching his breath. I could see his chest heaving from where I stood. And then he was up and running toward the rubble-pocked ruins.

Swearing, Simon dashed toward the motorcar, even as Mark was hastily reversing, and they roared away. I could hear the Vicar protesting, but they didn't stop. Leaving me alone with Alex Craig.

I went in to be certain the bleeding had stopped. His eyes were closed, his mouth a tight line. Blood was already seeping through my makeshift bandages, and I pulled off my apron and used it to tighten the bandaging and put more pressure on the wound. Finishing that, I went back to the open door, and gasped as a muddy, dripping Lieutenant Collier stepped toward me.

He had doubled back, unseen.

"And where's the Army now?" he demanded.

"You wasted your time. Craig is in no condition to row you anywhere, much less porter the boat as far as the water. And I'm not strong enough to help you carry it."

"I've changed my mind. Come on, into the motorcar with you."

"I won't go," I said. Backing into the narrow space, my hands behind me, I felt for a tool, anything I could use as a weapon. But Alex Craig was too tidy, there was nothing within easy reach.

"Look, I don't particularly like killing people, but I'll shoot him in the head this time if you don't move fast."

He leveled the revolver at the man on the floor.

I couldn't chance it. I said quickly, "Very well," and hurried toward the motorcar.

Alex Craig protested vehemently, trying to get to his feet, but Lieutenant Collier ignored him.

He stood with his revolver still pointing at the wounded man. "Can you crank the damned thing?"

I went to the front of the bonnet and did just that. Then I walked to the passenger's door and got in.

Only then did he turn away, moving swiftly, swinging himself into the seat beside me.

"Where are we going?" I asked, praying that he would tell me, and that Alex Craig would hear it, and was conscious enough to remember it.

"Dover," Lieutenant Collier said. He was cornered now, there wasn't a great deal of choice. But once in Dover, he might convince someone he'd lost his orders, and sail for France.

"Dover?" I repeated. "Why there?"

"I have friends there. They'll help me. They told me Britton had been brought back to England."

He was reversing now, and soon we were flying down the line of warehouses and turning up the hill toward the town.

And then the motor began to sputter.

Swearing, he stamped his foot on the gas pedal, trying to make the motorcar climb the hill. It did, catching well enough to make it, but a little past the lane that ran down to Abbey Hall, almost to where the gate to the ruins of Cranbourne Abbey stood open, it simply coughed several times and died.

Lieutenant Collier pounded his fists on the steering wheel in red-faced fury, and for an instant, I feared he might turn on me, blaming me for what had happened. But the town-dweller whose vehicle this was hadn't counted on the drive to Cranbourne, he hadn't seen the necessity of filling up with petrol.

The Lieutenant was out of his seat, flinging his door wide, and then coming around to drag me out as well. "It's your doing, all of this," he said savagely. "I told Britton I didn't want you killed, but he said you were dangerous. And he was right, damn it."

He had my arm in a bruising grip, and was shoving me ahead of him toward the open gate. Just in time I remembered the queue of children marching in that direction for a school outing. They'd be coming out soon, and the last thing I wanted was for this angry man to confront them.

"You can't do this," I said fiercely.

"Tell me I can't," he said through clenched teeth, still pulling me toward the gate.

"You'll be boxed in," I told him. "There's no other way out. They'll corner you, and I don't want to be caught in the crossfire." I prayed it was true that there wasn't a postern gate. "What's more, you've only four shots left."

I don't think he'd ever fired his revolver in anger. Not until today. He wasn't very good with it, but he had managed to bring down Alex Craig and shoot Simon.

He stopped so abruptly I stumbled. His hand was all that kept me from going down on my knees.

"There's a better way," he said, and abandoning the ruins, abandoning the commandeered motorcar, he started back the way we'd come. And I realized as I saw the lane ahead, that now, with no hope left, he was going to the Hall.

My fault. But I couldn't have let him come near those children. He carried me along with him, turning down the lane. It was no longer shaded by the trees, which were bare branches over our heads now. He seemed to come to his senses a bit, casting a look around, trying to see if anyone was watching. He tucked his revolver in his belt and said to me, "Don't try to escape. Hear me? I'll shoot the first person I see, if I can't shoot you."

I wasn't sure he meant it, but I couldn't take a chance. I let him march me along the abbey wall, and put my energies toward trying to think what to do.

How long would it take before Mark and Simon realized they were on a wild goose chase on the far side of the Cran and come back to look for me and for Collier? I tried to work it out. But Alex Craig had heard Collier say we were heading for Dover. Would they see the motorcar where it had been left, or take the turning for the main road through Cranbourne, heading for the coast? Not coming near it . . .

"Who was Corporal Britton to you?"

"A nasty little housebreaker," he said roughly. "They gave him to me for my batman. We both wanted to go to France, that was what we had in common, but the Army wouldn't hear of assigning another officer to the powder mill. And so there we were. I think he'd have blown up the mill himself, if he'd known how to do it. I kept him away from it as much as possible. And away from Ashton and everyone else."

"But why torment the Ashtons?" I asked breathlessly, trying to keep pace but finding it hard to do with my arm in his grip. That threw off my gait. "It's senseless."

"Damn it, it got out of *hand*. I thought if I gave the Army Philip Ashton, convinced them that he'd set off the explosion for his own reasons, they'd reward me by giving me back my rank and sending me to France. They'd overlooked him, but if I could make them believe—the bloody war's nearly over, for God's sake, and as soon as the Yanks got to the Front, I could see it wouldn't last much longer. I didn't want to be a Lieutenant with no battle experience for the rest of my life, when there were enough officers coming back from France to fill several peacetime armies. I'd live on a pittance, looked down on, no memoirs to write, nothing. I'd be a *nobody*."

"Even so, I don't see how you persuaded half a village to do your bidding." And yet, in his friendly, helpful way, he'd convinced me to trust him. I'd even gone back to look for that frog. How difficult would it be for such a man to work on the feelings of those who'd lost so much?

Almost as if he'd heard me, he was saying, "It wasn't as easy as I expected. Anonymous letters, a few whispers, a suggestion here or there—I thought they'd take root. In the end, I was driven to despair trying to find enough disgruntled people to persuade the rest that Ashton was guilty." He added sourly, "Even Inspector Brothers was slow off the mark, although I must say later on he was happy enough to get his own back against Worley for overturning some of his soundest cases. And then suddenly everyone was convinced Ashton was a monster. They weren't satisfied with his arrest. They wanted blood. It was like something out of the French Revolution, I couldn't control it any longer. Mrs. Branch and that confounded dog—she found one hen dead in her coop, and she went haring off to Constable Hood with her tale. I tried to tell her it was ill-advised, but she wouldn't listen. I sent the Benning woman an anonymous letter about the cigarettes, and she was adamant she'd seen just that herself. But there was talk of the Germans capitulating, and I was still in Kent. No closer to getting to France."

He sounded angry and put out, as if all the blame belonged to the survivors of the dead. No scrap of pity for the Ashtons, or for using grieving families. All I could think of was how the Ashtons would ever find a way back through this tangle. Unless Lieutenant Collier stood trial himself and people could see how completely they'd been used.

But how to get all of us out of this business alive?

I could see the house ahead now. It had seemed such a short distance, coming down the drive in Mark's motorcar. On foot, it seemed to take forever. I kept stumbling over my own boots.

Trying to think of a way to warn Mrs. Ashton and Clara, I considered breaking free and making a run for it. But he was angry enough now, he'd kill me and both of them.

He stopped just short of the door, catching his breath, looking up at the windows, as if he could tear the walls down and leave them nothing but a heap of stone. Like the mill.

And then he turned to me. "We'll knock at the door. You'll tell them that you've brought a friend of Mark's home with you. Anything to get us inside."

With my free hand I gestured toward his uniform, caked with mud, splotched with water. His face already bruising, his nose an ugly red. "You don't look like a friend."

He jerked my arm, and it hurt. "Tell them Craig had taken me out in his boat and there was trouble. I need to clean up before returning to Canterbury."

I was afraid that would work too well. But he was already pushing me toward the door. I stood there for a moment, my turn to catch my breath. My cap was awry, but I straightened it as best I could with one hand. Then I smoothed my skirts.

"Hurry," he said roughly, looking over his shoulder down the lane. "Get it over with."

I reached for the heavy knocker, lifted it, and let it drop. Hoping no one would hear it.

No one came.

"They're away. In Canterbury."

"Again," he snapped. "Harder this time."

And I did as he asked. I could hear the sound echoing in the house. After a moment the door opened.

"Mark—" Clara began, and then stopped short. "Sister Crawford?" she asked tentatively, her gaze moving from me to the disheveled man beside me. He'd managed a smile, but it was more ghastly than friendly.

"I'm so sorry," I began. "The Lieutenant here was trying out one of Alex Craig's boats, and it came to grief. I suggested bringing him here to clean up a bit." As far as I knew, she had never set eyes on the man who was liaison for the army at the mill. And so I didn't give his name straightaway.

"I thought you were in Canterbury," she said, frowning.

"We were. Mark and Simon are over by the ruins. They'll be coming back shortly."

"Yes, of course." She swung the door wide and we stepped in. Moving quickly, Lieutenant Collier shut the door behind us with some force, and Clara, on the point of leading us upstairs, already talking about the room he could use, stopped and turned to look at us in fright.

"Don't panic, Clara, please don't," I said. "This man means you no harm. You aren't a member of the family."

She stared at me as if I'd lost my mind.

Before the Lieutenant could speak, I added, "Go downstairs to the servants, and tell them we won't be requiring them for several hours. Keep them down there, if you can. Please? You must protect them."

She was on the point of arguing, when I said in Matron's voice, "Do as I say, Clara." I would have given anything to know where Helen Ashton was. I prayed she wasn't in her enclosed garden. It was a trap, and there would be bloodshed getting Lieutenant Collier out of there. Worse than the abbey ruins.

Standing her ground, Clara said in a worried voice. "Bess? What's happening?"

"Nothing to worry you about," I said. "If you do as I ask."

"But who is this man?"

"Someone the Ashtons knew in the past." I could feel the man beside me stirring impatiently. He had let me deal with Clara—I wasn't sure he knew who she was—because he would be getting his way without any trouble. He was as aware of those last four shots as I was. He didn't intend to waste them. And he wouldn't brook much more interference on her part. "Go on, Clara, please."

This time she turned and hurried toward the door leading down to the kitchen. She must have met Mrs. Byers coming up, because I could hear voices before Clara firmly closed the door behind her.

I had intended to take Captain Collier to an empty room, but I remembered suddenly that Mr. Heatherton-Scott had taken over the study for the time being. I didn't know if he'd left for Canterbury or not. I hesitated.

"The sitting room." He shoved me forward "Go on. It's that way. I know that much."

I had no choice but to lead him to the sitting room. As I opened the door, Mrs. Ashton looked up. "Bess, dear? I was just about to ring for Mrs. Byers, to bring up a pot—"

She broke off as Lieutenant Collier stepped into view.

But Mrs. Ashton was nothing if not brave. After a moment, she looked him up and down and said, "I thought we were done with you."

"He's been in Canterbury all along. Since the mill burned," I said, wanting her to understand some of what had happened.

He pushed me into the room and shut the door, standing with his back to it. "You never liked me. Nor I you," he said to her.

"Where is my son?" she asked.

"He's with Simon Brandon," I told her. "They didn't come with us."

"I see. Well, my husband is facing the hangman. You failed to burn us alive. What else are you planning?"

To my surprise, he said almost querulously, "I didn't intend it to end this way. But I've been cornered."

"Have you indeed?" She held out her hand. "Bess, come and sit beside me."

He no longer needed me as a shield. I wrenched my arm free and crossed the room without hurrying, to do as she asked. "He's armed," I said. "And no one else is."

"Shut up," he said to me. And drew the revolver. "I need to think."

We sat there, watching him, watching the uncertainty in his eyes as he held us at gunpoint, unclear about what he intended to do now. I think he'd expected her to beg or fall apart, giving him the motivation to shoot her, but in the face of her calm, he couldn't find a reason.

"You may as well sit down too," she said with a sigh.

But he kept his back to the door. "Who else is in the house, besides the woman Clara, and the staff?" he asked.

"There's a man in a wheelchair. He's staying with us at the moment," she said. "You won't find him a threat."

"Who is he?"

"A houseguest. He has problems with his legs. Sister Crawford here is teaching him how to exercise them. He can't come down the stairs on his own."

He digested that. To me he said, "I thought you were here to help clear Ashton. You were busy enough about it in France."

"I'd been asked to help there. But I keep returning to the Hall because of Mr. Heatherton-Scott's state of health."

"If you need money to get free of all this—and I expect you'd like to—I can help you there," Helen

Ashton said. "I have the money here in the house to pay my husband's attorneys."

He said nothing.

"I don't particularly want to die," she added. "And I expect you don't either. But how else is this to end? If you kill me, you lose a valuable hostage. If you don't kill me, you must go before my son returns and discovers you here. You can't have it both ways, you know. I've been told you're ambitious. You've said yourself you want to go to France. But think what you could do with a large sum of money in America? You could be anyone. Important. Well liked. I can help get you there."

"Shut up," he said for the second time, this time to Mrs. Ashton.

She shrugged. "As you wish." She reached for the book she'd been reading when we came into the room, and opened it to the page where she'd put it aside.

He stood there, ill at ease, and I thought to myself that this was as dangerous as his anger.

"If you hadn't come around asking me about Captain Collier," he said to me after a moment, "none of this would have happened. You do realize that."

"But I didn't know who you were. It didn't occur to me." And that was my mistake.

"It didn't occur to you that I'd sunk so low? Well, I had. Do you know what it's like to sit there day in and day out, speaking to boys and men, and even mothers who want me to talk their lad out of joining the Army? Conscription didn't get all of the eligible ones. They still come in and ask me to tell them the *truth* about France. What it's like over there. And I've never set foot across the Channel. Do you have any idea how galling that is? To be reduced in rank and left to molder in a cramped office on a back street, for the duration? I can fight, I know I could. But once the mill went up, I was never given the *chance*."

"But we didn't know," Mrs. Ashton said calmly. "There was no one to tell us, was there? We thought you were in London—or Scotland. We were never *told*."

In the distance I thought I caught the sound of a motorcar coming up the drive. I wasn't sure whether it was my imagination or not. What would happen if Mark and Simon walked through the outer door, and then came in here? What would this man do with his four shots? Mrs. Ashton and Mark, Simon and me. Or would he save one for himself?

What if it was Henry and Mr. Heatherton-Scott, instead?

Either his hearing wasn't as keen as mine, or it was indeed my imagination. I listened fiercely, but heard nothing more.

"You must hurry if you're to leave. Take me with you, I'll gladly go," I said.

But he shook his head. "I want to be compensated for all I've been through," he said after a moment. "I want someone else to suffer."

"My husband is in a prison cell, fighting for his life. Is that not enough for you?" Mrs. Ashton demanded.

All at once his expression altered. "I want someone else to suffer," he repeated. "If I can't reach Ashton, I can still do him harm. I can shoot you and his son, and there will be an end to it." He had made up his mind. And I didn't see how we could change it.

Mrs. Ashton reached out and took my hand. The book she'd pretended to read again slipped to the floor with a thud.

At that very same moment, there was a knock at the sitting room door.

Chapter Twenty

Lieutenant Collier looked from one to the other of us, his eyes wide. Decision was upon him, and it took a second to register. Then he backed away from the door, still keeping us in his sights.

All I could think of was Mark or Simon walking into this room and being shot.

I stood up and cried out, "Mark, no!"

The door opened, and the Lieutenant switched his revolver to point directly at whoever was coming in.

It swung wide, and there was Mr. Heatherton-Scott, in his wheelchair, maneuvering into the room, a frown on his face, and then stopping short half across the threshold as he saw the revolver in a stranger's hand.

"What the devil?" he said. "Who is this man?"

I had flung myself across the room, already halfway there, almost within reach of that weapon, when the lawyer gave me away, his surprised gaze swiveling in my direction, and Lieutenant Collier turned and fired wildly.

I could feel the bullet's breath as it took the cap from my head, but I was committed and I plowed into him with all my strength. I'd had to wrestle men in the throes of high fever back to their beds, but there was always another Sister near enough at hand to come to my aid and add her weight to mine.

There was no one here to help.

Or so I thought.

But the lawyer made up for his error by giving the wheels of his chair an almighty push, flying across the room, colliding with the Lieutenant and bringing him down. In the melee, I fought to reach the revolver, and he fired again. There was the sound of broken glass.

Only two more shots. But they would be enough to stop me and to kill the helpless man in the chair. Or Mrs. Ashton.

There were others in the room suddenly, I didn't know where they had come from, my eyes not leaving the revolver waving about even as I clutched the Lieutenant's forearm, struggling with him.

Someone swept past my head, this one in the khaki of a Sergeant-Major, and Simon told me, "*Move.*"

I dropped like a stone, crouching among pushing and shoving legs as Simon closed with Lieutenant Collier. He was fighting with frustrated fury, cursing and swearing as he resisted Simon.

The lawyer's chair was thrust back with some force, and Mark was there, adding his weight to Simon's, and then Simon, one hand still clamped over the Lieutenant's wrist, freed the other and hit Collier hard on the chin.

He went down like a sack, flailing still as he lost consciousness.

I crawled out of the way as Simon stepped back, the revolver in his hand.

He handed it to Mark, the senior officer here, and then helped me to my feet.

"Are you all right?" he demanded, hands on my shoulders, holding me steady.

Catching my breath, I reached up for my cap, and remembered. Then I saw it, trampled underfoot.

Mark had gone to his mother, and I heard her say in a strained voice, "Oh, dear, Mark. I fear this chair is ruined too."

I turned in Simon's grip and saw that one of the shots had gone through the back of the chair.

She was standing by the broken window, rather pale, but unhurt. Mark wordlessly pulled her into his arms, and to her surprise as well as ours, she began to laugh and cry at the same time.

Simon let me go, reached down for my cap, and handed it to me.

For the first time I looked around.

Lieutenant Collier was sprawled in a heap on the carpet, completely unconscious. The wheelchair, unceremoniously pushed to one side, was facing the other way. The door stood wide, and I could hear voices in the passage.

I said, all at once remembering, "There's Alex Craig . . ."

"He can wait," Mr. Heatherton-Scott said, his expression grim. "Will someone tell me what the he— what is going on here?"

I gave him the briefest possible explanation, and left the rest to Mark and Mrs. Ashton.

Simon, borrowing the still-running motorcar, drove me back to the River Cran, and I found the Vicar in the shed, leaning against the hull of the half-finished boat, and Alex Craig sitting up against the far wall.

He looked almost giddy with relief when he saw me coming toward him. "Thank God. But I thought you were on your way to Dover." He turned to Simon, just behind me. "Where's that bas— Collier?"

"In custody," Simon told him briefly. "It's finished. Thank you, Vicar, for staying with him."

"The motorcar ran out of petrol. Instead of Dover, we went to the Hall. It ended there," I explained.

"Is anyone else hurt?" the Vicar asked anxiously.

"A chair," I said, and he shook his head, as if my light remark was uncalled for.

I added, "He fired twice more inside the house, and hit the chair and a window." I knelt to have a look at my patient, but he was stable. Over my shoulder, I said to Simon, "If you and the Vicar can help him, we'll take him back to the Hall."

"I don't want to go there," Alex Craig said adamantly. "Not there."

"You don't have much choice," I told him. "You won't care too much for the journey even that far, but it will be easier than going all the way to Canterbury. Besides, they'll eventually send an ambulance for you, along with the police to take charge of Lieutenant Collier. And there's the Sergeant-Major's arm to see to as well."

He resisted, but it was too painful to do anything else but allow himself to be put into the waiting motorcar. The Vicar sat beside him, cushioning his bad arm from the jolting.

In the passenger's seat, I said to Simon, "How did you find us?"

"Craig told us you were on your way to Dover. We left the Vicar with him and set out. Clara was at the end of the lane—Mark stopped, and she ran over to us, telling us about the man you'd brought there, that she couldn't believe Mark had sent him to the house. She thought we were down by the sheds, and she was on her way there."

"How brave of her," I said, and meant it.

"We brought her back, she went around to the tradesman's entrance, and we waited until she was out of range. We were just coming to the door when we heard the shots."

Simon looked at me, grinning. "I fear the Major is not as fleet of foot as I am."

"He's recovering from his own wounds," I said, in Mark's defense. But I could picture Simon, first through the door and not waiting for order of battle as he charged toward the sitting room.

"Just as well you were fleet of foot," I went on. "I couldn't have held on much longer."

"There was a hole in your cap." He wasn't grinning now.

"I'd hoped you hadn't noticed."

He said nothing.

"You realize you could be up on charges for striking an officer."

"The Colonel will understand."

And so he would, I thought dryly.

Inspector Brothers was not best pleased. After I'd bandaged the wound in his arm, Simon had run into Canterbury to fetch him. We were a rather somber group, waiting for their return. Mark had locked the still-groggy Lieutenant into a broom closet, and from time to time in the silence we could hear him pounding furiously on the door.

It was stout enough to hold him. I'd seen it for myself.

We tried to tell the Inspector the whole story, although he interrupted constantly, as if he didn't believe us. Finally, Alex Craig, who was sitting in the study with us, having refused to go up to a bedroom, said testily, "For God's sake, Brothers, what else do you need? The Sergeant-Major here has no reason to protect the Ashtons, and neither do I. Heatherton-Scott is an officer of the court, and has no reason to lie. And Mr. Parry is a clergyman who was brought into the picture quite by accident. You may refuse to believe Sister Crawford, or Major Ashton, or his mother, but the four of us can't be discounted as easily. If nothing else, Collier is guilty of attempted murder for shooting me and two more counts for firing his revolver in a crowded room. You can sort out the rest later."

All the same, Brothers dragged his feet.

We could hear the outer door open, and Henry came walking in, a smile on his face like the cat that had just eaten the songbird in the cage.

"I've been to the clinic where Corporal Britton was a patient until his death. They allowed me to go through his things." I could well imagine how persuasive Henry must have been. Simon had been refused permission.

One arm had been behind his back, and Henry brought it out now, holding a cushion in his hand.

"Dear God," I said, getting up and crossing the room to take it from him. "Look, Simon, it's the pillow that nearly smothered Sister Morris. If only they'd allowed you to *search*." I handed it to Inspector Brothers. "It's proof that the corporal had attempted to kill a Sister in France. Now we're a little closer to connecting him to the murder of Sergeant Rollins as well. The Army will need to know this straightaway."

Henry wasn't finished. "There are letters in his kit too. They provide that proof. I expect he might have had a little blackmail in mind. Or believed he needed to protect himself if he was caught. I've read two of them."

He passed them to Inspector Brothers, who was looking a bit overwhelmed at this stage.

Simon spoke then.

"I've reported to the Army. While I was in Canterbury. They'll be sending someone from the Military Foot Police to the Hall as soon as possible. Collier is still a serving officer."

Inspector Brothers cleared his throat. "I'll need statements," he said doggedly.

Mr. Heatherton-Scott leaned forward and took up a sheaf of papers from Philip Ashton's desk top. "These statements were taken while we were waiting for you, Inspector. I believe you'll find them all in order. I made certain of that, with Mr. Parry here as my witness."

Inspector Brothers took them, staring down at them as if they might bite him. And well they might, for his obstruction of justice. He might find himself demoted to sergeant. And I think for the first time, he realized that.

In the end, the Army took Lieutenant Collier into custody, and we spent several hours closeted with a Major and two sergeants who had been dispatched to oversee this matter. Major Atkins went over the statements very carefully, compared Simon's notes and other evidence, and when he was satisfied, he told us that the charges against Lieutenant Collier were serious indeed. And they intended to look into the attack on Sister Morris and the death of Sergeant Rollins.

When they left it was after nine o'clock in the evening. We had a late supper in the dining room, all of us nearly too weary to eat. Alex Craig had wanted to go home, but he was running a slight fever, and I insisted that he choose between a hospital and here. To my surprise, he preferred to remain at the Hall.

The next morning, Simon and I ran him in to see a doctor for his shoulder, and he was clapped in hospital, willing or not.

Driving back to Abbey Hall, Simon looked across at me. "You've cleared Philip Ashton's good name."

"I hope so."

"Have you forgot you're due back in France tomorrow? Your transport leaves Dover tonight."

I had. I sat bolt upright in my seat. "There's no time to find a replacement for that cap with the bullet hole in it. How will I ever explain that to Matron?"

"Tell her it's a souvenir of an earlier battle."

I sighed. "There won't be time to go home. I've seen the Colonel Sahib twice, and my mother only once. I'll ask Mrs. Ashton to write to her and tell her why I never got to London, much less Somerset. And you must explain to my father as well. But leave out the worst of the details."

"He'll see them in the Army's report. Be sure of that."

"Oh well. There's nothing we can do, I expect."

"The war will be over in a few weeks, Bess. At most." He reached out and briefly put his hand over mine, where they were folded in my lap. "Your mother is counting the days."

And I knew she wasn't the only one . . .

Author's Note

There was in fact a terrible explosion and fire at the Oare Gunpowder Works near Faversham in Kent on 2 April 1916. Accounts vary, but more than a hundred men were killed. It was a tragedy for the people of The Swale both personally and economically, and it had dire consequences for the war effort barely two months before the bloody and fierce fighting at the Battle of the Somme.

We'd heard about this event many times during our visits to Kent. The Oare Gunpowder Works is now a lovely outdoor park where visitors can learn more about what happened and how gunpowder was made. It's well worth a visit. And there are the real graves of the real victims in Faversham.

Having lived in Delaware, where the Hagley Mills made gunpowder for du Pont and often dealt with sudden death, we were intrigued by what might happen to a small community when it is visited by such a calamity, natural or man-made, and how people cope when the inexplicable changes their world.

A Pattern of Lies is not the story of the Oare Works or its aftermath. Instead it is a look at a fictional village where the livelihood of many people depended on the powder mill, and the loss of life touched almost every household. We have borrowed some of the details from the 1916 event because they fit the story we wanted to tell. That is all we have borrowed. But we are reminded of what someone said in another more modern disaster: *When you can't blame God, what do you do?*

About the Author

Charles Todd is the author of the Bess Crawford mysteries, the Inspector Ian Rutledge mysteries, and two stand-alone novels. A mother and son writing team, they live in Delaware and North Carolina.

HARPER LUXE

THE NEW LUXURY IN READING

We hope you enjoyed reading
our new, comfortable print size and found it
an experience you would like to repeat.

Well — you're in luck!

HarperLuxe offers the finest in fiction and
nonfiction books in this same larger print size and
paperback format. Light and easy to read, HarperLuxe
paperbacks are for book lovers who want to see
what they are reading without the strain.

For a full listing of titles and
new releases to come, please visit our website:

www.HarperLuxe.com